MAZIRIAN THE MAGICIA

He could imprison a wizard in a tiny bottle, defeat the mightiest, most fearsome creatures, and make himself master of the elements. But how was he to capture and conquer the maiden of the woods?

THE SEEKER IN THE FORTRESS by Manly Wade Wellman

Harpist, swordsman, last survivor of Atlantis—could he find the secret no one else had mastered, the key to the sorcerer's innermost citadel?

AND THE MONSTERS WALK by John Jakes

They roam the streets of London, raised by an ancient spell of evil. Who will help a man with no magic to end their reign of terror?

THE WALL AROUND THE WORLD by Theodore Cogswell

It had been there as long as anyone could remember. Was it there to keep something out or to keep the warlocks in?

These are just a few of the exciting and imaginative realms explored in—

WIZARDS
ISAAC ASIMOV'S MAGICAL WORLDS
OF FANTASY #1

SIGNET Science Fiction You'll Enjoy

WIZARDS

Isaac Asimov's Magical Worlds of Fantasy #1

EDITED BY
Isaac Asimov,
Martin H. Greenberg
and Charles G. Waugh

A SIGNET BOOK

NEW AMERICAN LIBRARY

TIMES MIRROR

NAL BOOKS ARE AVAILABLE AT QUANTITY DISCOUNTS WHEN USED
TO PROMOTE PRODUCTS OR SERVICES. FOR INFORMATION PLEASE
WRITE TO PREMIUM MARKETING DIVISION, THE NEW AMERICAN
LIBRARY, INC., 1633 BROADWAY, NEW YORK, NEW YORK 10019.

Acknowledgments

"Mazirian the Magician," by Jack Vance. Copyright © 1950 by Jack Vance; copyright
renewed. Reprinted by permission of Kirby McCauley, Ltd.

"Please Stand By," by Ron Goulart. Copyright © 1961 by Mercury Press, Inc. From
THE MAGAZINE OF FANTASY AND SCIENCE FICTION. Reprinted by permission
of the author.

"What Good Is a Glass Dagger?" by Larry Niven. Copyright © 1972 by Mercury Press,
Inc. From THE MAGAZINE OF FANTASY AND SCIENCE FICTION. Reprinted by
permission of the author.

"The Eye of Tandyla," by L. Sprague de Camp. First published in FANTASTIC
ADVENTURES, Vol. 13, #5, for May, 1951, C#B. 294 742 by Ziff-Davis Publishing
Co. Copyright renewed by L. Sprague de Camp 1979 RE 26 977. Reprinted by
permission of the author.

"The White House Child," by Greg Bear. Copyright © 1979 by Terry Carr. Reprinted
by permission of the author.

"Semley's Necklace," by Ursula K. Le Guin. Copyright © 1964, 1975 by Ursula K. Le
Guin. Reprinted by permission of the author and the author's agent, Virginia Kidd.

"And the Monsters Walk," by John Jakes. Copyright © 1952 by Ziff-Davis Publishing
Co.; originally published in *Fantastic Adventures*, July, 1952; © renewed 1980 by John
Jakes. Reprinted by permission of the author.

"The Seeker in the Fortress," by Manley Wade Wellman. Copyright © 1979 by Gerald
W. Page and Hank Reinhardt. Reprinted by permission of Kirby McCauley, Ltd.

"The Wall Around the World," by Theodore Cogswell. Copyright © 1953 by Galaxy
Publishing Corporation; © renewed 1981 by Theodore R. Cogswell. Reprinted by permission
of the author.

"The People of The Black Circle," by Robert E. Howard. Copyright © 1934 by Popular
Fiction Company. Reprinted by permission of CONAN Properties Inc.

SIGNET, SIGNET CLASSIC, MENTOR, PLUME, MERIDIAN and NAL BOOKS
are published by The New American Library, Inc.,
1633 Broadway, New York, New York 10019

FIRST PRINTING, OCTOBER, 1983

1 2 3 4 5 6 7 8 9

PRINTED IN THE UNITED STATES OF AMERICA

CONTENTS

Introduction

WIZARDS

by Isaac Asimov

There is nothing really mysterious about the word "wizard." The first syllable "wiz" is used, in common slang these days, for anyone or anything that is uncommonly smart or impressive, and it sounds very much like "wise." In fact, it *is* a form of "wise," and a "wizard" is simply a "wise man."

Of course there's the suffix "-ard," which, along with its variant "-art," is usually used to indicate an excessive amount of something. A "coward" is one who is too easily cowed; a "braggart" is one who brags entirely too much; a "drunkard" is one who is too frequently drunk.

And a "wizard," then? Presumably, a wizard is one who is too wise for anyone's comfort.

How is that possible? In general, we tend to honor wisdom, to deify it almost. How can one be too wise?

It depends on the kind of Universe we live in. To almost all people in every generation—even our own—the Universe is a frightening and dangerous place. It is operated on an entirely whimsical, capricious, and even clearly malevolent basis, and we are the helpless prey of forces enormously greater than we can handle.

How else can we explain the storms that strike without warning, the droughts, the sudden onset of disease and plagues, the mischances of every kind?

Surely, the Universe must be under the control of beings who are as irrational, as erratic, as irascible, as human beings are at their worst; who are incredibly powerful and yet incredibly childish as well; who, even if basically well-disposed, are apt to explode into uncontrollable anger at some small offense or meaningless slight.

Even if we picture the Universe as under the control of an all-good, as well as all-powerful, being, he is apt to lose his temper, and then—watch out. Or, if he is so good that never for an instant is his goodness in question, one can only suppose the additional existence of competing forces of evil, that the all-good being is forced to allow the existence of (or that he chooses, for some inscrutable reason of his own, to allow to exist).

However we may slice it, the Universe seems to be a horrible madhouse. Yet might it not be possible to behave in such a way as to keep all these supernatural beings in good temper? You might kill animals and burn them so that a delicious smoke rises to the sky where these beings live and feeds them into good-natured satiation. Or you might sing endless songs of praise to these beings, flattering them into benevolence. Or you might find magic chants that either lull them to kindness or bind them into impotence.

Everything, however, must be done *just so*. The words, the gestures, the exact order of events, the whole ritual, must be correct, or the result will surely be worse than if you had done nothing at all.

But how do you discover what the ritual must be? Clearly, the only sources are the supernatural beings themselves. If some human being learns the secrets, he can control the Universe by flattering, bamboozling, or overpowering the supernatural beings.

Does any human being actually learn the secret? Well, you and I, being very clever people who live in the twentieth century and have had an excellent scientific education, know that they don't, that there are no secrets of this sort, that there are, indeed, no supernatural beings of this sort, no demons, afreets, jinn, nymphs, satyrs—but that's just you and I. To others not so well placed in space and time, and not so learned and sophisticated as we are, it is enough if someone *says* he has the secrets. If he is clever enough and daring enough to make those who watch and listen think he is indeed controlling the Universe, they will believe him. (Why not? Think how many millions fall for all the hoary old tricks and flim-flams from astrology to spoon-bending, plus everything in between.)

There are various names one can give the people who know the secrets whereby the Universe might be controlled, but one of them is "wizard."

People might feel grateful to the controllers of fate, for surely it is to them that one must turn to make sure that the rains come and the infections don't; they are the saviors, the answerers of questions, the bringers of good fortune, the helpers in time of disappointment and sickness.

Think of Merlin, the archetypical wizard of legend and perhaps the most popular of all. Who has a bad word for him?

Then why that "-ard" ending?

Is not a wizard just as capable of irascibility and loss of temper as any supernatural being? Might not a wizard have his feelings hurt? Might he not hunger for more power? In short, are not wizards just as dangerous as the beings they control?

Of course.

Wizardry is a double-edged sword, then, and if we deal with stories of wizards, which edge are we likely to harp on? Remember that catastrophe is more dramatic than peace; danger more dramatic than sleep; and—yes—evil is more dramatic than good. Writers, being human, and wanting to go where the readers are, are apt therefore to stress the evils and dangers of wizardry.

What you have in this book, then, are a group of stories that are full of drama, of danger, and of heart-stopping action. That's the best kind of stories to have as long as you're sitting comfortably in your favorite armchair or cuddled cozily in bed—so best wishes to you, and good reading.

MAZIRIAN THE MAGICIAN

by
Jack Vance

*Jack Vance first appeared in the science fiction maga-
zines in the late 1940s and quickly established a loyal
following, both for his sf and for his fantasy. Among his
many notable books are THE DYING EARTH (1950),
SHOWBOAT WORLD (1975), WYST: ALASTOR 1716
(1978), and THE BOOK OF DREAMS (1981), the
latter part of his popular "Demon Princes" series. He
is one of very few writers to have won the Edgar Award
of the Mystery Writers of America, the Hugo Award for
outstanding sf, and the Nebula Award of the Science
Fiction Writers of America. A writer's writer, he is highly
regarded by his peers and by his still-growing readership.*

*From his classic collection THE DYING EARTH,
"Mazirian the Magician" is an enchanting example of
Jack Vance's ability to write future fairy tales.*

Deep in thought, Mazirian the Magician walked his garden.
Trees fruited with many intoxications overhung his path, and
flowers bowed obsequiously as he passed. An inch above the

ground, dull as agates, the eyes of mandrakes followed the tread of his black-slippered feet. Such was Mazirian's garden—three terraces growing with strange and wonderful vegetations. Certain plants swam with changing iridescences; others held up blooms pulsing like sea-anemones, purple, green, lilac, pink, yellow. Here grew trees like feather parasols, trees with transparent trunks threaded with red and yellow veins, trees with foliage like metal foil, each leaf a different metal—copper, silver, blue tantalum, bronze, green iridium. Here blooms like bubbles tugged gently upward from glazed green leaves, there a shrub bore a thousand pipe-shaped blossoms, each whistling softly to make music of the ancient Earth, of the ruby-red sunlight, water seeping through black soil, the languid winds. And beyond the roqual hedge the trees of the forest made a tall wall of mystery. In this waning hour of Earth's life no man could count himself familiar with the glens, the glades, the dells and deeps, the secluded clearings, the ruined pavilions, the sun-dappled pleas-aunces, the gullys and heights, the various brooks, freshets, ponds, the meadows, thickets, brakes and rocky outcrops.

Mazirian paced his garden with a brow frowning in thought. His step was slow and his arms were clenched behind his back. There was one who had brought him puzzlement, doubt, and a great desire: a delightful woman-creature who dwelt in the woods. She came to his garden half-laughing and always wary, riding a black horse with eyes like golden crystals. Many times had Mazirian tried to take her; always her horse had borne her from his varied enticements, threats, and subterfuges.

Agonized screaming jarred the garden. Mazirian, hastening his step, found a mole chewing the stalk of a plant-animal hybrid. He killed the marauder, and the screams subsided to a dull gasping. Mazirian stroked a furry leaf and the red mouth hissed in pleasure.

Then: "K-k-k-k-k-k-k," spoke the plant. Mazirian stooped, held the rodent to the red mouth. The mouth sucked, the small body slid into the stomach-bladder underground. The plant gurgled, eructated, and Mazirian watched with satisfaction.

The sun had swung low in the sky, so dim and red that the stars could be seen. And now Mazirian felt a watching presence. It would be the woman of the forest, for thus had she disturbed him before. He paused in his stride, feeling for the direction of the gaze.

He shouted a spell of immobilization. Behind him the plant-animal froze to rigidity and a great green moth wafted to the ground. He whirled around. There she was, at the edge of the forest, closer than ever she had approached before. Nor did she move as he advanced. Mazirian's young-old eyes shone. He would take her to his manse and keep her in a prison of green glass. He would test her brain with fire, with cold, with pain and with joy. She should serve him with wine and make the eighteen motions of allurement by yellow lamp-light. Perhaps she was spying on him; if so, the Magician would discover immediately, for he could call no man friend and had forever to guard his garden.

She was but twenty paces distant—then there was a thud and pound of black hooves as she wheeled her mount and fled into the forest.

The Magician flung down his cloak in rage. She held a guard—a counter-spell, a rune of protection—and always she came when he was ill-prepared to follow. He peered into the murky depths, glimpsed the wanness of her body flitting through a shaft of red light, then black shade and she was gone . . . Was she a witch? Did she come of her own volition, or—more likely—had an enemy sent her to deal him inquietude? If so, who might be guiding her? There was Prince Kandive the Golden, of Kaiin, whom Mazirian had bilked of his secret of renewed youth. There was Azvan the Astronomer, there was Turjan—hardly Turjan, and here Mazirian's face lit in a pleasing recollection . . . He put the thought aside. Azvan, at least, he could test. He turned his steps to his workshop, went to a table where rested a cube of clear crystal, shimmering with a red and blue aureole. From a cabinet he brought a bronze gong and a silver hammer. He tapped on the gong and the mellow tone sang through the room and out, away and beyond. He tapped again and again. Suddenly Azvan's face shone from the crystal, beaded with pain and great terror.

"Stay the strokes, Mazirian!" cried Azvan. "Strike no more on the gong of my life!"

Mazirian paused, his hand poised over the gong.

"Do you spy on me, Azvan? Do you send a woman to regain the gong?"

"Not I, Master, not I. I fear you too well."

"You must deliver me the woman, Azvan; I insist."

"Impossible, Master! I know not who or what she is!"

Mazirian made as if to strike. Azvan poured forth such a torrent of supplication that Mazirian with a gesture of disgust threw down the hammer and restored the gong to its place.

Azvan's face drifted slowly away, and the fine cube of crystal shone blank as before.

Mazirian stroked his chin. Apparently he must capture the girl himself. Later, when black night lay across the forest, he would seek through his books for spells to guard him through the unpredictable glades. They would be poignant corrosive spells, of such a nature that one would daunt the brain of an ordinary man and two render him mad. Mazirian, by dint of stringent exercise, could encompass four of the most formidable, or six of the lesser spells.

He put the project from his mind and went to a long vat bathed in a flood of green light. Under a wash of clear fluid lay the body of a man, ghastly below the green glare, but of great physical beauty. His torso tapered from wide shoulders through lean flanks to long strong legs and arched feet; his face was clean and cold with hard flat features. Dusty golden hair clung about his head.

Mazirian stared at the thing, which he had cultivated from a single cell. It needed only intelligence, and this he knew not how to provide. Turjan of Miir held the knowledge, and Turjan—Mazirian glanced with a grim narrowing of the eyes at a trap in the floor—refused to part with his secret.

Mazirian pondered the creature in the vat. It was a perfect body; therefore might not the brain be ordered and pliant? He would discover. He set in motion a device to draw off the liquid and presently the body lay stark to the direct rays. Mazirian injected a minim of drug into the neck. The body twitched. The eyes opened, winced in the glare. Mazirian turned away the projector.

Feebly the creature in the vat moved its arms and feet, as if unaware of their use. Mazirian watched intently: perhaps he had stumbled on the right synthesis for the brain.

"Sit up!" commanded the Magician.

The creature fixed its eyes upon him, and reflexes joined muscle to muscle. It gave a throaty roar and sprang from the vat at Mazirian's throat. In spite of Mazirian's strength it caught him and shook him like a doll.

For all Mazirian's magic he was helpless. The mesmeric spell had been expended, and he had none other in his brain. In any event he could not have uttered the space-twisting syllables with that mindless clutch at his throat.

His hand closed on the neck of a leaden carboy. He swung and struck the head of his creature, which slumped to the floor.

Mazirian, not entirely dissatisfied, studied the glistening body at his feet. The spinal coordination had functioned well. At his table he mixed a white potion, and, lifting the golden head, poured the fluid into the lax mouth. The creature stirred, opened its eyes, propped itself on its elbows. The madness had left its face—but Mazirian sought in vain for the glimmer of intelligence. The eyes were as vacant as those of a lizard.

The Magician shook his head in annoyance. He went to the window and his brooding profile was cut black against the oval panes . . . Turjan once more? Under the most dire inquiry Turjan had kept his secret close. Mazirian's thin mouth curved wryly. Perhaps if he inserted another angle in the passage . . .

The sun had gone from the sky and there was dimness in Mazirian's garden. His white night-blossoms opened and their captive gray moths fluttered from bloom to bloom. Mazirian pulled open the trap in the floor and descended stone stairs. Down, down, down . . . At last a passage intercepted at right angles, lit with the yellow light of eternal lamps. To the left were his fungus beds, to the right a stout oak and iron door, locked with three locks. Down and ahead the stone steps continued, dropping into blackness.

Mazirian unlocked the three locks, flung wide the door. The room within was bare except for a stone pedestal supporting a glass-topped box. The box measured a yard on a side and was four or five inches high. Within the box—actually a squared passageway, a run with four right angles—moved two small creatures, one seeking, the other evading. The predator was a small dragon with furious red eyes and a monstrous fanged mouth. It waddled along the passage on six splayed legs, twitching its tail as it went. The other stood only half the size of the dragon—a strong-featured man, stark naked, with a copper fillet binding his long black hair. He moved slightly faster than his pursuer, which still kept relentless chase, using a measure of craft, speeding, doubling back, lurking at the angle in case the man should unwarily step around. By holding himself continually alert, the man was able to stay beyond the reach of the fangs. The man was Turjan, whom Mazirian by trickery had captured several weeks before, reduced in size and thus imprisoned.

Mazirian watched with pleasure as the reptile sprang upon the momentarily relaxing man, who jerked himself clear by the thickness of his skin. It was time, Mazirian thought, to give both rest and nourishment. He dropped panels across the passage,

separating it into halves, isolating man from beast. To both he
gave meat and pannikins of water.

Turjan slumped in the passage.

"Ah," said Mazirian, "you are fatigued. You desire rest?"

Turjan remained silent, his eyes closed. Time and the world
had lost meaning for him. The only realities were the gray
passage and the interminable flight. At unknown intervals came
food and a few hours rest.

"Think of the blue sky," said Mazirian, "the white stars,
your castle Miir by the river Derna; think of wandering free in
the meadows."

The muscles at Turjan's mouth twitched.

"Consider, you might crush the little dragon under your heel."

Turjan looked up. "I would prefer to crush your neck,
Mazirian."

Mazirian was unperturbed. "Tell me, how do you invest your
vat creatures with intelligence? Speak, and you go free."

Turjan laughed, and there was madness in his laughter.

"Tell you? And then? You would kill me with hot oil in a
moment."

Mazirian's thin mouth drooped petulantly.

"Wretched man, I know how to make you speak. If your
mouth were stuffed, waxed and sealed, you would speak! Tomorrow I take a nerve from your arm and draw coarse cloth along its
length."

The small Turjan, sitting with his legs across the passageway,
drank his water and said nothing.

"Tonight," said Mazirian with studied malevolence, "I add
an angle and change your run to a pentagon."

Turjan paused and looked up through the glass cover at his
enemy. Then he slowly sipped his water. With five angles there
would be less time to evade the charge of the monster, less of the
hall in view from one angle.

"Tomorrow," said Mazirian, "you will need all your agility."
But another matter occurred to him. He eyed Turjan speculatively.
"Yet even this I spare you if you assist me with another problem."

"What is your difficulty, febrile Magician?"

"The image of a woman-creature haunts my brain, and I
would capture her." Mazirian's eyes went misty at the thought.
"Late afternoon she comes to the edge of my garden riding a
great black horse—you know her, Turjan?"

"Not I, Mazirian." Turjan sipped his water.

Mazirian continued. "She has sorcery enough to ward away

Felojun's Second Hypnotic Spell—or perhaps she has some protective rune. When I approach, she flees into the forest."

"So then?" asked Turjan, nibbling the meat Mazirian had provided.

"Who may this woman be?" demanded Mazirian, peering down his long nose at the tiny captive.

"How can I say?"

"I must capture her," said Mazirian abstractedly: "What spells, what spells?"

Turjan looked up, although he could see the Magician only indistinctly through the cover of glass.

"Release me, Mazirian, and on my word as a Chosen Hierarch of the Maram-Or, I will deliver you this girl."

"How would you do this?" asked the suspicious Mazirian.

"Pursue her into the forest with my best Live Boots and a headful of spells."

"You would fare no better than I," retorted the Magician. "I give you freedom when I know the synthesis of your vat-things. I myself will pursue the woman."

Turjan lowered his head that the Magician might not read his eyes.

"And as for me, Mazirian?" he inquired after a moment.

"I will treat with you when I return."

"And if you do not return?"

Mazirian stroked his chin and smiled, revealing fine white teeth. "The dragon could devour you now, if it were not for your cursed secret."

The Magician climbed the stairs. Midnight found him in his study, poring through leather-bound tomes and untidy portfolios . . . At one time a thousand or more runes, spells, incantations, curses, and sorceries had been known. The reach of Grand Motholam—Ascolais, the Ide of Kauchique, Almery to the South, the Land of the Falling Wall to the East—swarmed with sorcerers of every description, of whom the chief was the Arch-Necromancer Phandaal. A hundred spells Phandaal personally had formulated—though rumor said that demons whispered at his ear when he wrought magic. Pontecilla the Pious, then ruler of Grand Motholam, put Phandaal to torment, and after a terrible night, he killed Phandaal and outlawed sorcery throughout the land. The wizards of Grand Motholam fled like beetles under a strong light; the lore was dispersed and forgotten, until now, at this dim time, with the sun dark, wilderness obscuring Ascolais, and the white city Kaiin half in ruins, only a few more than a hundred spells remained to the knowledge of man. Of these, Mazirian had access to seventy-three, and gradually, by stratagem and negotiation, was securing the others.

Mazirian made a selection from his books and with great effort forced five spells upon his brain: Phandaal's Gyrator, Felojun's Second Hypnotic Spell, The Excellent Prismatic Spray, The Charm of Untiring Nourishment, and the Spell of the Omnipotent Sphere. This accomplished, Mazirian drank wine and retired to his couch.

The following day, when the sun hung low, Mazirian went to walk in his garden. He had but short time to wait. As he loosened the earth at the roots of his moon-geraniums a soft rustle and stamp told that the object of his desire had appeared.

She sat upright in the saddle, a young woman of exquisite configuration. Mazirian slowly stooped, as not to startle her, put his feet into the Live Boots and secured them above the knee.

He stood up. "Ho, girl," he cried, "you have come again. Why are you here of evenings? Do you admire the roses? They are vividly red because live red blood flows in their petals. If today you do not flee, I will make you the gift of one."

Mazirian plucked a rose from the shuddering bush and advanced toward her, fighting the surge of the Live Boots. He had taken but four steps when the woman dug her knees into the ribs of her mount and so plunged off through the trees.

Mazirian allowed full scope to the life in his boots. They gave a great bound, and another, and another, and he was off in full chase.

So Mazirian entered the forest of fable. On all sides mossy boles twisted up to support the high panoply of leaves. At intervals shafts of sunshine drifted through to lay carmine blots on the turf. In the shade long-stemmed flowers and fragile fungi sprang from the humus; in this ebbing hour of Earth nature was mild and relaxed.

Mazirian in his Live Boots bounded with great speed through the forest, yet the black horse, running with no strain, stayed easily ahead.

For several leagues the woman rode, her hair flying behind like a pennon. She looked back and Mazirian saw the face over her shoulder as a face in a dream. Then she bent forward; the golden-eyed horse thundered ahead and soon was lost to sight. Mazirian followed by tracing the trail in the sod.

The spring and drive began to leave the Live Boots, for they had come far and at great speed. The monstrous leaps became shorter and heavier, but the strides of the horse, shown by the tracks, were also shorter and slower. Presently Mazirian entered a meadow and saw the horse, riderless, cropping grass. He stopped short. The entire expanse of tender herbiage lay before him. The trail of the horse leading into the glade was clear, but there was no trail leaving. The woman therefore had dismounted somewhere behind—how far he had no means of knowing. He walked toward the horse, but the creature shied and bolted through the trees. Mazirian made one effort to follow, and discovered that his Boots hung lax and flaccid—dead.

He kicked them away, cursing the day and his ill-fortune. Shaking the cloak free behind him, a baleful tension shining on his face, he started back along the trail.

In this section of the forest, outcroppings of black and green rock, basalt and serpentine, were frequent—forerunners of the crags over the River Derna. On one of these rocks Mazirian saw a tiny man-thing mounted on a dragon-fly. He had skin of a greenish cast; he wore a gauzy smock and carried a lance twice his own length.

Mazirian stopped. The Twk-man looked down stolidly.

"Have you seen a woman of my race passing by, Twk-man?"

"I have seen such a woman," responded the Twk-man after a moment of deliberation.

"Where may she be found?"

"What may I expect for the information?"

"Salt—as much as you can bear away."

The Twk-man flourished his lance. "Salt? No. Liane the Wayfarer provides the chieftain Dandanflores salt for all the tribe."

Mazirian could surmise the services for which the bandit-troubadour paid salt. The Twk-men, flying fast on their dragon-flies, saw all that happened in the forest.

"A vial of oil from my telanxis blooms?"

"Good," said the Twk-man. "Show me the vial."

Mazirian did so.

"She left the trail at the lightning-blasted oak lying a little before you. She made directly for the river valley, the shortest route to the lake."

Mazirian laid the vial beside the dragon-fly and went off toward the river oak. The Twk-man watched him go, then dismounted and lashed the vial to the underside of the dragon-fly, next to the skein of fine haft the woman had given him thus to direct Mazirian.

The Magician turned at the oak and soon discovered the trail over the dead leaves. A long open glade lay before him, sloping gently to the river. Trees towered to either side and the long sundown rays steeped one side in blood, left the other deep in black shadow. So deep was the shade that Mazirian did not see the creature seated on a fallen tree; and he sensed it only as it prepared to leap on his back.

Mazirian sprang about to face the thing, which subsided again to sitting posture. It was a Deodand, formed and featured like a handsome man, finely muscled, but with a dead black lusterless skin and long slit eyes.

"Ah, Mazirian, you roam the woods far from home," the black thing's soft voice rose through the glade.

The Deodand, Mazirian knew, craved his body for meat. How had the girl escaped? Her trail led directly past.

"I come seeking, Deodand. Answer my questions, and I undertake to feed you much flesh."

The Deodand's eyes glinted, flitting over Mazirian's body. "You may in any event, Mazirian. Are you with powerful spells today?"

"I am. Tell me, how long has it been since the girl passed? Went she fast, slow, alone or in company? Answer, and I give you meat at such time as you desire."

The Deodand's lips curled mockingly. "Blind Magician! She has not left the glade." He pointed, and Mazirian followed the direction of the dead black arm. But he jumped back as the Deodand sprang. From his mouth gushed the syllables of Phandaal's Gyrator Spell. The Deodand was jerked off his feet and flung high in the air, where he hung whirling, high and low, faster and slower, up to the tree-tops, low to the ground. Mazirian watched with a half-smile. After a moment he brought the Deodand low and caused the rotations to slacken.

"Will you die quickly or slow?" asked Mazirian. "Help me and I kill you at once. Otherwise you shall rise high where the pelgrane fly."

Fury and fear choked the Deodand.

"May dark Thial spike your eyes! May Kraan hold your living brain in acid!" And it added such charges that Mazirian felt forced to mutter countercurses.

"Up then," said Mazirian at last, with a wave of his hand. The black sprawling body jerked high above the tree-tops to revolve slowly in the crimson bask of setting sun. In a moment a mottled bat-shaped thing with hooked snout swept close and its beak tore the black leg before the crying Deodand could kick it away. Another and another of the shapes flitted across the sun.

"Down, Mazirian!" came the faint call. "I tell what I know."

Mazirian brought him close to earth.

"She passed alone before you came. I made to attack her but she repelled me with a handful of thyle-dust. She went to the end of the glade and took the trail to the river. This trail leads also past the lair of Thrang. So is she lost, for he will sate himself on her till she dies."

Mazirian rubbed his chin. "Had she spells with her?"

"I know not. She will need strong magic to escape the demon Thrang."

"Is there anything else to tell?"

"Nothing."

"Then you may die." And Mazirian caused the creature to revolve at ever greater speed, faster and faster, until there was only a blur. A strangled wailing came and presently the Deodand's frame parted. The head shot like a bullet far down the glade; arms, legs, viscera flew in all directions.

Mazirian went his way. At the end of the glade the trail led steeply down ledges of dark green serpentine to the River Derna. The sun had set and shade filled the valley. Mazirian gained the riverside and set off downstream toward a far shimmer known as Sanra Water, the Lake of Dreams.

An evil odor came to the air, a stink of putrescence and filth. Mazirian went ahead more cautiously, for the lair of Thrang the ghoul-bear was near, and in the air was the feel of magic—strong brutal sorcery his own more subtle spells might not contain.

The sound of voices reached him, the throaty tones of Thrang and gasping cries of terror. Mazirian stepped around a shoulder of rock, inspected the origin of the sounds.

Thrang's lair was an alcove in the rock, where a fetid pile of grass and skins served him for a couch. He had built a rude pen to cage three women, these wearing many bruises on their bodies and the effects of much horror on their faces. Thrang had taken them from the tribe that dwelt in silk-hung barges along the lake-shore. Now they watched as he struggled to subdue the woman he had just captured. His round gray man's face was contorted and he tore away her jerkin with his human hands. But she held away the great sweating body with an amazing dexterity. Mazirian's eyes narrowed. Magic, magic!

So he stood watching, considering how to destroy Thrang with no harm to the woman. But she spied him over Thrang's shoulder.

"See," she panted, "Mazirian has come to kill you."

Thrang twisted about. He saw Mazirian and came charging on all fours, venting roars of wild passion. Mazirian later wondered if the ghoul had cast some sort of spell, for a strange paralysis strove to bind his brain. Perhaps the spell lay in the sight of Thrang's raging graywhite face, the great arms thrust out to grasp.

Mazirian shook off the spell, if such it were, and uttered a spell of his own, and all the valley was lit by streaming darts of fire, lashing in from all directions to spit Thrang's blundering body in a thousand places. This was the Excellent Prismatic Spray—many-colored stabbing lines. Thrang was dead almost at once, purple blood flowing from countless holes where the radiant rain had pierced him.

But Mazirian heeded little. The girl had fled. Mazirian saw her white form running along the river toward the lake, and took up the chase, heedless of the piteous cries of the three women in the pen.

The lake presently lay before him, a great sheet of water whose further rim was but dimly visible. Mazirian came down to the sandy shore and stood seeking across the dark face of Sanra Water, the Lake of Dreams. Deep night with only a verge of afterglow ruled the sky, and stars glistened on the smooth surface. The water lay cool and still, tideless as all Earth's waters had been since the moon had departed the sky.

Where was the woman? There, a pale white form, quiet in the shadow across the river. Mazirian stood on the riverbank, tall and commanding, a light breeze ruffling the cloak around his legs.

"Ho, girl," he called. "It is I, Mazirian, who saved you from Thrang. Come close, that I may speak to you."

"At this distance I hear you well, Magician," she replied. "The closer I approach the farther I must flee."

"Why then do you flee? Return with me and you shall be mistress of many secrets and hold much power."

She laughed. "If I wanted these, Mazirian, would I have fled so far?"

"Who are you then that you desire not the secrets of magic?"

"To you, Mazirian, I am nameless, lest you curse me. Now I go where you may not come." She ran down the shore, waded slowly out till the water circled her waist, then sank out of sight. She was gone.

Mazirian paused indecisively. It was not good to use so many spells and thus shear himself of power. What might exist below the lake? The sense of quiet magic was there, and though he was not at enmity with the Lake Lord, other beings might resent a trespass. However, when the figure of the girl did not break the surface, he uttered the Charm of Untiring Nourishment and entered the cool waters.

He plunged deep through the Lake of Dreams, and as he stood on the bottom, his lungs at ease by virtue of the charm, he marveled at the fey place he had come upon. Instead of blackness a green light glowed everywhere and the water was but little less clear than air. Plants undulated to the current and with them moved the lake flowers, soft with blossoms of red, blue and yellow. In and out swam large-eyed fish of many shapes.

The bottom dropped by rocky steps to a wide plain where trees of the underlake floated up from slender stalks to elaborate fronds and purple water-fruits, and so till the misty wet distance veiled all. He saw the woman, a white water nymph now, her hair like dark fog. She half-swam, half-ran across the sandy floor of the water-world, occasionally looking back over her shoulder. Mazirian came after, his cloak streaming out behind.

He drew nearer to her, exulting. He must punish her for leading him so far . . . The ancient stone stairs below his workroom led deep and at last opened into chambers that grew ever vaster as one went deeper. Mazirian had found a rusted cage in one of these chambers. A week or two locked in the blackness would curb her willfulness. And once he had dwindled a woman small as his thumb and kept her in a little glass bottle with two buzzing flies . . .

A ruined white temple showed through the green. There were many columns, some toppled, some still upholding the pediment. The woman entered the great portico under the shadow of the architrave. Perhaps she was attempting to elude him; he must follow closely. The white body glimmered at the far end of the nave, swimming now over the rostrum and into a semi-circular alcove behind.

Mazirian followed as fast as he was able, half-swimming, half-walking through the solemn dimness. He peered across the murk. Smaller columns here precariously upheld a dome from which the keystone had dropped. A sudden fear smote him, then realization as he saw the flash of movement from above. On all sides the columns toppled in, and an avalanche of marble blocks tumbled at his head. He jumped frantically back.

The commotion ceased, the white dust of the ancient mortar

drifted away. On the pediment of the main temple the woman kneeled on slender knees, staring down to see how well she had killed Mazirian.

She had failed. Two columns, by sheerest luck, had crashed to either side of him, and a slab had protected his body from the blocks. He moved his head painfully. Through a chink in the tumbled marble he could see the woman, leaning to discern his body. So she would kill him? He, Mazirian, who had already lived more years than he could easily reckon? So much more would she hate and fear him later. He called his charm, the Spell of the Omnipotent Sphere. A film of force formed around his body, expanding to push aside all that resisted. When the marble ruins had been thrust back, he destroyed the sphere, regained his feet, and glared about for the woman. She was almost out of sight, behind a brake of long purple kelp, climbing the slope to the shore. With all his power he set out in pursuit.

T'sain dragged herself up on the beach. Still behind her came Mazirian the Magician, whose power had defeated each of her plans. The memory of his face passed before her and she shivered. He must not take her now.

Fatigue and despair slowed her feet. She had set out with but two spells, the Charm of Untiring Nourishment and a spell affording strength to her arms—the last permitting her to hold off Thrang and tumble the temple upon Mazirian. These were exhausted; she was bare of protection; but, on the other hand, Mazirian could have nothing left.

Perhaps he was ignorant of the vampire-weed. She ran up the slope and stood behind a patch of pale, wind-beaten grass. And now Mazirian came from the lake, a spare form visible against the shimmer of the water.

She retreated, keeping the innocent patch of grass between them. If the grass failed—her mind quailed at the thought of what she must do.

Mazirian strode into the grass. The sickly blades became sinewy fingers. They twined about his ankles, holding him in an unbreakable grip, while others sought to find his skin.

So Mazirian chanted his last spell—the incantation of paralysis, and the vampire grass grew lax and slid limply to earth. T'sain watched with dead hope. He was now close upon her, his cloak flapping behind. Had he no weakness? Did not his fibers ache, did not his breath come short? She whirled and fled across the meadow, toward a grove of black trees. Her skin chilled at the deep shadows, the somber frames. But the thud of the Magician's feet was loud. She plunged into the dread shade. Before all in the grove awoke she must go as far as possible.

Snap! A thong lashed at her. She continued to run. Another and another—she fell. Another great whip and another beat at her. She staggered up, and on, holding her arms before her face. Snap! The flails whistled through the air, and the last blow twisted her around. So she saw Mazirian.

He fought. As the blows rained on him, he tried to seize the whips and break them. But they were supple and springy beyond his powers, and jerked away to beat at him again. Infuriated by his resistance, they concentrated on the unfortunate Magician, who foamed and fought with transcendent fury, and T'sain was permitted to crawl to the edge of the grove with her life.

She looked back in awe at the expression of Mazirian's lust for life. He staggered about in a cloud of whips, his furious obstinate figure dimly silhouetted. He weakened and tried to flee, and then he fell. The blows pelted at him—on his head, shoulders, the long legs. He tried to rise but fell back.

T'sain closed her eyes in lassitude. She felt the blood oozing from her broken flesh. But the most vital mission yet remained. She reached her feet, and reelingly set forth. For a long time the thunder of many blows reached her ears.

Mazirian's garden was surpassingly beautiful by night. The star-blossoms spread wide, each of magic perfection, and the captive half-vegetable moths flew back and forth. Phosphorescent water-lilies floated like charming faces on the pond and the bush which Mazirian had brought from far Almery in the south tinctured the air with sweet fruity perfume.

T'sain, weaving and gasping, now came groping through the garden. Certain of the flowers awoke and regarded her curiously. The half-animal hybrid sleepily chittered at her, thinking to recognize Mazirian's step. Faintly to be heard was the wistful music of the blue-cupped flowers singing of ancient nights when a white moon swam the sky, and great storms and clouds and thunder ruled the seasons.

T'sain passed unheeding. She entered Mazirian's house, found the workroom where glowed the eternal yellow lamps. Mazirian's golden-haired vat-thing sat up suddenly and stared at her with his beautiful vacant eyes.

She found Mazirian's keys in the cabinet, and managed to claw open the trap door. Here she slumped to rest and let the pink gloom pass from her eyes. Visions began to come—Mazirian, tall and arrogant, stepping out to kill Thrang; the strange-hued flowers under the lake; Mazirian, his magic lost, fighting the whips . . . She was brought from the half-trance by the vat-thing timidly fumbling with her hair.

She shook herself awake, and half-walked, half-fell down the stairs. She unlocked the thrice-bound door, thrust it open with almost the last desperate urge of her body. She wandered in to clutch at the pedestal where the glass-topped box stood and Turjan and the dragon were playing their desperate game. She flung the glass crashing to the floor, gently lifted Turjan out and set him down.

The spell was disrupted by the touch of the rune at her wrist, and Turjan became a man again. He looked aghast at the nearly unrecognizable T'sain.

She tried to smile up at him.

"Turjan—you are free—"

"And Mazirian?"

"He is dead." She slumped wearily to the stone floor and lay limp. Turjan surveyed her with an odd emotion in his eyes.

"T'sain, dear creature of my mind," he whispered, "more noble are you than I, who used the only life you knew for my freedom."

He lifted her body in his arms.

"But I shall restore you to the vats. With your brain I build another T'sain, as lovely as you. We go."

He bore her up the stone stairs.

PLEASE STAND BY

by
Ron Goulart

*Ron Goulart has published scores of novels and hun-
dreds of short stories, the vast majority wonderful, zany
tales bursting with social satire. Goulart is sf's premier
humorist, and once addicted to his work, the reader is
hooked for life. Among his best books are AFTER
THINGS FELL APART (1970), GADGET MAN (1971),
SKYROCKET STEELE (1980), and the story collections
WHAT'S BECOME OF SCREWLOOSE? AND OTHER
INQUIRIES (1971) and NUTZENBOLTS AND MORE
TROUBLES WITH MACHINES (1975). He is even better at the shorter lengths, and a BEST OF GOULART
would be a treasure.*

*Perhaps the funniest story Ron Goulart ever wrote,
''Please Stand By'' recounts the difficulties of being
transformed into an elephant on national holidays!*

The art department secretary put her Christmas tree down and
kissed Max Kearny. ''There's somebody to see you,'' she said,
getting her coat the rest of the way on and picking up the tree again.

Max shifted on his stool. "On the last working day before Christmas?"

"Pile those packages in my arms," the secretary said. "He says it's an emergency."

Moving away from his drawing board Max arranged the gift packages in the girl's arms. "Who is it? A rep?"

"Somebody named Dan Padgett."

"Oh, sure. He's a friend of mine from another agency. Tell him to come on back."

"Will do. You'll have a nice Christmas, won't you, Max?"

"I think the Salvation Army has something nice planned."

"No, seriously, Max. Don't sit around some cold bar. Well, Merry Christmas."

"Same to you." Max looked at the rough layout on his board for a moment and then Dan Padgett came in. "Hi, Dan. What is it?"

Dan Padgett rubbed his palms together. "You still have your hobby?"

Max shook out a cigarette from his pack. "The ghost detective stuff? Sure."

"But you don't specialize in ghosts only?" Dan went around the room once, then closed the door.

"No. I'm interested in most of the occult field. The last case I worked on involved a free-lance resurrectionist. Why?"

"You remember Anne Clemens, the blonde?"

"Yeah. You used to go out with her when we worked at Bryan-Josephs and Associates. Skinny girl."

"Slender. Fashion model type." Dan sat in the room's chair and unbuttoned his coat. "I want to marry her."

"Right now?"

"I asked her two weeks ago but she hasn't given me an answer yet. One reason is Kenneth Westerland."

"The animator?"

"Yes. The guy who created Major Bowser. He's seeing Anne, too."

"Well," said Max, dragging his stool back from the drawing board. "I don't do lovelorn work, Dan. Now if Westerland were a vampire or a warlock I might be able to help."

"He's not the main problem. It's if Anne says yes."

"What is?"

"I can't marry her."

"Change of heart?"

"No." Dan tilted to his feet. "No." He rubbed his hands

together. "No, I love her. The thing is there's something wrong with me. I hate to bother you so close to Christmas, but that's part of it."

Max lit a fresh cigarette from the old one. "I still don't have a clear idea of the problem, Dan."

"I change into an elephant on all national holidays."

Max leaned forward and squinted one eye at Dan. "An elephant?"

"Middle-sized gray elephant."

"On national holidays?"

"More or less. It started on Halloween. It didn't happen again till Thanksgiving. Fortunately I can talk during it and I was able to explain to my folks that I wouldn't get home for our traditional Thanksgiving get-together."

"How do you dial the phone?"

"I waited till they called me. You can pick up a phone with your trunk. I found that out."

"Usually people change into cats or wolves."

"I wouldn't mind that," Dan said, sitting. "A wolf, that's acceptable. It has a certain appeal. I'd even settle for a giant cockroach, for the symbolic value. But a middle-sized gray elephant. I can't expect Anne to marry me when I do things like that."

"You don't think," said Max, crossing to the window and looking down at the late afternoon crowds, "that you're simply having hallucinations?"

"If I am they are pretty authentic. Thanksgiving Day I ate a bale of hay." Dan tapped his fingers on his knees. "See, the first time I changed I got hungry after a while. But I couldn't work the damned can opener with my trunk. So I figured I'd get a bale of hay and keep it handy if I ever changed again."

"You seemed to stay an elephant for how long?"

"Twenty-four hours. The first time—both times I've been in my apartment, which has a nice solid floor—I got worried. I trumpeted and stomped around. Then the guy upstairs, the queer ceramacist, started pounding on the floor. I figured I'd better keep quiet so nobody would call the cops and take me off to a zoo or animal shelter. Well, I waited around and tried to figure things out and then right on the nose at midnight I was myself again."

Max ground his cigarette into the small metal pie plate on his workstand. "You're not putting me on, are you?"

"No, Max." Dan looked up hopefully. "Is this in your line? I

don't know anyone else to ask. I tried to forget it. Now, though,
Christmas is nearly here. Both other times I changed was on a
holiday. I'm worried.''

"Lycanthropy," said Max. "That can't be it. Have you been
near any elephants lately?''

"I was at the zoo a couple of years ago. None of them bit me
or even looked at me funny.''

"This is something else. Look, Dan, I've got a date with a
girl down in Palo Alto on Christmas Day. But Christmas Eve I
can be free. Do you change right on the dot?''

"If it happens I should switch over right at midnight on the
twenty-fourth. I already told my folks I was going to spend these
holidays with Anne. And I told her I'd be with them.''

"Which leaves her free to see Westerland.''

"That son of a bitch.''

"Major Bowser's not a bad cartoon show.''

"Successful anyway. That dog's voice is what makes the
show. I hate Westerland and I've laughed at it." Dan rose.
"Maybe nothing will happen.''

"If anything does it may give me a lead.''

"Hope so. Well, Merry Christmas, Max. See you tomorrow
night.''

Max nodded and Dan Padgett left. Leaning over his drawing
board Max wrote *Hex?* on the margin of his layout.

He listened to the piped in music play Christmas carols for a
few minutes and then started drawing again.

The bale of hay crackled as Max sat down on it. He lit a
cigarette carefully and checked his watch again. "Half hour to
go," he said.

Dan Padgett poured some scotch into a cup marked Tom &
Jerry and closed the venetian blinds. "I felt silly carrying that
bale of hay up here. People expect to see you with a tree this
time of year.''

"You could have hung tinsel on it.''

"That'd hurt my fillings when I eat the hay." Dan poured
some more scotch and walked to the heater outlet. He kicked it
once. "Getting cold in here. I'm afraid to complain to the
landlady. She'd probably say—'Who else would let you keep an
elephant in your rooms? A little chill you shouldn't mind.' ''

"You know," said Max, "I've been reading up on lycanthropy.
A friend of mine runs an occult bookshop.''

"Non-fiction seems to be doing better and better.''

"There doesn't seem to be any recorded case of were-elephants."

"Maybe the others didn't want any publicity."

"Maybe. It's more likely somebody has put a spell on you. In that case you could change into most anything."

Dan frowned. "I hadn't thought of that. What time is it?"

"Quarter to."

"A spell, huh? Would I have to meet the person who did it? Or is it done from a distance?"

"Usually there has to be some kind of contact."

"Say," said Dan, lowering his head and stroking his nose, "you'd better not sit on the bale of hay. Animals don't like people fooling with their food." He was standing with his feet wide apart, his legs stiff.

Max carefully got up and moved back across the room. "Something?"

"No," said Dan. He leaned far forward, reaching for the floor with his hands. "I just have an itch. My stomach."

Max watched as Dan scratched his stomach with his trunk. "Damn."

Raising his head, the middle-sized gray elephant squinted at Max. "Hell, I thought it wouldn't happen again."

"Can I come closer?"

Dan beckoned with his trunk. "I won't trample you."

Max reached out and touched the side of the elephant. "You're a real elephant sure enough."

"I should have thought to get some cabbages, too. This stuff is pretty bland." He was tearing trunkfuls of hay from the bale and stuffing them into his mouth.

Max remembered the cigarette in his hand and lit it. He walked twice around the elephant and said, "Think back now, Dan. To the first time this happened. When was it?"

"I told you. Halloween."

"But that's not really a holiday. Was it the day after Halloween? Or the night itself?"

"Wait. It was before. It was the day after the party at Eando Carawan's. In the Beach."

"Where?"

"North Beach. There was a party. Anne knows Eando's wife. Her name is Eando, too."

"Why?"

"His name is Ernest and hers is Olivia. E-and-O. So they both called themselves Eando. They paint those pictures of bug-eyed children you can buy in all the stores down there. You should know them, being an artist yourself.''

Max grunted. ''Ernie Carawan. Sure, he used to be a freelance artist, specializing in dogs. We stopped using him because all his dogs started having bug-eyes.''

''You ought to see Olivia.''

''What happened at the party?''

''Well,'' said Dan, tearing off more hay, ''I get the idea that there was some guy at this party. A little round fat guy. About your height. Around thirty-five. Somebody said he was a stage magician or something.''

''Come on,'' said Max, ''elephants are supposed to have good memories.''

''I think I was sort of drunk at the time. I can't remember all he said. Something about doing me a favor. And a flash.''

''A flash?''

''The flash came to him like that. I told him to—to do whatever he did.'' Dan stopped eating the hay. ''That would be magic, though, Max. That's impossible.''

''Shut up and eat your hay. Anything is possible.''

''You're right. Who'd have thought I'd be spending Christmas as an elephant.''

''That magician for one,'' said Max. ''What's his name? He may know something.''

''His name?''

''That's right.''

''I don't know. He didn't tell me.''

''Just came up and put a spell on you.''

''You know how it is at parties.''

Max found the phone on a black table near the bookshelves. ''Where's the phone book?''

''Oh, yeah.''

''What?''

''It's not here. The last time I was an elephant I ate it.''

''I'll get Carawan's number from information and see if he knows who this wizard is.''

Carawan didn't. But someone at his Christmas Eve party did. The magician ran a sandal shop in North Beach. His name was Claude Waller. As far as anyone knew he was visiting his ex-wife in Los Angeles for Christmas and wouldn't be back until Monday or Tuesday.

* * *

Max reached for the price tag on a pair of orange leather slippers. The beaded screen at the back of the shop clattered.

"You a fagot or something, buddy?" asked the heavy-set man who came into the room.

"No, sir. Sorry."

"Then you don't want that pair of slippers. That's my fagot special. Also comes in light green. Who are you?"

"Max Kearny. Are you Claude Waller?"

Waller was wearing a loose brown suit. He unbuttoned the coat and sat down on a stool in front of the counter. "That's who I am. The little old shoemaker."

Max nodded.

"That's a switch on the wine commercial with the little old winemaker."

"I know."

"My humor always bombs. It's like my life. A big bomb. What do you want?"

"I hear you're a magician."

"No."

"You aren't?"

"Not anymore. My ex-wife, that flat-chested bitch, and I have reunited. I don't know what happened. I'm a tough guy. I don't take any crap."

"I'd say so."

"Then why'd I send her two hundred bucks to come up here?"

"Is there time to stop the check?"

"I sent cash."

"You're stuck then, I guess."

"She's not that bad."

"Do you know a guy named Dan Padgett?"

"No."

"How about Ernie Carawan?"

"Eando? Yeah."

"On Halloween you met Dan Padgett and a girl named Anne Clemens at the party the Carawans gave."

"That's a good act. Can you tell me what it says on the slip of paper in my pocket?"

"Do you remember talking to Dan? Could you have put some kind of spell on him?"

Waller slid forward off the stool. "That guy. I'll be damned. I did do it then."

"Do what?"

"I was whacked out of my mind. Juiced out of my skull, you know. I got this flash. Some guy was in trouble. This Padgett it was. I didn't think I'd really done anything. Did I?"

"He turns into an elephant on national holidays."

Waller looked at his feet. Then laughed. "He does. That's great. Why'd I do that do you suppose?"

"Tell me."

Waller stopped laughing. "I get these flashes all the time. It bugs my wife. She doesn't know who to sleep with. I might get a flash about it. Wait now." He picked up a hammer from his workbench and tapped the palm of his hand. "That girl. The blonde girl. What's her name?"

"Anne Clemens."

"There's something. Trouble. Has it happened yet?"

"What's supposed to happen?"

"Ouch," said Waller. He'd brought the hammer down hard enough to start a bruise. "I can't remember. But I know I put a spell on your friend so he could save her when the time came."

Max lit a cigarette. "It would be simpler just to tell us what sort of trouble is coming."

Waller reached out behind him to set the hammer down. He missed the bench and the hammer smashed through the top of a shoe box. "Look, Kearny. I'm not a professional wizard. It's like in baseball. Sometimes a guy's just a natural. That's the way I am. A natural, I'm sorry, buddy. I can't tell you anything else. And I can't take that spell off your friend. I don't even remember how I did it."

"There's nothing else you can remember about what kind of trouble Anne is going to have?"

Frowning, Waller said, "Dogs. A pack of dogs. Dogs barking in the rain. No, that's not right. I can't get it. I don't know. This Dan Padgett will save her." Waller bent to pick up the hammer. "I'm pretty sure of that."

"This is Tuesday. On Saturday he's due to change again. Will the trouble come on New Year's Eve?"

"Buddy, if I get another flash I'll let you know."

At the door Max said, "I'll give you my number."

"Skip it," said Waller. "When I need it, I'll know it."

The door of the old Victorian house buzzed and Max caught the doorknob and turned it. The stairway leading upstairs was lined with brown paintings of little girls with ponies and dogs. The light from the door opening upstairs flashed down across the bright gilt frames on which eagles and flowers twisted and curled together.

"Max Kearny?" said Anne Clemens over the stair railing.

"Hi, Anne. Are you busy?"

"Not at the moment. I'm going out later. I just got home from work a little while ago."

This was Wednesday night. Max hadn't been able to find Anne at home until now. "I was driving by and I thought I'd stop."

"It's been several months since we've seen each other," said the girl as Max reached the doorway to her apartment. "Come in."

She was wearing a white blouse and what looked like a pair of black leotards. She wasn't as thin as Max had remembered. Her blonde hair was held back with a thin black ribbon.

"I won't hold you up?" Max asked.

Anne shook her head. "I won't have to start getting ready for a while yet."

"Fine." Max got out his cigarettes and sat down in the old sofa chair Anne gestured at.

"Is it something about Dan, Max?" The single overhead light was soft and it touched her hair gently.

"In a way."

"Is it some trouble?" She was sitting opposite Max, straight up on the sofa bed.

"No," said Max. "Dan's got the idea, though, that you might be in trouble of some sort."

The girl moistened her lips. "Dan's too sensitive in some areas. I think I know what he means."

Max held his pack of cigarettes to her.

"No, thanks. Dan's worried about Ken Westerland, isn't he?"

"That's part of it."

"Max," said Anne, "I worked for Ken a couple of years ago. We've gone out off and on since then. Dan shouldn't worry about that."

"Westerland isn't causing you any trouble?"

"Ken? Of course not. If I seem hesitant to Dan it's only that I don't want Ken to be hurt either." She frowned, turning away. She turned back to Max and studied him as though he had suddenly appeared across from her. "What was I saying? Well, never mind. I really should be getting ready."

"If you need anything," said Max, "let me know."

"What?"

"I said that—"

"Oh, yes. If I need anything. Fine. If I'm going to dinner I should get started."

"You studying modern dance?"

Anne opened the door. "The leotards. No. They're comfortable. I don't have any show business leanings." She smiled quickly. "Thank you for dropping by, Max."

The door closed and he was in the hall. Max stood there long enough to light a cigarette and then went downstairs and outside.

It was dark now. The street lights were on and the night cold was coming. Max got in his car and sat back, watching the front steps of Anne's building across the street. Next to his car was a narrow empty lot, high with dark grass. A house had been there once and when it was torn down the stone stairs had been left. Max's eyes went up, stopping in nothing beyond the last step. Shaking his head and lighting a new cigarette he turned to watch Anne's apartment house.

The front of the building was covered with yards and yards of white wooden gingerbread. It wound around and around the house. There was a wide porch across the building front. One with a peaked roof over it.

About an hour later Kenneth Westerland parked his gray Mercedes sedan at the corner. He was a tall thin man of about thirty-five. He had a fat man's face, too round and plump-cheeked for his body. He was carrying a small suitcase.

After Westerland had gone inside Max left his car and walked casually to the corner. He crossed the street. He stepped suddenly across a lawn and into the row of darkness alongside Anne's building. Using a garbage can to stand on Max pulled himself up onto the first landing of the fire escape without use of the noisy ladder.

Max sat on the fire escape rail and, concealing the match flame, lit a cigarette. When he'd finished smoking it he ground out the butt against the ladder. Then he swung out around the edge of the building and onto the top of the porch roof. Flat on his stomach he worked up the slight incline. In a profusion of ivy and hollyhock Max concealed himself and let his left eye look up into the window.

This was the window of her living room and he could see Anne sitting in the chair he'd been sitting in. She was wearing a black cocktail dress now and her hair was down, touching her shoulders. She was watching Westerland. The suitcase was sitting on the rug between Max and the animator.

Westerland had a silver chain held between his thumb and forefinger. On the end of the chain a bright silver medallion spun.

Max blinked and ducked back into the vines. Westerland was hypnotizing Anne. It was like an illustration from a pulp magazine.

Looking in again Max saw Westerland let the medallion drop into his suit pocket. Westerland came toward the window and Max eased down.

After a moment he looked in. Westerland had opened the suitcase. It held a tape recorder. The mike was in Anne's hand. In her other she held several stapled together sheets of paper.

Westerland pushed her coffee table in front of Anne and she set the papers on it. Her eyes seemed focused still on the spot where the spinning disc had been.

On his knees by the tape machine Westerland fitted on a spool of tape. After speaking a few words into the mike he gave it back to the girl. They began recording what had to be a script of some kind.

From the way Westerland used his face he was doing different voices. Anne's expression never changed as she spoke. Max couldn't hear anything.

Letting himself go flat he slid back to the edge of the old house and swung onto the fire escape. He waited to make sure no one had seen him and went to work on the window that led to the escape. It wasn't much work because there was no lock on it. It hadn't been opened for quite a while and it creaked. Max stepped into the hall and closed the window. Then he went slowly to the door of Anne's apartment and put his ear against it.

He could hear the voices faintly now. Westerland speaking as various characters. Anne using only one voice, not her own. Max sensed something behind him and turned to see the door of the next apartment opening. A big girl with black-rimmed glasses was looking at him.

"What is it?" she said.

Max smiled and came to her door. "Nobody home I guess. Perhaps you'd like to subscribe to the *Seditionist Daily*. If I sell eight more subscriptions I get a stuffed panda."

The girl poked her chin. "A panda? A grown man like you shouldn't want a stuffed panda."

Max watched her for a second. "It is sort of foolish. To hell with them then. It's not much of a paper anyway. No comics and only fifteen words in the crossword puzzle. Good night, miss. Sorry to bother you. You've opened my eyes." He went down the stairs as the door closed behind him.

What he'd learned tonight gave him no clues as to Dan's problem. But it was interesting. For some reason Anne Clemens was the voice of Westerland's animated cartoon character, Major Bowser.

By Friday Max had found out that Westerland had once worked in night clubs as a hypnotist. That gave him no leads about why Dan Padgett periodically turned into an elephant.

Early in the afternoon Dan called him. "Max. Something's wrong."

"Have you changed already?"

"No, I'm okay. But I can't find Anne."

"What do you mean?"

"She hasn't showed up at work today. And I can't get an answer at her place."

"Did you tell her about Westerland? About what I found out the other night?"

"I know you said not to. But you also said I was due to save her from some trouble. I thought maybe telling her about Westerland was the way to do it."

"You're supposed to save her while you're an elephant. Damn it. I didn't want her to know what Westerland was doing yet."

"If it's any help Anne didn't know she was Major Bowser. And she thinks she went to dinner with Westerland on Wednesday."

"No wonder she's so skinny. Okay. What else did she say?"

"She thought I was kidding. Then she seemed to become convinced. Even asked me how much Westerland probably made off the series."

"Great," said Max, making heavy lines on his memo pad. "Now she's probably gone to him and asked him for her back salary or something."

"Is that so bad?"

"We don't know." Max looked at his watch. "I can take off right now. I'll go out to her place and look around. Then check at Westerland's apartment. He lives out on California Street. I'll call you as soon as I find out anything."

"In the meantime," said Dan, "I'd better see about getting another bale of hay."

*   *   *

There was no lead on Anne's whereabouts at her apartment, which Max broke into. Or at Westerland's, where he came in through the skylight.

At noon on Saturday Max was wondering if he should sit back and trust to Waller's prediction that Dan would save Anne when the time came.

He lit a new cigarette and wandered about his apartment. He looked through quite a few of the occult books he'd collected.

The phone rang.

"Yes?"

"This is Waller's Sandal Shop."

"The magician?"

"Right, buddy. That is you, Kearny?"

"Yes. What's happening?"

"I got a flash."

"So?"

"Go to Sausalito."

"And?"

"That's all the flash told me. You and your friend get over to Sausalito. Today. Before midnight."

"You haven't got any more details?"

"Sorry. My ex-wife got in last night and I've been too unsettled to get any full scale flashes." The line went dead.

"Sausalito?" said Dan when Max called him.

"That's what Waller says."

"Hey," said Dan. "Westerland's ex-wife."

"He's got one, too?"

"His wife had a place over there. I remember going to a party with Anne there once. Before Westerland got divorced. Could Anne be there?"

"Wouldn't Mrs. Westerland complain?"

"No, she's in Europe. It was in Herb Caen and—Max! The house would be empty now. Anne must be there. And in trouble."

The house was far back from the road that ran up through the low hills of Sausalito, the town just across the Golden Gate Bridge from San Francisco. It was a flat scattered house of redwood and glass.

Max and Dan had driven by it and parked the car. Max in the lead, they came downhill through a stretch of trees, descending toward the back of the Westerland house. It was late afternoon now and the great flat windows sparkled and went black and sparkled again as they came near. A high hedge circled the patio

and when Max and Dan came close their view of the house was
cut off.

"Think she's here?" Dan asked.

"We should be able to spot some signs of life," Max said.
"I'm turning into a first class peeping tom. All I do is watch
people's houses."

"I guess detective work's like that," said Dan. "Even the
occult stuff."

"Hold it," said Max. "Listen."

"To what?"

"I heard a dog barking."

"In the house?"

"Yep."

"Means there's somebody in there."

"It means Anne's in there probably. Pretty sure that was
Major Bowser."

"Hi, pals," said a high-pitched voice.

"Hello," said Max, turning to face the wide bald man behind
them.

"Geese Louise," the man said, pointing his police special at
them, "this sure saves me a lot of work. The boss had me out
looking for you all day. And just when I was giving up and
coming back here with my tail between my legs—well, here you
are."

"Who's your boss?"

"Him. Westerland. I'm a full-time pro gunman. Hired to get
you."

"You got us," said Max.

"Look, would you let me tell him I caught you over in Frisco?
Makes me seem more efficient."

"We will," said Max, "if you'll let us go. Tell him we used
karate on you. We can even break your arm to make it look
good."

"No," said the bald man. "Let it pass. You guys want too
many concessions. Go on inside."

Westerland was opening the refrigerator when his gunman
brought Max and Dan into the kitchen.

"You brought it off, Lloyd," said Westerland, taking a popsicle
from the freezer compartment.

"I studied those pictures you gave me."

"Where's Anne?" Dan asked.

Westerland squeezed the wrapper off the popsicle. "Here.
We've only this minute finished a recording session. Sit down."

When the four of them were around the white wooden table Westerland said, "You, Mr. Kearny."

Max took out his pack of cigarettes and put them on the table in front of him. "Sir?"

"Your detective work will be the ruin of you."

"All I did was look through a few windows. It's more acrobatics than detection."

"Nevertheless, you're on to me. Your overprotective attitude toward Miss Clemens has caused you to stumble on one of the most closely guarded secrets of the entertainment industry."

"You mean Anne's being the voice of Major Bowser?"

"Exactly," said Westerland, his round cheeks caving as he sucked the popsicle. "But it's too late. Residuals and reruns."

Dan tapped the tabletop. "What's that mean?"

"What else? I've completed taping the sound track for episode 78 F Major Bowser. I have a new series in the works. Within a few months the major will be released to secondary markets. That means I don't need Anne Clemens anymore."

Dan clenched his fists. "So let her go."

"Why did you ever need her?" Max asked, looking at Westerland.

"She's an unconscious talent," said Westerland, catching the last fragment of the popsicle off the stick. "She first did that voice one night over two years ago. After a party I'd taken her to. She'd had too much to drink. I thought it was funny. The next day she'd forgotten about it. Couldn't even remember the voice. Instead of pressing her I used my hypnotic ability. I had a whole sketch book full of drawings of that damned dog. The voice clicked. It matched. I used it."

"And made $100,000," said Dan.

"The writing is mine. And quite a bit of the drawing."

"And now?" said Max.

"She knows about it. She has thoughts of marrying and settling down. She asked me if $5,000 would be a fair share of the profits from the major."

"Is that scale for 78 shows?" Max said.

"I could look it up," said Westerland. He was at the refrigerator again. "Lemon, lime, grape, watermelon. How's grape sound? Fine. Grape it is." He stood at the head of the table and unwrapped the purple popsicle. "I've come up with an alternative. I intend to eliminate all of you. Much cheaper way of settling things."

"You're kidding," said Dan.

"Animators are supposed to be lovable guys like Walt Disney," said Max.

"I'm a businessman first. I can't use Anne Clemens anymore. We'll fix her first and you two at some later date. Lloyd, put these detectives in the cellar and lock it up."

Lloyd grinned and pointed to a door beyond the stove. Max and Dan were made to go down a long flight of wooden stairs and into a room that was filled with the smell of old newspapers and unused furniture. There were small dusty windows high up around the beamed ceiling.

"Not a very tough cellar," Dan whispered to Max.

"But you won't be staying here," said Lloyd. He kept his gun aimed at them and stepped around a fallen tricycle to a wide oak door in the cement wall. A padlock and chain hung down from a hook on the wall. Lloyd slid the bolt and opened the door. "The wine cellar. He showed it to me this morning. No wine left, but it's homey. You'll come to like it."

He got them inside and bolted the door. The chains rattled and the padlock snapped.

Max blinked. He lit a match and looked around the cement room. It was about twelve feet high and ten feet wide.

Dan made his way to an old cobbler's bench in the corner. "Does your watch glow in the dark?" he asked as the match went out.

"It's five thirty."

"The magician was right. We're in trouble."

"I'm wondering," said Max, striking another match.

"You're wondering what the son of a bitch is going to do to Anne."

"Yes," Max said, spotting an empty wine barrel. He turned it upside down and sat on it.

"And what'll he do with us?"

Max started a cigarette from the dying match flames. "Drop gas pellets through the ceiling, fill the room with water, make the walls squeeze in."

"Westerland's trickier than that. He'll probably hypnotize us into thinking we're pheasants and then turn us loose the day the hunting season opens."

"Wonder how Lloyd knew what we looked like."

"Anne's got my picture in her purse. And one I think we all took at some beach party once."

Max leaned back against the dark wall. "This is about a middle-sized room, isn't it?"

"I don't know. The only architecture course I took at school was in water color painting."

"In six hours you'll be a middle-sized elephant."

Dan's bench clattered. "You think this is it?"

"Should be. How else are we going to get out of here?"

"I smash the door like a real elephant would." He snapped his fingers. "That's great."

"You should be able to do it."

"But Max?"

"Yeah?"

"Suppose I don't change?"

"You will."

"We only have the word of an alcoholic shoemaker."

"He knew about Sausalito."

"He could be a fink."

"He's a real magician. You're proof of that."

"Max?"

"Huh?"

"Maybe Westerland hypnotized us into thinking I was an elephant."

"How could he hypnotize me? I haven't seen him for years."

"He could hypnotize you and then make you forget you were."

"Dan," said Max, "relax. After midnight if we're still in here we can think up excuses."

"How do we know he won't harm Anne before midnight?"

"We don't."

"Let's try to break out now."

Max lit a match and stood up. "I don't think these barrel staves will do it. See anything else?"

"Legs off this bench. We can unscrew them and bang the door down."

They got the wooden legs loose and taking one each began hammering at the bolt with them.

After a few minutes a voice echoed in. "Stop that ruckus."

"The hell with you," said Dan.

"Wait now," said Westerland's voice. "You can't break down the door. And even if you could Lloyd would shoot you. I'm sending him down to sit guard. Last night at Playland he won four Betty Boop dolls at the shooting gallery. Be rational."

"How come we can hear you?"

"I'm talking through an air vent."

"Where's Anne?" shouted Dan.

"Still in a trance. If you behave I may let her bark for you before we leave."

"You louse."

Max found Dan in the dark and caught his arm. "Take it easy." Raising his voice he said, "Westerland, how long do we stay down here?"

"Well, my ex-wife will be in Rome until next April. I hope to have a plan worked out by then. At the moment, however, I can't spare the time. I have to get ready for the party."

"What party?"

"The New Year's Eve party at the Leversons'. It's the one where Anne Clemens will drink too much."

"What?"

"She'll drink too much and get the idea she's an acrobat. She'll borrow a car and drive to the Golden Gate Bridge. While trying out her act on the top rail she'll discover she's not an acrobat at all and actually has a severe dread of heights. When I hear about it I'll still be at the Leversons' party. I'll be saddened that she was able to see so little of the New Year."

"You can't make her do that. Hypnotism doesn't work that way."

"That's what you say now, Padgett. In the morning I'll have Lloyd slip the papers under the door."

The pipe stopped talking.

Dan slammed his fist into the cement wall. "He can't do it."

"Who are the Leversons?"

Dan was silent for a moment. "Leverson. Joe and Jackie. Isn't that the art director at BBDO? He and his wife live over here. Just up from Sally Stanford's restaurant. It could be them."

"It's a long way to midnight," said Max. "But I have a feeling we'll make it."

"We have to save Anne," said Dan, "and there doesn't seem to be anything to do but wait."

"What's the damn time, Max?"

"Six thirty."

"Must be nearly eight by now."

"Seven fifteen."

"I think I still hear them up there."

*   *   *

"Now?"

"Little after nine."

"Only ten? Is that watch going?"

"Yeah, it's ticking."

"Eleven yet, Max?"

"In five minutes."

"They've gone, I'm sure."

"Relax."

"Look," said Dan, when Max told him it was quarter to twelve, "I don't want to step on you if I change."

"I'll duck down on the floor by your feet. Your present feet. Then when you've changed I should be under your stomach."

"Okay. After I do you hop on my back."

At five to twelve Max sat down on the stone floor. "Happy New Year."

Dan's feet shuffled, moved farther apart. "My stomach is starting to itch."

Max ducked a little. In the darkness a darker shadow seemed to grow overhead. "Dan?"

"I did it, Max." Dan laughed. "I did it right on time."

Max edged up and climbed on top of the elephant. "I'm aboard."

"Hang on. I'm going to push the door with my head."

Max hung on and waited. The door creaked and began to give.

"Watch it, you guys!" shouted Lloyd from outside.

"Trumpet at him," said Max.

"Good idea." Dan gave a violent angry elephant roar.

"Jesus!" Lloyd said.

The door exploded out and Dan's trunk slapped Lloyd into the side of the furnace. His gun sailed into a clothes basket. Max jumped down and retrieved it.

"Go away," he said to Lloyd.

Lloyd blew his nose. "What kind of prank is this?"

"If he doesn't go," said Max, "trample him."

"Let's trample him no matter what," said Dan.

Lloyd left.

"Hell," said Dan. "How do I get up those stairs?"

"You don't," said Max, pointing. "See there, behind that stack of papers. A door. I'll see if it's open."

"Who cares. I'll push it open."

"Okay. I'll go find a phone book and look up Leversons. Meet you in the patio."

Dan trumpeted and Max ran up the narrow wooden stairs.

The elephant careened down the grassy hillside. All around now New Year's horns were sounding.

"Only two Leversons, huh?" Dan asked again.

"It's most likely the art director. He's nearest the bridge."

They came out on Bridgeway, which ran along the water.

Dan trumpeted cars and people out of the way and Max ducked down, holding onto the big elephant ears.

They turned as the road curved and headed them for the Leverson home. "It better be this one," Dan said.

The old two story house was filled with lighted windows, the windows spotted with people. "A party sure enough," said Max.

In the long twisted driveway a motor started. "A car," said Dan, running up the gravel.

Max jumped free as Dan made himself a road block in the driveway.

Red tail lights tinted the exhaust of a small gray Jaguar convertible. Max ran to the car. Anne Clemens jerked the wheel and spun it. Max dived over the back of the car and, teetering on his stomach, jerked the ignition key off and out. Anne kept turning the wheel.

Max caught her by the shoulders, swung around off the car and pulled her up so that she was now kneeling in the driver's seat.

The girl shook her head twice, looking beyond Max.

He got the door open and helped her out. The gravel seemed to slide away from them in all directions.

"Duck," yelled Dan, still an elephant.

Max didn't turn. He dropped, pulling the girl with him.

A shot smashed a cobweb pattern across the windshield.

"You've spoiled it for sure," cried Westerland. "You and your silly damn elephant have spoiled my plan for sure."

The parking area lights were on and a circle of people was forming behind Westerland. He was standing twenty feet away from Max and Anne.

Then he fell over as Dan's trunk flipped his gun away from him.

Dan caught up the fallen animator and shook him.

Max got Anne to her feet and held onto her. "Bring her out of this, Westerland."

"In a pig's valise."

Dan tossed him up and caught him.

"Come on."

"Since you're so belligerent," said Westerland. "Dangle me closer to her."

Max had Lloyd's gun in his coat pocket. He took it out now and pointed it up at the swinging Westerland. "No wise stuff."

Westerland snapped his fingers near Anne's pale face.

She shivered once and fell against Max. He put his arms under hers and held her.

Dan suddenly dropped Westerland and, trumpeting once at the silent guests, galloped away into the night.

As his trumpet faded a siren filled the night.

"Real detectives," said Max.

Both Anne and Westerland were out. The guests were too far away to hear him.

A bush crackled behind him and Max turned his head.

Dan, himself again, came up to them. "Would it be okay if I held Anne?"

Max carefully transferred her. "She should be fine when she comes to."

"What'll we tell the law?"

"The truth. Except for the elephant."

"How'd we get from his place here?"

"My car wouldn't start. We figured he'd tampered with it. We hailed a passing motorist who dropped us here."

"People saw the elephant."

"It escaped from a zoo."

"What zoo?"

"Look," said Max, dropping the gun back into his pocket, "don't be so practical about this. We don't have to explain it. Okay?"

"Okay. Thanks, Max."

Max lit a cigarette.

"I changed back in only an hour. I don't think it will happen again, Max. Do you?"

"If it would make you feel any better I'll spend the night before Lincoln's Birthday with you and Anne."

"How about what?" said Anne. She looked up at Dan. "Dan? What is it?"

"Nothing much. A little trouble with Westerland. I'll explain."

Max nodded at them and went up the driveway to meet the approaching police. Somewhere in the night a final New Year's horn sounded.

WHAT GOOD IS A GLASS DAGGER?

by
Larry Niven

Larry Niven is simply amazing. Renowned for his "hard" science fiction like RINGWORLD (1970) and its sequel THE RINGWORLD ENGINEERS (1980), he is also a master of fantasy, and such books as THE FLYING SORCERERS (1971; with David Gerrold) and THE MAGIC GOES AWAY (1978) are tremendously popular. He has also teamed with Jerry Pournelle to form one of science fiction's most successful collaborative pairs. A frequent guest at sf conventions, he has won five Hugo Awards and one Nebula to date.

"What Good Is a Glass Dagger?" is the second of a series of stories in which Larry Niven tries to give a scientific explanation for magic. And as a bonus, he also throws in a new rationale for lycanthropy.

I

Twelve thousand years before the birth of Christ, in an age when miracles were somewhat more common, a warlock used an ancient secret to save his life.

In later years he regretted that. He had kept the secret of the

Warlock's Wheel for several normal lifetimes. The demon-sword
Glirendree and its stupid barbarian captive would have killed
him, no question of that. But no mere demon could have been as
dangerous as that secret.

Now it was out, spreading like ripples on a pond. The battle
between Glirendree and the Warlock was too good a tale not to
tell. Soon no man would call himself a magician who did not
know that magic could be used up. So simple, so dangerous a
secret. The wonder was that nobody had noticed it before.

A year after the battle with Glirendree, near the end of a
summer day, Aran the Peacemonger came to Shayl Village to
steal the Warlock's Wheel.

Aran was a skinny eighteen-year-old, lightly built. His face
was lean and long, with a pointed chin. His dark eyes peered out
from under a prominent shelf of bone. His short, straight dark
hair dropped almost to his brows in a pronounced widow's peak.
What he was was no secret; and anyone who touched hands with
him would have known at once, for there was short fine hair on
his palms. But had anyone known his mission, he would have
been thought mad.

For the Warlock was a leader in the Sorcerer's Guild. It was
known that he had a name; but no human throat could pronounce
it. The shadow demon who had been his name-father had later
been imprisoned in tattooed runes on the Warlock's own back:
an uncommonly dangerous bodyguard.

Yet Aran came well protected. The leather wallet that hung
from his shoulder was old and scarred, and the seams were
loose. By its look it held nuts and hard cheese and bread and
almost no money. What it actually held was charms. Magic
would serve him better than nuts and cheese, and Aran could
feed himself as he traveled, at night.

He reached the Warlock's cave shortly after sunset. He had
been told how to use his magic to circumvent the Warlock's
safeguards. His need for magic implied a need for voice and
hands, so that Aran was forced to keep the human shape; and
this made him doubly nervous. At moonrise he chanted the
words he had been taught, and drew a live bat from his pouch
and tossed it gently through the barred entrance to the cave.

The bat exploded into a mist of blood that drifted slant-wise
across the stone floor. Aran's stomach lurched. He almost ran
then; but he quelled his fear and followed it in, squeezing
between the bars.

Those who had sent him had repeatedly diagrammed the cave for him. He could have robbed it blindfolded. He would have preferred darkness to the flickering blue light from what seemed to be a captured lightning bolt tethered in the middle of the cavern. He moved quickly, scrupulously tracing what he had been told was a path of safety.

Though Aran had seen sorcerous tools in the training laboratory in the School for Mercantile Grammaree in Atlantis, most of the Warlock's tools were unfamiliar. It was not an age of mass production. He paused by a workbench, wondering. Why would the Warlock be grinding a glass dagger?

But Aran found a tarnish-blackened metal disc hanging above the workbench, and the runes inscribed around its rim convinced him that it was what he had come for. He took it down and quickly strapped it against his thigh, leaving his hands free to fight if need be. He was turning to go, when a laughing voice spoke out of the air.

"Put that down, you mangy son of a bitch—"

Aran converted to wolf.

Agony seared his thigh!

In human form Aran was a lightly built boy. As a wolf he was formidably large and dangerous. It did him little good this time. The pain was blinding, stupefying. Aran the wolf screamed and tried to run from the pain.

He woke gradually, with an ache in his head and a greater agony in his thigh and a tightness at his wrists and ankles. It came to him that he must have knocked himself out against a wall.

He lay on his side with his eyes closed, giving no sign that he was awake. Gently he tried to pull his hands apart. He was bound, wrists and ankles. Well, he had been taught a word for unbinding ropes.

Best not to use it until he knew more.

He opened his eyes a slit.

The Warlock was beside him, seated in lotus position, studying Aran with a slight smile. In one hand he held a slender willow rod.

The Warlock was a tall man in robust good health. He was deeply tanned. Legend said that the Warlock never wore anything above the waist. The years seemed to blur on him; he might have been twenty or fifty. In fact he was one hundred and ninety years old, and bragged of it. His condition indicated the power of his magic.

Behind him, Aran saw that the Warlock's Wheel had been returned to its place on the wall.

Waiting for its next victim? The real Warlock's Wheel was of copper; those who had sent Aran had known that much. But this decoy must be tarnished silver, to have seared him so.

The Warlock wore a dreamy, absent look. There might still be a chance, if he could be taken by surprise. Aran said, "Kplir—"

The Warlock lashed him across the throat.

The willow wand had plenty of spring in it. Aran choked and gagged; he tossed his head, fighting for air.

"That word has four syllables," the Warlock informed him in a voice he recognized. "You'll never get it out."

"Gluck," said Aran.

"I want to know who sent you."

Aran did not answer, though he had his wind back.

"You're no ordinary thief. But you're no magician either," the Warlock said almost musingly. "I heard you. You were chanting by rote. You used basic spells, spells that are easy to get right, but they were the right spells each time.

"Somebody's been using prescience and farsight to spy on me. Someone knows too many of my defenses," the ancient magician said gently. "I don't like that. I want to know who, and why."

When Aran did not reply, the Warlock said, "He had all the knowledge, and he knew what he was after, but he had better sense than to come himself. He sent a fool." The Warlock was watching Aran's eyes. "Or perhaps he thought a werewolf would have a better chance at me. By the way, there's silver braid in those cords, so you'd best stay human for the nonce."

"You knew I was coming."

"Oh, I had ample warning. Didn't it occur to you that I've got prescience and farsight too? It occurred to your master," said the Warlock. "He set up protections around you, a moving region where prescience doesn't work."

"Then what went wrong?"

"I foresaw the dead region, you ninny. I couldn't get a glimpse of what was stealing into my cave. But I could look around it. I could follow its path through the cavern. That path was most direct. I knew what you were after.

"Then, there were bare footprints left behind. I could study them before they were made. You waited for moonrise instead of trying to get in after dusk. On a night of the full moon, too.

"Other than that, it wasn't a bad try. Sending a werewolf was bright. It would take a kid your size to squeeze between the bars, and then a kid your size couldn't win a fight if something went wrong. A wolf your size could.''

"A lot of good it did me.''

"What I want to know is, how did they talk an Atlantean into this? They must have known what they were after. Didn't they tell you what the Wheel does?''

"Sucks up magic,'' said Aran. He was chagrined, but not surprised, that the Warlock had placed his accent.

"Sucks up *mana*,'' the Warlock corrected him. "Do you know what *mana* is?''

"The power behind magic.''

"So they taught you that much. Did they also tell you that when the *mana* is gone from a region, it doesn't come back? Ever?''

Aran rolled on his side. Being convinced that he was about to die, he felt he had nothing to lose by speaking boldly. "I don't understand why you'd want to keep it a secret. A thing like the Warlock's Wheel, it could make war obsolete! It's the greatest purely defensive weapon ever invented!''

The Warlock didn't seem to understand. Aran said, "You *must* have thought of that. Why, no enemy's curses could touch Atlantis, if the Warlock's Wheel were there to absorb it!''

"Obviously you weren't sent by the Atlantean Minister of Offense. He'd know better.'' The Warlock watched him shrewdly. "Or were you sent by the Greek Isles?''

"I don't understand.''

"Don't you know that Atlantis is tectonically unstable? For the last half a thousand years, the only thing that's kept Atlantis above the waves has been the spells of the sorcerer-kings.''

"You're lying.''

"You obviously aren't.'' The Warlock made a gesture of dismissal. "But the Wheel would be bad for any nation, not just Atlantis. Spin the Wheel, and a wide area is dead to magic for—as far as I've been able to tell—the rest of eternity. Who would want to bring about such a thing?''

"I would.''

"You would. Why?''

"We're sick of war,'' Aran said roughly. Unaware that he had said *we*. "The Warlock's Wheel would end war. Can you imagine an army trying to fight with nothing but swords and daggers? No hurling of death spells. No prescients spying out the enemy's battle plans. No killer demons beating at unseen protective walls.''

Aran's eyes glowed. "Man to man, sword against sword, blood and bronze, and no healing spells. Why, no king would ever fight on such terms! We'd give up war forever!"

"Some basic pessimism deep within me forces me to doubt it."

"You're laughing at me. You don't *want* to believe it," Aran said scornfully. "No more *mana* means the end of your youth spells. You'd be an old man, too old to live!"

"That must be it. Well, let's see who you are." The Warlock touched Aran's wallet with the willow wand, let it rest there a few moments. Aran wondered frantically what the Warlock could learn from his wallet. If the lockspells didn't hold, then—

They didn't, of course. The Warlock reached in, pulled out another live bat, then several sheets of parchment marked with what might have been geometry lessons and with script printed in a large, precise hand.

"Schoolboy script," he commented. "Lines drawn with pain-ful accuracy, mistakes scraped out and redrawn . . . The idiot! He forgot the hooked tail on the Whirlpool design. A wonder it didn't eat him." The Warlock looked up. "Am I being attacked by children? These spells were prepared by half a dozen apprentices!"

Aran didn't answer; but he lost hope of concealing anything further.

"They have talent, though. So. You're a member of the Peacemongers, aren't you? All the army-age youngsters. I'll wager you're backed by half the graduating class of the School of Mercantile Grammaree. They must have been watching me for months now, to have my defenses down so pat.

"And you want to end the war against the Greek Isles. Did you think you'd help matters by taking the Warlock's Wheel to Atlantis? Why, I'm half minded to let you walk out with the thing. It would serve you right for trying to rob me."

He looked hard into Aran's eyes. "Why, you'd do it, wouldn't you? Why? I said *why?*"

"We could still use it."

"You'd sink Atlantis. Are the Peacemongers traitors now?"

"I'm no traitor." Aran spoke low and furious. "We want to change Atlantis, not destroy it. But if we owned the Warlock's Wheel, the Palace would listen to us!"

He wriggled in his tight bonds, and thought once again of the word that would free him. Then, convert to werewolf and run! Between the bars, down the hill, into the woods and freedom.

"I think I'll make a conservative of you," the Warlock said
suddenly.

He stood up. He brushed the willow wand lightly across
Aran's lips. Aran found that he could not open his mouth. He
remembered now that he was entirely in the Warlock's power—
and that he was a captured thief.

The Warlock turned, and Aran saw the design on his back. It
was an elaborately curlicued five-sided tattoo in red and green
and gold inks. Aran remembered what he had been told of the
Warlock's bodyguard.

"Recently I dreamed," said the Warlock. "I dreamed that I
would find a use for a glass dagger. I thought that the dream
might be prophetic, and so I carved—"

"That's silly," Aran broke in. "What good is a glass dagger?"

He had noticed the dagger on the way in. It had a honed
square point and honed edges and a fused-looking hilt with a
guard. Two clamps padded with fox leather held it in place on
the work table. The uppermost cutting edge was not yet finished.

Now the Warlock removed the dagger from its clamps. While
Aran watched, the Warlock scratched designs on the blade with a
pointed chunk of diamond that must have cost him dearly. He
spoke low and softly to it, words that Aran couldn't hear. Then
he picked it up like—a dagger.

Frightened as he was, Aran could not quite believe what the
Warlock was doing. He felt like a sacrificial goat. There was
mana in sacrifice . . . and more *mana* in human sacrifice . . . but
he wouldn't. He wouldn't!

The Warlock raised the knife high, and brought it down hard
in Aran's chest.

Aran screamed. He had felt it! A whisper of sensation, a slight
ghostly tug—the knife was an insubstantial shadow. But there
was a knife in Aran the Peacemonger's heart! The hilt stood up
out of his chest!

The Warlock muttered low and fast. The glass hilt faded and
was gone, apparently.

"It's easy to make glass invisible. Glass is half invisible
already. It's still in your heart," said the Warlock. "But don't
worry about it, Don't give it a thought. Nobody will notice.
Only, be sure to spend the rest of your life in *mana*-rich territory.
Because if you ever walk into a place where magic doesn't
work—well, it'll reappear, that's all."

Aran struggled to open his mouth.

"Now, you came for the secret of the Warlock's Wheel, so

you might as well have it. It's just a simple kinetic sorcery, but open-ended.'' He gave it. ''The Wheel spins faster and faster until it's used up all the *mana* in the area. It tends to tear itself apart, so you need another spell to hold it together—'' and he gave that, speaking slowly and distinctly. Then he seemed to notice that Aran was flopping about like a fish. He said, ''Kplirapranthry.''

The ropes fell away. Aran stood up shakily. He found he could speak again, and what he said was, ''Take it out. Please.''

''Now, there's one thing about taking that secret back to Atlantis. I assume you still want to? But you'd have to describe it before you could use it as a threat. You can see how easy it is to make. A big nation like Atlantis tends to have enemies, doesn't it? And you'd be telling them how to sink Atlantis in a single night.''

Aran pawed at his chest, but he could feel nothing. ''Take it out.''

''I don't think so. Now we face the same death, wolf boy. Goodby, and give my best to the School for Mercantile Grammaree. And, oh yes, don't go back by way of Hvirin Gap.''

''Grandson of an ape!'' Aran screamed. He would not beg again. He was wolf by the time he reached the bars, and he did not touch them going through. With his mind he felt the knife in his chest, and he heard the Warlock's laughter following him down the hill and into the trees.

When next he saw the Warlock, it was thirty years later and a thousand miles away.

II

Aran traveled as a wolf, when he could. It was an age of greater magic; a werewolf could change shape whenever the moon was in the sky. In the wolf shape Aran could forage, reserving his remaining coins to buy his way home.

His thoughts were a running curse against the Warlock.

Once he turned about on a small hill, and stood facing north toward Shayl Village. He bristled, remembering the Warlock's laugh; but he remembered the glass dagger. He visualized the Warlock's throat, and imagined the taste of arterial blood; but the glowing, twisting design on the Warlock's back flashed at the back of Aran's eyes, and Aran tasted defeat. He could not fight a shadow demon. Aran howled, once, and turned south.

Nildiss Range, the backbone of a continent, rose before him as he traveled. Beyond the Range was the sea, and a choice of boats to take him home with what he had learned of the Warlock. Perhaps the next thief would have better luck . . .

And so he came to Hvirin Gap.

Once the range had been a formidable barrier to trade. Then, almost a thousand years ago, a sorcerer of Rynildissen had worked an impressive magic. The Range had been split as if by a cleaver. Where the mountains to either side sloped precipitously upward, Hvirin Gap sloped smoothly down to the coast, between rock walls flat enough to have a polished look.

Periodically the bandits had to be cleaned out of Hvirin Gap. This was more difficult every year; for the spells against banditry didn't work well there, and swords had to be used instead. The only compensation was that the dangerous mountain dragons had disappeared too.

Aran stopped at the opening. He sat on his haunches, considering.

For the Warlock might have been lying. He might have thought it funny to send Aran the long way over Nildiss Range.

But the dragon bones. Where magic didn't work, dragons died. The bones were there, huge and reptilian. They had fused with the rock of the pass somehow, so that they looked tens of millions of years old.

Aran had traveled the Gap in wolf form. If Hvirin Gap was dead of magic, he should have been forced into the man form. Or would he find it impossible to change at all?

"But I can go through as a wolf," Aran thought. "That way I can't be killed by anything but silver and platinum. The glass dagger should hurt, but—

"Damn! I'm invulnerable, but is it *magic?* If it doesn't work in Hvirin Gap—" and he shuddered.

The dagger had never been more than a whisper of sensation, that had faded in half an hour and never returned. But Aran knew it was there. Invisible, a knife in his heart, waiting.

It might reappear in his chest, and he could still survive—as a wolf. But it would hurt! And he could never be human again.

Aran turned and padded away from Hvirin Gap. He had passed a village yesterday. Perhaps the resident magician could help him.

"A glass dagger!" the magician chortled. He was a portly, jolly, balding man, clearly used to good living. "Now I've heard everything. Well, what were you worried about? It's got a handle, doesn't it? Was it a complex spell?''

"I don't think so. He wrote runes on the blade, then stabbed me with it.''

"Fine. You pay in advance. And you'd better convert to wolf, just to play safe.'' He named a sum that would have left Aran without money for passage home. Aran managed to argue him down to something not far above reason, and they went to work.

The magician gave up some six hours later. His voice was hoarse, his eyes were red from oddly colored, oddly scented smokes, and his hands were discolored with dyes. "I can't touch the hilt, I can't make it visible, I can't get any sign that it's there at all. If I use any stronger spell, it's likely to kill you. I quit, wolf boy. Whoever put this spell on you, he knows more than a simple village magician.''

Aran rubbed his chest where the skin was stained by mildly corrosive dyes. "They call him the Warlock.''

The portly magician stiffened. "The Warlock? *The* Warlock? And you didn't think to tell me. Get out.''

"What about my money?''

"I wouldn't have tried it for ten times the fee! Me, a mere hedge-magician, and you turned me loose against the Warlock! We might both have been killed. If you think you're entitled to your money, let's go to the headman and state our case. Otherwise, get out.''

Aran left, shouting insults.

"Try other magicians if you like,'' the other shouted after him. "Try Rynildissen City! But tell them what they're doing first!''

III

It had been a difficult decision for the Warlock. But his secret was out and spreading. The best he could do was see to it that world sorcery understood the implications.

The Warlock addressed the Sorcerers' Guild on the subject of *mana* depletion and the Warlock's Wheel.

"Think of it every time you work magic,'' he thundered in what amounted to baby talk after his severely technical description of the Wheel. "Only finite *mana* in the world, and less of it every year, as a thousand magicians drain it away. There were beings who ruled the world as gods, long ago, until the raging power of their own being used up the *mana* that kept them alive.

"One day it'll all be gone. Then all the demons and dragons and unicorns, trolls and rocs and centaurs will vanish quite away, because their metabolism is partly based on magic. Then all the dream-castles will evaporate, and nobody will ever know they were there. Then all the magicians will become tinkers and smiths, and the world will be a dull place to live. You have the power to bring that day nearer!"

That night he dreamed.

A duel between magicians makes a fascinating tale. Such tales are common—and rarely true. The winner of such a duel is not likely to give up trade secrets. The loser is dead, at the very least.

Novices in sorcery are constantly amazed at how much preparation goes into a duel, and how little action. The duel with the Hill Magician started with a dream, the night after the Warlock's speech made that duel inevitable. It ended thirty years later.

In that dream the enemy did not appear. But the Warlock saw a cheerful, harmless-looking fairy castle perched on an impossible hill. From a fertile, hummocky landscape, the hill rose like a breaking wave, leaning so far that the castle at its crest had empty space below it.

In his sleep the Warlock frowned. Such a hill would topple without magic. The fool who built it was wasting *mana*.

And in his sleep he concentrated, memorizing details. A narrow path curled up the hillside. Facts twisted, dreamlike. There was a companion with him; or there wasn't. The Warlock lived until he passed through the gate; or he died at the gate, in agony, with great ivory teeth grinding together through his rib cage.

He woke himself up trying to sort it out.

The shadowy companion was necessary, at least as far as the gate. Beyond the enemy's gate he could see nothing. A Warlock's Wheel must have been used there, to block his magic so thoroughly.

Poetic justice?

He spent three full days working spells to block the Hill Magician's prescient sense. During that time his own sleep was dreamless. The other's magic was as effective as his own.

IV

Great ships floated at anchor in the harbor.

There were cargo ships whose strange demonic figureheads had limited power of movement, just enough to reach the rats that tried to swarm up the mooring lines. A large Atlantean passenger liner was equipped with twin outriggers made from whole tree trunks. By the nearest dock a magician's slender yacht floated eerily above the water. Aran watched them all rather wistfully.

He had spent too much money traveling over the mountains. A week after his arrival in Rynildissen City he had taken a post as bodyguard/watchdog to a rug merchant. He had been down to his last coin, and hungry.

Now Lloraginezee the rug merchant and Ra-Harroo his secretary talked trade secrets with the captain of a Nile cargo ship. Aran waited on the dock, watching ships with indifferent patience.

His ears came to point. The bearded man walking past him wore a captain's kilt. Aran hailed him: "Ho, Captain! Are you sailing to Atlantis?"

The bearded man frowned. "And what's that to you?"

"I would send a message there."

"Deal with a magician."

"I'd rather not," said Aran. He could hardly tell a magician that he wanted to send instructions on how to rob a magician. Otherwise the message would have gone months ago.

"I'll charge you more, and it will take longer," the bearded man said with some satisfaction. "Who in Atlantis, and where?"

Aran gave him an address in the city. He passed over the sealed message pouch he had been carrying for three months now.

Aran too had made some difficult decisions. In final draft his message warned of the tectonic instability of the continent, and suggested steps the Peacemongers could take to learn if the Warlock had lied. Aran had not included instructions for making a Warlock's Wheel.

Far out in the harbor, dolphins and mermen played rough and complicated games. The Atlantean craft hoisted sail. A wind rose from nowhere to fill the sails. It died slowly, following the passenger craft out to sea.

Soon enough, Aran would have the fare. He would almost have it now, except that he had twice paid out sorcerer's fees, with the result that the money was gone and the glass dagger was not. Meanwhile, Lloraginezee did not give trade secrets to his bodyguard. He knew that Aran would be on his way as soon as he had the money.

Here they came down the gangplank: Lloraginezee with less waddle than might be expected of a man of his girth; the girl walking with quiet grace, balancing the rug samples on her head. Ra-Harroo was saying something as Aran joined them, something Aran may have been intended to hear.

"Beginning tomorrow, I'll be off work for five days. *You* know," she told Lloraginezee—and blushed.

"Fine, fine," said Lloraginezee, nodding absently.

Aran knew too. He smiled but did not look at her. He might embarrass her . . . and he knew well enough what Ra-Harroo looked like. Her hair was black and short and coarse. Her nose was large but flat, almost merging into her face. Her eyes were brown and soft, her brows dark and thick. Her ears were delicately formed and convoluted, and came to a point. She was a lovely girl, especially to another of the wolf people.

They held hands as they walked. Her nails were narrow and strong, and the fine hair on her palm tickled.

In Atlantis he would have considered marrying her, had he the money to support her. Here, it was out of the question. For most of the month they were friends and co-workers. The night life of Rynildissen City was more convenient for a couple, and there were times when Lloraginezee could spare them both.

Perhaps Lloraginezee made such occasions. He was not of the wolf people. He probably enjoyed thinking that sex had reared its lovely, disturbing head. But sex could not be involved—except at a certain time of the month. Aran didn't see her then. She was locked up in her father's house. He didn't even know where she lived.

He found out five nights later.

He had guarded Lloraginezee's way to Adrienne's House of Pleasures. Lloraginezee would spend the night . . . on an air mattress floating on mercury, a bed Aran had only heard described. A pleasant sleep was not the least of pleasures.

The night was warm and balmy. Aran took a long way home, walking wide of the vacant lot behind Adrienne's. That broad, flat plot of ground had housed the palace of Shilbree the Dreamer, three hundred years ago. The palace had been all magic, and quite an achievement even in its day. Eventually it had . . . worn out, Shilbree would have said.

One day it was gone. And not even the simplest of spells would work in that vacant lot.

Someone had told Aran that households of wolf people occupied several blocks of the residential district. It seemed to be true, for he caught identifying smells as he crossed certain paths.

He followed one, curious to see what kind of house a wealthy werewolf would build in Rynildissen.

The elusive scent led him past a high, angular house with a brass door . . . and then it was too late, for another scent was in his nostrils and in his blood and brain. He spent that whole night howling at the door. Nobody tried to stop him. The neighbors must have been used to it; or they may have known that he would kill rather than be driven away.

More than once he heard a yearning voice answering from high up in the house. It was Ra-Harroo's voice. With what remained of his mind, Aran knew that he would be finding apologies in a few days. She would think he had come deliberately

Aran howled a song of sadness and deprivation and shame.

V

The first was a small village called Gath, and a Guild 'prentice who came seeking black opals. He found them, and free for the taking too, for Gath was dead empty. The 'prentice sorcerer wondered about that, and he looked about him, and presently he found a dead spot with a crumbled castle in it. It might have been centuries fallen. Or it might have been raised by magic, and collapsed when the *mana* went out of it, yesterday or last week.

It was a queer tale, and it got around. The 'prentice grew rich on the opals, for black opals are very useful for cursing. But the empty village bothered him.

"I thought it was slavers at first," he said once, in the Warlock's hearing as it turned out. "There were no corpses, none anywhere. Slave traders don't kill if they can help it.

"But why would a troop of slavers leave valuables lying where they were? The opals were all over the street, mixed with hay. I think a jeweler must have been moving them in secret when—*something* smashed his wagon. But why didn't they pick up the jewels?"

It was the crumbled castle the Warlock remembered three years later, when he heard about Shiskabil. He heard of that one directly, from a magpie that fluttered out of the sky onto his shoulder and whispered, "Warlock?"

And when he had heard, he went.

Shiskabil was a village of stone houses within a stone wall. It must have been abandoned suddenly. Dinners had dried or rotted on their plates; meat had been burnt to ash in ovens. There were no living inhabitants, and no dead. The wall had not been breeched. But there were signs of violence everywhere: broken furniture, doors with broken locks or splintered hinges, crusted spears and swords and makeshift clubs, and blood. Dried black blood everywhere, as if it had rained blood.

Clubfoot was a younger Guild member, thin and earnest. Though talented, he was still a little afraid of the power he commanded through magic. He was not happy in Shiskabil. He walked with shoulders hunched, trying to avoid the places where blood had pooled.

"Weird, isn't it? But I had a special reason to send for you," he said. "There's a dead region outside the wall. I had the idea someone might have used a Warlock's Wheel there."

A rectangular plot of fertile ground, utterly dead, a foretaste of a world dead to magic. In the center were crumbled stones with green plants growing between.

The Warlock circled the place, unwilling to step where magic did not work. He had used the Wheel once before, against Glirendree, after the demon-sword had killed his shadow demon. The Wheel had sucked the youth from him, left the Warlock two hundred years old in a few seconds.

"There was magic worked in the village," said Clubfoot. "I tried a few simple spells. The *mana* level's very low. I don't remember any famous sorcerers from Shiskabil; do you?"

"No."

"Then whatever happened here was done by magic." Clubfoot almost whispered the word. Magic could be very evil—as he knew.

They found a zigzag path through the dead borderline, and a faintly live region inside. At a gesture from the Warlock, the crumbled stones stirred feebly, trying to rise.

"So it was somebody's castle," said Clubfoot. "I wonder how he got this effect?"

"I thought of something like it once. Say you put a heavy kinetic spell on a smaller Wheel. The Wheel would spin very fast, would use up mana in a very tight area—"

Clubfoot was nodding. "I see it. He could have run it on a track, a close path. It would give him a kind of hedge against magic around a live region."

"And he left the border open so he could get his tools in and out. He zigzagged the entrance so no spells could get through. Nobody could use farsight on him. I wonder . . ."

"I wonder what he had to hide?"

"I wonder what happened in Shiskabil," said the Warlock.

And he remembered the dead barrier that hid the Hill Magician's castle. His leisurely duel with a faceless enemy was twelve years old.

It was twenty-three years old before they found the third village.

Hathzoril was bigger than Shiskabil, and better known. When a shipment of carvings in ivory and gem woods did not arrive, the Warlock heard of it.

The village could not have been abandoned more than a few days when the Warlock arrived. He and Clubfoot found meals half cooked, meals half eaten, broken furniture, weapons that had been taken from their racks, broken doors—

"But no blood. I wonder why?"

Clubfoot was jittery. "Otherwise it's just the same. The whole population gone in an instant, probably against their will. Ten whole years; no, more. I'd half forgotten . . . You got here before I did. Did you find a dead area and a crumbled castle?"

"No. I looked."

The younger magician rubbed his birth-maimed foot—which he could have cured in half an hour, but it would have robbed him of half his powers. "We could be wrong. If it's him, he's changed his techniques."

That night the Warlock dreamed a scrambled dream in pyrotechnic colors. He woke thinking of the Hill Magician.

"Let's climb some hills," he told Clubfoot in the morning. "I've got to know if the Hill Magician has something to do with these empty villages. We're looking for a dead spot on top of a hill."

That mistake almost killed him.

The last hill Clubfoot tried to climb was tumbled, crumbled soil and rock that slid and rolled under his feet. He tried it near sunset, in sheer desperation, for they had run out of hills and patience.

He was still near the base when the Warlock came clambering to join him. "Come down from there!" he laughed. "Nobody would build on this sand heap."

Clubfoot looked around, and shouted, "Get out of here! You're older!"

The Warlock rubbed his face and felt the wrinkles. He picked his way back in haste and in care, wanting to hurry, but fearful of breaking fragile bones. He left a trail of fallen silver hair.

Once beyond the *mana*-poor region, he cackled in falsetto.

"My mistake. I know what he did now. Clubfoot, we'll find the dead spot inside the hill."

"First we'll work you a rejuvenation spell." Clubfoot laid his tools out on a rock. A charcoal block, a silver knife, packets of leaves . . .

"That border's bad. It sucks up *mana* from inside. He must have to move pretty often. So he raised up a hill like a breaking wave. When the magic ran out the hill just rolled over the castle and covered up everything. He'll do it again, too."

"Clever. What do you think happened in Hathzoril Village?"

"We may never know." The Warlock rubbed new wrinkles at the corners of his eyes. "Something bad, I think. Something very bad."

VI

He was strolling through the merchants' quarter that afternoon, looking at rugs.

Normally this was a cheerful task. Hanging rugs formed a brightly colored maze through this part of the quarter. As Aran the rug merchant moved through the maze, well-known voices would call his name. Then there would be gossip and canny trading.

He had traded in Rynildissen City for nearly thirty years, first as Lloraginezee's apprentice, later as his own man. The finest rugs and the cheapest, from all over this continent and nearby islands, came by ship and camel's back to Rynildissen City. Wholesalers, retailers, and the odd nobleman who wished to furnish a palace would travel to Rynildissen City to buy. Today they glowed in the hot sunlight . . . but today they only depressed him. Aran was thinking of moving away.

A bald man stepped into view from behind a block of cured sphinx pelts.

Bald as a roc's egg he was, yet young, and in the prime of muscular good health. He was shirtless like a stevedore, but his pantaloons were of high quality and his walk was pure arrogance. Aran felt he was staring rather rudely. Yet there was something familiar about the man.

He passed Aran without a glance.

Aran glanced back once, and was jolted. The design seemed to leap out at him: a five-sided multicolored tattoo on the man's back.

Aran called, "Warlock!"

He regretted it the next moment. The Warlock turned on him the look one gives a presumptuous stranger.

The Warlock had not changed at all, except for the loss of his hair. But Aran remembered that thirty years had passed; that he himself was a man of fifty, with the hollows of his face filled out by rich living. He remembered that his greying hair had receded, leaving his widow's peak as a shock of hair all alone on his forehead. And he remembered, in great detail, the circumstances under which he had met the Warlock.

He had spent a thousand nights plotting vengeance against the Warlock; yet now his only thought was to get away. He said, "Your pardon, sir—"

But something else occurred to him, so that he said firmly, "But we *have* met."

"Under what circumstance? I do not recall it," the Warlock said coldly.

Aran's answer was a measure of the self-confidence that comes with wealth and respect. He said, "I was robbing your cave."

"Were you!" The Warlock came closer. "Ah, the boy from Atlantis. Have you robbed any magicians lately?"

"I have adopted a somewhat safer way of life," Aran said equably. "And I do have reason for presuming on our brief acquaintance."

"Our brief—" The Warlock laughed so that heads turned all over the marketplace. Still laughing, he took Aran's arm and led him away.

They strolled slowly through the merchants' quarter, the Warlock leading. "I have to follow a certain path," he explained. "A project of my own. Well, my boy, what have you been doing for thirty years?"

"Trying to get rid of your glass dagger."

"Glass dagger? . . . Oh, yes, I remember. Surely you found time for other hobbies?"

Aran almost struck the Warlock then. But there was something he wanted from the Warlock; and so he held his temper.

"My whole life has been warped by your damned glass dagger," he said. "I had to circle Hvirin Gap on my way home. When I finally got here I was out of money. No money for passage to Atlantis, and no money to pay for a magician, which meant that I couldn't get the glass knife removed.

"So I hired out to Lloraginezee the rug merchant as a bodyguard/watchdog. Now I'm the leading rug merchant in

Rynildissen City, I've got two wives and eight children and a few grandchildren, and I don't suppose I'll ever get back to Atlantis.''

They bought wine from a peddler carrying two fat wineskins on his shoulders. They took turns drinking from the great copper goblet the man carried.

The Warlock asked, "Did you ever get rid of the knife?"

"No, and you ought to know it! What kind of a spell did you *put* on that thing? The best magicians in this continent haven't been able to so much as *touch* that knife, let alone pull it out. I wouldn't be a rug merchant if they had."

"Why not?"

"Well, I'd have earned my passage to Atlantis soon enough, except that every time I heard about a new magician in the vicinity I'd go to him to see if he could take that knife out. Selling rugs was a way to get the money to pay the magicians. Eventually I gave up on the magicians and kept the money. All I'd accomplished was to spread your reputation in all directions."

"Thank you," the Warlock said politely.

Aran did not like the Warlock's amusement. He decided to end the conversation quickly. "I'm glad we ran into each other," he said, "because I have a problem that is really in your province. Can you tell me something about a magician named Wavyhill?"

It may be that the Warlock stiffened. "What is it that you want to know?"

"Whether his spells use excessive power."

The Warlock lifted an interrogatory eyebrow.

"You see, we try to restrict the use of magic in Rynildissen City. The whole nation could suffer if a key region like Rynildissen City went dead to magic. There'd be no way to stop a flood, or a hurricane, or an invasion of barbarians. Do you find something amusing?"

"No, no. But could a glass dagger possibly have anything to do with your conservative attitude?"

"That's entirely my own business, Warlock. Unless you'd care to read my mind?"

"No, thank you. My apologies."

"I'd like to point out that more than just the welfare of Rynildissen City is involved. If this region went dead to magic, the harbor mermen would have to move away. They have quite an extensive city of their own, down there beyond the docks. Furthermore, they run most of the docking facilities and the *entire* fishing industry—"

"Relax. I agree with you completely. You know that," the magician laughed. "You ought to!"

"Sorry. I preach at the drop of a hat. It's been ten years since anyone saw a dragon near Rynildissen City. Even further out, they're warped, changed. When I first came here the dragons had a mercenary's booth in the city itself! What are you doing?"

The Warlock had handed the empty goblet back to the vendor and was pulling at Aran's arm. "Come this way, please. Quickly, before I lose the path."

"Path?"

"I'm following a fogged prescient vision. I could get killed if I lose the path—or if I don't, for that matter. Now, just what was your problem?"

"That," said Aran, pointing among the fruit stalls.

The troll was an ape's head on a human body, covered from head to toe in coarse brown hair. From its size it was probably female, but it had no more breasts than a female ape. It held a wicker basket in one quite human hand. Its bright brown eyes glanced up at Aran's pointing finger—startlingly human eyes— then dropped to the melon it was considering.

Perhaps the sight should have roused reverence. A troll was ancestral to humanity: *Homo habilis*, long extinct. But they were too common. Millions of the species had been fossilized in the drylands of Africa. Magicians of a few centuries ago had learned that they could be reconstituted by magic.

"I think you've just solved one of my own problems," the Warlock said quietly. He no longer showed any trace of amusement.

"Wonderful," Aran said without sincerity. "My own problem is, how much *mana* are Wavyhill's trolls using up? The *mana* level in Rynildissen City was never high to start with. Wavyhill must be using terrifically powerful spells just to keep them walking." Aran's fingertips brushed his chest in an unconscious gesture. "I'd hate to leave Rynildissen City, but if magic stops working here I won't have any choice."

"I'd have to know the spells involved. Tell me something about Wavyhill, will you? Everything you can remember."

To most of Rynildissen City the advent of Wavyhill the magician was very welcome.

Once upon a time troll servants had been common. They were terrifically strong. Suffering no pain, they could use hysterical strength for the most mundane tasks. Being inhuman, they could work on official holidays. They needed no sleep. They did not steal.

But Rynildissen City was old, and the *mana* was running low. For many years no troll had walked in Rynildissen City. At the gate they turned to blowing dust.

Then came Wavyhill with a seemingly endless supply of trolls, which did *not* disintegrate at the gate. The people paid him high prices in gold and in honors.

"For half a century thieves have worked freely on holidays," Aran told the Warlock. "Now we've got a trollish police force again. Can you blame people for being grateful? They made him a Councilman—over my objections. Which means that there's very little short of murder that Wavyhill can't do in Rynildissen City."

"I'm sorry to hear that. Why did you say *over your objections?* Are you on the Council?"

"Yes. I'm the one who rammed through the laws restricting magic in Rynildissen City. And failed to ram through some others, I might add. The trouble is that Wavyhill doesn't make the trolls in the city. Nobody knows where they come from. If he's depleting the *mana* level, he's doing it somewhere else."

"Then what's your problem?"

"Suppose the trolls use up *mana* just by existing? . . . I should be asking, *do they?*"

"I think so," said the Warlock.

"I *knew* it. Warlock, will you testify before the Council? Because—"

"No, I won't."

"But you've got to! I'll never convince anyone by myself. Wavyhill is the most respected magician around, and he'll be testifying against me! Besides which, the Council all own trolls themselves. They won't want to believe they've been suckered, and they have been if we're right. The trolls will collapse as soon as they've lowered the *mana* level enough."

At that point Aran ran down, for he had seen with what stony patience the Warlock was waiting for him to finish.

The Warlock waited three seconds longer, using silence as an exclamation point. Then he said, "It's gone beyond that. Talking to the Council would be like shouting obscenities at a forest fire. I could get results that way. You couldn't."

"Is he *that* dangerous?"

"I think so."

Aran wondered if he was being had. But the Warlock's face

was so grave . . . and Aran had seen that face in too many
nightmares. *What am I doing here?* he wondered. *I had a
technical question about trolls. So I asked a magician . . . and
now . . .*

"Keep talking. I need to know more about Wavyhill. And
walk faster," said the Warlock. "How long has he been here?"

"Wavyhill came to Rynildissen City seven years ago. Nobody
knows where he came from; he doesn't have any particular
accent. His palace sits on a hill that looks like it's about to fall
over. What are you nodding at?"

"I know that hill. Keep talking."

"We don't see him often. He comes with a troupe of trolls, to
sell them; or he comes to vote with the Council on important
matters. He's short and dark—."

"That could be a seeming. Never mind, describe him anyway.
I've never seen him."

"Short and dark, with a pointed nose and a pointed chin and
very curly dark hair. He wears a dark robe of some soft material,
a tall pointed hat, and sandals, and he carries a sword."

"Does he!" The Warlock laughed out loud.

"What's the joke? I carry a sword myself sometimes.—Oh,
that's right, magicians have a *thing* about swordsmen."

"That's not why I laughed. It's a trade joke. A sword can be a
symbol of masculine virility."

"Oh?"

"You see the point, don't you? A sorcerer doesn't need a
sword. He knows more powerful protections. When a sorcerer
takes to carrying a sword, it's pretty plain he's using it as a cure
for impotence."

"And it works?"

"Of course it works. It's straight one-for-one similarity magic,
isn't it? But you've got to take the sword to bed with you!"
laughed the Warlock. But his eyes found a troll servant, and his
laughter slipped oddly.

He watched as the troll hurried through a gate in a high white
wall. They had passed out of the merchants' quarter.

"I think Wavyhill's a necromancer," he said abruptly.

"Necromancer. What is it? It sounds ugly."

"A technical term for a new branch of magic. And it is ugly.
Turn sharp left here."

They ducked into a narrow alley. Two- and three-story houses
leaned over them from both sides. The floor of the alley was

filthy, until the Warlock snarled and gestured. Then the dirt and garbage flowed to both sides.

The Warlock hurried them deep into the alley. "We can stop here, I think. Sit down if you like. We'll be here for some time—or I will."

"Warlock, are you playing games with me? What does this new dance have to do with a duel of sorcery?"

"A fair question. Do you know what lies that way?"

Aran's sense of direction was good, and he knew the city. "The Judging Place?"

"Right. And that way, the vacant lot just this side of Adrienne's House of Pleasures—you know it? The deadest spot in Rynildissen City. The palace of Shilbree the Dreamer once stood there."

"*Might* I ask—"

"The courthouse is void of *mana* too, naturally. Ten thousand defendants and thirty thousand lawyers all praying for conviction or acquittal doesn't leave much magic in *any* courthouse. If I can keep either of those spots between me and Wavyhill, I can keep him from using farsight on me."

Aran thought about it. "But you have to know where he is."

"No. I only have to know where I ought to be. Most of the time, I don't. Wavyhill and I have managed to fog each other's prescient senses pretty well. But I'm supposed to be meeting an unknown ally along about now, and I've taken great care that Wavyhill can't spy on me.

"You see, I invented the Wheel. Wavyhill has taken the Wheel concept and improved it in at least two ways that I know of. Naturally he uses up *mana* at a ferocious rate.

"He may also be a mass murderer. And he's my fault. That's why I've got to kill him."

Aran remembered then that his wives were waiting dinner. He remembered that he had decided to end this conversation hours ago. And he remembered a story he had been told, of a layman caught in a sorcerer's duel, and what had befallen him.

"Well, I've got to be going," he said, standing up. "I wish you the best of luck in your duel, Warlock. And if there's anything I can do to help . . ."

"Fight with me," the Warlock said instantly.

Aran gaped. Then he burst out laughing.

The Warlock waited with his own abnormal patience. When he had some chance of being heard, he said, "I dreamed that an ally would meet me during this time. That ally would accompany me to the gate of Wavyhill's castle. I don't have many of those

Larry Niven

dreams to help me, Aran. Wavyhill's good. If I go alone, my
forecast is that I'll be killed.''

"Another ally," Aran suggested.

"No. Too late. The time has passed."

"Look." Aran slapped his belly with the flat of his hand. The
flesh rippled. "It's not that much extra weight," he said, "for a
man. I'm not *unsightly*. But as a wolf I'd look ten years pregnant!
I haven't turned wolf in years.

"What am I doing? I don't have to convince you of anything,"
Aran said abruptly. And he walked away fast.

The Warlock caught him up at the mouth of the alley. "I
swear you won't regret staying. There's something you don't
know yet."

"Don't follow me too far, Warlock. You'll lose your path."
Aran laughed in the magician's face. "Why should I fight by
your side? If you really need me to win, I couldn't be more
delighted! I've seen your face in a thousand nightmares, you and
your glass dagger! So die, Warlock. It's my dinner time."

"Shh," said the Warlock. And Aran saw that the Warlock was
not looking at him, but over his shoulder.

Aran felt the urge to murder. But his eyes flicked to follow the
Warlock's gaze, and the imprecations died in his throat.

It was a troll. Only a troll, a male, with a tremendous pack on
its back. Coming toward them.

And the Warlock was gesturing to it. Or were those magical
passes?

"Good," he said. "Now, I could tell you that it's futile to
fight fate, and you might even believe me, because I'm an
expert. But I'd be lying. Or I could offer you a chance to get rid
of the dagger—"

"Go to Hell. I learned to live with that dagger—"

"Wolf man, if you never learn anything else from me, learn
never to blaspheme in the presence of a magician! Excuse me."
The troll had walked straight to the mouth of the alley. Now the
Warlock took it by the arm and led it inside. "Will you help me?
I want to get the pack off its back."

They lifted it down, while Aran wondered at himself. Had he
been bewitched into obedience? The pack was very heavy. It
took all of Aran's strength, even though the Warlock bore the
brunt of the load. The troll watched them with blank brown eyes.

"Good. If I tried this anywhere else in the city, Wavyhill
would know it. But this time I know where he is. He's in

Adrienne's House of Pleasures, searching for me, the fool! He's already searched the courthouse.

"Never mind that. Do you know of a village named Gath?"

"No."

"Or Shiskabil?"

"No. Wait." A Shiska had bought six matching green rugs from him once. "Yes. A small village north of here. Something . . . happened to it . . ."

"The population walked out one night, leaving all their valuables and a good deal of unexplained blood."

"That's right." Aran felt sudden horrible doubt. "It was never explained."

"Gath was first. Then Shiskabil, then Hathzoril. Bigger cities each time. At Hathzoril he was clever. He found a way to hide where his palace had been, and he didn't leave any blood."

"But what does he *do*? Where do the people go?"

"What do you know about *mana*, Aran? You know that it's the power behind magic, and you know it can be used up. What else?"

"I'm not a magician. I sell rugs."

"*Mana* can be used for good or evil; it can be drained, or transferred from one object to another, or from one man to another. Some men seem to carry *mana* with them. You can find concentrations in oddly shaped stones, or in objects of reverence, or in meteoroids.

"There is much *mana* associated with murder," said the Warlock. "Too much for safety, in my day. My teacher used to warn us against working near the site of a murder, or the corpse of a murdered man, or murder weapons—as opposed to weapons of war, I might add. War and murder are different in intent.

"Necromancy uses murder as a source of magic. It's the most powerful form of magic—so powerful that it could never have developed until now, when the *mana* level everywhere in the world is so low.

"I think Wavyhill is a necromancer," said the Warlock. And he turned to the troll. "We'll know in a moment."

The troll stood passive, its long arms relaxed at its sides, watching the Warlock with strangely human brown eyes and with a human dignity that contrasted oddly with its low animal brow and hairy body. It did not flinch as the Warlock dropped a kind of necklace over its head.

The change came instantly. Aran backed away, sucking air. The Warlock's necklace hung around a man's neck—a man in his middle thirties, blond-haired and bearded, wearing a porter's kilt—and that man's belly had been cut wide open by one clean swing of a sword or scimitar. Aran caught the smell of him: he had been dead for three or four days, plus whatever time the preserving effects of magic had been at work on him. Yet he stood, passively waiting, and his expression had not changed.

"Wavyhill has invented a kind of perpetual motion," the Warlock said dryly; but he backed away hastily from the smell of the dead man. "There's enough power in a murdered man to make him an obedient slave, and plenty left over to cast on him the seeming of a troll. He takes more *mana* from the environment, but what of that? When the *mana* runs out in Gath, Wavyhill's trolls kill their masters. Then twice as many trolls move on to Shiskabil. In Hathzoril they probably used strangling cords; they wouldn't spill any blood that way, and they wouldn't bleed themselves. I wonder where he'll go after Rynildissen?"

"Nowhere! We'll tell the Council!"

"And Wavyhill a Councilman? No. And you can't spread the word to individual members, because eventually one of them would tip Wavyhill that you're slandering him."

"They'd believe *you.*"

"All it takes is one who doesn't. Then he tells Wavyhill, and Wavyhill turns loose the trolls. No. You'll do three things," said the Warlock in tones not of command but of prophecy. "You'll go home. You'll spend the next week getting your wives and children out of Rynildissen City."

"My gods, yes!"

"I swore you wouldn't regret hearing me out. The third thing, if you so decide, is to join me at dawn, at the north gate, a week from today. Come by way of Adrienne's House of Pleasures," the Warlock ordered, "and stay awhile. The dead area will break your trail.

"Do that today, too. I don't want Wavyhill to follow you by prescience. Go *now,*" said the Warlock.

"I can't decide!"

"Take a week."

"I may not be here. How can I contact you?"

"You can't. It doesn't matter. I'll go with you or without you." Abruptly the Warlock stripped the necklace from the neck of the standing corpse, turned and strode off down the alley. Following the path.

The dead man was a troll again. It followed Aran with large, disturbingly human brown eyes.

VII

That predawn morning, Adrienne's House of Pleasures was wrapped in thick black fog. Aran the rug merchant hesitated at the door; then, shivering, squared his shoulders and walked out into it.

He walked with his sword ready for tapping or killing. The fog grew lighter as he went, but no less dense. Several times he thought he saw monstrous vague shapes pacing him. But there was no attack. At dawn he was at the north gate.

The Warlock's mounts were either lizards enlarged by magic or dragons mutated by no magic. They were freaks, big as twin bungalows. One carried baggage; the other, two saddles in tandem.

"Mount up," the Warlock urged. "We want to get there before nightfall." Despite the chill of morning he was bare to the waist. He turned in his saddle as Aran settled behind him. "Have you lost weight?"

"I fasted for six days, and exercised too. And my wives and children are four days on their way to Atlantis by sea. You can guess what pleasures I chose at Adrienne's."

"I wouldn't have believed it. Your belly's as flat as a board."

"A wolf can fast for a long time. I ate an unbelievable meal last night. Today I won't eat at all."

The fog cleared as they left Rynildissen, and the morning turned clear and bright and hot. When Aran mentioned it, the Warlock said, "That fog was mine. I wanted to blur things for Wavyhill."

"I thought I saw shapes in the fog. Were those yours too?"

"No."

"Thanks."

"Wavyhill meant to frighten you, Aran. He wouldn't attack you. He *knows* you won't be killed before we reach the gate."

"That explains the pack lizards. I wondered how you could possibly expect to sneak up on him."

"I don't. He knows we're coming. He's waiting."

The land was rich in magic near Wavyhill's castle. You could tell by the vegetation: giant mushrooms, vying for variety of shape and color; lichens growing in the shapes of men or beasts; trees with contorted trunks and branches, trees that moved menacingly as the pack-lizards came near.

"I could make them talk," said the Warlock. "But I couldn't trust them. They'll be Wavyhill's allies."

In the red light of sunset, Wavyhill's castle seemed all rose marble, perched at the top of a fairy mountain. The slender tower seemed made for kidnapped damsels. The mountain itself, as Aran saw it now for the first time, was less a breaking wave than a fist raised to the sky in defiance.

"We couldn't use the Wheel here," said the Warlock. "The whole mountain would fall on us."

"I wouldn't have let you use the Wheel."

"I didn't bring one."

"Which way?"

"Up the path. He knows we're coming."

"Is your shadow demon ready?"

"Shadow demon?" The Warlock seemed to think. "Oh. For a moment I didn't know what you were talking about. That shadow demon was killed in the battle with Glirendree, thirty years ago."

Words caught in Aran's throat, then broke loose in a snarl. *"Then why don't you put on a shirt?"*

"Habit. I've got lots of strange habits. Why so vehement?"

"I don't know. I've been staring at your back since morning. I guess I was counting on the shadow demon." Aran swallowed. "It's just us, then?"

"Just us."

"Aren't you even going to take a sword? Or a dagger?"

"No. Shall we go?"

The other side of the hill was a sixty degree slope. The narrow, meandering path could not support the lizard beasts. Aran and the Warlock dismounted and began to climb.

The Warlock said, "There's no point in subtlety. We know we'll get as far as the gate. So does Wavyhill . . . excuse me." He threw a handful of silver dust ahead of them. "The road was about to throw us off. Apparently Wavyhill doesn't take anything for granted."

But Aran had only the Warlock's word for it; and that was the only danger that threatened their climb.

There was a rectangular pond blocking the solid copper gates. An arched bridge led across the pond. They were approaching the bridge when their first challenger pushed between the gates.

"What is it?" Aran whispered. "I've never *heard* of anything like it."

"There isn't. It's a changed one. Call it a snail dragon . . ."

. . . A snail dragon. Its spiral shell was just wide enough to block the gate completely. Its slender, supple body was fully exposed, reared high to study the intruders. Shiny leaflike scales covered the head and neck; but the rest of the body was naked, a soft greyish-brown. Its eyes were like black marbles. Its teeth were white and pointed, and the longest pair had been polished to a liquid glow.

From the other side of the small arched bridge, the Warlock called, "Ho, guardian! Were you told of our coming?"

"No," said the dragon. "Were you welcome, I would have been told."

"Welcome!" The Warlock guffawed. "We came to kill your master. Now, the interesting thing is that he knows of our coming. Why did he not warn you?"

The snail dragon tilted its mailed head.

The Warlock answered himself. "He knows that we will pass this gate. He suspects that we must pass over your dead body. He chose not to tell you so."

"That was kind of him." The dragon's voice was low and very gravelly, a sound like rocks being crushed.

"Kind, yes. But since we are foredoomed to pass, why not step aside? Or make for the hills, and we will keep your secret."

"It cannot be."

"You're a changed one, snail dragon. Beasts whose energy of life is partly magical, breed oddly where the *mana* is low. Most changed ones are not viable. So it is with you," said the Warlock. "The shell could not protect you from a determined and patient enemy. Or were you counting on speed to save you?"

"You raise a salient point," said the guardian. "If I were to leave now, what then? My master will very probably kill you when you reach his sanctum. Then, by and by, this week or the next, he will wonder how you came to pass his guardian. Then, next week or the week following, he will come to see, or to remove the discarded shell. By then, with luck and a good tail wind, I could be halfway to the woods. Perchance he will miss me in the tall grass," said the bungalow-sized beast. "No. Better to take my chances here in the gate. At least I know the direction of attack."

"Damn, you're right," said the Warlock. "My sympathies, snail dragon."

And he set about fixing the bridge into solidity. Half of it, the half on the side away from the gate, really was solid. The other half was a reflected illusion, until the Warlock—did things.

"The dead border runs under the water," he told Aran. "Don't fall into it."

The snail dragon withdrew most of itself into its shell. Only his scaly head showed now, as Aran and the Warlock crossed.

Aran came running.

He was still a man. It was not certain that Wavyhill knew that Aran was a werewolf. It *was* certain that they would pass the gate. So he reserved his last defense, and came at the dragon with a naked sword.

The dragon blew fire.

Aran went through it. He carried a charm against dragon fire.

But he couldn't *see* through it. It shocked hell out of him when teeth closed on his shoulder. The dragon had stretched incredibly. Aran screamed and bounced his blade off the metallic scales and—the teeth loosed him, snapped ineffectually at the Warlock, who danced back laughing, waving—

But the Warlock had been unarmed!

The dragon collapsed. His thick neck was cut half in two, behind the scales. The Warlock wiped his weapon on his pantaloons and held it up.

Aran felt suddenly queasy.

The Warlock laughed again. " 'What good is a glass dagger?' The fun thing about being a magician is that everyone always expects you to use magic."

"But, but—"

"It's just a glass dagger. No spells on it, nothing Wavyhill could detect. I had a friend drop it in the pond two days ago. Glass in water is near enough to invisible to fool the likes of Wavyhill."

"Excuse my open mouth. I just don't like glass daggers. Now what?"

The corpse and shell of the snail dragon still blocked the gate.

"If we try to squeeze around, we could be trapped. I suppose we'll have to go over."

"Fast," said Aran.

"Right, fast. Keep in mind that he could be *anywhere*." The Warlock took a running start and ran/climbed up the curve of the shell.

Aran followed almost as quickly.

In his sanctum, the snail dragon had said. The picture he had evoked was still with Aran as he went up the shell. Wavyhill would be hidden in his basement or his tower room, in some place of safety. Aran and the Warlock would have to fight their way through whatever the enemy could raise against them, while Wavyhill watched to gauge their defenses. There were similar tales of magicians' battles . . .

Aran was ravenously hungry. It gave him a driving energy he hadn't had in years, decades. His pumping legs drove a body that seemed feather-light. He reached the top of the shell just as the Warlock was turning full about in apparent panic.

Then he saw them: a horde of armed and armored skeletons coming at them up a wooden plank. There must have been several score of them. Aran shouted and drew his sword. *How do you kill a skeleton?*

The Warlock shouted too. Strange words, in the Guild language.

The skeletons howled. A whirlwind seemed to grip them and lift them and fling them forward. Already they were losing form, like smoke rings. Aran turned to see the last of them vanishing into the Warlock's back.

My name is legion. They must have been animated by a single demon. And the Warlock had pulled that demon into a demon trap, empty and waiting for thirty years.

The problem was that both Aran and the Warlock had been concentrating on the plural demon.

The Warlock's back was turned, and Aran could do nothing. He spotted Wavyhill gesticulating from across the courtyard, in the instant before Wavyhill completed his spell.

Aran turned to shout a warning; and so he saw what the spell did to the Warlock. The Warlock was old in an instant. The flesh seemed to fade into his bones. He looked bewildered, spat a mouthful of blackened pebbles—no, teeth—closed his eyes and started to fall.

Aran caught him.

It was like catching an armload of bones. He eased the Warlock onto his back on the great snail shell. The Warlock's breathing was stertorous; he could not have long to live.

"Aran the Merchant!"

Aran looked down. "What did you do to him?"

The magician Wavyhill was dressed as usual, in dark robe and sandals and pointed hat. A belt with a shoulder loop held his big-hilted sword just clear of the ground. He called, "That is precisely what I wish to discuss. I have found an incantation that behaves as the Warlock's Wheel behaves, but directionally. Is this over your head?"

"I understand you."

"In layman's terms, I've sucked the magic from him. That leaves him two hundred and twenty-six years old. I believe that gives me the win.

"My problem is whether to let you live. Aran, do you understand what my spell will do to you?"

Aran did, but—"Tell me anyway. Then tell me how you found out."

"From some of my colleagues, of course, after I determined that you were my enemy. You must have consulted an incredible number of magicians regarding the ghostly knife in your heart."

"More than a dozen. Well?"

"Leave in peace. Don't come back."

"I have to take the Warlock."

"He is my enemy."

"He's my ally. I won't leave him," said Aran.

"Take him then."

Aran stooped. He was forty-eight years old, and the bitterness of defeat had replaced the manic energy of battle. But the Warlock was little more than a snoring mummy, dry and light. The problem would be to get the fragile old man down from the snail shell.

Wavyhill was chanting!

Aran stood—in time to see the final gesture. Then the spell hit him.

For an instant he thought that the knife had truly reappeared in his heart. But the pain was all through him! like a million taut strings snapping inside him! The shape of his neck changed grindingly; all of his legs snapped forward; his skull flattened, his eyes lost color vision, his nose stretched, his lips pulled back from bared teeth.

The change had never come so fast, had never been more complete. A blackness fell on Aran's mind. It was a wolf that rolled helplessly off the giant snail shell and into the courtyard. A wolf bounced heavily and rolled to its feet, snarled deep in its throat and began walking stiff-legged toward Wavyhill.

Wavyhill was amazed! He started the incantation over, speaking very fast, as Aran approached. He finished as Aran came within leaping distance.

This time there was no change at all. Except that Aran leapt, and Wavyhill jumped back just short of far enough, and Aran tore his throat out.

*   *   *

For Aran the nightmare began then. What had gone before was as sweet dreams.

Wavyhill should have been dead. His severed carotid arteries pumped frantically, his windpipe made horrid bubbling sounds, and—Wavyhill drew his sword and attacked.

Aran the wolf circled and moved in and slashed—and backed away howling, for Wavyhill's sword had run him through the heart. The wound healed instantly. Aran the wolf was not surprised. He leapt away, and circled, and slashed and was stabbed again, and circled . . .

It went on and on.

Wavyhill's blood had stopped flowing. He'd run out. Yet he was still alive. So was his sword, or so it seemed. Aran never attacked unless it seemed safe, but the sword bit him every time. And every time he attacked, he came away with a mouthful of Wavyhill.

He was going to win. He could not help but win. His wounds healed as fast as they were made. Wavyhill's did not. Aran was stripping the flesh from the magician's bones.

There was a darkness on his brain. He moved by animal cunning. Again and again he herded Wavyhill back onto the slippery flagstones where Wavyhill had spilled five quarts of his blood. Four feet were surer than two. It was that cunning that led him to bar Wavyhill from leaving the courtyard. He tried. He must have stored healing magic somewhere in the castle. But Aran would not let him reach it.

He had done something to himself that would not let him die. He must be regretting it terribly. Aran the wolf had crippled him now, slashing at his ankles until there was not a shred of muscle left to work the bones. Wavyhill was fighting on his knees. Now Aran came closer, suffering the bite of the sword to reach the magician . . .

Nightmare.

Aran the Peacemonger had been wrong. If Aran the rug merchant could work on and on, stripping the living flesh from a man in agony, taking a stab wound for every bite—if Aran could suffer such agonies to do this to *anyone*, for *any* cause—

Then neither the end of magic, nor anything else, would ever persuade men to give up war. They would fight on, with swords and stones and whatever they could find, for as long as there were men.

The blackness had lifted from Aran's brain. It must have been the sword: the *mana* in an enchanted sword had replaced the *mana* sucked from him by Wavyhill's variant of the Warlock's Wheel.

And, finally, he realized that the sword was fighting alone.

Wavyhill was little more than bloody bones. He might not be dead, but he certainly couldn't move. The sword waved itself at the end of the stripped bones of his arm, still trying to keep Aran away.

Aran slid past the blade. He gripped the hilt in his teeth and pulled it from the magician's still-fleshy hand. The hand fought back with a senseless determined grip, but it wasn't enough.

He had to convert to human to climb the dragon shell.

The Warlock was still alive, but his breathing was a thing of desperation. Aran laid the blade across the Warlock's body and waited.

The Warlock grew young. Not as young as he had been, But he no longer looked—dead. He was in the neighborhood of seventy years old when he opened his eyes, blinked, and asked, "What happened?"

"You missed all the excitement," said Aran.

"I take it you beat him. My apologies. It's been thirty years since I fought Glirendree. With every magician in the civilized world trying to duplicate the Warlock's Wheel, one or another was bound to improve on the design."

"He used it on me, too."

"Oh?" The Warlock chuckled. "I suppose you're wondering about the knife."

"It did come to mind. Where is it?"

"In my belt. Did you think I'd leave it in your chest? I'd had a dream that I would need it. So I kept it. And sure enough—"

"But it was in my heart!"

"I made an image of it. I put the image in your heart, then faded it out."

Aran's fingernails raked his chest. "You miserable son of an ape! You let me think that knife was in me for thirty years!"

"You came to my house as a thief," the Warlock reminded him. "Not an invited guest."

Aran the merchant had acquired somewhat the same attitude toward thieves. With diminished bitterness he said, "Just a little magician's joke, was it? No wonder nobody could get it out. All right. Now tell me why Wavyhill's spell turned me into a wolf."

The Warlock sat up carefully. He said, "What?"

"He waved his arms at me and sucked all the *mana* out of me, and I turned into a wolf. I even lost my human intelligence. Probably my invulnerability too. If he hadn't been using an enchanted sword he'd have cut me to ribbons."

"I don't understand that. You should have been frozen into human form. Unless . . ."

Then, visibly, the answer hit him. His pale cheeks paled further. Presently he said, "You're not going to like this, Aran."

Aran could see it in the Warlock's face, seventy years old and very tired and full of pity. "Go on," he said.

"The Wheel is a new thing. Even the dead spots aren't *that* old. The situation has never come up before, that's all. People automatically assume that werewolves are people who can turn themselves into wolves.

"It seems obvious enough. You can't even make the change without moonlight. You keep your human intelligence. But there's never been proof, one way or another, until now."

"You're saying I'm a wolf."

"Without magic, you're a wolf," the Warlock agreed.

"Does it matter? I've spent most of my life as a man," Aran whispered. "What difference does it make—oh. Oh, yes."

"It wouldn't matter if you didn't have children."

"Eight. And they'll have children. And one day the *mana* will be gone everywhere on Earth. Then what, Warlock?"

"You know already."

"They'll be wild dogs for the rest of eternity!"

"And nothing anyone can do about it."

"Oh, yes, there is! I'm going to see to it that no magician ever enters Rynildissen again!" Aran stood up on the dragon's shell. "Do you hear me, Warlock? Your kind will be barred. Magic will be barred. We'll save the *mana* for the sea people and the dragons!"

It may be that he succeeded. Fourteen thousand years later, there are still tales of werewolves where Rynildissen City once stood. Certainly there are no magicians.

THE EYE OF TANDYLA

by
L. Sprague de Camp

L. Sprague de Camp has been entertaining science fiction and fantasy readers for more than forty-five years. Although he is proficient at all types of speculative fiction, one of his characteristics is a well-developed sense of humor that has earned him a devoted following. His major works have spanned the decades from sf's "Golden Age" to the present: LEST DARKNESS FALL (1941), ROGUE QUEEN (1951), THE INCOMPLETE ENCHANTER (1942; with Fletcher Pratt), TALES FROM GAVAGAN'S BAR (1953, with Pratt), THE WHEELS OF IF (1948), THE BEST OF L. SPRAGUE DE CAMP (1977), and THE GREAT FETISH (1978), among many others. In addition, he has co-written a large number of Conan the Barbarian tales, some from short stories and fragments left to us by Conan's creator, Robert E. Howard.

A droll parody of sword and sorcery quest, "The Eye of Tandyla" is an enjoyable story which might make an even more enjoyable movie.

One day—so long ago that mountains have arisen since, with cities on their flanks—

Derezong Taash, sorcerer to King Vuar the capricious, sat in his library reading the Collected Fragments of Lontang and drinking the green wine of Zhysk. He was at peace with himself and the world, for nobody had tried to murder him for ten whole days, by natural means or otherwise. When tired of puzzling out the cryptic glyphs, Derezong would gaze over the rim of his goblet at his demon-screen, on which the great Shuazid (before King Vuar took a capricious dislike to him) had depicted Derezong's entire stable of demons, from the fearful Fernazot down to the slightest sprite that submitted to his summons.

One wondered, on seeing Derezong, why even a sprite should bother. For Derezong Taash was a chubby little man (little for a Lorska, that is) with white hair framing a round youthful face. When he had undergone the zompur-treatment, he had carelessly forgotten to name his hair among the things for which he wanted eternal youth—an omission which had furnished his fellow magicians with fair scope for ribald ridicule.

On this occasion, Derezong Taash planned, when drunk enough, to heave his pudgy form out of the reading-chair and totter in to dinner with his assistant, Zhamel Seh. Four of Derezong's sons should serve the food as a precaution against Derezong's ill-wishers, and Zhamel Seh should taste it first as a further precaution.

And then the knock upon the door and the high voice of King Vuar's most insolent page: "My lord sorcerer, the king will see you forthwith!"

"What about?" grumbled Derezong Taash.

"Do I know where the storks go in winter? Am I privy to the secrets of the living dead of Sedo? Has the North Wind confided to me what lies beyond the ramparts of the Riphai?"

"I suppose not." Derezong yawned, rose, and toddled throneward. He glanced back over his shoulders as he went, disliking to walk through the halls of the palace without Zhamel to guard his back against a sudden stab.

The lamplight gleamed upon King Vuar's glabrous pate, and the king looked up at Derezong Taash from under his hedge of heavy brows. He sat upon his throne in the audience chamber, and over his head upon the wall was fastened the hunting-horn of the great King Zynah, Vuar's father.

After his preliminary prostration, Derezong Taash observed something else that had escaped his original notice: that on a small table in front of the throne, which usually bore a vase of flowers, there now reposed a silver plate, and on the plate the head of the Minister of Commerce, wearing that witlessly blank expression that heads are wont to do when separated from their proper bodies.

Evidently King Vuar was not in his jolliest mood.

"Yes, O King?" said Derezong Taash, his eyes swivelling nervously from the head of the late minister to that of his sovereign.

King Vuar said: "Good my lord, my wife Ilepro, whom I think you know, has a desire that you alone can satisfy."

"Yes, Sire?"

The king said: "She wishes that jewel that forms the third eye of the goddess Tandyla. You know that temple in Lotor?"

"Yes, Sire."

"This small-souled buckster," said Vuar, indicating the head, "said, when I put the proposal to him, that the gem could not be bought, wherefore I caused his length to be lessened. This hasty act I now regret, for it transpires that he was right. Therefore, our only remaining course is to steal the thing."

"Y-yes, Sire."

The king rested his long chin upon his fist and his agate eyes saw distant things. The lamplight gleamed upon the ring of gray metal on his finger, a ring made from the heart of a falling star, and of such might as a magic-repellant that not even the sendings of the wizards of Lotor had power to harm its wearer.

He continued: "We can either essay to seize it openly, which would mean war, or by stealth. Now, although I will go to some trouble to gratify the whims of Ilepro, my plans do not include a Lotrian war. At least, not until all other expedients have been attempted. You, therefore, are hereby commissioned to go to Lotor and obtain this jewel."

"Yes indeed, Sire," said Derezong with a heartiness that was, to say the least, a bit forced. Any thoughts of protest that he might have entertained had some minutes since been banished by the sight of the unlucky minister's head.

"Of course," said Vuar in tones of friendly consideration, "should you feel your own powers inadequate, I'm sure the King of Zhysk will lend me his wizard to assist you. . . ."

"Never, Sire!" cried Derezong, drawing himself up to his full five-five. "That bungling beetlehead, far from helping, would be but an anchor stone about my neck!"

King Vuar smiled a lupine smile, though Derezong could not perceive the reason. "So be it, then."

Back in his own quarters Derezong Taash rang for his assistant. After the third ring Zhamel Seh sauntered in, balancing his big bronze sword by the pommel on his palm.

"Some day," said Derezong, "you'll amputate some poor wight's toe showing off that trick, and I only hope it will be yours. We leave tomorrow on a mission."

Zhamel Seh grasped his sword securely by the hilt and grinned down upon his employer. "Good! Whither?"

Derezong Taash told him.

"Better yet! Action! Excitement!" Zhamel swished the air with his sword. "Since you put the geas upon the queen's mother have we sat in these apartments like barnacles on a pile, doing nought to earn King Vuar's bounty."

"What's wrong with that? I plague none and nobody plagues me. And now with winter coming on, we must journey forth to the ends of rocky Lotor to try to lift this worthless bauble the king's sack of a favorite has set her silly heart upon."

"I wonder why?" said Zhamel. "Since she's Lotri by birth, you'd think she'd wish to ward her land's religious symbols instead of stealing them away for her own adornment."

"One never knows. Our own women are unpredictable enough, and as for Lotris . . . But let's to the task of planning our course and equipage."

They rode east to fertile Zhysk on the shores of the Tritonian Sea, and in the city of Bienkar sought out Derezong's friend, Goshap Tuzh the lapidary, from whom they solicited information to forearm them against adversity.

"This jewel," said Goshap Tuzh, "is about the size of a small fist, egg-shaped without facets, and of a dark purple hue. When seen from one end, it displays rays like a sapphire, but seven instead of six. It forms the pupil of the central eye of the statue of Tandyla, being held in place by leaden prongs. As to what other means, natural or otherwise, the priests of Tandyla employ to guard their treasure, I know not, save that they are both effective and unpleasing. Twenty-three attempts have been made to pilfer the stone in the last five centuries, all terminating fatally for the thieves. The last time I, Goshap Tuzh, saw the body of the thief . . ."

As Goshap told the manner in which the unsuccessful thief had been used, Zhamel gagged and Derezong looked into his wine with an expression of distaste, as if some many-legged creeping thing swam therein—although he and his assistant were by no means the softest characters in a hard age.

"Its properties?" said Derezong Taash.

"Considerable, though perhaps over-rated by distant rumor. It is the world's most sovereign antidemonic, repelling even the dread Tr'lang himself, who is of all demons the deadliest."

"Is it even stronger than King Vuar's ring of starmetal?"

"Much. However, for our old friendship, let me advise you to change your name and take service with some less exacting liege lord. There's no profit in seeking to snatch this Eye."

Derezong Taash ran his fingers through his silky-white hair and beard. "True, he ever wounds me by his brutally voiced suspicions of my competence, but to relinquish such luxe as I enjoy were not so simple. Where else can I obtain such priceless books and enrapturing women for the asking? Nay, save when he becomes seized of these whimsies, King Vuar's a very good master indeed."

"But that's my point. When do you know his caprice notorious may not be turned against you?"

"I know not; betimes I think it must be easier to serve a barbarian king. Barbarians, being wrapped in a mummy-cloth of custom and ritual, are more predictable."

"Then why not flee? Across the Tritonian Sea lies lordly Torrutseish, where one of your worth would soon rise—"

"You forget," said Derezong, "King Vuar holds hostages: my not inconsiderable family. And for them I must stick it out, though the Western Sea swallow the entire land of Pusaad as it predicted in the prophecies."

Goshap shrugged. " 'Tis your affair. I do but indigitate that you are one of these awkward intermediates: Too tub-like ever to make a prow swordsman, and unable to attain the highest grade of magical adeptry because you'll not forswear the delights of your zenana."

"Thank you, good Goshap," said Derezong, sipping the green wine. "Howsoever, I live not to attain preeminence in some austere regimen disciplinary, but to enjoy life. And now who's a reliable apothecary in Bienkar from whom I can obtain a packet of syr-powder of highest grade and purity?"

"Dualor can furnish you. What semblance do you propose upon yourselves to cast?"

"I thought we'd go as a pair of traders from Parsk. So, if you hear of a couple traversing Lotor accompanied by vast uproar and vociferation, fail not to show the due surprise."

Derezong Taash bought his syr-powder with squares of gold bearing the stamp of King Vuar, then returned to their inn where he drew his pentacles and cast his powder and recited the Incantation of the Nines. At the end, both he and Zhamel Seh were both lying helpless on the floor, with their appearance changed to that of a pair of dark hawk-nosed fellows in the fluttery garb of Parsk, with rings in their ears.

When they recovered their strength, they rode forth. They crossed the desert of Reshape without suffering excessively either from thirst, or from the bites of venomous serpents, or from attacks of spirits of the waste. They passed through the Forest of Antro without being assailed by brigands, sword-toothed cats, or the Witch of Antro. And at last they wound among the iron hills of Lator.

As they stopped for one night, Derezong said: "By my reckoning and according to what passersby have told us, the temple should lie not more than one day's journey ahead. Hence, it were time to try whether we can effect our direption by surrogate instead of in our own vulnerable persons." And he began drawing pentacles in the dirt.

"You mean to call up Feranzot?" asked Zhamel Seh.

"The same."

Zhamel shuddered. "Some day you'll leave an angle of a pentacle unclosed, and that will be the end of us."

"No doubt. But to assail this stronghold of powers chthonian by any but the mightiest means were an even surer passport to extinction. So light the rushes and begin."

"I can fancy nothing riskier than dealing with Feranzot," grumbled Zhamel, "save perhaps invoking the terrible Tr'lang himself." But he did as he was bid.

They went through the Incantation of Br'tong, as reconstructed by Derezong Taash from the Fragments of Lontang, and the dark shape of Feranzot appeared outside the main pentacle, wavering and rippling. Derezong felt the heat of his body sucked forth by the cold of the daev, and felt the overwhelming depression the thing's presence engendered. Zhamel Seh, for all his thews, cowered.

"What would you?" whispered Feranzot.

Derezong Taash gathered his weakened forces and replied: "You shall steal the jewel in the middle eye of the statue of the goddess Tandyla in the nearby temple thereof and render it to me."

"That I cannot."

"And why not?"

"First, because the priests of Tandyla have traced around their temple a circle of such puissance that no sending or semblance or spirit, save the great Tr'lang, can cross it. Second, because the Eye itself is surrounded by an aura of such baleful influence that not I, nor any other of my kind, nor even Tr'lang himself, can exert a purchase upon it on this plane. May I return to my own dimension now?"

"Depart, depart, depart . . . Well, Zhamel, it looks as though we should be compelled to essay this undelightsome task ourselves."

Next day they continued their ride. The hills became mountains of uncommon ruggedness, and the road a mere trail cut into cliffs of excessive steepness. The horses, more accustomed to the bison-swarming plains of windy Lorsk, misliked the new topography, and rubbed their riders' legs painfully against the cliffside in their endeavor to keep away from the edge.

Little sun penetrated these gorges of black rock, which began to darken almost immediately after noon. Then the sky clouded over and the rocks became shiny with cold mist. The trail crossed the gorge by a spidery bridge suspended from ropes. The horses balked.

"Not that I blame them," said Derezong Taash, dismounting. "By the red-hot talons of Vrazh, it takes the thought of my fairest concubine to nerve me to cross!"

When led in line with Zhamel belaboring their rumps from the rear, the animals crossed, though unwillingly. Derezong, towing them, took one brief look over the side of the bridge at the white thread of water foaming far below and decided not to do that again. Feet and hooves resounded hollowly on the planking and echoed from the cliffsides, and the wind played with the ropes as with the strings of a great harp.

On the other side of the gorge, the road continued its winding upward way. They passed another pair, a man and a woman, riding down the trail, and had to back around a bend to find a place with room enough to pass. The man and the woman went by looking somberly at the ground, barely acknowledging with the grunt the cheerful greeting Derezong tossed at them.

Then the road turned sharply into a great cleft in the cliff, wherein their hooffalls echoed thrice as loud as life and they could scarcely see to pick their way. The bottom of the cleft sloped upward, so that in time they came out upon an area of tumbled stones with a few dwarfed trees. The road ran dimly on through the stones until it ended in a flight of steps, which in turn led up to the Temple of Tandyla itself. Of this temple of ill repute, the travellers could see only the lower parts, for the upper ones disappeared into the cloud floor. What they could see of it was all black and shiny and rising to sharp peaks.

Derezong remembered the unpleasant attributes ascribed to the goddess, and the even more disagreeable habits credited to her priests. It was said, for instance, that the worship of Tandyla, surely a sinister enough figure in the Pusaadian pantheon, was a mere blind to cover dark rites concerning the demon Tr'lang, who in elder days had been a god in his own right. That was before the towering Lorskas, driven from the mainland by the conquering Hauskirik, had swarmed across the Tritonian Sea to Pusaad, before that land had begun its ominous subsidence.

Derezong Taash assured himself that gods and demons alike were not usually so formidable as their priests, from base motives of gain, tried to make them out. Also, that wild tales of the habits of priests usually turned out to be at least somewhat exaggerated. Although he did not fully believe his own assurances, they would have to suffice for want of better.

In front of the half-hidden temple, Derezong Taash pulled up, dismounted, and with Zhamel's help weighted down the reins of their beasts with heavy stones to hinder them from straying.

As they started for the steps Zhamel cried: "Master!"

"What is't?"

"Look upon us!"

Derezong looked and saw that the semblance of traders from Parsk had vanished, and that they were again King Vuar's court magician and his assistant, plain for all to see. They must have stepped across that line that Fernazot had warned them of.

Derezong took a sharp look at the entrance, and half-hidden in the inadequate light he saw two men flanking the doorway. His eye caught the gleam of polished bronze. But if these doorkeepers had observed the change in the looks of the visitors, they gave no sign.

Derezong Taash drove his short legs up the shiny black steps. The guards came into full view, thick-bodied Lotris with beetling brows. Men said they were akin to the savages of Ierarne in the far Northeast, who knew not horse-taming and fought with sharpened stone. These stood staring straight ahead, each facing the other like statues. Derezong and Zhamel passed between them.

They found themselves in a vestibule where a pair of young Lotri girls said: "Your boots and swords, sirs."

Derezong lifted off his baldric and handed it to the nearest, scabbard and all; then pulled off his boots and stood barefoot with the grass he had stuffed into them to keep them from chafing sticking out from between his toes. He was glad to feel the second sword hanging down his back inside his shirt.

"Come on," said Derezong Taash, and led the way into the naos of the temple.

It was much like other temples: a big rectangular room smelling of incense, with a third of the area partitioned off by a railing, behind which rose the huge black squat statue of Tandyla. The smooth basalt of which it was carved reflected feebly the highlights from the few lamps, and up at the top, where its head disappeared into the shadows, a point of purple light showed where the jewel in its forehead caught the rays.

A couple of Lotris knelt before the railing, mumbling prayers. A priest appeared from the shadows on one side, waddled across the naos behind the railing. Derezong half expected the priest to turn on him with a demand that he and Zhamel follow him into the sanctum of the high priest, but the priest kept on walking and disappeared into the darkness on the other side.

Derezong Taash and his companion advanced, a slow step at a time, towards the railing. As they neared it, the two Lotris completed their devotions and rose. One of them dropped something that jingled into a large tub-like receptacle behind the railing, and the two squat figures walked quickly out.

For the moment, Derezong and Zhamel were entirely alone in the big room, though in the silence they could hear faint motions and voices from other parts of the temple. Derezong brought out his container of syr-powder and sprinkled it while racing through the Incantation of Ansuan. When he finished, there stood between himself and Zhamel a replica of himself.

Derezong Taash climbed over the railing and trotted on the tips of his plump toes around behind the statue. Here in the shadows, he could see doors in the walls. The statue sat with its back almost but not quite touching the wall behind it, so that an active man, by bracing his back against the statue and his feet against the wall, could lever himself up. Though Derezong was "active" only in a qualified sense, he slipped into the gap and squirmed into a snugly-fitting fold in the goddess's stone draperies. Here he lay, hardly breathing, until he heard Zhamel's footfalls die away.

The plan was that Zhamel should walk out of the temple, accompanied by the double of Derezong. The guards, believing that the temple was now deserted of visitors, would relax. Derezong would steal the stone; Zhamel should raise a haro outside, urging the guards to "Come quickly!" and while their attention was thus distracted, Derezong would rush out.

Derezong Taash began to worm his way up between the statue and the wall. It was hard going for one of his girth, and sweat ran out from under his cap of fisher-fur and down his face. Still no interruption.

He arrived on a level with the shoulder and squirmed out on to that projection, holding the right ear for safety. The slick stone was cold under his bare feet. By craning his neck, he could see the ill-favored face of the goddess in profile, and by stretching he could reach the jewel in her forehead.

Derezong Taash took out of his tunic a small bronze pry-bar he had brought along for this purpose. With it he began to pry up the leaden prongs that held the gem in place, carefully lest he mar the stone or cause it to fall to the floor below. Every few pries, he tested it with his finger. Soon it felt loose.

The temple was quiet.

Around the clock he went with his little bar, prying. Then the stone came out, rubbing gently against the smooth inner surfaces of the bent-out leaden prongs. Derezong Taash reached for the inside of his tunic, to hide the stone and the bar. But the two objects proved too much for his pudgy fingers to handle at once. The bar came loose and fell with a loud ping—ping down the front of the statue, bouncing from breast to belly to lap, to end with a sonorous clank on the stone floor in front of the image.

Derezong Taash froze rigid. Seconds passed and nothing happened. Surely the guards had heard . . .

But still there was silence.

Derezong Taash secured the jewel in his tunic and squirmed back over the shoulder to the darkness behind the statue. Little by little, he slid down the space between statue and wall. He reached the floor. Still no noise save an occasional faint sound such as might have been made by the temple servants preparing dinner for their masters. He waited for the diversion promised by Zhamel Seh.

He waited and waited. From somewhere came the screech of a man in the last agonies.

At last, giving up, Derezong Taash hurried around the hip of the statue. He scooped up the pry-bar with one quick motion, climbed back over the railing, and tiptoed toward the exit.

There stood the guards with swords out, ready for him.

Derezong Taash reached back over his shoulder and pulled out his second sword. In a real fight, he knew he would have little hope against one hardened and experienced swordfighter, let alone two. His one slim chance lay in bursting through them by a sudden berserk attack and keeping on running.

He expected such adroit and skillful warriors to separate and come at him from opposite sides. Instead, one of them stepped forward and took an awkward swipe at him. Derezong parried with a clash of bronze and struck back. Clang! clang! went the blades, and then his foe staggered back, dropped his sword with a clatter, clutched both hands to his chest, and folded up in a heap on the floor. Derezong was astonished; he could have sworn he had not gotten home.

Then the other man was upon him. At the second clash of blades, that of the guard spun out of his hand, to fall ringingly to the stone pave. The guard leaped back, turned and ran, disappearing through one of the many ambient doors.

Derezong Taash glanced at his sword, wondering if he had not known his own strength all this time. The whole exchange had taken perhaps ten seconds, and so far as he could tell in the dim light, no blood besmeared his blade. He was tempted to test the deadness of the fallen guard by poking him, but lacked both time and ruthlessness to do so. Instead, he ran out of the vestibule and looked for Zhamel and the double of himself.

No sign of either. The four horses were still tethered a score of paces from the steps of the temple. The stones were sharp under Derezong's bare and unhardened soles.

Derezong hesitated, but only for a flash. He was in a way fond of Zhamel Seh, and his assistant's brawn had gotten him out of trouble about as often as Zhamel's lack of insight had gotten them into it. On the other hand, to plunge back into the temple in search of his erratic aide would be rash to the point of madness. And he did have definite orders from the king.

He sheathed his sword, scrambled on to the back of his horse, and cantered off, leading the other three beasts by their bridles.

During the ride down the narrow deft, Derezong had time to think, and the more he thought the less he liked what he thought. The behavior of the guards was inexplicable on any grounds but their being drunk or crazy, and he did not believe either. Their failure to attack him simultaneously; their failure to note the fall of the pry-bar; the ease with which he, an indifferent swordsman, had bested them; the fact that one fell down without being touched; their failure to yell for help . . .

Unless they planned it that way. The whole thing had been too easy to account for by any other hypothesis. Maybe they wanted him to steal the accursed bauble.

At the lower end of the cleft, where the road turned out on to the side of the cliff forming the main gorge, he pulled up, dismounted, and tied the animals, keeping an ear cocked for the sound of pursuers echoing down the cleft. He took out the Eye of Tandyla and looked at it. Yes, when seen end-on it showed the rayed effect promised by Goshap Tuzh. Otherwise, it exhibited no special odd or unnatural properties. So far.

Derezong Taash set it carefully on the ground and backed away from it to see it from a greater distance. As he backed, the stone moved slightly and started to roll towards him.

At first he thought he had not laid it down on a level enough place, and leaped to seize it before it should roll over the edge into the gulf. He put it back and heaped a little barrier of pebbles and dust around it. Now it should not roll!

But when he backed again it did, right over his little rampart. Derezong Taash began to sweat anew, and not, this time, from physical exertion. The stone rolled toward him, faster and faster. He tried to dodge by shrinking into a recess in the cliff-wall. The stone swerved and came to rest at the toe of one of his bare feet, like a pet animal asking for a pat on the head.

He scooped out a small hole, laid the gem in it, placed a large stone over the hole, and walked away. The large stone shook and the purple egg appeared, pushing aside the pebbles in its path as if it were being pulled out from under the rock by an invisible cord. It rolled to his feet again and stopped.

Derezong Taash picked up the stone and looked at it again. It did not seem to have been scratched. He remembered that the demand for the stone originated with an Ilepro, the King's wife.

With a sudden burst of emotion, Derezong Taash threw the stone from him, towards the far side of the gorge.

By all calculation, the gem should have followed a curved path, arching downward to shatter against the opposite cliff. Instead, it slowed in midflight over the gorge, looped back, and flew into the hand that had just thrown it.

Derezong Taash did not doubt that the priests of Tandyla had laid a subtle trap for King Vuar in the form of this jewel. What it would do to the king and to the kingdom of Lorsk if Derezong carried out his mission, he had no idea. So far as he knew, it was merely an antidemonic, and therefore should protect Vuar instead of harming him. Nevertheless, he was sure something unpleasant was planned, of which he was less than eager to be the agency. He placed the gem on a flat rock, found a stone the size of his head, raised it in both hands, and brought it down upon the jewel.

Or so he intended. On the way down, the stone struck a projecting shelf of rock, and a second later Derezong was capering about like a devil-dancer of Dzen, sucking his mashed fingers and cursing the priests of Tandyla in the names of the most fearful demons in his repertory. The stone lay unharmed.

For, Derezong reasoned, these priests must have put upon the gem not only a following-spell, but also the Incantation of Duzhateng, so that every effort on the part of Derezong to destroy the object would rebound to his own damage. If he essayed some more elaborate scheme of destruction, he would probably end up with a broken leg. The Incantation of Duzhateng could be lifted only by a complicated spell for which Derezong did not have the materials, which included some very odd and repellant substances indeed.

Now, Derezong Taash knew that there was only one way in which he could both neutralize these spells and secure the jewel so that it should plague him no more, and that was to put it back in the hole in the forehead of the statue of Tandyla and hammer down the leaden prongs that held it in its setting. Which task, however, promised to present more difficulties than the original theft. For if the priests of Tandyla had meant Derezong to steal the object, they might show greater acumen in thwarting his attempt to return it, than they had in guarding it in the first place.

One could but try. Derezong Taash put the jewel into his tunic, mounted his horse (leaving the other still tethered) and rode back up the echoing cleft. When he came out upon the little plateau upon which squatted the temple of Tandyla, he saw that he had indeed been forestalled. Around the entrance to the temple stood a double row of guards, the bronze scales of their cuirasses glimmering faintly in the fading light. The front rank carried shields of mammoth hide and big bronze swords, while those in the rear bore long pikes which they held in both hands and thrust between the men of the front rank. They thus presented a formidable hedge to any attacker, who had first to get past the spear-points and then deal with the swords.

One possibility was to gallop at them in the hope that one or two directly in one's way would flinch aside, opening a path by which one could burst through the serried line. Then, one could ride on into the temple and perhaps get the gem back into place before being caught up with. If not, there would be a great smash, some battered guards, a wounded horse, and a thoroughly skewered and sliced sorcerer all tangled in a kicking heap.

Derezong Taash hesitated, then thought of his precious manuscripts awaiting him in King Vuar's palace, which he could never safely enter again unless he brought either the gem or an acceptable excuse for not having it. He kicked his mount into motion.

As the animal cantered toward the line, the spear-points got closer and larger and sharper-looking, and Derezong Taash saw that the guards were not going to flinch aside and obligingly let him through. Then, a figure came out of the temple and ran down the steps to the rear of the guards. It wore a priest's robe, but just before the shock of impact Derezong recognized the rugged features of Zhamel Seh.

Derezong Taash hauled on his reins, and the horse skidded to a halt with its nose a scant span from the nearest point. Derezong—living in a stirrupless age—slid forward until he bestrode the animal's neck. Clutching its mane with his left hand, he felt for the gem with his right.

"Zhamel!" he called. "Catch!"

He threw. Zhamel leaped high and caught the stone before it had time to loop back.

"Now put it back!" cried Derezong.

"What? Art mad?"

"Put it back, speedily, and secure it!"

Zhamel, trained to obey commands no matter how bizarre, dashed back into the temple, albeit wagging his head as if in sorrow for his master's loss of sanity. Derezong Taash untangled himself from his horse's mane and pulled the beast back out of reach of the spears. Under their lacquered helmets, the heads of the guards turned this way and that in evident perplexity. Derezong surmised that they had been given one simple order—to keep him out—and that they had not been told how to cope with fraternization between the stranger and one of their own priests.

As the guards did not seem to be coming after him, Derezong sat on his horse, eyes on the portal. He'd given Zhamel a fair chance to accomplish his mission and escape, though he thought little of the youth's chances. If Zhamel tried to push or cut his way through the guards, they would make mincemeat of him, unarmored as he was. And he, Derezong, would have to find and train another assistant, who would probably prove as unsatisfactory as his predecessor. Still, Derezong could not leave the boy utterly to his fate.

Then, Zhamel Seh ran down the steps carrying a long pike of the kind held by the rear-rank guards. Holding this pike level, he ran at the guards as though he were about to spear one in the back. Derezong, knowing that such a scheme would not work, shut his eyes.

But just before he reached the guards, Zhamel Seh dug the point of the pike into the ground and pole-vaulted. Up he went, legs jerking and dangling like those of a man being hanged, over the lacquered helmets and the bronze swords and the mammoth hide shields. He came down in front of the guards, breaking one of their pikes with a loud snap, rolled to his feet, and ran towards Derezong Taash. The latter had already turned his horse around.

As Zhamel caught hold of the edge of the saddle pad, an uproar arose behind them as priests ran out of the temple shouting. Derezong drummed with his bare heels on the stallion's ribs and set off at a canter, Zhamel swinging along in great leaps beside him. They wended their way down the cleft while the sound of hooves wafted after them.

Derezong Taash wasted no breath in questions while picking his way down the trail. At the bottom, where the cleft ended on one side of the great gorge, they halted for Zhamel to mount his own horse, then continued as fast as they dared. The echoes of the pursuers' hooves came down the cleft with a deafening clatter.

At the suspension-bridge, the horses balked again, but Derezong mercilessly pricked and slapped his mount with his sword until the beast trotted out upon the swaying walkway. The cold wind hummed through the ropes and the daylight was almost gone.

At the far end, with a great sigh of relief, Derezong Taash looked back. Down the cliffside road came a line of pursuers, riding at reckless speed.

He said: "Had I but time and materials, I'd cast a spell on yonder bridge that should make it look as 'twere broken and dangling useless."

"What's wrong with making it broken and useless in very truth?" cried Zhamel, pulling his horse up against the cliffside and hoisting himself so that he stood upon his saddle.

He swung his sword at the cables. As the first of the pursuers reached the far side of the bridge, the structure sagged and fell away with a great swish of ropes and clatter of planks. The men from the temple set up an outcry, and an arrow whizzed across the gap to shatter against the rock. Derezong and Zhamel resumed their journey.

A fortnight later, they sat in the garden back of the shop of Goshap Tuzh the lapidary in sunny Bienkar. Zhamel Seh told his part of the tale:

". . . so on my way out, this little Lotri cast her orbs upon me once again. Now, thought I, there'll be time in plenty to perform the Master's work and make myself agreeable in this quarter as well—"

"Young cullion!" growled Derezong into his wine.

"—so I followed her. And in truth all was going in most propitious and agreeable wise, when who should come in but one of these chinless wonders in cowl and robe, and went for me with a knife. I tried to fend the fellow off, and fear that in the fracas his neck by ill hap got broke. So, knowing there might be trouble, I borrowed his habit and sallied forth therein, to find that Master, horses, and Master's double had all gone."

"And how time had flown!" said Derezong Taash in sarcastic tones. "I trust at least that the young Lotri has cause to remember this episode with pleasure. The double no doubt being a mere thing of shadow and not a being rational, walked straight out and vanished when it crossed the magical barrier erected by the priests."

"And," continued Zhamel, "there were priests and guards rushing about chittering like a pack of monkeys. I rushed about as if I were one of them, saw them range the guards around the portal, and then the Master returned and threw me the stone. I grasped the situation, swarmed up the statue, popped Tandyla's third eye back into its socket, and hammered the prongs in upon it with the pommel of my dagger. Then I fetched a pike from the armory, pausing but to knock senseless a couple of Lotris who sought to detain me for interrogation, and you know the rest."

Derezong Taash rounded out the story and said: "Good Goshap, perchance you can advise our next course, for I fear that should we present ourselves before King Vuar in proper persons, without the gem, he'd have our heads set tastefully on silver platters ere were our explanation finished. No doubt, remorse would afterwards o'erwhelm him, but that would help us not."

"Since he holds you in despite, why not leave him, as I've urged before?" said Goshap.

Derezong Taash shrugged. "Others, alas, show a like lack of appreciation, and would prove no easier masters. For had these priests of Tandyla confided in my ability to perform a simple task like carrying their gemstone from Lotor to Lorsk, their plot would doubtless have borne its intended fruit. But fearing lest I should lose or sell it on the way, they put a supernumerary spell upon it—"

"How could they, when the stone has anti-magical properties?"

"Its anti-magical properties comprise simple antidemonism, whereas the following-spell and the Incantation of Duzhateng are sympathetic magic, not sorcerous. At any rate, they caused it to follow me hither and thither, thus arousing my already awakened suspicions to the feverpitch." He sighed and took a pull on the green wine. "What this sorry world needs is more confidence. But say on, Goshap."

"Well, then, why not write him a letter setting forth the circumstances? I'll lend you a slave to convey it to Lorsk in advance of your persons, so that when you arrive, King Vuar's wrath shall have subsided."

Derezong pondered. "Sage though I deem your suggestion, it faces one obstacle insurmountable. Namely: That of all the men at the court of Lorsk, but six can read; and among these King Vuar is not numbered. Whereas of the six, at least five are among my enemies who'd like nought better than to see me tumbled from my place. And should the task of reading my missive to the king devolve on one of these, you can fancy how he'd distort my harmless pictographs to my discredit. Could we trick old Vuar into thinking we'd performed our task, as by passing off on him a stone similar to that he expects of us? Know you of such?"

"Now there," said Goshap, "is a proposal indeed. Let me cogitate . . . Last year, when the bony specter of want came upon the land, King Daior placed his best crown in pawn to the Temple of Kelk, for treasure wherewith to still the clamorings of his people. Now, this crown bears at its apex a purple star sapphire of wondrous size and fineness, said to have been shaped by the gods before the Creation for their own enjoyment, and being in magnitude and hue not unlike that which forms the Eye of Tandyla. And the gem has never been redeemed, wherefore the priests of Kelk have set the crown on exhibition, thereby mulcting the curious of further offerings. But as to how this well-guarded gem shall be transferred from this crown to your possession, ask me not, and in truth I had liefer know nought of the matter."

Next day, Derezong Taash cast upon himself and Zhamel Seh

the likeness of Atlantes, from the misty mountain range in the desert of Gautha, far to the East across the Tritonian Sea, where it was said in Pusaad that there were men with snakes for legs and others with no heads but faces in their chests.

Zhamel Seh grumbled: "What are we, magicians or thieves? Perhaps if we succeed in this, the King of Torrutseish across the Tritonian Sea has some bauble he specially fancies, that we could rob him of."

Derezong Taash did not argue the point, but led the way to the square fronted by the Temple of Kelk. They strode up to the temple with the Atlantean swagger, and into where the crown lay upon a cushion on a table with a lamp to illuminate it and two seven-foot Lorskas to guard it, one with a drawn sword and the other with a nocked arrow. The guards looked down over their great black beards at the red-haired Atlanteans in their blue cloaks and armlets of orichalc who pointed and jabbered as they saw the crown. And then the shorter Atlantean, that was Derezong Taash beneath the illusion, wandered out, leaving the other to gape.

Scarcely had the shorter Atlas passed the portal than he gave a loud squawk. The guards, looking that way, saw his head in profile projecting past the edge of the doorway and looking upward as though his body were being bent backward, while a pair of hands gripped his throat.

The guards, not knowing that Derezong was strangling himself, rushed to the portal. As they neared it, the head of the assailed Atlantean disappeared from view, and they arrived to find Derezong Taash in his proper form strolling up to the entrance. All the while behind them the powerful fingers of Zhamel Seh pried loose the stone from King Daior's crown.

"Is aught amiss, sirs?" said Derezong to the guards, who stared about wildly as Zhamel Seh came out of the temple behind them. As he did so, he also dropped his Atlantean disguise and became another Lorska like the guards, though not quite so tall and bushy-bearded.

"If you seek an Atlas," said Derezong in answer to their questions, "I saw two such issue from your fane and slink off into yonder alley with furtive gait. Perhaps it behooves you to see whether they have committed some depredation in your hallowed precincts?"

As the guards rushed back into the temple to see, Derezong Taash and his assistant made off briskly in the opposite direction.

Zhamel Seh muttered: "At least, let's hope we shall not have to return this jewel to the place whence we obtained it!"

Derezong and Zhamel reached Lezohtr late at night, but had not even finished greeting their loving concubines when a messenger informed Derezong Taash that the king wanted him at once.

Derezong Taash found King Vuar in the audience room, evidently freshrisen from his bed for he wore nought but his crown and bearskin wrapped about his bony body. Ilepro was there, too, clad with like informality, and with her were her ever-present Lotrian quartet.

"You have it?" said King Vuar, lifting a bushy brow that boded no good for a negative answer.

"Here, Sire," said Derezong, heaving himself up off the floor and advancing with the jewel from the crown of King Daior.

King Vuar took it in his finger-tips and looked at it in the light of the single lamp. Derezong Taash wondered if the king would think to count the rays to see if there were six or seven; but he reassured himself with the thought that King Vuar was notoriously weak in higher mathematics.

The king extended the jewel towards Ilepro. "Here, Madam," he said. "And let us hope that with this transaction ends your incessant plaint."

"My lord is as generous as the sun," said Ilepro in her thick Lotrian accent. " 'Tis true I have a little more to say, but not for servile ears." She spoke in Lotrian to her four attendants, who scuttled out.

"Well?" said the king.

Ilepro stared into the sapphire and made a motion with her free hand, meanwhile reciting something in her native tongue. Although she went too fast for Derezong Taash to understand, he caught a word several times repeated, that shook him to the core. The word was "Tr'lang".

"Sire!" he cried. "I fear this northern witch is up to no good—"

"What?" roared King Vuar. "You hlipend my wife, and before my very optics? I'll have your head—"

"But Sire! King! Look!"

The king broke into his tirade long enough to look, and never resumed it. For the flame of the lamp had shrunk to a bare spark. Cold eddies stirred the air of the room, in the midst of which the gloom thickened into shadow and the shadow into substance. At first, it seemed a shapeless darkness, a sable fog, but then a pair of glowing points appeared, palpable eyes, at twice the height of a man.

Derezong's mind sought for exorcisms while his tongue clove to the roof of his mouth with terror. For his own Ferenzot was but a kitten compared to this, and no pentacle protected him.

The eyes grew plainer, and lower down horny talons threw back faint highlights from the feeble flame of the lamp. The cold in the room was as if an iceberg had walked in, and Derezong smelt an odor as of burning feathers.

Ilepro pointed at the king and cried something in her own language. Derezong thought he saw fangs as a great mouth opened and Tr'lang swept forward towards Ilepro. She held the jewel in front of her, as if to ward off the daev. But it paid no attention. As the blackness settled around her, she gave a piercing scream.

The door now flew open again and the four Lotri women rushed back in. Ilepro's screams continued, diminuendo, with a curious effect of distance, as if Tr'lang were dragging her far away. All that could be seen was a dwindling shapeless shape of shadow in the middle of the floor.

The foremost of the Lotris cried "Ilepro!" and sprang towards the shape, shedding wraps with one hand while tugging out a great bronze sword with the other. As the other three did likewise, Derezong Taash realized that they were not women at all, but burly male Lotris given a superficially feminine look by shaving their beards and padding their clothes in appropriate places.

The first of the four swung his sword through the place where the shape of Tr'lang had been, but without meeting resistance other than that of air. Then he turned toward the king and Derezong.

"Take these alive!" he said in Lotrian. "They shall stand surety for our safe departure."

The four moved forward, their swords ready and their free hands spread to clutch like the talons of the just-departed demon. Then the opposite door opened and in came Zhamel Seh with an armful of swords. Two he tossed to Derezong Taash and King Vuar, who caught them by the hilts; the third he gripped in his own large fist as he took his place beside the other two.

"Too late," said another Lotri. "Slay them and run's our only chance."

Suiting the deed to the declaration, he rushed upon the three Lorskas. Clang! Clang! went the swords as the seven men slashed and parried in the gloom. King Vuar had whirled his bearskin around his left arm for a shield and fought naked save for his crown. While the Lorskas had an advantage of reach, they were handicapped by the king's age and Derezong's embonpoint and mediocrity of swordsmanship.

Though Derezong cut and thrust nobly, he found himself pushed back towards a corner, and felt the sting of a flesh-wound in the shoulder. And whatever the ignorant might think of a wizard's powers, it was quite impossible to fight physically for one's life and cast a spell at the same time.

The king bellowed for help, but no answer came, for in these inner chambers the thick stone walls and hangings deadened sound before it reached the outer rooms of the palace where King Vuar's guards had their stations. Like the others, he, too, was driven back until the three were fighting shoulder to shoulder in the corner. A blade hit Derezong's head flatsides and made him dizzy, while a metallic sound told that another blow had gotten home on the king's crown, and a yelp from Zhamel Seh revealed that he also had been hurt.

Derezong Taash found himself fast tiring. Each breath was a labor, and the hilt was slippery in his aching fingers. Soon they'd beat down his guard and finish him, unless he found some more indirect shift by which to make head against them.

He threw his sword, not at the Lotri in front of him, but at the little lamp that flickered on the table. The lamp flew off with a clatter and went out as Derezong Taash dropped on all fours and crept after his sword. Behind him in the darkness he could hear the footsteps and the hard breathing of men, afraid to strike for fear of smiting a friend and afraid to speak lest they reveal themselves to a foe.

Derezong Taash felt along the wall until he came to the hunting-horn of King Zynah. Wrenching the relic from the wall he filled his lungs and blew a tremendous blast.

The blast of the horn resounded deafeningly in the confined space. Derezong took several steps, lest one of the Lotris locate him by sound and cut him down in the dark, and blew again. With loud tramplings and clankings, the guards of King Vuar approached. The door burst open and in they came with weapons ready and torches high.

"Take them!" said King Vuar, pointing at the Lotris.

One of the Lotris tried to resist, but a guardsman's sword sheared the hand from his arm as he swung, and the Lotri yelled and sank to the floor to bleed to death. The others were subdued with little trouble.

"Now," said the king, "I can give you the boon of a quick

death, or I can turn you over to the tormentors for a slower and much more interesting one. Do you confess your plans and purposes in full, the former alternative shall be permitted you. Speak.''

The Lotri who had led the others when they entered the room said: "Know, King, that I am Paanuvel, the husband of Ilepro. The others are gentlemen of the court of Ilepro's brother Konesp, High Chief of Lotor.''

"Gentlemen!" snorted King Vuar.

"As my brother-in-law has no sons of his own, he and I concocted this sublime scheme for bringing his kingdom and yours under the eventual united rule of my son Pendetr. This magician of yours was to steal the Eye of Tandyla, so that, when Ilepro conjured up the daev Tr'lang, the monster would not assail her as she'd be protected by the gem's powers; it would, instead, dispose of you. For she knew that no lesser creature of the outer dimensions could assail you whilst you wear the ring of starmetal. Then she'd proclaim the child Pendetr king, as you've already named him heir, with herself as regent till he comes of age. But the antisorcellarious virtues of this jewel are evidently not what they once were, for Tr'lang engulfed my wife though she thrust the gem in its maw.''

"You have spoken well and frankly," said King Vuar, "though I question the morality of turning your wife over to me, yourself being not only alive but present here in disguise. However, the customs of the Lotris are not ours. Lead them out, guards, and take off their heads.''

"One more word, King," said Paanuvel. "For myself I care little, now that my beloved Ilepro's gone. But I ask that you make not the child Pendetr suffer for his father's faulty schemes.''

"I will think on't. Now, off with you and with your heads.'' The king turned to Derezong Taash, who was mopping at his flesh-wound. "What is the cause of the failure of the Eye of Tandyla?''

Derezong, in fear and trembling, told the true tale of their foray into Lotor and their subsequent theft of the sapphire in Bienkar.

"Aha!" said King Vuar. "So that's what we get for not counting the rays seen in the stone!''

He paused to pick up the jewel from where it lay upon the floor, and the quaking Derezong foresaw his own severance, like that which the Lotris were even now experiencing.

Then Vuar smiled thinly. "A fortunate failure, it seems," said the king. "I am indebted to you both, first for your shrewdness in penetrating the plans of the Lotris to usurp the throne of Lorsk, second for fighting beside me to such good purpose this night.

"Howsoever, we have here a situation fraught with some slight embarrassment. For King Daior is a good friend of mine, which friendship I would not willingly forego. And even though I should return the gem to him with explanation and apology, the fact that my servants purloined it in the first place would not sit well with him. My command to you, therefore, is to return at once to Bienkar—"

"Oh, no!" cried Derezong Taash, the words escaping involuntarily from him under the impetus of strong emotion.

"—return to Bienkar," continued the king as if he had not heard, "and smuggle the jewel back to its original position in the crown of the King of Zhysk, without letting anyone know that you are involved either in the disappearance of the stone or in its eventual restoration. For such accomplished rogues as you and your apprentice have shown yourselves to be, this slight feat will pose no serious obstacle. And so goodnight, my lord sorcerer."

King Vuar threw his bearskin about him and tramped off to his apartments, leaving Derezong and Zhamel staring at one another with expressions of mingled horror and a vast dismay.

THE WHITE HORSE CHILD

by
Greg Bear

Greg Bear is a young (born in 1951) American writer who is rapidly achieving recognition as an excellent storyteller and craftsman. His novels include HEGIRA (1979), PSYCHLONE (1979), and the very interesting BEYOND HEAVEN'S RIVER (1980). His short stories have appeared in such publications as ANALOG, UNIVERSE, and NEW DIMENSIONS. Mr. Bear lives in California and has worked as a planetarium operator, a most fitting occupation for a science fiction writer.

"The White Horse Child" is a memorable story about the wizardry of writing, normality, and children, and how the three often don't mix.

When I was seven years old, I met an old man by the side of the dusty road between school and farm. The late afternoon sun had cooled and he was sitting on a rock, hat off, hands held out to the gentle warmth, whistling a pretty song. He nodded at me as I walked past. I nodded back. I was curious, but I knew better than to get involved with strangers. Nameless evils seemed to attach themselves to strangers, as if they might turn into lions when no one but a little kid was around.

"Hello, boy," he said.

I stopped and shuffled my feet. He looked more like a hawk than a lion. His clothes were brown and gray and russet, and his hands were pink like the flesh of some rabbit a hawk had just plucked up. His face was brown except around the eyes, where he might have worn glasses; around the eyes he was white, and this intensified his gaze. "Hello," I said.

"Was a hot day. Must have been hot in school," he said.

"They got air conditioning."

"So they do, now. How old are you?"

"Seven," I said. "Well, almost eight."

"Mother told you never to talk to strangers?"

"And Dad, too."

"Good advice. But haven't you seen me around here before?" I looked him over. "No."

"Closely. Look at my clothes. What color are they?"

His shirt was gray, like the rock he was sitting on. The cuffs, where they peeped from under a russet jacket, where white. He didn't smell bad, but he didn't look particularly clean. He was smooth-shaven, though. His hair was white and his pants were the color of the dirt below the rock. "All kinds of colors," I said.

"But mostly I partake of the landscape, no?"

"I guess so," I said.

"That's because I'm not here. You're imagining me, at least part of me. Don't I look like somebody you might have heard of?"

"Who are you supposed to look like?" I asked.

"Well, I'm full of stories," he said. "Have lots of stories to tell little boys, little girls, even big folk, if they'll listen."

I started to walk away.

"But only if they'll listen," he said. I ran. When I got home, I told my older sister about the man on the road, but she only got a worried look and told me to stay away from strangers. I took her advice. For some time afterward, into my eighth year, I avoided that road and did not speak with strangers more than I had to.

The house that I lived in, with the five other members of my family and two dogs and one beleaguered cat, was white and square and comfortable. The stairs were rich, dark wood overlaid with worn carpet. The walls were dark oak paneling up to a foot above my head, then white plaster, with a white plaster ceiling. The air was full of smells—bacon when I woke up, bread and soup and dinner when I came home from school, dust on weekends when we helped clean.

Sometimes my parents argued, and not just about money, and those were bad times; but usually we were happy. There was talk about selling the farm and the house and going to Mitchell where Dad could work in a computerized feed-mixing plant, but it was only talk.

It was early summer when I took the dirt road again. I'd forgotten about the old man. But in almost the same way, when the sun was cooling and the air was haunted by lazy bees, I saw an old woman. Women strangers are less malevolent than men, and rarer. She was sitting on the gray rock, in a long green skirt summer-dusty, with a daisy-colored shawl and a blouse the precise hue of cottonwoods seen in a late hazy day's muted light.

"Hello, boy," she said.

"I don't recognize you, either," I blurted, and she smiled.

"Of course not. If you didn't recognize him, you'd hardly know me."

"Do you know him?" I asked. She nodded. "Who was he? Who are you?"

"We're both full of stories. Just tell them from different angles. You aren't afraid of us, are you?"

I was, but having a woman ask the question made all the difference. "No," I said. "But what are you doing here? And how do you know—?"

"Ask for a story," she said. "One you've never heard of before." Her eyes were the color of baked chestnuts, and she squinted into the sun so that I couldn't see her whites. When she opened them wider to look at me, she didn't have any whites.

"I don't want to hear stories," I said softly.

"Sure you do. Just ask."

"It's late. I got to be home."

"I knew a man who became a house," she said. "He didn't like it. He stayed quiet for thirty years, and watched all the people inside grow up, and be just like their folks, all nasty and dirty and leaving his walls to flake, and the bathrooms were unbearable. So he spit them out one morning, furniture and all, and shut his doors and locked them."

"What?"

"You heard me. Upchucked. The poor house was so disgusted he changed back into a man, but he was older and he had a cancer and his heart was bad because of all the abuse he had lived with. He died soon after.''

I laughed, not because the man had died but because I knew such things were lies. ''That's silly,'' I said.

''Then here's another. There was a cat who wanted to eat butterflies. Nothing finer in the world for a cat than to stalk the grass, waiting for black and pumpkin butterflies. It crouches down and wriggles its rump to dig in the hind paws, then it jumps. But a butterfly is no sustenance for a cat. It's practice. There was a little girl about your age—might have been your sister, but she won't admit it—who saw the cat and decided to teach it a lesson. She hid in the taller grass with two old kites under each arm and waited for the cat to come by stalking. When it got real close, she put on her mother's dark glasses, to look all bug-eyed, and she jumped up flapping the kites. Well, it was just a little too real, because in a trice she found herself flying, and she was much smaller than she had been, and the cat jumped at her. Almost got her, too. Ask your sister about that sometime. See if she doesn't deny it.''

''How'd she get back to be my sister again?''

''She became too scared to fly. She lit on a flower and found herself crushing it. The glasses broke, too.''

''My sister did break a pair of Mom's glasses once.''

The woman smiled.

''I got to be going home.''

''Tomorrow you bring me a story, okay?''

I ran off without answering. But in my head, monsters were already rising. If she thought I was scared, wait until she heard the story I had to tell! When I got home my oldest sister, Barbara, was fixing lemonade in the kitchen. She was a year older than I, but acted as if she were grown-up. She was a good six inches taller and I could beat her if I got in a lucky punch, but no other way—so her power over me was awesome. But we were usually friendly.

''Where you been?'' she asked, like a mother.

''Somebody tattled on you,'' I said.

Her eyes went doe-scared, then wizened down to slits. ''What're you talking about?''

''Somebody tattled about what you did to Mom's sunglasses.''

''I already been whipped for that,'' she said nonchalantly. ''Not much more to tell.''

''Oh, but *I* know more.''

''Was *not* playing doctor,'' she said. The youngest, Sue-Ann, weakest and most full of guile, had a habit of telling the folks somebody or other was playing doctor. She didn't know what it meant—I just barely did—but it had been true once, and she held it over everybody as her only vestige of power.

"No," I said, "but I know what you were doing. And I won't tell anybody."

"You don't know nothing," she said. Then she accidentally poured half a pitcher of lemonade across the side of my head and down my front. When Mom came in I was screaming and swearing like Dad did when he fixed the cars, and I was put away for life plus ninety years in the bedroom I shared with younger brother Michael. Dinner smelled better than usual that evening, but I had none of it. Somehow, I wasn't brokenhearted. It gave me time to think of a scary story for the country-colored woman on the rock.

School was the usual mix of hell and purgatory the next day. Then the hot, dry winds cooled and the bells rang and I was on the dirt road again, across the southern hundred acres, walking in the lees and shadows of the big cottonwoods. I carried my Road-Runner lunch pail and my pencil box and one book—a handwriting manual I hated so much I tore pieces out of it at night, to shorten its lifetime—and I walked slowly, to give my story time to gel.

She was leaning up against a tree, not far from the rock. Looking back, I can see she was not so old as a boy of eight years thought. Now I see her lissome beauty and grace, despite the dominance of gray in her reddish hair, despite the crow's-feet around her eyes and the smile-haunts around her lips. But to the eight-year-old she was simply a peculiar crone. And he had a story to tell her, he thought, that would age her unto graveside.

"Hello, boy," she said.

"Hi." I sat on the rock.

"I can see you've been thinking," she said.

I squinted into the tree shadow to make her out better. "How'd you know?"

"You have the look of a boy that's been thinking. Are you here to listen to another story?"

"Got one to tell, this time," I said.

"Who goes first?"

It was always polite to let the woman go first so I quelled my haste and told her she could. She motioned me to come by the tree and sit on a smaller rock, half-hidden by grass. And while the crickets in the shadow tuned up for the evening, she said, "Once there was a dog. This dog was a pretty usual dog, like the ones that would chase you around home if they thought they could get away with it—if they didn't know you, or thought you were up to something the big people might disapprove of. But this dog lived in a graveyard. That is, he belonged to the caretaker. You've seen a graveyard before, haven't you?''

"Like where they took Grandpa."

"Exactly," she said. "With pretty lawns, and big white and gray stones, and for those who've died recently, smaller gray stones with names and flowers and years cut into them. And trees in some places, with a mortuary nearby made of brick, and a garage full of black cars, and a place behind the garage where you wonder what goes on." She knew the place, all right. "This dog had a pretty good life. It was his job to keep the grounds clear of animals at night. After the gates were locked, he'd be set loose, and he wandered all night long. He was almost white, you see. Anybody human who wasn't supposed to be there would think he was a ghost, and they'd run away.

"But this dog had a problem. His problem was, there were rats that didn't pay much attention to him. A whole gang of rats. The leader was a big one, a good yard from nose to tail. These rats made their living by burrowing under the ground in the old section of the cemetery."

That did it. I didn't want to hear any more. The air was a lot colder than it should have been, and I wanted to get home in time for dinner and still be able to eat it. But I couldn't go just then.

"Now the dog didn't know what the rats did, and just like you and I, probably, he didn't much care to know. But it was his job to keep them under control. So one day he made a truce with a couple of cats that he normally tormented and told them about the rats. These cats were scrappy old toms and they'd long since cleared out the competition of other cats, but they were friends themselves. So the dog made them a proposition. He said he'd let them use the cemetery any time they wanted, to prowl or hunt in or whatever, if they would put the fear of God into a few of the rats. The cats took him up on it. 'We get to do whatever we want,' they said, 'whenever we want, and you won't bother us.' The dog agreed.

"That night the dog waited for the sounds of battle. But they never came. Nary a yowl." She glared at me for emphasis. "Not a claw scratch. Not even a twitch of tail in the wind." She took a deep breath, and so did I. "Round about midnight the dog went out into the graveyard. It was very dark and there wasn't wind, or bird, or speck of star to relieve the quiet and the dismal, inside-of-a-box-camera blackness. He sniffed his way to the old part of the graveyard, and met with the head rat, who was sitting on a slanty, cracked wooden grave marker. Only his eyes and a tip of tail showed in the dark, but the dog could smell him. 'What happened to the cats?' he asked. The rat shrugged his haunches. 'Ain't seen any cats,' he said. 'What did you think—that you could scare us out with a couple of cats? Ha. Listen—if there had been any cats here tonight, they'd have been strung and hung like meat in a shed, and my youn'uns would have grown fat on—' ''

"No-o-o!" I screamed, and I ran away from the woman and the tree until I couldn't hear the story any more.

"What's the matter?" she called after me. "Aren't you going to tell me your story?" Her voice followed me as I ran.

It was funny. That night, I wanted to know what happened to the cats. Maybe nothing had happened to them. Not knowing made my visions even worse—and I didn't sleep well. But my brain worked like it had never worked before.

The next day, a Saturday, I had an ending—not a very good one in retrospect—but it served to frighten Michael so badly he threatened to tell Mom on me.

"What would you want to do that for?" I asked. "Cripes, I won't ever tell you a story again if you tell Mom!"

Michael was a year younger and didn't worry about the future. "You never told me stories before," he said, "and everything was fine. I won't miss them."

He ran down the stairs to the living room. Dad was smoking a pipe and reading the paper, relaxing before checking the irrigation on the north thirty. Michael stood at the foot of the stairs, thinking. I was almost down to grab him and haul him upstairs when he made his decision and headed for the kitchen. I knew exactly what he was considering—that Dad would probably laugh and call him a little scaredy cat. But Mom would get upset and do me in proper.

She was putting a paper form over the kitchen table to mark it for fitting a tablecloth. Michael ran up to her and hung onto a pants leg while I halted at the kitchen door, breathing hard, eyes threatening eternal torture if he so much as peeped. But Michael didn't worry about the future much.

"Mom," he said.

"Cripes!" I shouted, high-pitching on the *i*. Refuge awaited me in the tractor shed. It was an agreed-upon hiding place. Mom didn't know I'd be there, but Dad did, and he could mediate.

It took him a half-hour to get to me. I sat in the dark behind a workbench, practicing my pouts. He stood in the shaft of light falling from the unpatched chink in the roof. Dust motes May-poled around his legs. "Son," he said. "Mom wants to know where you got that story."

Now, this was a peculiar thing to be asked. The question I'd expected had been, "Why did you scare Michael?" or maybe, "What made you think of such a thing?" But no. Somehow, she had plumbed the problem, planted the words in Dad's mouth, and impressed upon him that father-son relationships were temporarily suspended.

"I made it up," I said.

"You've never made up that kind of story before."

"I just started."

He took a deep breath. "Son, we get along real good, except when you lie to me. We know better. Who told you that story?"

This was uncanny. There was more going on than I could understand—there was a mysterious, adult thing happening. I had no way around the truth. "An old woman," I said.

Dad sighed even deeper. "What was she wearing?"

"Green dress," I said.

"Was there an old man?"

I nodded.

"Christ," he said softly. He turned and walked out of the shed. From outside, he called me to come into the house. I dusted off my overalls and followed him. Michael sneered at me.

" 'Locked them in coffins with old dead bodies,' " he mimicked. "Phhht! You're going to get it."

The folks closed the folding door to the kitchen with both us outside. This disturbed Michael, who'd expected instant vengeance. I was too curious and worried to take revenge on him, so he skulked out the screen door and chased the cat around the house. "Lock you in a coffin!" he screamed.

Mom's voice drifted from behind the louvred doors. "Do you hear that? The poor child's going to have nightmares. It'll warp him."

"Don't exaggerate," Dad said.

"Exaggerate what? That those filthy people are back? Ben, they must be a hundred years old now! They're trying to do the same thing to your son that they did to your brother . . . and just look at *him!* Living in sin, writing for those hell-spawned girlie magazines.''

''He ain't living in sin, he's living alone in an apartment in New York City. And he writes for all kinds of places.''

''They tried to do it to you, too! Just thank God your aunt saved you.''

''Margie, I hope you don't intend—''

''Certainly do. She knows all about them kind of people. She chased them off once, she can sure do it again!''

All hell had broken loose. I didn't understand half of it, but I could feel the presence of Great Aunt Sybil Danser. I could almost hear her crackling voice and the shustle of her satchel of Billy Grahams and Zondervans and little tiny pamphlets with shining light in blue offset on their covers.

I knew there was no way to get the full story from the folks short of listening in, but they'd stopped talking and were sitting in that stony kind of silence that indicated Dad's disgust and Mom's determination. I was mad that nobody was blaming me, as if I were some idiot child not capable of being bad on my own. I was mad at Michael for precipitating the whole mess.

And I was curious. Were the man and woman more than a hundred years old? Why hadn't I seen them before, in town, or heard about them from other kids? Surely I wasn't the only one they'd seen on the road and told stories to. I decided to get to the source. I walked up to the louvred doors and leaned my cheek against them. ''Can I go play at George's?''

''Yes,'' Mom said. ''Be back for evening chores.''

George lived on the next farm, a mile and a half east. I took my bike and rode down the old dirt road going south.

They were both under the tree, eating a picnic lunch from a wicker basket. I pulled my bike over and leaned it against the gray rock, shading my eyes to see them more clearly.

''Hello, boy,'' the old man said. ''Ain't seen you in a while.''

I couldn't think of anything to say. The woman offered me a cookie and I refused with a muttered, ''No, thank you, ma'am.''

''Well then, perhaps you'd like to tell us your story.''

''No, ma'am.''

''No story to tell us? That's odd. Meg was sure you had a story in you someplace. Peeking out from behind your ears maybe, thumbing its nose at us.''

The woman smiled ingratiatingly. ''Tea?''

''There's going to be trouble,'' I said.

''Already?'' The woman smoothed the skirt in her lap and set a plate of nut bread into it. "Well, it comes sooner or later, this time sooner. What do you think of it, boy?"

"I think I got into a lot of trouble for not much being bad," I said. "I don't know why."

"Sit down then," the old man said. "Listen to a tale, then tell us what's going on."

I sat down, not too keen about hearing another story but out of politeness. I took a piece of nut bread and nibbled on it as the woman sipped her tea and cleared her throat. "Once there was a city on the shore of a broad, blue sea. In the city lived five hundred children and nobody else, because the wind from the sea wouldn't let anyone grow old. Well, children don't have kids of their own, of course, so when the wind came up in the first year the city never grew any larger."

"Where'd all the grownups go?" I asked. The old man held his fingers to his lips and shook his head.

"The children tried to play all day, but it wasn't enough. They became frightened at night and had bad dreams. There was nobody to comfort them because only grownups are really good at making nightmares go away. Now, sometimes nightmares are white horses that come out of the sea, so they set up guards along the beaches, and fought them back with wands made of blackthorn. But there was another kind of nightmare, one that was black and rose out of the ground, and those were impossible to guard against. So the children got together one day and decided to tell all the scary stories there were to tell, to prepare themselves for all the nightmares. They found it was pretty easy to think up scary stories, and every one of them had a story or two to tell. They stayed up all night spinning yarns about ghosts and dead things, and live things that shouldn't have been, and things that were neither. They talked about death and about monsters that suck blood, about things that live way deep in the earth and long, thin things that sneak through cracks in doors to lean over the beds at night and speak in tongues no one could understand. They talked about eyes without heads, and vice versa, and little blue shoes that walk across a cold empty white room, with no one in them, and a bunk bed that creaks when it's empty, and a printing press that produces newspapers from a city that never was. Pretty soon, by morning, they'd told all the scary stories. When the black horses came out of the ground the next night, and the white horses from the sea, the children greeted them with cakes and ginger ale, and they held a big party. They also invited the pale sheet-things from the clouds, and everyone ate hearty and had a good time. One white horse let a little boy ride on it, and took him wherever he wanted to go. So there were no more bad dreams in the city of children by the sea.''

I finished the piece of bread and wiped my hands on my crossed legs. ''So that's why you tried to scare me,'' I said.

She shook her head. ''No. I never had a reason for telling a story, and neither should you.''

''I don't think I'm going to tell stories any more,'' I said. ''The folks get too upset.''

''Philistines,'' the old man said, looking off across the fields.

''Listen, young man. There is nothing finer in the world than the telling of tales. Split atoms if you wish, but splitting an infinitive—and getting away with it—is far nobler. Lance boils if you wish, but pricking pretensions is often cleaner and always more fun.''

.''Then why are Mom and Dad so mad?''

The old man shook his head. ''An eternal mystery.''

''Well, I'm not so sure,'' I said. ''I scared my little brother pretty bad and that's not nice.''

''Being scared is nothing,'' the old woman said. ''Being bored, or ignorant—now that's a crime.''

''I still don't know. My folks say you have to be a hundred years old. You did something to my uncle they didn't like, and that was a long time ago. What kind of people are you, anyway?''

The old man smiled. ''Old, yes. But not a hundred.''

''I just came out here to warn you. Mom and Dad are bringing out my great aunt, and she's no fun for anyone. You better go away.'' With that said, I ran back to my bike and rode off, pumping for all I was worth. I was between a rock and a hard place. I loved my folks but I itched to hear more stories. Why wasn't it easier to make decisions?

That night I slept restlessly. I didn't have any dreams, but I kept waking up with something pounding at the back of my head, like it wanted to be let in. I scrunched my face up and pressed it back.

At Sunday breakfast, Mom looked across the table at me and put on a kind face. ''We're going to pick up Auntie Danser this afternoon, at the airport,'' she said.

My face went like warm butter.

''You'll come with us, won't you?'' she asked. ''You always did like the airport.''

''All the way from where she lives?'' I asked.

''From Omaha,'' Dad said.

I didn't want to go, but it was more a command than a request. I nodded and Dad smiled at me around his pipe.

"Don't eat too many biscuits," Mom warned him. "You're putting on weight again."

"I'll wear it off come harvest. You cook as if the whole crew was here, anyway."

"Auntie Danser will straighten it all out," Mom said, her mind elsewhere. I caught the suggestion of a grimace on Dad's face, and the pipe wriggled as he bit down on it harder.

The airport was something out of a TV space movie. It went on forever, with stairways going up to restaurants and big smoky windows which looked out on the screaming jets, and crowds of people, all leaving, except for one pear-shaped figure in a cotton print dress with fat ankles and glasses thick as headlamps. I knew her from a hundred yards.

When we met, she shook hands with Mom, hugged Dad as if she didn't want to, then bent down and gave me a smile. Her teeth were yellow and even, sound as a horse's. She was the ugliest woman I'd ever seen. She smelled of lilacs. To this day lilacs take my appetite away.

She carried a bag. Part of it was filled with knitting, part with books and pamphlets. I always wondered why she never carried a Bible—just Billy Grahams and Zondervans. One pamphlet fell out and Dad bent to pick it up.

"Keep it, read it," Auntie Danser instructed him. "Do you good." She turned to Mom and scrutinized her from the bottom of a swimming pool. "You're looking good. He must be treating you right."

Dad ushered us out the automatic doors into the dry heat. Her one suitcase was light as a mummy and probably just as empty. I carried it and it didn't even bring sweat to my brow. Her life was not in clothes and toiletry but in the plastic knitting bag.

We drove back to the farm in the big white station wagon. I leaned my head against the cool glass of the rear seat window and considered puking. Auntie Danser, I told myself, was like a mental dose of castor oil. Or like a visit to the dentist. Even if nothing was going to happen her smell presaged disaster, and like a horse sniffing a storm, my entrails worried.

Mom looked across the seat at me—Auntie Danser was riding up front with Dad—and asked, "You feeling okay? Did they give you anything to eat? Anything funny?"

I said they'd given me a piece of nut bread. Mom went, "Oh, Lord."

"Margie, they don't work like that. They got other ways."
Auntie Danser leaned over the back seat and goggled at me.
"Boy's just worried. I know all about it. These people and I
have had it out before."

Through those murky glasses, her flat eyes knew me to my
young, pithy core. I didn't like being known so well. I could see
that Auntie Danser's life was firm and predictable, and I made a
sudden commitment. I liked the man and woman. They caused
trouble, but they were the exact opposite of my great-aunt. I felt
better, and I gave her a reassuring grin. "Boy will be okay," she
said. "Just a colic of the upset mind."

Michael and Barbara sat on the front porch as the car drove
up. Somehow a visit by Auntie Danser didn't bother them as
much as it did me. They didn't fawn over her but they accepted
her without complaining—even out of adult earshot. That made
me think more carefully about them. I decided I didn't love them
any the less, but I couldn't trust them, either. The world was
taking sides and so far on my side I was very lonely. I didn't
count the two old people on my side, because I wasn't sure they
were—but they came a lot closer than anybody in the family.

Auntie Danser wanted to read Billy Graham books to us after
dinner, but Dad snuck us out before Mom could gather us
together—all but Barbara, who stayed to listen. We watched the
sunset from the loft of the old wood barn, then tried to catch the
little birds that live in the rafters. By dark and bedtime I was
hungry, but not for food. I asked Dad if he'd tell me a story
before bed.

"You know your Mom doesn't approve of all that fairy-tale
stuff," he said.

"Then no fairy tales. Just a story."

"I'm out of practice, son," he confided. He looked very sad.
"Your mom says we should concentrate on things that are real
and not waste our time with make-believe. Life's hard. I may
have to sell the farm, you know, and work for that feed-mixer in
Mitchell."

I went to bed and felt like crying. A whole lot of my family had
died that night, I didn't know exactly how, or why. But I was
mad.

I didn't go to school the next day. During the night I'd had a
dream, which came so true and whole to me that I had to rush to
the stand of cottonwoods and tell the old people. I took my lunch
box and walked rapidly down the road.

They weren't there. On a piece of wire braided to the biggest tree they'd left a note on faded brown paper. It was in a strong, feminine hand, sepia-inked, delicately scribed with what could have been a goose-quill pen. It said: "We're at the old Hauskopf farm. Come if you must."

Not "Come if you can." I felt a twinge. The Hauskopf farm, abandoned fifteen years ago and never sold, was three miles farther down the road and left on a deep-rutted fork. It took me an hour to get there.

The house still looked deserted. All the white paint was flaking, leaving dead gray wood. The windows stared. I walked up the porch steps and knocked on the heavy oak door. For a moment I thought no one was going to answer. Then I heard what sounded like a gust of wind, but inside the house, and the old woman opened the door. "Hello, boy," she said. "Come for more stories?"

She invited me in. Wildflowers were growing along the base-boards and tiny roses peered from the brambles that covered the walls. A quail led her train of inch-and-a-half fluffball chicks from under the stairs, into the living room. The floor was carpeted but the flowers in the weave seemed more than patterns. I could stare down and keep picking out detail for minutes. "This way, boy," the woman said. She took my hand. Hers was smooth and warm but I had the impression it was also hard as wood.

A tree stood in the living room, growing out of the floor and sending its branches up to support the ceiling. Rabbits and quail and a lazy-looking brindle cat looked at me from tangles of roots. A wooden bench surrounded the base of the tree. On the side away from us, I heard someone breathing. The old man poked his head around, and smiled at me, lifting his long pipe in greeting. "Hello, boy," he said.

"The boy looks like he's ready to tell us a story, this time," the woman said.

"Of course, Meg. Have a seat, boy. Cup of cider for you? Tea? Herb biscuit?"

"Cider, please," I said.

The old man stood and went down the hall to the kitchen. He came back with a wooden tray and three steaming cups of mulled cider. The cinnamon tickled my nose as I sipped.

"Now. What's your story?"

"It's about two hawks," I said. I hesitated.

"Go on."

"Brother hawks. Never did like each other. Fought for a strip of land where they could hunt."

"Yes?"

"Finally, one hawk met an old, crippled bobcat that had set up a place for itself in a rockpile. The bobcat was learning itself magic so it wouldn't have to go out and catch dinner, which was awful hard for it now. The hawk landed near the bobcat and told it about his brother, and how cruel he was. So the bobcat said, 'Why not give him the land for the day? Here's what you can do.' The bobcat told him how he could turn into a rabbit, but a very strong rabbit no hawk could hurt."

"Wily bobcat," the old man said, smiling.

" 'You mean, my brother wouldn't be able to catch me?' the hawk asked. 'Course not,' the bobcat said. 'And you can teach him a lesson. You'll tussle with him, scare him real bad—show him what tough animals there are on the land he wants. Then he'll go away and hunt somewhere else.' The hawk thought that sounded like a fine idea. So he let the bobcat turn him into a rabbit and he hopped back to the land and waited in a patch of grass. Sure enough, his brother's shadow passed by soon, and then he heard a swoop and saw the claws held out. So he filled himself with being mad and jumped up and practically bit the tail feathers off his brother. The hawk just flapped up and rolled over on the ground, blinking and gawking with his beak wide. 'Rabbit,' he said, 'that's not natural. Rabbits don't act that way.'

" 'Round here they do,' the hawk-rabbit said. 'This is a tough old land, and all the animals here know the tricks of escaping from bad birds like you.' This scared the brother hawk, and he flew away as best he could, and never came back again. The hawk-rabbit hopped to the rockpile and stood up before the bobcat, saying, 'It worked real fine. I thank you. Now turn me back and I'll go hunt my land.' But the bobcat only grinned and reached out with a paw and broke the rabbit's neck. Then he ate him, and said, 'Now the land's mine, and no hawks can take away the easy game.' And that's how the greed of two hawks turned their land over to a bobcat."

The old woman looked at me with wide, baked-chestnut eyes and smiled. "You've got it," she said. "Just like your uncle. Hasn't he got it, Jack?" The old man nodded and took his pipe from his mouth. "He's got it fine. He'll make a good one."

"Now, boy, why did you make up that story?"

I thought for a moment, then shook my head. "I don't know," I said. "It just came up."

"What are you going to do with the story?"

I didn't have an answer for that question, either.

"Got any other stories in you?"

I considered, then said. "Think so."

A car drove up outside and Mom called my name. The old woman stood and straightened her dress. "Follow me," she said. "Go out the back door, walk around the house. Return home with them. Tomorrow, go to school like you're supposed to do. Next Saturday, come back and we'll talk some more."

"Son? You in there?"

I walked out the back and came around to the front of the house. Mom and Auntie Danser waited in the station wagon. "You aren't allowed out here. Were you in that house?" Mom asked. I shook my head.

My great aunt looked at me with her glassed-in flat eyes and lifted the corners of her lips a little. "Margie," she said, "go have a look in the windows."

Mom got out of the car and walked up the porch to peer through the dusty panes. "It's empty, Sybil."

"Empty, boy, right?"

"I don't know," I said. "I wasn't inside."

"I could hear you, boy," she said. "Last night. Talking in your sleep. Rabbits and hawks don't behave that way. You know it, and I know it. So it ain't no good thinking about them that way, is it?"

"I don't remember talking in my sleep," I said.

"Margie, let's go home. This boy needs some pamphlets read into him."

Mom got into the car and looked back at me before starting the engine. "You ever skip school again, I'll strap you black and blue. It's real embarrassing having the school call, and not knowing where you are. Hear me?"

I nodded.

Everything was quiet that week. I went to school and tried not to dream at night, and did everything boys are supposed to do. But I didn't feel like a boy. I felt something big inside, and no amount of Billy Grahams and Zondervans read at me could change that feeling.

I made one mistake, though. I asked Auntie Danser why she never read the Bible. This was in the parlor one evening after dinner and cleaning up the dishes. "Why do you want to know, boy?" she asked.

"Well, the Bible seems to be full of fine stories, but you don't carry it around with you. I just wondered why."

"Bible is a good book," she said. "The only good book. But it's difficult. It has lots of camouflage. Sometimes—" She stopped. "Who put you up to asking that question?"

"Nobody," I said.

"I heard that question before, you know," she said. "Ain't the first time I been asked. Somebody else asked me, once."

I sat in my chair, stiff as a ham.

"Your father's brother asked me that once. But we won't talk about him, will we?"

I shook my head.

Next Saturday I waited until it was dark and everyone was in bed. The night air was warm but I was sweating more than the warm could cause as I rode my bike down the dirt road, lamp beam swinging back and forth. The sky was crawling with stars, all of them looking at me. The Milky Way seemed to touch down just beyond the road, like I might ride straight up it if I went far enough.

I knocked on the heavy door. There were no lights in the windows and it was late for old folks to be up, but I knew these two didn't behave like normal people. And I knew that just because the house looked empty from the outside didn't mean it was empty within. The wind rose up and beat against the door, making me shiver. Then it opened. It was dark for a moment and the breath went out of me. Two pairs of eyes stared from the black. They seemed a lot taller this time. "Come in, boy," Jack whispered.

Fireflies lit up the tree in the living room. The brambles and wildflowers glowed like weeds on a sea floor. The carpet crawled, but not to my feet. I was shivering in earnest now and my teeth chattered.

I only saw their shadows as they sat on the bench in front of me. "Sit," Meg said. "Listen close. You've taken the fire and it glows bright. You're only a boy but you're just like a pregnant woman now. For the rest of your life you'll be cursed with the worst affliction known to humans. Your skin will twitch at night. Your eyes will see things in the dark. Beasts will come to you and beg to be ridden. You'll never know one truth from another. You might starve, because few will want to encourage you. And if you do make good in this world, you might lose the gift and search forever after, in vain. Some will say the gift isn't special.

Beware them. Some will say it is special and beware them, too. And some—"

There was a scratching at the door. I thought it was an animal for a moment. Then it cleared its throat. It was my great-aunt.

"Some will say you're damned. Perhaps they're right. But you're also enthused. Carry it lightly, and responsibly."

"Listen in there. This is Sybil Danser. You know me. Open up."

"Now stand by the stairs, in the dark where she can't see," Jack said. I did as I was told. One of them—I couldn't tell which—opened the door and the lights went out in the tree, the carpet stilled, and the brambles were snuffed. Auntie Danser stood in the doorway, outlined by star glow, carrying her knitting bag. "Boy?" she asked. I held my breath.

"And you others, too."

The wind in the house seemed to answer. "I'm not too late," she said. "Damn you, in truth, damn you to hell! You come to our towns, and you plague us with thoughts no decent person wants to think. Not just fairy stories, but telling the way people live, and why they shouldn't live that way! Your very breath is tainted! Hear me?" She walked slowly into the empty living room, feet clonking on the wooden floor. "You make them write about us, and make others laugh at us. Question the way we think. Condemn our deepest prides. Pull out our mistakes and amplify them beyond all truth. What right do you have to take young children and twist their minds?"

The wind sang through the cracks in the walls. I tried to see if Jack or Meg was there, but only shadows remained.

"I know where you come from, don't forget that! Out of the ground! Out of the bones of old, wicked Indians! Shamans and pagan dances and worshiping dirt and filth! I heard about you from the old squaws on the reservation. Frost and Spring, they called you, signs of the turning year. Well, now you got a different name! Death and demons, I call you, hear me?"

She seemed to jump at a sound but I couldn't hear it. "Don't you argue with me!" she shrieked. She took her glasses off and held out both hands. "Think I'm a weak old woman, do you? You don't know how deep I run in these communities! I'm the one who had them books taken off the shelves. Remember me? Oh, you hated it—not being able to fill young minds with your pestilence. Took them off high school shelves, and out of lists— burned them for junk! Remember? That was me. I'm not dead yet! Boy, where are you?"

"Enchant her," I whispered to the air. "Magic her. Make her go away. Let me live here with you."

"Is that you, boy? Come with your aunt, now. Come with, come away!"

"Go with her," the wind told me. "Send your children this way, years from now. But go with her."

I felt a kind of tingly warmth and knew it was time to get home. I snuck out the back way and came around to the front of the house. There was no car. She'd followed me on foot all the way from the farm. I wanted to leave her there in the old house, shouting at the dead rafters, but instead I called her name and waited.

She came out crying. She knew.

"You poor, sinning boy," she said, pulling me to her lilac bosom.

SEMLEY'S NECKLACE

by
Ursula K. Le Guin

Ursula K. Le Guin is one of science fiction's most renowned and honored writers—she has won (to date) three Nebulas, four Hugos, the National Book Award, two Jupiters, and the Gandalf Life Award, among others. She was also the Guest of Honor at the 1975 World Science Fiction Convention in Australia. Her classic works include THE LEFT HAND OF DARKNESS (1969), THE LATHE OF HEAVEN (1971), and THE DIS-POSSESSED: AN AMBIGUOUS UTOPIA (1974). Some of her finest short stories can be found in THE WIND'S TWELVE QUARTERS (1975). She is also a leading critic of the field.

A poignant fairy tale, "Semley's Necklace" exemplifies Arthur C. Clarke's first law—to the beholder an advanced science appears to be magic.

How can you tell the legend from the fact on these worlds that lie so many years away?—planets without names, called by their people simply The World, planets without history, where the past is the matter of myth, and a returning explorer finds his own doings of a few years back have become the gestures of a god. Unreason darkens that gap of time bridged by our lightspeed ships, and in the darkness uncertainty and disproportion grow like weeds.

In trying to tell the story of a man, an ordinary League scientist, who went to such a nameless half-known world not many years ago, one feels like an archaeologist amid millennial ruins, now struggling through choked tangles of leaf, flower, branch and vine to the sudden bright geometry of a wheel or a polished cornerstone, and now entering some commonplace, sunlit doorway to find inside it the darkness, the impossible flicker of a flame, the glitter of a jewel, the half-glimpsed movement of a woman's arm.

How can you tell fact from legend, truth from truth?

Through Rocannon's story the jewel, the blue glitter seen briefly, returns. With it let us begin, here:

Galactic Area 8, No. 62: FOMALHAUT II.
High-Intelligence Life Forms: Species Contacted:
Species I.
  A. Gdemiar (singular Gdem): Highly intelligent, fully hominoid nocturnal troglodytes, 120–135 cm. in height, light skin, dark head-hair. When contacted these cave-dwellers possessed a rigidly stratified oligarchic urban society modified by partial colonial telepathy, and a technologically oriented Early Steel culture. Technology enhanced to Industrial, Point C, during League Mission of 252–254. In 254 an Automatic Drive ship (to-from New South Georgia) was presented to oligarchs of the Kiriensea Area community. Status C-Prime.
  B. Fiia (singular Fian): Highly intelligent, fully hominoid, diurnal, av. ca. 130 cm. in height, observed individuals generally light in skin and hair. Brief contacts indicated village and nomadic communal societies, partial colonial telepathy, also some indication of short-range TK. The race appears a-technological and evasive, with minimal and fluid culture-patterns. Currently untaxable. Status E-Query.

  Species II.
  Liuar (singular Liu): Highly intelligent, fully hominoid, diurnal, av. height above 170 cm., this species possesses a fortress/village, clan-descent society, a blocked technology (Bronze), a feudal-

*heroic culture. Note horizontal social cleavage into 2 pseudo-
races: (a) Olgyior, "midmen," light-skinned and dark-haired;
(b) Angyar, "lords," very tall, dark-skinned, yellow-haired—*

"That's her," said Rocannon, looking up from the *Abridged
Handy Pocket Guide to Intelligent Life-forms* at the very tall,
dark-skinned, yellow-haired woman who stood halfway down the
long museum hall. She stood still and erect, crowned with bright
hair, gazing at something in a display case. Around her fidgeted
four uneasy and unattractive dwarves.

"I didn't know Fomalhaut II had all those people besides the
trogs," said Ketho, the curator.

"I didn't either. There are even some 'Unconfirmed' species
listed here, that they never contacted. Sounds like time for a
more thorough survey mission to the place. Well, now at least
we know what she is."

"I wish there were some way of knowing *who* she is. . . ."

She was of an ancient family, a descendant of the first kings
of the Angyar, and for all her poverty her hair shone with the
pure, steadfast gold of her inheritance. The little people, the
Fiia, bowed when she passed them, even when she was a
barefoot child running in the fields, the light and fiery comet of
her hair brightening the troubled winds of Kirien.

She was still very young when Durhal of Hallan saw her,
courted her, and carried her away from the ruined towers and
windy halls of her childhood to his own high home. In Hallan on
the mountainside there was no comfort either, though splendor
endured. The windows were unglassed, the stone floors bare; in
coldyear one might wake to see the night's snow in long, low
drifts beneath each window. Durhal's bride stood with narrow
bare feet on the snowy floor, braiding up the fire of her hair and
laughing at her young husband in the silver mirror that hung in their
room. That mirror, and his mother's bridal-gown sewn with a
thousand tiny crystals, were all his wealth. Some of his lesser
kinfolk of Hallan still possessed wardrobes of brocaded clothing,
furniture of gilded wood, silver harness for their steeds, armor
and silver mounted swords, jewels and jewelry—and on these
last Durhal's bride looked enviously, glancing back at a gemmed
coronet or a golden brooch even when the wearer of the orna-
ment stood aside to let her pass, deferent to her birth and
marriage-rank.

Fourth from the High Seat of Hallan Revel sat Durhal and his bride Semley, so close to Hallanlord that the old man often poured wine for Semley with his own hand, and spoke of hunting with his nephew and heir Durhal, looking on the young pair with a grim, unhopeful love. Hope came hard to the Angyar of Hallan and all the Western Lands, since the Starlords had appeared with their houses that leaped about on pillars of fire and their awful weapons that could level hills. They had interfered with all the old ways and wars, and though the sums were small there was terrible shame to the Angyar in having to pay a tax to them, a tribute for the Starlords' war that was to be fought with some strange enemy, somewhere in the hollow places between the stars, at the end of years. "It will be your war too," they said, but for a generation now the Angyar had sat in idle shame in their revel-halls, watching their double swords rust, their sons grow up without ever striking a blow in battle, their daughters marry poor men, even midmen, having no dowry of heroic loot to bring a noble husband. Hallanlord's face was bleak when he watched the fair-haired couple and heard their laughter as they drank bitter wine and joked together in the cold, ruinous, resplendent fortress of their race.

Semley's own face hardened when she looked down the hall and saw, in seats far below hers, even down among the half breeds and the midmen, against white skins and black hair, the gleam and flash of precious stones. She herself had brought nothing in dowry to her husband, not even a silver hairpin. The dress of a thousand crystals she had put away in a chest for the wedding-day of her daughter, if daughter it was to be.

It was, and they called her Haldre, and when the fuzz on her little brown skull grew longer it shone with steadfast gold, the inheritance of the lordly generations, the only gold she would ever possess. . . .

Semley did not speak to her husband of her discontent. For all his gentleness to her, Durhal in his pride had only contempt for envy, for vain wishing, and she dreaded his contempt. But she spoke to Durhal's sister Durossa.

"My family had a great treasure once," she said. "It was a necklace all of gold, with the blue jewel set in the center—sapphire?"

Durossa shook her head, smiling, not sure of the name either. It was late in warmyear, as these Northern Angyar called the summer of the eight-hundred-day year, beginning the cycle of months anew at each equinox; to Semley it seemed an outlandish calendar, a mid-mannish reckoning. Her family was at an end, but it had been older and purer than the race of any of these northwestern marchlanders, who mixed too freely with the Olgyior. She sat with Durossa in the sunlight on a stone windowseat high up in the Great Tower, where the older woman's apartment was. Widowed young, childless, Durossa had been given in second marriage to Hallanlord, who was her father's brother. Since it was a kinmarriage and a second marriage on both sides she had not taken the title of Hallanlady, which Semley would some day bear; but she sat with the old lord in the High Seat and ruled with him his domains. Older than her brother Durhal, she was fond of his young wife, and delighted in the bright-haired baby Haldre.

"It was bought," Semley went on, "with all the money my forebear Leynen got when he conquered the Southern Fiefs—all the money from a whole kingdom, think of it, for one jewel! Oh, it would outshine anything here in Hallan, surely, even those crystals like koob-eggs your cousin Issar wears. It was so beautiful they gave it a name of its own; they called it the Eye of the Sea. My great-grandmother wore it."

"You never saw it?" the older woman asked lazily, gazing down at the green mountainslopes where long, long summer sent its hot and restless winds straying among the forests and whirling down white roads to the seacoast far away.

"It was lost before I was born."

"No, my father said it was stolen before the Starlords ever came to our realm. He wouldn't talk of it, but there was an old midwoman full of tales who always told me the Fiia would know where it was."

"Ah, the Fiia I should like to see!" said Durossa. "They're in so many songs and tales; why do they never come to the Western Lands?"

"Too high, too cold in winter, I think. They like the sunlight of the valleys of the south."

"Are they like the Clayfolk?"

"Those I've never seen; they keep away from us in the south. Aren't they white like midmen, and misformed? The Fiia are fair; they look like children, only thinner, and wiser. Oh, I wonder if they know where the necklace is, who stole it and where he hid it! Think, Durossa—if I could come into Hallan Revel and sit down by my husband with the wealth of a kingdom round my neck, and outshine the other women as he outshines all men!"

Durossa bent her head above the baby, who sat studying her own brown toes on a fur rug between her mother and aunt.

"Semley is foolish," she murmured to the baby; "Semley who shines like a falling star, Semley whose husband loves no gold but the gold of her hair. . . ."

And Semley, looking out over the green slopes of summer toward the distant sea, was silent.

But when another coldyear had passed, and the Starlords had come again to collect their taxes for the war against the world's end—this time using a couple of dwarfish Clayfolk as interpreters, and so leaving all the Angyar humiliated to the point of rebellion—and another warmyear too was gone, and Haldre had grown into a lovely, chattering child, Semley brought her one morning to Durossa's sunlit room in the tower. Semley wore an old cloak of blue, and the hood covered her hair.

"Keep Haldre for me these few days, Durossa," she said, quick and calm. "I'm going south to Kirien."

"To see your father?"

"To find my inheritance. Your cousins of Harget Fief have been taunting Durhal. Even that halfbreed Parna can torment him, because Parna's wife has a satin coverlet for her bed, and a diamond earring, and three gowns, the dough-faced black-haired trollop! while Durhal's wife must patch her gown—"

"Is Durhal's pride in his wife, or what she wears?"

But Semley was not to be moved. "The Lords of Hallan are becoming poor men in their own hall. I am going to bring my dowry to my lord, as one of my lineage should."

"Semley! Does Durhal know you're going?"

"My return will be a happy one—that much let him know," said young Semley, breaking for a moment into her joyful laugh; then she bent to kiss her daughter, turned, and before Durossa could speak, was gone like a quick wind over the floors of sunlit stone.

Married women of the Angyar never rode for sport, and Semley had not been from Hallan since her marriage; so now, mounting the high saddle of a windsteed, she felt like a girl again, like the wild maiden she had been, riding half-broken steeds on the north wind over the fields of Kirien. The beast that bore her now down from the hills of Hallan was of finer breed, striped coat fitting sleek over hollow, buoyant bones, green eyes slitted against the wind, light and mighty wings sweeping up and down to either side of Semley, revealing and hiding, revealing and hiding the clouds above her and the hills below.

On the third morning she came to Kirien and stood again in the ruined courts. Her father had been drinking all night, and, just as in the old days, the morning sunlight poking through his fallen ceilings annoyed him, and the sight of his daughter only increased his annoyance. "What are you back for?" he growled, his swollen eyes glancing at her and away. The fiery hair of his youth was quenched, grey strands tangled on his skull. "Did the young Halla not marry you, and you've come sneaking home?"

"I am Durhal's wife. I came to get my dowry, father."

The drunkard growled in disgust; but she laughed at him so gently that he had to look at her again, wincing.

"It is true, father, that the Fiia stole the necklace Eye of the Sea?"

"How do I know? Old tales. The thing was lost before I was born, I think. I wish I never had been. Ask the Fiia if you want to know. Go to them, go back to your husband. Leave me alone here. There's no room at Kirien for girls and gold and all the rest of the story. The story's over here; this is the fallen place, this is the empty hall. The sons of Leynen all are dead, their treasures are all lost. Go on your way, girl."

Grey and swollen as the web-spinner of ruined houses, he turned and went blundering toward the cellars where he hid from daylight.

Leading the striped windsteed of Hallan, Semley left her old home and walked down the steep hill, past the village of the midmen, who greeted her with sullen respect, on over fields and pastures where the great, wing-clipped, half-wild herilor grazed, to a valley that was green as a painted bowl and full to the brim with sunlight. In the deep of the valley lay the village of the Fiia, and as she descended leading her steed the little, slight people ran up toward her from their huts and gardens, laughing, calling out in faint, thin voices.

"Hail Halla's bride, Kirienlady, Windborne, Semley the Fair!"

They gave her lovely names and she liked to hear them, minding not at all their laughter; for they laughed at all they said. That was her own way, to speak and laugh. She stood tall in her long blue cloak among their swirling welcome.

"Hail Lightfolk, Sundwellers, Fiia friends of men!"

They took her down into the village and brought her into one of their airy houses, the tiny children chasing along behind. There was no telling the age of a Fian once he was grown; it was hard even to tell one from another and be sure, as they moved about quick as moths around a candle, that she spoke always to the same one. But it seemed that one of them talked with her for a while, as the others fed and petted her steed, and brought water for her to drink, and bowls of fruit from their gardens of little trees. "It was never the Fiia that stole the necklace of the Lords of Kirien!" cried the little man. "What would the Fiia do with gold, Lady? For us there is sunlight in warmyear, and in coldyear the remembrance of sunlight; the yellow fruit, the yellow leaves in endseason, the yellow hair of our lady of Kirien; no other gold."

"Then it was some midman stole the thing?"

Laughter rang long and faint about her. "How would a midman dare? O Lady of Kirien, how the great jewel was stolen no mortal knows, not man nor midman nor Fian nor any among the Seven Folk. Only dead minds know how it was lost, long ago when Kireley the Proud whose great-granddaughter is Semley walked alone by the caves of the sea. But it may be found perhaps among the Sunhaters."

"The Clayfolk?"

A louder burst of laughter, nervous.

"Sit with us, Semley, sunhaired, returned to us from the north." She sat with them to eat, and they were as pleased with her graciousness as she with theirs. But when they heard her repeat that she would go to the Clayfolk to find her inheritance, if it was there, they began not to laugh; and little by little there were fewer of them around her. She was alone at last with perhaps the one she had spoken with before the meal. "Do not go among the Clayfolk, Semley," he said, and for a moment her heart failed her. The Fian, drawing his hand down slowly over his eyes, had darkened all the air about him. Fruit lay ash-white on the plate; all the bowls of clear water were empty.

"In the mountains of the far land the Fiia and the Gdemiar parted. Long ago we parted," said the slight, still man of the Fiia. "Longer ago we were one. What we are not, they are. What we are, they are not. Think of the sunlight and the grass and the trees that bear fruit, Semley; think that not all roads that lead down lead up as well."

"Mine leads neither down nor up, kind host, but only straight on to my inheritance. I will go to it where it is, and return with it."

The Fian bowed, laughing a little.

Outside the village she mounted her striped windsteed, and, calling farewell in answer to their calling, rose up into the wind of afternoon and flew southwestward toward the caves down by the rocky shores of Kiriensea.

She feared she might have to walk far into those tunnel-caves to find the people she sought, for it was said the Clayfolk never came out of their caves into the light of the sun, and feared even the Greatstar and the moons. It was a long ride; she landed once to let her steed hunt tree-rats while she ate a little bread from her saddlebag. The bread was hard and dry by now and tasted of leather, yet kept a faint savor of its making, so that for a moment, eating it alone in a glade of the southern forests, she heard the quiet tone of a voice and saw Durhal's face turned to her in the light of the candles of Hallan. For a while she sat daydreaming of that stern and vivid young face, and of what she would say to him when she came home with a kingdom's ransom around her neck: "I wanted a gift worthy of my husband, Lord. . . ." Then she pressed on, but when she reached the coast the sun had set, with the Greatstar sinking behind it. A mean wind had come up from the west, starting and gusting and veering, and her windsteed was weary fighting it. She let him glide down on the sand. At once he folded his wings and curled his thick, light limbs under him with a thrum of purring. Semley stood holding her cloak close at her throat, stroking the steed's neck so that he flicked his ears and purred again. The warm fur comforted her hand, but all that met her eyes was grey sky full of smears of cloud, grey sea, dark sand. And then running over the sand a low, dark creature—another—a group of them, squatting and running and stopping.

She called aloud to them. Though they had not seemed to see her, now in a moment they were all around her. They kept a distance from her windsteed; he had stopped purring, and his fur rose a little under Semley's hand. She took up the reins, glad of his protection but afraid of the nervous ferocity he might display. The strange folk stood silent, staring, their thick bare feet planted in the sand. There was no mistaking them: they were the height of the Fiia and in all else a shadow, a black image of those laughing people. Naked, squat, stiff, with lank hair and grey-white skins, dampish-looking like the skins of grubs; eyes like rocks.

"You are the Clayfolk?"

"Gdemiar are we, people of the Lords of the Realms of Night." The voice was unexpectedly loud and deep, and rang out pompous through the salt, blowing dusk; but, as with the Fiia, Semley was not sure which one had spoken.

"I greet you, Nightlords. I am Semley of Kirien, Durhal's wife of Hallan. I come to you seeking my inheritance, the necklace called Eye of the Sea, lost long ago."

"Why do you seek it here, Angya? Here is only sand and salt and night."

"Because lost things are known of in deep places," said Semley, quite ready for a play of wits, "and gold that came from earth has a way of going back to the earth. And sometimes the made, they say, returns to the maker." This last was a guess; it hit the mark.

"It is true the necklace Eye of the Sea is known to us by name. It was made in our caves long ago, and sold by us to the Angyar. And the blue stone came from the Clayfields of our kin to the east. But these are very old tales, Angya."

"May I listen to them in the places where they are told?"

The squat people were silent a while, as if in doubt. The grey wind blew by over the sand, darkening as the Greatstar set; the sound of the sea loudened and lessened. The deep voice spoke again: "Yes, lady of the Angyar. You may enter the Deep Halls. Come with us now." There was a changed note in his voice, wheedling. Semley would not hear it. She followed the Claymen over the sand, leading on a short rein her sharp-taloned steed.

At the cave-mouth, a toothless, yawning mouth from which a stinking warmth sighed out, one of the Claymen said, "The air-beast cannot come in."

"Yes," said Semley.

"No," said the squat people.

"Yes. I will not leave him here. He is not mine to leave. He will not harm you, so long as I hold the reins."

"No," deep voices repeated; but others broke in, "As you will," and after a moment of hesitation they went on. The cave-mouth seemed to snap shut behind them, so dark was it under the stone. They went in single file, Semley last.

The darkness of the tunnel lightened, and they came under a ball of weak white fire hanging from the roof. Farther on was another, and another; between them long black worms hung in festoons from the rock. As they went on these fire-globes were set closer, so that all the tunnel was lit with a bright, cold light.

Semley's guides stopped at a parting of three tunnels, all blocked by doors that looked to be of iron. "We shall wait, Angya," they said, and eight of them stayed with her, while three others unlocked one of the doors and passed through. It fell to behind them with a clash.

Straight and still stood the daughter of the Angyar in the white, blank light of the lamps; her windsteed crouched beside her, flicking the tip of his striped tail, his great folded wings

stirring again and again with the checked impulse to fly. In the
tunnel behind Semley the eight Claymen squatted on their hams,
muttering to one another in their deep voices, in their own
tongue.

The central door swung clanging open. "Let the Angya enter
the Realm of Night!" cried a new voice, booming and boastful.
A Clayman who wore some clothing on his thick grey body
stood in the doorway, beckoning to her. "Enter and behold the
wonders of our lands, the marvels made by hands, the works of
the Nightlords!"

Silent, with a tug at her steed's reins, Semley bowed her head
and followed him under the low doorway made for dwarfish
folk. Another glaring tunnel stretched ahead, dank walls dazzling
in the white light, but, instead of a way to walk upon, its floor
carried two bars of polished iron stretching off side by side as far
as she could see. On the bars rested some kind of cart with metal
wheels. Obeying her new guide's gestures, with no hesitation
and no trace of wonder on her face, Semley stepped into the cart
and made the windsteed crouch beside her. The Clayman got in
and sat down in front of her, moving bars and wheels about. A
loud grinding noise arose, and a screaming of metal on metal,
and then the walls of the tunnel began to jerk by. Faster and
faster the walls slid past, till the fireglobes overhead ran into a
blur, and the stale warm air became a foul wind blowing the
hood back off her hair.

The cart stopped. Semley followed the guide up basalt steps
into a vast anteroom and then a still vaster hall, carved by
ancient waters or by the burrowing Clayfolk out of the rock, its
darkness that had never known sunlight lit with the uncanny cold
brilliance of the globes. In grilles cut in the walls huge blades
turned and turned, changing the stale air. The great closed space
hummed and boomed with noise, the loud voices of the Clayfolk,
the grinding and shrill buzzing and vibration of turning blades
and wheels, the echoes and re-echoes of all this from the rock.
Here all the stumpy figures of the Claymen were clothed in
garments imitating those of the Starlords—divided trousers, soft
boots, and hooded tunics—though the few women to be seen,
hurrying servile dwarves, were naked. Of the males many were
soldiers, bearing at their sides weapons shaped like the terrible
light-throwers of the Starlords, though even Semley could see
these were merely shaped iron clubs. What she saw, she saw
without looking. She followed where she was led, turning her
head neither to left nor right. When she came before a group of

Claymen who wore iron circlets on their black hair her guide halted, bowed, boomed out, "The High Lords of the Gdemiar!"

There were seven of them, and all looked up at her with such arrogance on their lumpy grey faces that she wanted to laugh.

"I come among you seeking the lost treasure of my family, O Lords of the Dark Realm," she said gravely to them. "I seek Leynen's prize, the Eye of the Sea." Her voice was faint in the racket of the huge vault.

"So said our messengers, Lady Semley." This time she could pick out the one who spoke, one even shorter than the others, hardly reaching Semley's breast, with a white, fierce face. "We do not have this thing you seek."

"Once you had it, it is said."

"Much is said, up there where the sun blinks."

"And words are borne off by the winds, where there are winds to blow. I do not ask how the necklace was lost to us and returned to you, its makers of old. Those are old tales, old grudges. I only seek to find it now. You do not have it now; but it may be you know where it is."

"It is not here."

"Then it is elsewhere."

"It is where you cannot come to it. Never, unless we help you."

"Then help me. I ask this as your guest."

"It is said, *The Angyar take; the Fiia give; the Gdemiar give and take.* If we do this for you, what will you give us?"

"My thanks, Nightlord."

She stood tall and bright among them, smiling. They all stared at her with a heavy, grudging wonder, a sullen yearning.

"Listen, Angya, this is a great favor you ask of us. You do not know how great a favor. You cannot understand. You are of a race that will not understand, that cares for nothing but wind-riding and crop-raising and sword-fighting and shouting together. But who made your swords of the bright steel? We, the Gdemiar! Your lords come to us here and in the Clayfields and buy their swords and go away, not looking, not understanding. But you are here now, you will look, you can see a few of our endless marvels, the lights that burn forever, the car that pulls itself, the machines that make our clothes and cook our food and sweeten our air and serve us in all things. Know that all these things are beyond your understanding. And know this: we, the Gdemiar, are the friends of those you call the Starlords! We came with them to Hallan, to Reohan, to Hul-Orren, to all your castles, to help them speak to you. The lords to whom you, the proud Angyar, pay tribute, are our friends. They do us favors as we do them favors! Now, what do your thanks mean to us?"

"That is your question to answer," said Semley, "not mine. I have asked my question. Answer it, Lord."

For a while the seven conferred together, by word and silence. They would glance at her and look away, and mutter and be still. A crowd grew around them, drawn slowly and silently, one after another till Semley was encircled by hundreds of the matted black heads, and all the great booming cavern floor was covered with people, except a little space directly around her. Her windsteed was quivering with fear and irritation too long controlled, and his eyes had gone very wide and pale, like the eyes of a steed forced to fly at night. She stroked the warm fur of his head, whispering, "Quietly now, brave one, bright one, windlord. . . ."

"Angya, we will take you to the place where the treasure lies." The Clayman with the white face and iron crown had turned to her once more. "More than that we cannot do. You must come with us to claim the necklace where it lies, from those who keep it. The airbeast cannot come with us. You must come alone."

"How far a journey, Lord?"

His lips drew back and back. "A very far journey, Lady. Yet it will last only one long night."

"I thank you for your courtesy. Will my steed be well cared for this night? No ill must come to him."

"He will sleep till you return. A greater windsteed you will have ridden, when you see that beast again! Will you not ask where we take you?"

"Can we go soon on this journey? I would not stay long away from my home."

"Yes. Soon." Again the grey lips widened as he stared up into her face.

What was done in those next hours Semley could not have retold; it was all haste, jumble, noise, strangeness. While she held her steed's head a Clayman stuck a long needle into the golden-striped haunch. She nearly cried out at the sight, but her steed merely twitched and then, purring, fell asleep. He was carried off by a group of Clayfolk who clearly had to summon up their courage to touch his warm fur. Later on she had to see a needle driven into her own arm—perhaps to test her courage, she thought, for it did not seem to make her sleep; though she was not quite sure. There were times she had to travel in the rail-

carts, passing iron doors and vaulted caverns by the hundred and
hundred; once the rail-cart ran through a cavern that stretched off
on either hand measureless into the dark, and all that darkness
was full of great flocks of herilor. She could hear their cooing,
husky calls, and glimpse the flocks in the front-lights of the cart;
then she saw some more clearly in the white light, and saw that
they were all wingless, and all blind. At that she shut her eyes.
But there were more tunnels to go through, and always more
caverns, more grey lumpy bodies and fierce faces and booming
boasting voices, until at last they led her suddenly out into the
open air. It was full night; she raised her eyes joyfully to the
stars and the single moon shining, little Heliki brightening in the
west. But the Clayfolk were all about her still, making her climb
now into some new kind of cart or cave, she did not know
which. It was small, full of little blinking lights like rushlights,
very narrow and shining after the great dank caverns and the
starlit night. Now another needle was stuck in her, and they told
her she would have to be tied down in a sort of flat chair, tied
down head and hand and foot.

"I will not," said Semley.

But when she saw that the four Claymen who were to be her
guides let themselves be tied down first, she submitted. The
others left. There was a roaring sound, and a long silence; a
great weight that could not be seen pressed upon her. Then there
was no weight; no sound; nothing at all.

"Am I dead?" asked Semley.

"Oh no, Lady," said a voice she did not like.

Opening her eyes, she saw the white face bent over her, the
wide lips pulled back, the eyes like little stones. Her bonds had
fallen away from her, and she leaped up. She was weightless,
bodiless; she felt herself only a gust of terror on the wind.

"We will not hurt you," said the sullen voice or voices.
"Only let us touch you, Lady. We would like to touch your hair.
Let us touch your hair. . . ."

The round cart they were in trembled a little. Outside its one
window lay blank night, or was it mist, or nothing at all? One
long night, they had said. Very long. She sat motionless and
endured the touch of their heavy grey hands on her hair. Later
they would touch her hands and feet and arms, and once her
throat: at that she set her teeth and stood up, and they drew back.

"We have not hurt you, Lady," they said. She shook her
head.

When they bade her, she lay down again in the chair that

bound her down; and when light flashed golden, at the window, she would have wept at the sight, but fainted first.

"Well," said Rocannon, "now at least we know what she is."

"I wish there were some way of knowing *who* she is," the curator mumbled. "She wants something we've got here in the Museum, is that what the trogs say?"

"Now, don't call 'em trogs," Rocannon said conscientiously; as a hilfer, an ethnologist of the High Intelligence Life-forms, he was supposed to resist such words. "They're not pretty, but they're Status C Allies. . . . I wonder why the Commission picked them to develop? Before even contacting all the HILF species? I'll bet the survey was from Centaurus—Centaurans always like nocturnals and cave dwellers. I'd have backed Species II, here, I think."

"The troglodytes seem to be rather in awe of her."

"Aren't you?"

Ketho glanced at the tall woman again, then reddened and laughed. "Well, in a way. I never saw such a beautiful alien type in eighteen years here on New South Georgia. I never saw such a beautiful woman anywhere, in fact. She looks like a goddess." The red now reached the top of his bald head, for Ketho was a shy curator, not given to hyperbole. But Rocannon nodded soberly, agreeing.

"I wish we could talk to her without those tr—Gdemiar as interpreters. But there's no help for it." Rocannon went toward their visitor, and when she turned her splendid face to him he bowed down very deeply, going right down to the floor on one knee, his head bowed and his eyes shut. This was what he called his All-Purpose Intercultural Curtsey, and he performed it with some grace. When he came erect again the beautiful woman smiled and spoke.

"She say, Hail, Lord of Stars," growled one of her squat escorts in Pidgin-Galactic.

"Hail, Lady of the Angyar," Rocannon replied. "In what way can we of the Museum serve the lady?"

Across the troglodytes' growling her voice ran like a brief silver wind.

"She say, Please give her necklace which treasure her blood-kin-forebears long long."

"Which necklace?" he asked, and understanding him, she pointed to the central display of the case before them, a magnificent thing, a chain of yellow gold, massive but very delicate in workmanship, set with one big hot-blue sapphire. Rocannon's eyebrows went up, and Ketho at his shoulder murmured, "She's got good taste. That's the Fomalhaut Necklace—famous bit of work."

She smiled at the two men, and again spoke to them over the heads of the troglodytes.

"She say, O Starlords, Elder and Younger Dwellers in House of Treasures, this treasure her one. Long long time. Thank you."

"How did we get the thing, Ketho?"

"Wait; let me look it up in the catalogue. I've got it here. Here. It came from these trogs—trolls—whatever they are: Gdemiar. They have a bargain-obsession, it says; we had to let 'em buy the ship they came here on, an AD-4. This was part payment. It's their own handiwork."

"And I'll bet they can't do this kind of work anymore, since they've been steered to Industrial."

"But they seem to feel the thing is hers, not theirs or ours. It must be important, Rocannon, or they wouldn't have given up this time-span to her errand. Why, the objective lapse between here and Fomalhaut must be considerable!"

"Several years, no doubt," said the hilfer, who was used to star-jumping. "Not very far. Well, neither the *Handbook* nor the *Guide* gives me enough data to base a decent guess on. These species obviously haven't been properly studied at all. The little fellows may be showing her simple courtesy. Or an interspecies war may depend on this damn sapphire. Perhaps her desire rules them, because they consider themselves totally inferior to her. Or despite appearances she may be their prisoner, their decoy. How can we tell? . . . Can you give the thing away, Ketho?"

"Oh, yes. All the Exotica are technically on loan, not our property, since these claims come up now and then. We seldom argue. Peace above all, until the War comes. . . ."

"Then I'd say give it to her."

Ketho smiled. "It's a privilege," he said. Unlocking the case, he lifted out the great golden chain; then, in his shyness, he held it out to Rocannon, saying, "You give it to her."

So the blue jewel first lay, for a moment, in Rocannon's hand.

His mind was not on it; he turned straight to the beautiful, alien woman, with his handful of blue fire and gold. She did not raise her hands to take it, but bent her head, and he slipped the necklace over her hair. It lay like a burning fuse along her golden-brown throat. She looked up from it with such pride, delight, and gratitude in her face that Rocannon stood wordless, and the little curator murmured hurriedly in his own language, "You're welcome, you're very welcome." She bowed her golden head to him and to Rocannon. Then, turning, she nodded to her squat guards—or captors?—and, drawing her worn blue cloak about her, paced down the long hall and was gone. Ketho and Rocannon stood looking after her.

"What I feel . . ." Rocannon began.

"Well?" Ketho inquired hoarsely, after a long pause.

"What I feel sometimes is that I . . . meeting these people from worlds we know so little of, you know, sometimes . . . that I have as it were blundered through the corner of a legend, or a tragic myth, maybe, which I do not understand. . . ."

"Yes," said the curator, clearing his throat. "I wonder . . . I wonder what her name is."

Semley the Fair, Semley the Golden, Semley of the Necklace. The Clayfolk had bent to her will, and so had even the Starlords in that terrible place where the Clayfolk had taken her, the city at the end of the night. They had bowed to her, and given her gladly her treasure from amongst their own.

But she could not yet shake off the feeling of those caverns about her where rock lowered overhead, where you could not tell who spoke or what they did, where voices boomed and grey hands reached out—Enough of that. She had paid for the necklace; very well. Now it was hers. The price was paid, the past was the past.

Her windsteed had crept out of some kind of box, with his eyes filmy and his fur rimed with ice, and at first when they had left the caves of the Gdemiar he would not fly. Now he seemed all right again, riding a smooth south wind through the bright sky toward Hallan. "Go quick, go quick," she told him, beginning to laugh as the wind cleared away her mind's darkness. "I want to see Durhal soon, soon. . . ."

And swiftly they flew, coming to Hallan by dusk of the second day. Now the caves of the Clayfolk seemed no more than last year's nightmare, as the steed swooped with her up the thousand steps of Hallan and across the Chasmbridge where the forests fell away for a thousand feet. In the gold light of evening in the flightcourt she dismounted and walked up the last steps between the stiff cavern figures of heroes and the two gatewards, who bowed to her, staring at the beautiful, fiery thing around her neck.

In the Forehall she stopped a passing girl, a very pretty girl, by her looks one of Durhal's close kin, though Semley could not call to mind her name. "Do you know me, maiden? I am Semley, Durhal's wife. Will you go tell the Lady Durossa that I have come back?"

For she was afraid to go on in and perhaps face Durhal at once, alone; she wanted Durossa's support.

The girl was gazing at her, her face very strange. But she murmured, "Yes, Lady," and darted off toward the Tower.

Semley stood waiting in the gilt, ruinous hall. No one came by; were they all at table in the Revel-hall? The silence was uneasy. After a minute Semley started toward the stairs to the Tower. But an old woman was coming to her across the stone floor, holding her arms out, weeping.

"O Semley, Semley!"

She had never seen the grey-haired woman, and shrank back.

"But Lady, who are you?"

"I am Durossa, Semley."

She was quiet and still, all the time that Durossa embraced her and wept, and asked if it were true the Clayfolk had captured her and kept her under a spell all these long years, or had it been the Fiia with their strange arts? Then, drawing back a little, Durossa ceased to weep.

"You're still young, Semley. Young as the day you left here. And you wear round your neck the necklace. . . ."

"I have brought my gift to my husband Durhal. Where is he?"

"Durhal is dead."

Semley stood unmoving.

"Your husband, my brother, Durhal Hallanlord was killed seven years ago in battle. Nine years you had been gone. The Starlords came no more. We fell to warring with the Eastern Halls, with the Angyar of Log and Hull-Orren. Durhal, fighting, was killed by a midman's spear, for he had little armor for his body, and none at all for his spirit. He lies buried in the fields above Orren Marsh."

Semley turned away. "I will go to him, then," she said, putting her hand on the gold chain that weighed down her neck. "I will give him my gift."

"Wait, Semley! Durhal's daughter, your daughter, see her now, Haldre the Beautiful!"

It was the girl she had first spoken to and sent to Durossa, a girl of nineteen or so, with eyes like Durhal's eyes, dark blue. She stood beside Durossa, gazing with those steady eyes at this woman Semley who was her mother and was her own age. Their age was the same, and their gold hair, and their beauty. Only Semley was a little taller, and wore the blue stone on her breast.

"Take it, take it. It was for Durhal and Haldre that I brought it from the end of the long night!" Semley cried this aloud, twisting and bowing her head to get the heavy chain off, dropping the necklace so it fell on the stones with a cold, liquid clash. "O take it, Haldre!" she cried again, and then, weeping aloud, turned and ran from Hallan, over the bridge and down the long, broad steps, and, darting off eastward into the forest of the mountainside like some wild thing escaping, was gone.

AND THE MONSTERS WALK

by
John Jakes

John Jakes is known to millions of readers as the author of the best-selling BICENTENNIAL SERIES of novels about America's past. However, before his current successes, he was an excellent writer of suspense, Western, fantasy, and science fiction stories for the genre magazines. Especially noteworthy novels in the sf field are BLACK IN TIME (1970), ON WHEELS (1973) and SIX-GUN PLANET (1970). A definitive sf collection of his shorter stories is THE BEST OF JOHN JAKES (1977). He is also fondly remembered in the fantasy field for his tales of "Brak the Barbarian."

"And the Monsters Walk" is a superior hardboiled supernatural thriller which, oddly enough, has never been anthologized. An oversight which we are pleased to correct.

We were somewhere in the Channel, with France lying to starboard and the country of England on the other hand. Both were lost in the fog and darkness of that impenetrable night. The freighter *Queen of Madagascar* rolled on the oily swells, and hundreds of gallons of water thundered across the lonely decks with each rise and fall.

The ship was a ship of strangers. The men were not English or American or even European. They were odd hues: swarthy, some of them, others yellowish with the cast of the Orient. At mess I sat alone, an Englishman working my way homeward by the only trade I knew—the sea.

And here we were, that strange, murderous crew with the slashed scarred faces, the dark furtive eyes, the pistols and the knives. One day out from England. Twenty-four hours. And my curiosity had risen to a fever pitch. I had to know what we carried in that sealed main hold. Once, off Algiers, when the hatch was open, I caught a whiff from down there. Standing in the bright sun, I swore it was a smell of bones and age. A smell of dead men. The vague thought of our being a monstrous coffin-ship intrigued me, played on my curiosity—a characteristic in me which, if not particularly worthy, provided for a life that was far from dull.

There was an opening into the main hold from a lower deck. Not a regular entrance-way or anything of the like. A makeshift iron door, probably cut from the bulkhead by a torch and refitted into its original frame.

No one guarded that door, you see. On our first day out, Captain Bezahrov had informed the crew that the penalty for entering the hold was instantaneous death. But there I was, crazy with curiosity, and yet lucky, too. Because what I found gave me knowledge that more important men longed for—later. Lucky, in a hellish sort of a way.

I stole through the rocking corridors, finished with my watch. From the faraway forecastle, echoing down the dismal metal companionways, came a wordless primitive song. One of the crewmen singing of his homeland, probably. It counterpointed the thunder of the waves in the black sea outside, and made my spine crawl.

I listened for a few moments, hesitating before the door. No footsteps sounded. No voices spoke anywhere near. Carefully, I eased the crude handle upward and inched the bulkhead door open. It was well oiled. It made no sound.

The hold was dark. At once, that overpowering stench of age and evil decay struck me. I stepped inside, inserting my penknife to keep the door ajar. I had nothing to lose. I don't mean that in a bragging sense. A life is certainly something to part with. But no wife, no children to care for. And curiosity burned high and insistent. There was just enough of an element of chance. I just *might* get away with it—

I flicked on my pocket torch and looked around, excited. They *did* look like coffins! Row on row of rough wooden boxes. I stepped closer and peered at the markings. *T. Nedros. Importer, 8 Ryster Lane, London, England.* I checked several of the strange packing cases. The address was always the same. All of them to this mysterious T. Nedros, Importer.

The boxes had lids, and those lids were only fastened down with cheap wire. What more could I ask? Holding my torch steady, I unwound the twists of wire and pushed back the lid. I leaned forward to peer at the contents.

And then the nightmare began.

I looked into that box for perhaps forty-five seconds. It couldn't have been longer. But what I saw could easily drive a man mad. A . . . a *shape*—could I call it that?—lay within. Nearly seven feet in length, I realized, estimating the length of the box. A shape in human form, but not human at all. A shadow shape, with monstrous furred hands and a blur of darkness for the head, in which burned two smoky red eyes, wide open, staring up blankly at the roof of the hold.

A . . . a *thing*, it was. A creature from some more ancient world, when spirits of evil trod the earth. A creature not of our time, not of the world of civilized men. A demon reshaped in human mold, dug from God knows what sorcerer's burying ground and boxed up and—this was the most horrible—loaded on a ship for London! The others must contain the same sort of monstrosity, I realized.

I retched. The death-smell filled my nostrils.

All in the forty-five seconds or less, flashing through my brain like flickering pictures on a screen. Like a man seeing his entire life in the moment before he dies. And I was dying then, in a sense. Dying and being re-born into a world of terrors unfit for humans to endure.

Quickly, then, the rest happened. I heard the sounds of the door, of feet clanging on the metal plates, of harsh foreign curses. Hands threw me quickly to the floor. I peered up. Lights had come on in the hold.

Captain Bezahrov stood over me, hands clenched in fury. "Marlow," he said quietly, holding his teeth together in rage, "you are a fool. You should have known that we would be wise enough to prepare an alarm system on the bridge for something as important as this.''

I said nothing. From far away came the wild and lonely drumming of the sea. My only chance was to make a break for it. With an effort, I sprang to my feet.

Bezahrov caught me when I was only half-risen. He towered above me, his round face jerked awry by the livid scar lying alongside his nose. A light far above him threw a dim halo around his cap, and I wondered how the angel Satan had looked when he fell from Paradise.

Bezahrov's pistol came sweeping down, butt first. I tried to dodge, but it was no use. He hit me several times and, in a pain-filled delirium, I felt hands lift me and carry me. Upward. *The deck!*

But I had known the penalty. I had known, and they did not have to speak of it. Abruptly, I felt wind lashing my face, and a fine rain. The waves thundered more loudly. A few more steps. The hands lifted me. *Lifted* . . .

And then the hands were gone. I hung in space for a moment and then I fell like a plummet, without thought, straight down to the black raging waters of the Channel. I struck the water and my mind went dark.

Slowly, I began to drift back into consciousness, stripes of gray light creeping across my eyes. I awoke as if from a pleasant sleep. I kept my eyes closed as the first coherent thoughts crossed my mind. I had no knowledge of how I managed to come out of that angry sea alive.

I recalled the thing in the box, and that same feeling of dread and loathing swept over me. And then I remembered the nightmare fall into the depths of the Channel. *By God, Marlow*, my mind said, *you have no right to be alive.*

But I was alive. That, or hell was a place to lie quietly between blankets. I opened my eyes. I felt no pain. My head was clear and my thoughts orderly. Or as orderly as they could be, with the vision of what I had seen gnawing at the back of my mind.

The room was bleak, with only the bed, a washstand, a chair and a writing desk. I blinked with astonishment. Neat and dry, my clothes, complete to cap and pea jacket, hung on the back of the chair.

I got out of bed, feeling chill air on my naked body. Dressing hastily, I approached the window under the slanting roof and raised the blind. Outside lay a gray and dismal sky brooding over the desolate roofs and docks of London's East End.

Then I was in London, and alive! But *how?* Already the nightmare had begun to take shape. I started walking back and forth across the room, trying to find an answer. But there was no answer. Not even a logical puzzle. Just a series of mad, frightening events—random, inexplicable.

After a few moments I saw the piece of paper on the writing desk. I snatched it up and read the lines inked in a small, almost childish hand. The words only added to the madness surrounding me.

We are your friends, it ran. *Do not question the fact that you are alive. We will contact you.*

I stared at the paper and questions flooded over me again. I stopped after a moment. It was futile. Two immediate things could be done. I was in London. I could find out exactly where I was, and I could go to Scotland Yard and tell them of the things I had seen.

I left the room, went down a short chilly hall, and downstairs into the main room of the lodging house. In the dim light, a fat, blowzy red-haired woman dozed at the desk.

"I'd like to know how I got here," I said to her, almost afraid to learn.

She looked at me out of eyes surrounded by wrinkles, and laughed coarsely. "Don't ask me, mate. I suppose you like your nip too much, like most of them. Blind when they come in, and afterwards they all want to know how they arrived."

"I wasn't drunk," I insisted. "Someone brought me here. When was it?"

"What's your name?"

"Marlow. Steven Marlow."

She consulted the spotted pages of the register. "Two nights ago. Monday."

"Who brought me?" I repeated.

"How should I know that?" she said, irritated. "I wasn't working then. Mr. Sudbury was here Monday night. He'd know who brought you in, I suppose." I could see from her face that she was still convinced I had come to the lodging house in a stupor.

"Then when can I talk to Mr. Sudbury?" I persisted.

"You can't," she said triumphantly. "He quit last night."

"Q—quit?" I stammered. The thing was becoming too confused even to think about.

"Yes, quit! Listen, matey, we don't ask questions around here. Mr. Sudbury only worked here three weeks. How do I know he wasn't wanted by the coppers? How do I know he didn't have some girl in trouble?" She threw up her hands. "I don't. But we don't ask questions, see. Why don't you just forget it and start off where you were before you got hold of the stuff?"

Angrily, I turned from the desk and walked out of the place. A sign above the door read *Bane's Rest*. Well, there wasn't any information to be had from the woman. I glared at her through the window, leaning on her elbows, her frowzy red hair bobbing as she nodded off to sleep.

I started off down the narrow street. I needed sanity. A touch of it, just a tiny bit of it.

Scotland Yard brought sanity to me. The office of Inspector Rohm, to whom I was sent after I gave many evasive answers to the question—for what did I need the Yard?—proved to be a bare little cubbyhole, not much more cheerful than the bedroom in which I had awakened.

Inspector Rohm was a thin, scholarly-looking man with sandy hair, erect posture, and sharp blue eyes. He sat in his chair and listened to my story. I poured it all out, incoherently, even wildly, while he sat there as if listening to a learned paper on physics. The only part I omitted concerned the note from my rescuers, whoever they were.

When I finished, Inspector Rohm peered at me with his blue eyes and said, "Is that *all?*"

"Yes," I said, "and it's the truth."

Rohm laughed. "I doubt that," he said gently. "My friend, we are bothered with many cranks and lunatics here, but I have never heard such a fantastic story."

"But I saw the thing!"

"Granted such creatures existed," he continued, "why would you come to us?"

And there he had me stopped. Why indeed? Except that I had sensed terrible evil in that thing on the ship, in all the cases in the hold, in fact. And evil had its opposite in good, and the law represented the most accessible source of that good.

I could not convey to him in words the impending sense of danger and unearthly evil I had felt on the *Queen of Madagascar*. I sat there, helpless under his critical gaze, twisting my cap in my hands.

"I . . . I don't know," I said. "I'm only a seaman, sir. I . . .

well . . . I felt that it meant trouble for us, somehow . . . for England . . . for the world. Evil, you understand . . ."

Rohm laughed again. "No, I'm afraid we'll have to have something a bit more concrete than that."

"But can't you check my story?" I pleaded. "Can't you check on the ship and her cargo?"

He thought a minute, and I suppose he finally decided to accept my suggestion, because he was a man who was meticulous about his duty, leaving no alternative open, no matter how impossible.

"All right. I'll ring up Customs."

After a few minutes on the phone, talking in clipped monosyllables, he turned back to me, pulling out a cigarette and lighting it. "Well, Marlow, the cargo from the *Queen of Madagascar* arrived all right, consigned to a perfectly legitimate importer named Nedros in Ryster Lane."

"What was the cargo?" I asked quietly.

"The usual run of Oriental stuff. Carpets, cloth goods, wines, water pipes." He smiled a bit sardonically. "For the curio shops. Items to give your parlor that odd touch, you know." When he laughed this time, it was in appreciation of his own humor.

"I saw that thing in the box," I insisted.

He shook his head. "No," he said with finality, "the cargo was as stated. That has been verified."

'But I knew the name of the person it was being sent to," I said. "I was on that ship!"

"Very true. But as for the rest, Mr. Marlow, you are either lying or in need of help from a psychiatrist. And now, I'm rather busy. If that's all, I'd appreciate your leaving."

"All right," I said, rising. "That's all, I suppose."

I walked out, feeling his eyes in my back, branding me a liar and a madman. The world had gone insane. Somehow, those *things* had left the *Queen of Madagascar* before she reached port. I knew there were many of them. I had looked into that box, and smelled the hold. I knew they threatened danger, vast and terrible danger, but no one cared. I knew they were somewhere in England now, in London, perhaps. And no one would pay any attention . . .

But I had that note in my pocket! I had come back out of the sea. And even if I had not, no one could have looked into the blank, hellish red eyes of that thing lying there in the iron hold of that storm-lashed ship and not known that here was greater evil than mankind had seen for centuries.

I went to a pub and tried to drink. Amid the laughter and the clink of mugs, I tried to sop up nightmare in alcohol. But it didn't work. I would drink for a bit, concentrating on the warm, light-headed feeling it produced. And then, I'd think of the shape in the box, and I would be sober again, as if I had not touched a drop.

I went back to Bane's Rest in the East End that night. I had no place else to go. The room was dark and chill, and I stared at the ceiling all night. I could not sleep.

Next morning my head was filled with a buzzing born of weariness, and my arms and legs felt as though they were lead. A little after seven I put on my cap and jacket and left the Rest to get some breakfast. An ample supply of pound notes had been left in the pocket of my coat by those responsible for the note, it seemed.

As I walked along I couldn't help noticing the early-morning mist and the rooftops against the sky beyond. Gray—all gray— suggestive of a hideous dead quality, as if a malignant living mold shrouded London. I bought several newspapers and pro- ceeded to find an inexpensive restaurant. Black taxis and other traffic moved briskly on the streets, and well-dressed men in bowlers, carrying umbrellas, moved on the walks, looking very content and complacent. I envied them in their security.

Over an egg and tea in the dimly lit white tile interior of the restaurant, I examined the newspapers. The huge headline of the first paper jerked my attention away from my food and filled me with fresh dread.

Lord Wolters Slain, the words shouted. *Harley Square Home Devastated. Mysterious Killers Still at Large.*

Lord Wolters. I knew the name, of course. Everyone did. In the Cabinet he was perhaps the most important man, particularly valuable to England in these times of stress because of his military experience. Defense needed an able guiding hand, and Lord Wolters provided it. Or he had. Now he was dead. And somehow it formed a link in my mind with the horror on the *Queen of Madagascar.*

I read the other accounts. They said much the same thing. But the third paper gave a bit of news that made me grow cold again. An unofficial report, it said, from servants of Lord Wolters, hinted that the corpse was mangled and dismembered, and that whole sections of the house had been demolished, including several walls.

There must be a connection. There *had* to be. Madness was slowly breaking loose in the streets of London. In such a time of world crisis, the death of Lord Wolters and the strange cargo out of the East united to form—what?

I could not say, exactly. But I knew some meaning lurked there. A dreadful meaning.

Another item on a back page confirmed my suspicions. A fisherman had been killed in a little village on the Channel coast. Before he died, he babbled insanely of monstrous, gigantic shapes coming out of the water, rising from the waves at night, and overwhelming him. A back page! No one would notice it.

This was two nights ago, the same night I was dropped over the side of the *Queen*. Those . . . *things* . . . came ashore and Captain Bezahrov loaded the long boxes with the regular cargo Inspector Rohm had named as checked by Customs. The things made their way to London, and Lord Wolters died. I had to see Harley Square. Every moment drew me deeper into the pattern, all the more frightening because I knew only vaguely what it was, and not why, or from where.

I left the papers on the table and hurried from the restaurant. A few minutes after eight o'clock I stood in the center of a crowd of the curious outside of the iron fence before the home of Lord Wolters. Scotland Yard was already on duty, guarding the doors. I could see nothing of the ruined interior of the house.

"Have they taken him away?" I asked a man next to me.

"Yes, a few minutes ago." The man scowled harshly and sucked on his pipe. "Only he wasn't on a stretcher. The hospital men brought out a big canvas sack. I hear he was in small pieces, all torn up. Devil's work, it sounds like."

I turned away, feeling the chill of the morning fog on me. *Devil's work.* Yes, living devils. My nose twitched, and I finally took conscious thought of the odor hanging over the whole square. Decay and festering rot. The smell in the ship's hold. The smell of the things. They *had* been here!

I listened for a bit and heard people talking about the odor. It puzzled them, but not one ventured a guess as to what it was. I wanted to seize them one by one; scream at them that I knew. But they never would have believed me, and the police would probably have run me off, less politely than Inspector Rohm had done.

Someone tugged at my sleeve. I turned, half-expecting to see the man with the pipe I had spoken to only a moment before. But another man stood there, a wizened, rat-like little man in filthy clothes and a checked cap. One milky blue eye peered at me from a stubbled triangular face. The other was covered by a dirty black patch. The man leaned close to me.

"Mr. Marlow," he said in a wheezing voice. His breath reeked of alcohol.

"Yes, my name's Marlow."

"I got a message for you."

Perhaps they were contacting me at last. "Who's it from?" I asked quickly.

The man with the patch cackled softly. "Him Who Doesn't Walk."

"Him—" The words stuck in my mouth. "Look here," I said angrily, "who are you and who's this man you're talking about?"

"Him Who Doesn't Walk," the fellow repeated in his shrill whisper. "He says to tell you he knows you're alive when you're not supposed to be. He says it won't be long, though. He says you haven't got much more time."

"Time? Time for what?"

The blue eye winked at me. "Time to live, Mr. Marlow. Time to live."

Angrily I reached out for him, intending to grab him and haul him off to some alley and beat the truth out of him about this incoherent babble of someone called Him Who Doesn't Walk. But as if it were a perfectly timed signal, the man turned away and someone to the rear of the crowd shoved abruptly.

I stumbled forward, bumping against two ladies who were in turn pushed against the iron fence. I fought to get my balance, and finally pulled myself erect. One of the women was adjusting her hat and glaring at me as she pinned it in place.

"Look here, sonny—" she exclaimed loudly.

"I'm sorry, madam," I blurted back, and turned again to where I had been standing. I searched the crowd, but I didn't see the man. I pushed my way out and stood in the middle of the square, surrounded by the gloomy gray fronts of the old houses. The man with the patch was nowhere in sight.

I started walking. One more incident, one more name on the role of horror and impossibility. Him Who Doesn't Walk. And not much time for me to live. Evidently these men weren't connected with my rescuers. Evidently they did not want me to remain alive because I knew of the cargo of the ship, and linked it with the slaying of Lord Wolters. And by some means, they could watch my every move, as my rescuers could evidently also do. I walked on, smoking a cigarette thoughtfully.

What could I do? Where could I run? I had so little information, and yet it was enough to warrant my dying. And how soon would the attack come? And from where?

I stopped at a news kiosk to light another cigarette. A man approached me, this time well-dressed, in a gray overcoat and bowler. He had a slender, scholarly face with intense black eyes, a straight nose, thin lips and a deeply bronzed complexion. He could have been any age from forty to seventy. His face was strange, decidedly not English.

"Excuse me," he said. "Do you have a light?" I nodded, holding the match to his cigarette. I had a wild desire to run. He might be the very killer with orders to put a knife in my back.

"Let's walk a bit," he said softly. His voice was accented with strange, resonant tones, as if an Oriental were trying to speak perfect English. He put his hand on my elbow and piloted me down a side street. Then he relaxed his grip and puffed his cigarette. I waited ready to turn on him at the first sign of danger.

"I sent you that note, Marlow," he said quietly, staring straight ahead. "I dragged you out of the sea and put you up at *Bane's Rest*. My name is Gerasmin."

The name meant nothing to me. "Can . . . can you explain anything about what's going on?" I stammered. "You said in the note you . . . you were my friends. Where are the others?"

"There is only one other," Gerasmin said, with a hint of sadness in his voice. "Her name is Angela. If you will come to my rooms, we will explain a few things to you."

"How do I know you don't want to kill me once you get me there?"

"You don't," he replied. "You must take that chance. But I can only say we trusted you and kept you from dying. You could do the same for us."

"All right," I said. "To your rooms." I wanted, more than anything, to get at the roots of the situation, and I determined to keep alert for trouble while I learned as much as possible.

Gerasmin had rooms in one of the better West End hotels. I felt out of place in my sailor's jacket and cap as we rode the lift to the fifth floor. He led me down a dim, thickly-carpeted hallway and into a spacious, well-furnished suite. Large glass windows, stretching from ceiling to floor, looked out upon the street.

The girl he had called Angela stood by the window, smoking and staring out at the gray sky. She was slender and nicely built, with dark hair drawn tightly back over her head. A very lovely young woman as she turned and looked at me with frank brown eyes.

"This must be Mr. Marlow," she said warmly. Her smile was weary, though, as if from strain. "How are you?" I heard the click as the door was locked behind me.

"Fine, thanks," I said, feeling awkward. Gerasmin threw his hat and topcoat onto a chair and moved to the liquor cabinet. "Sit down, Marlow, I'll fix us drinks. Scotch do for you?"

"Yes, that'll be fine." I twisted my cap in my hands. I wanted answers. The curiosity was pulsing through me again, almost eclipsing the terrors of the last thirty-six hours.

We said nothing until Gerasmin handed out the drinks. Then he lit another cigarette with a steady hand and said, "Marlow, we pulled you out of the sea two nights ago."

"How?"

"Perhaps I can explain by telling you a little about Angela and me. I am an Indian by birth, and I spent much time in Tibet. Consequently, I have studied certain realms of knowledge that would not be recognized as valid at Oxford." He tapped his skull, smiling. "Spirit matters, Marlow. Movement of matter by thought. It can be done. And second sight, if you want to call it that. I can see anywhere, at any time."

His words were calm and quiet, and yet the meaning struck home with the force of blows. Here he was, this dark-skinned man with the ageless face, in a hotel room in London, telling me in clipped British accents that he had powers that I never knew existed; powers only hinted at in ancient legends.

"I'm afraid I can't believe you," I said weakly, like a man in shock.

He smiled. "No, I imagine not. You see that?" He was pointing to a small blue vase standing on top of a radio-phonograph console. "Watch it, Marlow. Watch it carefully." He closed his eyes and drew his lips together tightly. His ageless face assumed a rigid quality. I turned my eyes to the vase.

And suddenly—*it vanished*.

Amazed, I turned back to Gerasmin. His eyes were open again and a lazy smile lay on his lips. He weighed an object in his left hand. The blue vase.

"That," he said, "was relatively easy. I saw you on the *Queen of Madagascar*, saw you dropped over the rail. I brought you out of the sea, to this room, and took you by cab to the Rest."

What was the man saying? A sorcerer . . . he must be that, an ancient sorcerer reborn. This was not the modern world of London. And yet it was, with a new and frightening dimension added, a dimension of magic and witchcraft—the supernatural.

"Why did you rescue me?" I stammered. "And how did you know about me in the first place?"

"We, or rather Gerasmin here, had been watching the *Queen*," Angela explained, "ever since she set out from India with her cargo of demons. That's what they are, Marlow. Creations of sorcery."

"And I just happened to be on board. Is that it?"

"Yes." She nodded. "The *Queen* needed one more crewman. They were undermanned as it was, since all of them but you were hirelings in the scheme. Only Captain Bezahrov and his mates, though, knew what the cargo was. And when Gerasmin saw you about to die, he decided to save you, in the hope that you would join us."

The questions were coming faster. "Where . . . where did those things come from?"

"The monsters?" Gerasmin said quietly. "From India, Tibet, Russia—all the dark corners of the East. They have been in the process of creation for ten years or so, by men who still practice the black arts. In a hundred shops in a hundred cities, men worked to fashion and animate them. They are actual demons, Mr. Marlow, children of what you call Hell. They were common in ancient times. The men who created them did not know their purpose in the Plan. They were paid, and they did their evil work."

"But what for?" I asked. "I still don't see that."

"It's a scheme that's been under way for years," Angela said, almost in a whisper. The smoke from her cigarette made a filmy halo around her head. "A scheme to take over the western world. My father and Gerasmin unearthed it in India twelve years ago. My father was Colonel Hilary St. Giles Saunders."

I nodded. The name was famous in the Indian Colonial Regiments.

Her face grew strained and harsh. "The leader of the organization discovered my father and Gerasmin. Father was killed in

Bombay. Gerasmin escaped and we are the only two people who now have full knowledge of the organization.''

"To take over the Western world?" I choked. "That seems incredible.''

"It's possible," Gerasmin breathed. "It's too possible, with their power. Marlow, the secrets of the East are undreamed of. Those things have monstrous strength. They cannot easily be killed. We have been alone, Angela and I. Now, if you'll join us, there'll be three. There's not a great deal we can do, but we can at least try. We must try! Angela and I have been waiting for years for the scheme to come off. And now it's under way, and London is the starting point.''

"From the East," I murmured. "Russia?"

Gerasmin smiled. "Yes, partly. They're even blatant about the fact. It's been written in their books for years. Captain Bezahrov is perhaps the second most important man in the organization. He is pure Russian. The real leader is a mixture of the worst elements in all the Eastern races.''

"Would that have anything to do with Him Who Doesn't Walk?" I said.

Angela started. "How did you know that name?"

I explained about the incident in Harley Square, and the man with the patch over his eye.

Gerasmin snapped his fingers and got to his feet. "Then they're on to you. It was only a matter of time, since they can see anywhere just as easily as I can. Yes, Him Who Doesn't Walk is the leader. I've never seen him, but I know he is a cripple and can't use his legs, if he has any legs at all.''

"Where is he?" I said. The thing was beginning to fall together, damnably, horribly, and I realized that I was now alone, cut off—almost forced into alliance with these two. I had little choice, even though they seemed hopelessly pitiful in their efforts, just the two of them.

"He's somewhere under London," Angela said, gesturing. "In sewers, deep underground, in hidden rooms—everywhere. We've picked up bits of information here and there, and evidently London is honeycombed with tunnels and subterranean chambers he and his followers have made over the years.''

"Can't you get Scotland Yard to work?" I said, forgetting for a moment my own experience.

Gerasmin smiled grimly. "You tried it, Marlow. We saw you try, and we let you go ahead because we knew what would happen. They called you insane. We face the same problem.

And now that Him Who Doesn't Walk is on to you, we may not have much time to work."

He said it calmly, impassively. And I realized that they were bound to me now, instead of the other way around. They had taken me in on a chance of my joining them, and had thereby exposed themselves to a heightened possibility of sudden death. I felt instinctively closer to them, and I couldn't help watching Angela. She was a very beautiful woman to find in such a lunatic's game.

"Look, Marlow," Gerasmin said, "we don't have much chance, I admit. Lord Wolters is already out of the way. God knows who is next. That item about the dead fisherman went unnoticed. Nobody will listen to us, and we're entirely alone. But we'd like to have you in."

I gazed at him closely, at those ageless black eyes and the fine dark hair resting sleekly on his head. A gentleman of this and other worlds, fighting against an army of hellish creatures born of magic. Then I looked at Angela.

"I'm in, if you want me."

I walked to the liquor cabinet to refill my drink, gesturing as I moved. "And you don't look so bad from here. You seem to take care of everything. I suppose you even had Mr. Sudbury move on, as a precaution."

Angela laughed softly again and moved to the window. "He's a very intelligent fellow, Gerasmin, this Mr. Marlow."

"Where can we start?" I asked. "Or can we start—do anything at all?"

"Now that you are with us," Gerasmin said briskly, "there will be two of us for the actual work. I never wanted to operate alone, and I did not want to expose Angela to danger. She's too valuable."

"I'm afraid I won't be much help," I told them. "I don't have any power—"

"We won't worry about that. I think the first thing is to find out how we get into the underground and see if we can scout some of the rooms belonging to Him Who Doesn't Walk. We'll ask around in the pubs. I have a few friends, although I have a strong hunch the entrance to the underground is through the shop of T. Nedros in Ryster Lane. He—"

"*Gerasmin!*" Angela spoke sharply at the window. We hurried over and looked down. Two cabs had pulled up before the hotel, and half a dozen men were getting out. Their heads were covered and we could not see their faces. I felt sweat run down my armpits, and for some reason I remembered the words of the man with the patch.

"Can you go into their minds?" Angela whispered.

Gerasmin nodded, closing his eyes. A moment later he opened them. "They're from the organization, all right. Him Who Doesn't Walk has seen us together and has decided to finish us all at one time. Come on!"

He ran to the closet, pulled it open, and took two large pistols from the top shelf. He gave one to Angela and one to me. Unbuttoning his suit coat, he loosened the brass hilts of the two knives in his waistband. Then, after a minute's thought, he took the pistol from Angela and dropped it into his own pocket.

"They're coming fast," he said. "We'll try the regular way out." He headed for the hall, jerked the door open and started down the fire escape. I ran ahead and pulled the door open, but I stopped short, seeing the figure in the coat and bowler two flights below.

"One's coming up here." I looked out again and caught a glimpse of a dark, upraised face glaring at me as the man climbed. "They look human enough. But there's another one down in the alley."

Gerasmin started back toward the rooms, with Angela and me close behind. Gerasmin indicated the open door from which we had just come. "In here. We'll try—"

There was a thunderous explosion, and a shot tore past my ear. Angela screamed softly and I whirled, pistol in hand. The quartet of killers had come around the bend of the hall and was closing in.

I dropped to one knee, sighted and fired. One of the men fell but the other three came on, coats thrown open and hands bringing out knives. They were men with dark, alien features, like the crew on the *Queen of Madagascar*. They were perhaps fifty yards down the hall, which was already filled with ropes of acrid smoke and echoes of shots. A woman screamed in the distance. I remember two heads popping out of doors and drawing back hastily.

Gerasmin fired over my shoulder, carefully and steadily. The second of the killers fell. Almost immediately I fired again, and the third staggered and bumped against the wall, screeching in an unfamiliar singsong language, clutching his arm where a dark, ugly stain began to grow. Abruptly, Angela cried out and we whirled in time to see the fire escape door come open. The first of the men from the alley flung his knife at us, his mouth twisted into a thick-lipped snarl.

I shoved Gerasmin roughly and he tumbled into the open door of the suite. I flattened myself out, feeling the rough carpet slam into my face as the knife whispered by overhead. From the corner of my eye, I saw it bury itself in the woodwork a dozen inches above my head, whirring.

We were holding our own; they hadn't been expecting us to be prepared, I suppose. This had evidently been the first move to eliminate Gerasmin, as well as me. The Indian leaned around the doorframe and triggered another shot. The knife-thrower was blown backwards through the fire escape door. He slammed into the railing, was thrown off balance, and went tumbling over the guard rail. His shriek dwindled as he fell toward the stones of the alley.

An alarm bell jangled down the corridor. I started to get to my feet, and just as I did Angela jerked the knife from the wall, her eyes wide with fright. She lashed out over my head. I ducked instinctively and heard a savage groan. When I turned again, I saw the fourth man of the quartet staggering back, an expression of bewilderment on his dark, primitive face. His head tilted back and the bowler fell off. He turned around, took a few steps, fell incongruously like a graceful ballet dancer, and lay still.

Angela's shoulders were shaking. She stared down at the knife with its blade stained a bright liquid red. Her left hand was pressed to her cheek, white-knuckled. "I had to," she breathed, not to us but to some great invisible jury of righteous men. "I had to kill him. He was almost on you . . ." She managed to glance at me, and then she began to sob, her shoulders slumping. "I've never killed anyone before. I've never . . ." Her words were obliterated by the crying.

Gerasmin put his arm around her and led her back into the apartment. I followed, the smoking gun hanging from my hand. I was beginning to relax, feeling the strain seep out of my muscles. The three of us were in the vestibule, Gerasmin in the lead, when he stepped back suddenly and faced us. His dark eyes were those of a man who had looked into the pit. I caught that hideous odor again. Death . . . decay . . .

"Him Who Doesn't Walk has been watching his agents die," Gerasmin breathed with harsh intensity. "Now he's sent—"

"What's wrong?" I snapped.

"Don't waste words. Stand close to me. We'll have to leave here. The thing's been transported right into the sitting room."

He drew the sobbing girl closer and I moved in toward them. Thank God she was too upset to realize what was going on.

Something tore the vestibule curtains aside and I saw it, towering there, its red smoky eyes glaring with dull fires of infinite evil, its body a thing of shadow, misshapen and vile in form, its great furred hands reaching out for us, its mouth emitting snuffling sounds. Again the power of Him Who Doesn't Walk struck home as I realized that this thing had been transported *by thought* to this very room, to destroy us.

It took a step forward. Its hands stretched toward us. I looked frantically to Gerasmin, but his eyes were closed, his lips clamped together tightly, and that vacant mindless expression lay on his face. Tiny dots of sweat glistened on his dark forehead. Angela sobbed wordlessly. *Hurry up*, my mind screamed, *for God's sake, hurry up!*

My flesh crawled. The thing took another step. Gerasmin groaned loudly. The furry hands reached for us and the stench grew overpowering. My mind swam, blank and incoherent, and I wanted to fall forward in weak helplessness. I wanted to stop the terrible effort and let myself be drawn into that thing of ancient evil. Dimly, I heard Gerasmin's whispered words and I held on for a moment longer.

"*We're going . . .*"

Then my mind whirled all the more. The room tilted crazily. Gerasmin and Angela fell away, and I swam over and over in a swirling gray vacuum where a furious wind shrieked. I moved my arms wildly, trying to catch hold of something. My stomach pushed toward my throat and the wind tearing at my skin brought real pain.

Gradually, a kind of sea-sick rocking sensation filled me. The grayness broke apart and portions of a scene sifted through. The gray vanished bit by bit, and I stared at the brick wall across the tiny alleyway, watching it heave from side to side and gradually come to rest.

Gerasmin was looking around, examining the alleyway. A hundred yards to our right lay a street. "We are five or six blocks from the hotel," he mused, staring at the crowds passing on the street. "That should do. We'll get a cab."

Angela gazed at me, quiet now, only her eyes showing the agony she had experienced. They were reddish and raw-looking. Gerasmin seized my hand. "Put your gun away, Marlow. You too, Angela. We must get out of here."

Angela dropped the knife, still clutched in her hand, into her purse. I nodded and clumsily put my pistol into the pocket of my pea jacket. Without a word we started toward the alley mouth. "That wasn't easy," Gerasmin said as we walked. "Three humans a distance of six blocks . . ." He shook his head and closed his eyes tightly. "I get a ferocious pain in my head . . ."

I wondered about the effort it must have been to lift me from the Channel, miles away, and bring me all the way to London. Evidently he had thought me valuable to do such a thing, and it drew me closer to them.

We stepped out onto the street and began walking toward the corner. The crowd eddied around us, oblivious of the things we had seen and been through. It made me laugh inwardly, a bit crazily. If they knew, what would any one of them do? It was hard to say, but I wondered how long they would remain sane.

"What was in the room?" Angela asked wearily.

"One of *them*," Gerasmin answered.

"From the ship?"

Gerasmin nodded, and I saw her shudder.

"Look," I said, pointing. "There's a cab. Shall we get it?"

They indicated that we should, and minutes later we were cruising through London streets, relatively safe from attack. Only the watching mind of Him Who Doesn't Walk could be on us now. We still had to be careful.

"Now," Gerasmin said, adjusting his necktie, "we'll start getting information about the entrance to the underground."

"It seems pretty risky going in there now," I countered. "We'd be in greater danger of being killed."

"He's right," Angela said softly.

"They will keep trying to kill us," Gerasmin said, staring at the panel closing the driver off from us, "no matter what we do or where we are. We can at least make some effort to find out more about their plans. Perhaps we might run across something. You see, Marlow—" He stared at me with those incredibly ancient eyes. "We don't have much chance to live anyway. We might as well make our remaining hours count."

I thought about that a minute. I tried to smile. "All right. We'll see for how much it'll count, then."

"Good. The pubs. We'll start there, so . . ."

I didn't need the end of the sentence. I leaned forward, slid the panel back and spoke to the driver. "We want to go somewhere near Ryster Lane."

"Whereabouts, guv'nor?" he said, not turning his head. "What number in the Lane?"

"Not *in* the Lane," I corrected. "A few blocks from it."

"All right, guv'nor. Where?"

"Any place. You pick the spot."

He turned around and stared at me in a peculiar manner. "Suit yourself," he said, shaking his head. They all thought we were insane. We, Gerasmin, Angela Saunders and I—mad, and removed from society. Yet we saw horrible realities where supposedly saner men could not.

I slid the panel shut and leaned back, lighting a cigarette. Gerasmin had closed his eyes and was resting his head in his hands. He'd been at it a long time, and I supposed every effort of his mind put on the strain a bit more.

Angela sat between us. Her head was nodding in exhaustion, dropping slowly toward my shoulder. Once she awoke with a start and smiled hazily, questioningly. I said, "Go ahead. Rest." Her expression was one of grateful weariness as she dropped off, her hair fanning out on the shoulder of my jacket.

I leaned back deeper into the seat and shut my eyes. A little rest, even in the joggling cab, would do me good.

Twenty minutes later the cabby let us out in a narrow street four blocks from Ryster Lane. Gerasmin paid him. I glanced at my watch. A few minutes past noon. We looked around. The houses were old, falling into ruin. Here and there newer facades intruded among these ancient moldering wrecks. A greengrocer in one place, a phonograph shop in another. Somewhere in the distance a boat horn hooted on the Thames. Not too far away, I decided.

"Down there." I pointed to the left, to a pub in the next block. We started walking, our heels clicking on the stone sidewalks. A strange trio we were as we went into that smoky, beery place. The bartender glanced at us sleepily, moved away from the two seedy-looking customers, men of middle age in the garb of workmen, and came to wait on us.

We each ordered a lager, Angela with obvious distaste. Gerasmin called the barkeep by name, and they exchanged a few words of greeting. Then the barkeep moved away to fetch the drinks. I leaned closer to Gerasmin, fidgeting, wanting to get some concrete action.

"Why can't you send your mind up to Nedros's place," I asked, "and take a look around? It would save a lot of time, and we're short of that."

"And Him Who Doesn't Walk would know somebody was

spying. He can feel other minds watching him," Gerasmin replied in a whisper.

"Well, then, I suspect he can probably see us right here, too, and find out what we're doing."

"No." The dark head shook back and forth. "There's been a mental shield around us, the three of us, ever since we came out in that alley. It's hard to keep up, but Him Who Doesn't Walk can't see or hear us. That's one trick we've got over him, I think. As far as he's concerned, Claud has been talking to empty air."

"Careful," Angela whispered suddenly. Claud, the barkeep, was returning with three pints of beer. He set them down with great precision, so that none of the fluffy white foam spilled.

"There you are, chum," he said to Gerasmin, rumbling the words loudly. Gerasmin paid him and leaned across the bar in a confidential manner. He crooked his finger and Claud caught on, glancing at the two working men, then drawing in close.

"I want to ask you a couple of questions, Claud. If you answer the last one right, there's ten quid in it for you."

Claud laughed under his breath, his thick red face spreading itself into a grin. "Go ahead, chum. Let's have your questions."

"This one is a point of information," Gerasmin said. "How far is Ryster Lane from here?"

Claud jerked a thick thumb. "Three blocks. Towards the river."

"Good." Gerasmin took a sip of the lager and I followed suit. Angela left hers untouched, watching the barkeep Claud intently. "Here's the next," Gerasmin said. "Have you ever heard of a person called Him Who Doesn't Walk?"

Claud blanched. His eyes grew wide and round; his hands clutched the edge of the bar. I had a strange eerie feeling, as if some strange force, or power, or *mind* were trying, straining to peer at us, but could not. As if it were fighting a barrier, smashing wrathfully against it to see what was going on beyond.

"Look, chum," Claud breathed in terror, "I don't want no trouble. Why don't you and your friends go someplace else?"

Gerasmin fingered the notes. In my growing impatience, I wanted to reach out and grab the barkeep's throat and shake the truth out of him. But Gerasmin remained cool and careful, displaying the pound notes only a few inches from Claud's florid face.

"Have you heard that name?" Gerasmin repeated.

Claud licked his lips and eyed the notes. "Yes."

"This is the important question," Gerasmin said smoothly. "Answer it and the money's yours."

"Let's hear it first."

"There's an importer in Ryster Lane. Nedros. Is that shop the entrance to . . ." Gerasmin hesitated. His eyes and voice grew hard. ". . . *the underground?*"

Claud breathed heavily, not answering. His eyes darted around the room, and I could see him taking in the tawdriness of his pub, thinking of the tawdriness and the struggle in his existence. He looked at the money again.

"I don't—" he began.

"Ten pounds," Gerasmin murmured, "is ten pounds."

"Sure," Claud blurted out suddenly. "Nedros's place is the entrance. But I only *heard* that. I don't know for sure. Remember that—I just heard it." He snatched the money from Gerasmin, his tone growing strident. "You and your friends better go."

Gerasmin smiled thinly and motioned to Angela and me. We walked out of the pub, leaving Claud staring down at the notes in his hand. Poor devil, I thought. He'll be wondering when he's going to get a knife in the back every day for the next five years.

Angela glanced at the clouds, darker now. It was only early afternoon, but it might as well have been the deep of night. We stood on the walk, clearing the stuffy smell of the pub from our heads. Angela spoke abruptly.

"Look, you two. Wherever we go from here, I'm coming along."

"Don't be foolish," Gerasmin said.

"I'm perfectly serious."

"We've seen things no man should," I said to her, "let alone a woman."

"You forget, Mr. Marlow," she replied, her tone hardening, "my father died in India because of what is going on now. I have a right to be part of your work. I've got a score to settle. Woman or not, my father died because of Him Who Doesn't Walk."

"This doesn't seem like a good place to argue about it," I said, glancing back into the pub. The two working men were staring curiously.

"You're right," Gerasmin put in. "We'll find a place to stay until after dark. And then we'll try our luck at getting into the shop of Mr. Nedros."

"I'm going with you," Angela said again, determined.

We did not reply as we moved off along the walk. The room

we rented was in a rooming house two blocks from the pub. We sat in the chill, dismal place all afternoon, playing cards with a pack we had been lucky enough to find at the desk. None of us said much. The ominous sky beyond the cheap yellowed window curtains threw a pall over our spirits, and now and again we heard the mournful sound of a hooter, on the river.

About six I went out for some food and the latest papers. I read them hastily on my way back to the rooming house, my throat growing tight and dry, my stomach growing cold. I raced up the stairs, forgetting about the sacks of food, and threw the papers down in front of Angela and Gerasmin. "More of it," was all I could say.

They glanced at me worriedly and bent over the papers. One lead story covered the killings in the hotel under a headline that began: *Mass Slaying.* But the most terrible piece of news concerned Sir Guy Folversham, Minister of the Exchequer. He had been slain around noon on his country estate. Torn to bits and left dead and mutilated in his eight-car garage. A gardener reported having seen something fleeing across the fields that looked like, ". . . *a great shadow*," the story said.

Gerasmin ground out his cigarette with deliberate anger. "Again," he breathed savagely. "They'll have the country wrecked in a week, at this rate. All the leaders being murdered." He slammed his fist into his palm.

"To Nedros," I said. "Let's get started."

He nodded, rising and checking his pistol. Angela once again brought up the subject of her accompanying us, and Gerasmin argued with her briefly.

"I'm going," she insisted.

"All right," he said, irritably, slipping into his topcoat. "We must stop wasting time. Come with us, but if we signal for you to turn back, return here and don't question us. Is that clear?"

She nodded, silent and stern-faced.

We set off through a heavy fog. I felt depressed, overwhelmed by the odds facing us. Our heels clicked on the cobbles, and the bellow of fog horns sounded dismally in our ears. A flickering street lamp illuminated the sign indicating Ryster Lane. We moved down the crooked little way, examining each of the shadowed doorways.

Finally I tugged at Gerasmin's arm and pointed. "Here." A numeral above the door said 8. We stepped into the doorway. The shop lay in darkness, its two windows curtained top to bottom. Heavy gold lettering on the glass proclaimed, *T. Nedros Importer*.

"Not much of a shop," Angela whispered.

"Doesn't need to be," I said, "for what's behind it."

Gerasmin tried the door. It was locked, of course. Without a word he closed his eyes, his lips drew tight and his brow wrinkled with strain. Angela seized my arm, staring at the Indian in the shadowed gloom. Gerasmin groaned and we heard a faint click. He sighed and relaxed, his shoulders slumping as he leaned forward to test the door again. It swung open imperceptibly.

"Come on," he said. "The lock's broken."

We had no sooner stepped into the darkened interior, reeking of incense and the smell of musty cloth and wood, than a bare bulb in the ceiling flared on, revealing the angular glare of dust-covered glass cases, empty of goods. Evidently T. Nedros did no importing at all to speak of. I snatched my gun from my pocket and shoved Angela behind me.

A voice cut through the silence. "Do not use the weapons, gentlemen."

We whirled around.

A section of empty wall shelving stood aside. The entrance framed a monstrously gross man in dirty gray trousers and filthy white shirt. His head was round and laden with fold upon pendulous fold of yellowish fat. Small eyes darted nervously at us, and a tiny pink tongue, like a snake's, flicked over his lips. The naked light bulb shone on his damp black hair, and I smelled the sickening odor of lemon cologne. His fat fingers were curled around a heavy .45 caliber automatic.

"I have a warning system set up," he said tonelessly. "It arouses me when anyone steps through my front door."

"You're Nedros?" I questioned.

"That is correct. But I have not had the pleasure of meeting *you*."

"We'll forego that pleasure," Gerasmin said, coldly.

"I will be quick about it," Nedros said, his cheeks quivering. "I do not know you, but I can guess why you are here. No one would come here who did not belong to the organization, unless they were spies. You could not be here on business of a commercial nature, since I do not actually carry on that kind of business." He laughed ponderously, then sobered again. "I must, of course, kill you."

My stomach twisted and coiled into writhing knots. Suddenly, I felt something cold touch my free hand, which hung at my side. Nedros could not see that hand, and I felt experimentally. A cold, sharp edge. A *knife!* One from the hotel! I wanted to turn and speak to Angela, to burst out my thanks. But instead I slid the knife up my sleeve and waited tensely.

"Let me have your weapons," Nedros ordered. He indicated Gerasmin. "You first."

Gerasmin took one cat-like step forward and started to bring his pistol up. Nedros reached out, smashing down with the barrel of his weapon and knocking the gun to the floor with a clatter. His thick lips quivered. "If I were not going to kill you," he breathed, "I would punish you for being so foolish. I would punish you painfully. You!" he snarled in my direction. "Your weapon!"

I began walking forward, feeling the knife pressing against my fingertips, up inside my sleeve. Nedros shifted his gun to his left hand and extended his right to take the pistol. I took more steps, as if I were out for a Sunday walk.

"That's far enough," he said, not knowing whether to expect an attack or not. His one moment of hesitation, thrown off guard by my feigned carelessness, was enough. His trigger finger began to whiten. I whipped up my gun, striking the barrel of his weapon aside. It roared loudly and one of the glass cases tinkled and smashed. By that time I had slipped the knife out, and as quickly as I could I drove it into his chest.

He gasped, his tiny eyes widening. His gun exploded again as his finger jerked spasmodically, but the bullet buried itself in the floor. He peered down curiously at the ugly red blotch widening on his dirty white shirt. Abruptly, his eyes closed, as if he had fallen asleep. His legs collapsed. His whole fleshy body quivered once in obscene ripples, and lay still.

Angela watched with a terrified expression. I pulled her gently forward, and she shielded her eyes as we stepped across the corpse of the gross and very dead Mr. Nedros and into the room beyond.

It was a plain room, with only a bed, a table and chairs and a lavatory behind a screen painted with Japanese figures. A green light bulb was set high in one wall. Evidently the alarm. In the opposite wall was a heavy gray iron door studded with large round rivets.

Gerasmin breathed deeply. "This looks like the entrance. From now on we've got to be more careful than ever." I stepped forward and pulled up the massive handle. The door swung open noiselessly.

Stairs descended, shrouded in darkness. Far, far down in the distance was a vague gleam of light.

I turned to Angela. "Do you feel up to it?"

She nodded. "Of course." I could see that her hands were trembling though. "Go on," she said.

I took the lead, my heart pounding at triphammer speed as we started down those stairs that led into a pit of darkness and God knows what unnamed horrors.

The steps were narrow and steep, so that we had to go down them almost sideways. We tried to make as little noise as possible, holding our pistols ready. The gleam of lights grew larger, but with terrible slowness. It seemed as though we were going downward for hour after hour. My legs began to tire. Once, Angela stumbled and almost fell. I turned in time, catching my balance in time to keep her from going down and sending me tumbling with her. She breathed tensely a moment, clutching my arms, her face quite near mine. Then she said, "I'm all right. Let's keep going."

We were like three heroes from ancient legend making the traditional descent into hell, except that we were not heroic. We were frightened; even Gerasmin had been edgy since the encounter with the killers at the hotel. What lay down where the light beckoned, we couldn't tell. One thing was certain, however. We were in the underground. The horrible stench of those *things* filled the air.

The light turned out to be a small blue bulb set in the wall at the bottom of the stairs. I turned back to them and whispered, "We're almost at the bottom. A tunnel runs on from here."

"Let's wait a minute and get our breath," Gerasmin replied. I nodded, stepping off the lowest step and helping Angela down. She leaned against me. We examined the corridor ahead, our nostrils filled with that timeless reek of dead life reborn.

The corridor stretched into the distance, lit every hundred yards or so by one of those blue bulbs. They shone like blurred rows of streetlamps. The corridor evidently had no end. It stretched away into shadows.

Gerasmin and Angela indicated that they were ready. We started out again. We tramped on down that hall for another long space of time, the blue bulbs marching past, one after another. At last Gerasmin whispered, "Look up ahead, Marlow. The corridor ends!"

Perhaps we had stumbled into some by-way designed to throw

prowlers off the track. But how could that be? There had been no cross corridors anywhere along the passage. "No," I replied, "there must be a door." I walked faster, conscious of the fact that we were deep in the earth; above us lay London, where perhaps, even now, more hideous crimes were taking place. We were in the stronghold of Him Who Doesn't Walk, and though Gerasmin's mind kept a shield around us, I had the feeling that we were close to death.

The corridor did not end with a door. It turned abruptly to the right for a few feet, and to the left again. As I rounded the first turn, I jammed myself back against the wall. Gerasmin and Angela pulled up short. Light spilled down the corridor, evidently from a room a few feet to the left of the next turning. I listened and heard the harsh tones of a voice I recognized.

"*All right, old boy,*" the voice said, "*so you do argue with him, wot does it get you? A berth in the river, is all.*"

A heavier, deeper voice mumbled something in reply; I could not make it out.

"That voice belongs to the man with the patch on his eye," I whispered to the two behind me. "You remember—the one who gave me the message from Him Who Doesn't Walk, in Harley Square?"

"Hear anything else?" Gerasmin asked.

"Another voice. This must be a stop on the route to the center of operations."

"We'll have to rush them," Gerasmin said.

I nodded. "Angela, you stay here until we get them cleaned out." I silenced her with a wave of my hand. "You ready?"

Gerasmin said that he was. He hesitated only a moment. Here again, beyond the bend of the tunnel, lay possible death. I was becoming numb with the thought of it; I think I had counted myself a dead man soon after waking up in *Bane's Rest*. I brought my pistol up, feeling the sweat on my palms, and started along the corridor at a dead run. Gerasmin kept pace behind me.

As we rounded the turn, an alarm bell began to ring. I cursed myself. Of course they'd have them. And the corridor was thirty feet long! I was halfway down it when the alarm went off. They'd have plenty of time to get ready. I broke into the room and slid out flat on the floor, firing. Two men crouched behind a large table, firing back. One was the man with the patch, who recognized me and cackled with laughter, because he thought we were trapped. The other, a swarthy, thick-set man wearing gold earrings and a thin black moustache, fired at us with one hand. His other was frantically pressing an alarm switch on the table.

The few moments that it lasted were filled with noise and smoke. I aimed and shot, and the swarthy man's hand, pressing hard on the buzzer, disappeared in a welter of blood. He reared up above the table top, and Gerasmin's shot sheared half his head away.

The man with the patch screamed and tossed his gun down. "Don't kill me," he begged. "Give a lad a sporting chance." He raised his hands over his head, but I watched his one milk-blue eye rolling wildly. He was listening for someone—

The room contained doorways to half a dozen corridors leading off in all directions. From down one of them, I knew, would come men to finish us. Gerasmin pressed forward and shoved his gun against the one-eyed man's neck.

"I want you to talk," he whispered, "and immediately. The friends you signaled won't be here in time to save your life."

"I don't know much, your honor," the man whined. "Honest to living Jesus, I don't, your honor."

Gerasmin jammed the barrel tight against the man's throat. "The next attack. When will it be? The next killing. What will it be?"

The man writhed against the wall. "Please, your honor . . ." His one eye blinked wildly.

"Tell me!" Gerasmin snarled. I caught a whiff of fetid air from a corridor at the opposite side of the room. Not the smell of the beasts. The river smell. Perhaps that corridor was a way out, leading to the Thames. I noted it quickly in my mind and turned back to Gerasmin and the one-eyed man who was cringing now, trembling against the wall. In the distance, down another corridor, I heard footsteps running. Still far away, though.

"I'll kill you before they get here," Gerasmin raged. "Tell me! The next attack!"

"Tomorrow . . ." the man wheezed. "Tomorrow, I think that's it, your honor."

"You'd better be sure."

"That's it," the man fairly screamed. "Don't shoot, your honor, I'm sure. Captain Bezahrov himself told me, just an hour or so ago."

"What time?"

"Ten o'clock, tomorrow morning."

"Where?"

"Number . . . Number Ten, Downing Street . . ."

"Good God!" I exclaimed. *"The Prime Minister!"*

"That's what we wanted to know," Gerasmin said. "You'd better get Angela."

I had completely forgotten about her. I went back into the corridor, softly calling her name. And then I stopped. The tunnel was filled with that overpowering stench—and a section of the floor was gone.

I knelt down and found an iron ladder leading down into darkness. The smell rising from the hole made me choke. Angela was gone! Fear raced through me. I started down the ladder, but heard Gerasmin call me.

"Marlow! They're coming!"

"Angela's gone!" I shouted back. "She's—"

A volley of shouts cut off the rest. I stood for a moment, my mind raging, torn in two directions. Angela, lovely, frightened Angela was gone into the darkness, gone with the monster taint lingering in the air behind her. Someone watched the corridor, not with his mind but in actuality. Something had risen up out of the dark ground and *taken* Angela—

Shots were roaring back in the tiny room. I heard Gerasmin's anguished scream: *"Marlow!"*

I raced back. The man with the black patch had fled. Gerasmin was crouched behind the table, firing down a corridor. Answering shots filled the room, bullets smacking into the walls.

I ran across the room on my knees and dropped down beside him, triggering a couple of shots.

"We've got to get word back about the Prime Minister," he whispered. "We've got to go back *now.*"

I indicated the corridor directly behind of us. "Do you smell the river there, or is it my imagination?"

His teeth were clenched together. "I smell it. We'll have to run for it. I'm—I'm too tired to try with my mind." The corridor from which the shots had come was silent now. But we heard a soft rustling of feet. They were stealing closer . . . closer . . . Gerasmin pulled at my sleeve and, bent over, we ran toward the corridor.

Bullets whispered in the air around us, but we got safely into the darkness and we kept running. They came after us, but our shots kept them off. No blue bulbs lit this corridor. Finally we slammed into another iron door. The strong odor of the river filtered through a thick wire grill.

My hands moved over the door; I found a wheel. "Here," I whispered, and began to turn it. Gradually the door swung open.

We stepped out onto the slippery mud bank of the river. I let go of the door and it closed automatically. Breathing hard, we pulled ourselves up the slope until we were directly above the door, and we lay there with our guns ready, waiting.

The killers did not come out.

Finally I began to breathe more easily. I looked around. The embankment stretched away in either direction. Lights lined the opposite shore, and a tug moved past us in the stream, its whistle sounding. My mind relaxed a little then. We were out of that hellish underground—out of the nightmare world of dark corridors and death at every turn. Two thoughts struck me suddenly. The assassination scheduled for tomorrow at ten, and Angela. I turned to Gerasmin quickly.

He lay stretched out on his stomach, as if tired. I spoke to him. He didn't answer. I spoke again, and again silence. My back grew cold. I reached out and touched him. I turned him over, and saw with horror the dark ugly stains on the front of his coat. He stared at me, his eyes wide open.

He was dead.

I heard the tug's whistle cry out mournfully a second time.

The night closed upon me, and I felt death and horror creeping near. I realized now just how alone I was. Gerasmin lay dead, all that strange ancient power gone—cut off. Mighty as he was, his mind had not been quick enough to stop the bullets that tore life out of him. The shield was down, too. No longer could I move unobserved. Him Who Doesn't Walk could watch me any hour of the day or night.

And Angela. The frightening thoughts struck me, one after another. She was down there in the underground, perhaps already dead. I had a wild urge to go back, and I started scrabbling on the bank to find the entrance. But I couldn't locate it anywhere. Perfectly concealed. The wet clay of the slope was everywhere the same.

Marlow alone. Marlow against them, the unseen ones, all the more terrible because they *were* unseen. I realized dimly that there was only one way for me to stay alive; one way for me to be strong enough and quick enough to elude them for a time. I had to hate them. I had to hate them with every anguished fiber of my soul. Hate would make me move faster, and even though I might move into a rain of bullets or the arms of one of those shadowy things, still, on the other hand, I might spend my time deliberating and die all the sooner.

Slowly, methodically, I began to think about them. I concentrated on Gerasmin's corpse, stared at the blood thickening and darkening on his coat. I remembered Angela. I pictured her writhing under a hundred obscene tortures; pictured her starving; pictured her dead, that lovely face racked by fear and unspeakable sights. I felt tension gathering in my body; focusing. The thoughts sang loud and clear as I pictured the man with the patch and his sly, lecherous warning in Harley Square, and the news of next morning's proposed slaughter.

My hate bubbled-up, seethed and became a constant fire of anger within me. It was personal now, very personal. I had forgotten the other men who had died. I wanted to be there when Bezahrov arrived at 10 Downing Street. I wanted to stand up to Bezahrov and fight him and kill him for the beast he was, he and all of them.

But a bit of rationality got through to me, thank God. I went away from the bank, much as I did not want to. With one last look at Gerasmin's corpse and a promise uttered silently to him, I walked away from the river. I had one person to turn to now; one—whether he wanted to help me or not. I would force him to help me. I would transfuse my hate into his body and his mind and show him that he had no other choice.

I checked a phone directory for the address of Inspector Rohm. A cab carried me to his flat. Two flights up dingy red-carpeted stairs, three doors down the hall smelling of tobacco and liquor and sweat, and I knocked on his door. I heard his voice from within saying, "Just a moment." I took out my pistol again.

The pistol greeted him when he opened the door. His sharp blue eyes took it in, and darted to my face. "Do you remember me?" I said. "Steven Marlow. The man with the insane story?"

"I remember you, certainly," he replied, his scholarly face a bit pale.

I gestured with the gun. "Let me in."

He stepped back and I went into the flat, closing the door behind me. Rohm blinked and I gestured again. "Get your coat on."

"Where are we going?"

"Number 10, Downing Street."

"*Number 10—*" he choked. "You are mad!"

"This is part of my story," I said evenly. "A story that is not mad, a story that is not insane or unbelievable. If you don't come with me, the Prime Minister will die at ten tomorrow morning, exactly as Lord Wolters and Sir Guy Folversham died. I'm forcing you to come with me so that others will eventually believe what I say. I'm forcing you because it's the only way you'll see that what I say is true."

"What if I don't?" he asked quietly.

"I'll kill you, Inspector. Do you believe me?"

He stared at me from those probing eyes for a long minute. "No," he said finally. "But I'll get my coat."

We hailed another cab. I pushed the pistol toward the driver and told him I was taking over. With Inspector Rohm beside me, we drove to Downing Street and parked the cab. Then I began talking, while the dark hours of night raced by and the stars lay hidden behind mourning-robes of clouds. I poured out the story, the part he had heard and the part he had not heard. I told it all, every detail, every instant.

And then I said, "Now do you believe me?"

"No," he said quietly. "I don't. Are you going to kill me for thinking it's too incredible?"

"Damn you!" I shouted at him. "It won't stop here. They'll burn Europe and they'll destroy America, systematically, because it will be too incredible that such a thing could ever happen. And then they'll pour out of the East, out of Russia, and the few poor devils left alive won't ever have a chance to live like decent human beings again!"

"I am willing to take one precaution," he said as dawn began to etch itself gray on the eastern sky. A horn honked in the distance. "Lord Wolters and Folversham have died, so we can't really afford to take chances. I'd like to ring up the Yard and get a squad of men."

"Machine guns," I insisted. "Get machine guns."

"And I'll have to ring up my superior to request that the Prime Minister be removed from here for the morning. I'll need a telephone for that. I'll believe you that much Marlow—do that much for you. You haven't committed any crime *yet*."

"Get to the phone," I said, thanking God for his sense of duty; his determination to leave none of the possibilities unaccounted for. If he couldn't see the greater danger, he could at least provide for the one at hand.

I began to sweat. The morning grew brighter, or as bright as another of those lead-gray days could be. The Prime Minister was no longer at 10 Downing Street when the appointed hour came. I had seen him leave, quiet, impressive, dignified. We had to keep off those obscene things! Men like this were worth it. Ordinary men, everywhere, were worth it.

Officers were stationed in every room. The officers were armed with machine guns. I stood with Rohm, smoking nervously, wishing that I were somewhere else, wishing I could wake up from this hell's dream. From another room came the metallic chime of a clock. The hour was ten.

They came up through the floor, six of them, materializing like foul black shadows, swirling, tumbling, roiling up. Captain Bezahrov came that way too, into our room, and it was madly incredible to see a human *coming up from the underground*.

The machine guns exploded in a roaring thunder and the things broke apart in blood and screams and decaying filth. Bezahrov whirled around once and sprawled on the floor, spilling out his life. They had been transported up through the ground, *thought* into this building on their mission of destruction, only to meet quick, furious death.

We bent over Bezahrov, dying, his scarred face twitching convulsively. There were rapid questions and whispered desperate answers. A bomb. Under London. Demolish half the city. Noon. Two days from now. Noon.

"Rohm?" I whispered, "we've got to get into the underground."

He turned to me. His voice suddenly faded away into the distance and I saw his horrible sharp eyes peering into mine. *"Yes, Marlow,"* he whispered, so the others could not hear, *"into the underground."* His voice died suddenly and he stared at me.

I tried to say something. I could not. I could not speak. My throat was tight and dry and I could not say a word. In a sick horror, I heard Rohm dismiss his men, sending them back to Scotland Yard. And then I heard a voice whisper in my brain:

"Come, Marlow. Into the underground. I want to kill you before I go. You have caused me much trouble. I want to kill you *myself.*"

The voice of Inspector Rohm. The *mind* of Inspector Rohm taking me over, holding me speechless, immobile. Holding, gripping. *The bomb*—I wanted to scream. Dimly I saw the officers moving toward the street. Inspector Rohm stared at me. Inspector Rohm—

Him Who Doesn't Walk.

I heard the wild laughter of the man who called himself Inspector Rohm. It echoed a dirge in my brain until I lost consciousness.

The pattern became clear as I awoke. Somehow, in a period of half-consciousness before I opened my eyes, a mind seemed to be telling me things I wanted to know, telling me in order to torment me before I reached the end. Why did I think I had been sent to him especially, out of all others, at Scotland Yard? He had willed it. Then he had sent me away. When I returned again, he had been forced to protect the Prime Minister, because he did not want me to suspect. Did I understand?

A laugh.

He had allowed Bezahrov to die, he had not cancelled the attack even though he knew it would fail, in order to take me. He did his duty as Inspector Rohm and the Prime Minister lived. And Him Who Doesn't Walk dismissed the officers. They had not been close enough to hear Bezahrov's whispered words, you see. Thus he took me into the underground, to kill me before the bomb went off. All along, he had been watching, been waiting at certain points along the trail. Damnably clever.

The thoughts came faster now, vengeful. *Where now?* Paris, Berlin, America, anywhere. Step by step. The high ones commanded it.

Where were they? I felt my muscles aching as if some monstrous thought-hand held them. The masters were in Russia; in the East. The masters wanted the world. Had not they told us that so many times?

We were alone in the underground and no one would know about the bomb to go off in two days. Inspector Rohm could arrange to die as a hero. Strange, eh? But I did not understand him, quite . . . the Prime Minister allowed to live that I might die . . . once again I caught a conception of the violent, gigantic force of evil in Him Who Doesn't Walk. It was vindictive; personal—

Wake up, Marlow!

I opened my eyes. I was standing in a room similar to the one in which we had fought with the man with the patch. There before me floated the torso of Inspector Rohm, alive, peering at me. But—but—Great God—*he had no legs!*

From the waist down there was nothing but emptiness—invisibility. I saw the trousers, socks, shoes and shorts on the floor. The monstrous vision hung before me, grinning at me. Him Who Doesn't Walk held a pistol.

"Now, Mr. Marlow," he said quietly, "you have thirty seconds before I shoot you down." His voice was soft. "You're peering so intently at my legs." He laughed at the last word. "Thought, Mr. Marlow. The power of brain. Life where there is no life. Inspector Rohm walked on legs of *mind.*"

Mind . . . desperately, I sought for the answer. I felt it gnawing at my brain, another voice, trying to get through, trying to break the wall. I felt the weight of the pistol still in my pocket. Him Who Doesn't Walk did not think I could use it. Could I? If the voice . . . if the voice . . .

"Thirty seconds, Mr. Marlow—counting from *now.*"

I felt the sweat standing out on my face. The voice . . . the voice was coming closer, rushing with a sound of other ancient voices flying on the wind from lonely temples on snowy peaks. The spirits of men who had touched holiness, goodness, coming toward me, summoned by that prime voice to add their strength, coming, if only I could let them in. But how? I was not calling them. Who was?

"Twenty seconds. Prepare yourself, Mr. Marlow. Pray to God who does not exist." He laughed shortly and cocked the pistol. "I am going to enjoy slaying you, Mr. Marlow. You have interfered so much . . ."

Come! Come! From a thousand ancient lands someone is calling for strength. Strength and a moment of life . . . straining, fighting . . . screaming his thoughts in an effort to penetrate . . .

"Fifteen seconds, Mr. Marlow."

I am coming . . . I am trying . . . I am coming . . . call me by name . . .

I can't, I thought wildly, I don't know of these things. I don't know of powers like this.

"Ten seconds."

You must call me by name.

I can't.

Can you hear me?

Yes.

Call me by name. It rests with you. You are afraid.

Yes, I am.

Do not listen to your fear. Think of me . . . think of me . . . who am I? I am here for a moment in eternity, waiting, watching. Call me . . . the spirits of good men have filled me . . . I am yours . . . call me, the desperate voice shrieked.

"Five seconds. Goodbye, Mr. Marlow." Him Who Doesn't Walk laughed.

His finger whitened upon the trigger.

No . . . no . . . I thought. *No* . . . I waited for the bullet, and in that instant I pushed down the nauseous fear flooding over me and thought clearly . . . of course . . . of course . . . the one . . .

"*Gerasmin!*" I screamed, throwing myself forward.

Him Who Doesn't Walk started and cursed. "You fool! Gerasmin is de—"

But he was not. I had thought his name and summoned him and he stood in the room, pale, shadowy, filmy of body, one hand pointing accusingly at Him Who Doesn't Walk, and the blood still running on his chest. His lips were tight, and his eyes were closed, and that ageless face seemed to radiate a kind of unearthly light.

Him Who Doesn't Walk turned on the apparition and started firing. Wildly. It vanished as quickly as it had come, like a puff of magician's smoke. By that time, though, I had my pistol out. I shot with hateful accuracy, aiming at the figure before me, wanting to tear the legless horror to bits. Finally the smoke and the noise diminished and I looked down. I knew I would never see his true face. Inspector Rohm's face had certainly not been his.

And I had blown his head away.

I heard a rushing of wind in my mind, of the spirits, of the entities, going back to their temples against the roof of the world, back to their ancient books of goodness and truth and wisdom and light. Another sound mingled in—the voice of Gerasmin returning to the mystic realm of the dead, with a syllable of farewell. It was no word I could utter or write down, yet I understood it. He had given me the strength to call upon him, and the ancient forgotten power.

I glanced at my watch. Ten-thirty. I began to walk through the underground. At fifteen minutes before eleven, I found the bomb mechanism and broke the wires. At eleven-eight, I found Angela locked in a cell off one of the main corridors, sleeping drugged and her hair disheveled, her face thin and pale. Perhaps Him Who Doesn't Walk had forgotten her in his fury to get me. Not stopping to wonder why, I thanked God she was still alive and carried her out of the underground, up through the shop of T. Nedros into the daylight. Behind me as I walked, I heard countless scurryings. The servants, the lackeys of hell were leaving, returning to their holes, their driving life force gone. The master was dead and I hoped that another would not call them forth for ten thousand years.

They put our story in the newspapers. Not with our names, because I did not want that, and the government supported me. They told how the real Inspector Rohm—his corpse—was found by the landlady in a closet in his flat the afternoon after I destroyed Him Who Doesn't Walk. They burned out the underground with flame throwers, too, destroying the last remnants of the things I first saw that night on the *Queen of Madagascar*.

And for us, then, Angela and me, it was over. We were free. I gave up the sea and took up a landsman's trade. We married a year later, and now we have our own home and a small son growing up. Once a year we go down to the cliffs of England and stand looking out at the dark Channel and the dark sky and the darker world beyond. We remember that it came once. We remember that it is written in their books. We stand on the cliffs in the wind once a year and watch the East.

We must not forget.

THE SEEKER IN THE FORTRESS

by
Manly Wade Wellman

Manly Wade Wellman is one of the great veterans of the science fiction/fantasy field, appearing in the sf magazines as early as 1927. He is best known for his stories featuring John the Ballad Singer, but the bulk of his writing has consisted of excellent novels for younger readers. His best work has been at the shorter lengths and can be found in his collections WHO FEARS THE DEVIL? (1963) and WORSE THINGS WAITING (1973). A noted historian of the state of North Carolina, he is still going strong and producing quality work at (as these words are written) the age of seventy-nine.

One of a series of stories about the last Atlantean, "The Seeker in the Fortress" pits wizard against warrior in an exciting tale of rescue.

Trombroll the wizard had set his fortress in what had been a small, jagged crater, rather like an ornate stopper in the crumpled neck of a wineskin. Up to it on all sides came the tumbled, clotted lips of the cone. Above and within them it lodged, a sheaf of round towers with, on the tallest, a fluttering banner of red, purple and black. At the lower center, where the fitted gray rocks of the walls fused with the jumbled gray rocks of the crater, stood a mighty double door of black metal. Slits in the towers seemed ready to rain point-blanked missiles, smoking floods of boiling oil. In the distance rose greater heights, none close enough to command the fortress. On the slope below the door, Prince Feothro of Deribana stood among his captains and councillors and shrugged inside his elegant armor. The plain behind him was thronged with his horsemen and footmen, his heavy engines of war. But just then he could not think of how to use them.

"What is there to do?" he almost whined into the gilded face-bars of his helmet and, as though in answer, a mighty voice boomed from a speaking trumpet on the battlement.

"Greetings, Prince, and shortly farewell. Do you give your princely pledge to a parley?"

"It is given," called back Feothro.

The black gates opened ringingly. Out paced a figure in elaborate ceremonial mail, to halt halfway down.

"I am a herald speaking with the voice of mighty Trombroll," said this man. "Trombroll is supreme in magic. The winds and the thunder fight his battles."

"Trombroll has plagued the world long enough," returned Feothro, sternly enough. "He threatens plague and famine, and demands tribute to hold them back. Tell him we've come to destroy him. These armies are the allied might of Deribana and Varlo, sworn to end Trombroll's reign of evil. Varlo's King Zapaun who is as my father, has pledged his thrice lovely daughter, the Princess Yann, to be my consort. Let Trombroll come out and fight."

"Why should he?" inquired the herald. "We have wells of water, stores of provisions. And we have also that exemplary triumph of beauty, the Princess Yann herself."

"Princess Yann!" howled Feothro. "You lie!"

"Cast your eyes upward to where our banner flies."

All looked aloft. Two guards were visible, escorting between them a slender figure in a bright red garment. Then all three drew back out of sight.

"That was Yann," babbled Feothro. "How possibly—"

"Trombroll's accomplished spies brought word of your advance against him, also word that Princess Yann was being sent to you. Her escort was ambushed, and she was brought here." A pause, to let it sink in. "Prince Feothro, you see how impossible your situation is. If you storm us, if you seek to enter this one gateway, the unhappy Princess will die an intricate death even now being invented for her. You wouldn't let that happen to her. We give you until sunrise tomorrow to lead your host away."

With which, the herald returned through the gate. The black portals clashed shut behind him.

Feothro called upon the names of half a dozen gods, in hope that at least one would hear him. "We must do something!" he half wailed to his chieftains to both sides. "Do something, I say!"

"Do what?" asked a silver-mailed subordinate, not very helpfully.

If Feothro had a reply to that, which is highly improbable, he did not give it. He looked to where two spearmen marched an upstanding stranger toward him.

"My Lord," said one of the two, saluting, "this man has been prowling here and there among the various commands, and he only laughs at questions."

Feothro regarded the stranger with what he hoped was a terrifying scowl. He saw one as tall as himself, but broader-shouldered, deeper-chested, leaner-waisted. The fellow wore dusty sandals and a shabby blue tunic with points of white. He carried a long sword at his belt, and behind his shoulder rode a gold-mounted harp. His features were saturnine and his hair tumbled in a dark mane.

"A spy for Trombroll, no doubt," Feothro snarled.

A shake of the head. "Not I. I was passing through and saw your army gathered. I strolled over to see what was afoot."

"Looking for trouble, were you?" suggested Feothro.

"I never look for trouble. It's everywhere."

"What's your name and people, and lie no more than you can help."

Amused white teeth flashed. "I'm an Atlantean—"

"A lie at once," charged Feothro. "Atlantis is drowned, and all Atlanteans with it."

"Except for me," said the other easily. "I was swept over the sea, with a broken gate for raft, came ashore, and have wandered ever since. My name's Kardios."

A chief leaned to Feothro. "My Lord, that name is known to me. Kardios is much talked of, as an adventurer among monsters."

Again Feothro surveyed Kardios. "If that's true, if you came here only to see what we do, what then?"

Kardios shrugged, and the strings of his harp whispered. "I heard your problem. Trombroll defies you in his fortress, and you don't dare attack for fear of what he'll do to your princess. Maybe I happened along in good time to help you."

"Then you know we can't storm their gate," said Feothro testily. "How would you mount the siege?"

"That's a good question," said Kardios, using the locution for perhaps the first time in the history of the world. "I hesitate to answer it, since you know that Trombroll's spies are apt to be listening. Maybe I wouldn't exactly mount a siege?"

"If you bring Princess Yann back safely, name your reward," said Feothro, not very graciously. "If you fail—"

"Oh," said Kardios, "if I come back, I'll have her with me. Have I leave to begin?"

"Don't go beyond this host," said Feothro. "Not beyond sight of this fortress."

"Naturally." Kardios turned on his heel and headed down slope among the gathered armed bands.

As he did so, he twitched his harp forward and swept its strings. He made up words to sing, no louder than he himself could hear:

> *"The keep is strong, the keep is tall,*
> *Its gates are black as sin,*
> *It bids defiance unto all*
> *Who seek to enter in."*

He liked that, and played and sang it again as he strode on past the rearmost elements of Feothro's besieging myriad. Some distance behind him followed the two spearmen, obviously told off to keep him in sight. Kardios headed around the foot of the slope, to where he could see the other side of the fortress. No gates there, only more slits for arrows and darts and lances to be cast down. Pondering this, Kardios smiled. Again he twanged the harp:

> *"Here, mysteries are grim and deep,*
> *Here, secrets men may shun,*
> *But never have I known a keep*
> *Without more gates than one."*

Something twitched beside his sandal, and he looked down. A frog, only a frog, prettily patterned in green. Kardios nodded to it. "Thank you, little brother," he said. "You may have solved a problem."

The frog hopped into some coarse green bush, the only vegetation Kardios had seen on the whole rocky crater. Dropping to one knee, he poked into the matted growth. Sure enough, it was damp where roots delved into earth. He glanced around, to see that his two escorting guardsmen were gazing, not at him, but up at the towers. Swiftly he dived into the brush as into a pool. Crouching low, he crept along the way the frog had shown him.

A tunnel of sorts was there, with water trickling on its floor. It was not too narrow for his shoulders. As he entered on hands and knees, he was encouraged by a patch of dim light ahead. On and on he worked his way, many times his own length, until his head came out into a gloomy upright shaft, with golden radiance above. He nodded congratulations to himself. The channel joined one of the wells of which he had heard Trombroll's herald boast.

It was faced with smooth, damp stones. Climbing them would be a dire danger, even for as active a climber as Kardios. He studied the shaft narrowly and saw that a rope dangled into it. Presumably a bucket hung below. Kardios drew his sword, reached out to the point, and pulled a loop of the rope to him. He tugged at it experimentally. Perhaps it would bear his weight. It must. He sheathed the sword, caught the rope in both hands, and swung out upon it.

Up he swarmed, hand over hand, helping himself now and then with a toe in a crevice of the stone-faced wall. It was not far to the top. He caught the lip of the curb, drew himself upon it, and found himself looking into the beady eyes of a squat, puffy-faced fellow in scale armor.

"What are you doing in the well?" challenged this one.

"Weren't you told about it, you fool?" snapped Kardios in his turn. "I did the bidding of our master Trombroll, I fetch news of the besiegers. Here, help me out."

A fat hand caught his wrist and Kardios sprang out upon stone flagging. Above them rose the torchlit roof of a cavern. The man glowered at Kardios.

"I don't know you," he said. "You're not of the garrison."

"I'm Trombroll's spy captain, noddlehead," said Kardios. "Since you saw me come in, you'll bear me witness with him. Now, look down into the well. See what treasure I brought with me, lashed to the rope below."

The man bent to look down. Kardios caught him by elbow and

ankle and flung him headlong into the shaft. So swiftly did he
fall that he had no time to howl. He only splashed, far below.

Now Kardios had time to see the cave into which he had won.
Against the rough walls were bracketed blazing torches of pitchy
wood. He saw bins and trestles piled with stores, he saw rows of
tall earthenware jars of oil and wine. Plainly, this was one of
Trombroll's well-stored larders. He dipped his hand into a wine
jar, then another and another, drinking appreciatively of the best
of them. He tore a barley loaf in two, bit into it, and helped it
along with a morsel from a huge mottled cheese. Feeling refreshed,
he moved along toward where must be a door.

He found it, made of heavy wooden slabs and iron bolts. He
tried it. It was locked.

"Is that you, Smar?" challenged someone from the other side.
"Your tour of duty has long to run before I let you out."

"Help in here, friend," said Kardios at once. "Smar fell
down the well."

"Who's in yonder?" demanded the one outside.

Kardios heard a key grate in a lock. As the door swung
inward, Kardios ducked behind it. In came another armored sentry,
sword in hand. Kardios kicked the door shut again. As he did so,
his own blade flashed out and he pushed the point close to the
sentry's hairy throat.

"One sound or move without my leave and you're off duty
forever," Kardios warned. "Drop that sword. Thank you. Now,
where are we here?"

"Where but in Trombroll's deepest cellar?" gulped the sentry.

"Deepest cellar, eh? What's above here?"

"The guard chamber, and, above that, the concourse. Higher
still, defenses and Trombroll's quarters."

Kardios's extended sword was pale and keen. The sentry
sweated as he looked at it.

"How many men in the guard chamber?" Kardios inquired.

"Men?" repeated his captive. "Just now, no men." Almost a
smile with that.

"A guard chamber unguarded?" said Kardios, scowling.

"No men are there, none at all."

"You wouldn't say that curious thing if it hadn't an element
of truth," judged Kardios. "Turn your back."

The sentry obeyed. Kardios yanked open the fastening of the
coat of mail and dragged it free. He lifted off the combed helmet
and set it on his own head. "Now, cross your hands behind
you."

Kardios bound the wrists with the man's own belt. He made a
gag of a dagger sheath from that belt, and took a bunch of keys.

"I don't kill unless I must, and so you may live if you stay
here without struggling free for, say, an hour," said Kardios,
and cautiously opened the door. He saw a passage, heavily faced
with cut stones and lighted by more torches but with no sign of
life. Into the passage he stepped and closed the door behind him.

He donned the mail jacket. It fit loosely, but that was better
than tightness. He left the door unlocked behind him and went
onward.

Steps led into a dark niche, and Kardios mounted them. At the
top was another locked door. He found a key for it and went
through into what must be that guard chamber where, he had
been assured, no men would be found just then.

It was a square, lofty apartment, with arms of all sorts racked
against its walls and dangling from its beams. There were rows
of shields, barred with Trombroll's garish colors of red, purple
and black. Lances were clumped in sheafs, swords hung in
bunches like gleaming soup vegetables. There were bales of
armored jackets such as Kardios himself had captured to wear,
and heaps of helmets, combed and plumed. If Trombroll had
followers enough to bear all these arms, his fortress was well
garrisoned.

Light shone from a cluster of lamps upon a great table of
polished black wood, and on benches and chairs around this
lounged, not men but women, young women. A dozen of them,
variously and attractively clad in gold-mounted breastplates and
greaves, with shining helmets bracketing their flowerlike faces.
They had weapons, too—curved swords, short-handled axes.
One held in her hand a stout, polished pole to which was
attached by a chain a lethal-seeming globe studded with fanglike
spikes. This one rose from her seat. She was tall, cleanly
symmetrical, and her blue eyes flashed loftily.

"Sentry, have you forgotten that we are not to be intruded
upon without order from Lord Trombroll?" she addressed him.
"We know your sort, and the unsoldierly motives that bring you
here. Speak your business, if any, and get out."

"And be glad you're able to get out," added another, almost
as tall and fully as beautiful. The armor the girls wore might
have protected them, here and there, against attack, but not very
thoroughly against admiration. All of them had their shapely
hands on their weapons.

"Shall I go before I sing you a song?" asked Kardios, summoning the most agreeable smile of which he was capable. He took his harp in his hands and touched the strings. He hoped words would come:

> *"Each is armored, each has a blade,*
> *Whetted and bright and keen,*
> *Each is a splendid warrior maid,*
> *Fair as a gracious queen. . . ."*

He deplored the scanning of that, but not so his audience. They squealed applause.

"Beautiful!" cried the one who had first addressed him. "We were so bored here. We don't know you, do we? What's your name, harp-striker?"

"Call me Kardios."

"If I call you Kardios, call me Elwa. I'm under-officer of this guard force. We're here because Trombroll won't put men on guard over Princess Yann. He fears they'll fall in love with her and help her escape, though I don't see why."

"Princess Yann?" said Kardios, as though the name were strange to him. "I'm new in this fortress—"

"And welcome, at least to us," beamed one of the girls.

"I didn't know she was here, in this guard chamber."

"We'd call you stupid if you weren't so handsome and melodious a singer," said Elwa, with a smile. "What's the rest of your song? For there must be more."

"Of course," said Kardios, who had been making up a second verse. He struck tender chords and sang again:

> *"Who dares face them with dauntless heart?*
> *A smile or a tender glance*
> *Would strike him down like a deadly dart,*
> *A trenchant sword or a lance."*

More applause, far more than Kardios thought his effort deserved. The girls flocked around him like doves to a handful of bread crumbs. Their smiles and tender glances might well accomplish the fate he had sung about. Elwa poured wine from a patterned jug into a silver-banded cup.

"Drink, Kardios," she bade, handing it to him. "I think I can guess why you came here—to see if we're as appetizing as rumored."

He drank. The wine was better than that in the cellars. "Far more appetizing," he made haste to assure her.

"More, do you think, than Yann in the cage yonder?"

She gestured toward the far end of the chamber. It was closed off with bars that seemed forged of gold. In the shadows within lurked something, somebody. Kardios took a step that way.

"No," warned Elwa, lifting her flaillike mace across his chest. "Trombroll wants no man of his following to look at her or speak to her. If we have to kill you, we'll sorrow, but we must."

"Which hardly encourages me to try speech with her," said Kardios, sitting on a bench to sip more wine. "Of course, if Trombroll should find me here—"

"We'll see he doesn't find you," promised a girl whose armor seemed uncomfortably tight on her splendid, tawny body. "Sing some more, it's prosy on duty down here."

"Prosy on duty," repeated Kardios, with his most agreeable smile. "That's like poetry, my dear. I'll dedicate this song to you."

He swept the strings and began:

> *"If Trombroll's wise, as people say,*
> *And shrewd, as people guess,*
> *Then why does Trombroll stay away*
> *From all this loveliness?"*

> *"Why does he keep to his towers*
> *When he could enter here,*
> *All among these lovely flowers—"*

Three loud thumps rang from the ceiling overhead.

"He's coming," breathed Elwa. "Quick, Kardios, get behind these cloaks."

She hustled him to a corner behind a garment-hung rack. Peeping out, Kardios saw a strangely spiny figure descend, as on an invisible cord, from a trapdoor above. All the girls snapped becomingly to attention.

"What report of my prisoner?" asked a deep, dull voice, like water flowing under snow.

"She stays quiet, says nothing, noble Lord Trombroll," said Elwa.

"I've come to take her away for an important interview," croaked Trombroll.

Peering between two cloaks, Kardios studied the wizard. Trombroll was in armor from toe to neck, a bizarre armor indeed. It was of drab metal and it bristled all over with ugly spikes and blades, so that Trombroll looked like a profusely spiny lizard. Even the backs of his gauntlets sprouted points. No sane man would grapple Trombroll.

Only his face was bare and, in Kardios's opinion, Trombroll would have done well to cover that, too. The nose stuck out like one of the armor spikes, and beneath it was a wide, taut-lipped mouth and a chin that slanted so far back as to be almost no chin at all. By contrast, Trombroll's brow bulged as though ready to burst. His gloomily gray hair fell to his shoulders and was bound with a fillet studded ostentatiously with many-colored jewels. Trombroll's eyes, pale as a crocodile's, fixed on the cage at the far end of the room.

"Bring her out," he ordered.

Two of the prettiest hastened to obey. One of them opened the cage door with a huge key. There was a murmur of argument, and then both the warrior maids reached in and fetched the prisoner out, holding her by the wrists. They marched her toward where Trombroll waited.

At once Kardios saw why Elwa and the others had spoken so disparagingly of Yann. She was smaller than the smallest of them, and considerably fairer than the fairest. Her flaming red gown was snug enough to accentuate every contour of her supple, dainty figure. Her lustrous dark hair was dressed in two winglike sweeps. Her blue eyes were large, though not large enough to be out of proportion to her rosy, round-chinned face. As she was led up to Trombroll, those eyes regarded him with concentrated dislike.

He laughed gratingly. One of his gloved hands took her by the chin. It looked like a sea urchin on a pink seashell.

"Princess," he said, "that fool who says you're betrothed to him lingers outside, not knowing whether to go or stay. It would be discourteous to leave you shut up here while you wait for him to make up his mind. I thought to offer you some entertainment."

"You'll please let me go," she said, in a voice that would, as Kardios thought, sing delightfully. She shrank from Trombroll's spiny person.

"I venture to assure you of the contrary. Wait until you see what is prepared for you, above here."

He shifted his grip to her elbow. "Relax in my hold," he said, "and here we go."

With that, he rose in the air, carrying Yann with him. They soared like leaves in a gale. They vanished through the trapdoor in the ceiling. All the warrior maids gazed upward after them, so intently that they were not aware that Kardios had come out from hiding.

"What Trombroll sees in her I can't understand," said Elwa acidly. She turned and saw Kardios. "It's all right, he's gone."

Kardios looked up at the trap. It was closed from above, apparently by a simple lid. "Where did he take her?"

"None of us knows that," said Elwa. "His apartments are far above here—this guard room is in the cellar of the fortress, and the towers reach high, high above us."

"I'd like to see," said Kardios, tossing aside the captured helmet and shucking off the shirt of mail.

All gazed with admiration at his revealed muscles of chest and arm. "Armor is so cumbersome," said one. "Shall we take off ours?"

"If my duty did not call me away, that would be delightful," smiled Kardios as he sprang lightly upon the table.

The trap door was at arm's length above his head. He prodded upward with his sword point. The lid shifted at the pressure, and he edged it clear of the opening. Pallid light was visible above him. Quickly he sheathed his sword and bestowed his harp at his back.

"Lovely ladies," he said, "I'd stay with you for hours if it weren't for that duty, but—"

With that, he leaped upward. His hand clutched through the trap and hooked on its rim. He heard them all gasp as he hauled himself powerfully upward, got hold with his other hand, and dragged his body to where he could get a knee upon the surface overhead. Next moment, he had hoisted himself clear of the trap and upon a paved floor.

His first sensation was of space, vast space, enough for an arena such as some nations used for bloody contests between armed men and fierce beasts. As he stood up, he half expected to see some great, abhorrent creature stealing toward him. But he was all alone on that bare, broad floor, with pale, plastered walls distantly all around him, up to a ceiling that gave off flickers of light. No sight of Trombroll or Yann. He looked this way and that.

He saw an uneven line slanting up the wall nearest him. It was a flight of railless stairs mounting to a corner, where another flight went across the adjacent wall to meet yet another. Those stairs mounted all the way around, and at the upper end of the highest flight appeared a dark blotch, a cavelike passage of some sort. That was the only hint of a way out of this mighty enclosure.

Kardios headed for the stairs. His feet struck sound from the floor and it echoed back to him. He hoped nobody was listening. He reached the bottom of the stairs. They were of cut stone, and narrow—room for only one to mount them. If he met somebody coming down, there would be no passing. As he walked up, the floor below dropped away. It would be a considerable fall down there. Kardios asked himself how he would accomplish the mission for which he had so lightly volunteered.

So close did he press to the wall, his hand against it and his eyes on those narrow steps, that he was not aware of other movement until it was almost upon him from above. Then he looked, to where four armored men descended, one behind the other. They bore jagged weapons that combined deadly features of both sword and axe.

"Who are you?" one of them growled. "Give the watchword."

"Never mind watchwords," replied Kardios. "I'm on special duty, I have a message for Trombroll."

"He went sailing from below, up to his own place," said another. "Had somebody with him, I thought. What's your message?"

"It's not for underlings," said Kardios.

"We know our orders," blustered the first speaker, burly and shaggy-jawed. "And we don't know you." He descended close and held out a big hand. "Give me your sword, you're under arrest until you can account for yourself."

"Arrest me if you dare," said Kardios, sliding his own weapon into view.

A grumbling laugh. "You fool, we're four to your one."

"Not as many as that, my friend," said Kardios, and shot out his point, swift as the head of a snake. It drove between joints of armor, and he cleared it as the big man tumbled from the stairs.

"Only three to one now," said Kardios, flashing his teeth.

The others came down toward him, but two of them could not stand side by side on the stairs. One slashed at Kardios, who parried expertly. Another dropped to his knees just behind his fellow and tried to stab past him at Kardios.

That made things difficult enough for laughter on the part of Kardios. He fended off a blow from the man standing erect, disengaged and lunged at the kneeling one. A howl of pain told him he had struck home. Up whirled his sword to pierce the belly of the other. He pushed close to the wall and let both of them go slamming overside in a fall many times a man's height.

"And now," said Kardios, his eyes twinkling at the remaining adversary, "it's only one against one. I never counted that as serious odds at all."

But that fourth man had seen three of his comrades perish in almost as many breaths. He turned and fled up the steps. Kardios followed, shaking drops of blood from his sword.

Where the steps turned at a corner was a door. The fugitive dragged it open and darted through like a frightened rabbit, slamming the door behind him. When Kardios came to that point, he could barely see the crack where the door closed. There was no knob or latch, and he could not pry it open with his sword. He negotiated the turn of the stairs and went on upward. The stairs at this new angle seemed narrower, if anything. Kardios forebore to look down.

There was movement, off there in the broad emptiness above the floor so far beneath. He spared a glance.

It flew. It was something woolly white, as big, perhaps, as a man, sliding here and there on outflung ribbed wings. It made a graceful arc as it headed toward Kardios. He saw that it had a face of some sort, bright black eyes anyway, and flaps of ears like a donkey's. As it came winging close, he saw that it had claws, too, both on its drawn-up legs and at the knuckle ends of its wings.

It swooped in at him, like a bat after a beetle.

Kardios ducked low, one knee to a stair. As the fluffy bulk struck the wall against which he had just stood, he smelled its stale odor. A thin shriek buzzed his ears. The flying thing retreated with a clumsy flip-flop of wings, Kardios glimpsed a splash of blood, like a ribbon across its bushy white chest. It recovered, dipped its wings right and left, and came at him again.

"You learn slowly, don't you?" Kardios addressed it, rising with his back pressed to the wall, his sword dancing before him.

It flew upon him. He saw the jaws gape, the rows of gleaming, daggerlike teeth. A bite from them might take off a man's arm or leg. The head craned forward in flight, driving close.

And Kardios reaped that head from its neck, as a harvester fells a tussock of grain with his sickle. Blood spurted into his own face as he watched his enemy go down, its wings not even fluttering.

Kardios mopped his lean, bloody cheeks. He wondered what that thing had been, where it had come from and why. Then he told himself that wondering was profitless. He resumed his climb of the stairs.

They grew ever narrower and steeper. Or they seemed to, which just now amounted to much the same thing. He felt like a spider that crept along a crack in a rock. The steps made a turn at another corner, and he took the new direction. Above him the ceiling glowed. If he looked at it, his vision would blur. On he went, on, on. He turned at the next corner. Three corners, he was on the ascent's last stage. There above him would be the way out of this dizzying ordeal.

A rumble above. Down the steps jumped and rolled something. A great stone cylinder, as big as a barrel, straight at him.

There was only one thing to do, and Kardios did it. As the rushing, whirling weight almost reached and struck him, he leaped high and let it thunder beneath him. He had a sense that its sides were inscribed with characters or diagrams, but could not be sure. As he came down on the stairs he almost lost footing, but dropped to his knees and one hand, while the cylinder tumbled away below him.

Instantly he was up again. Without pausing to think, he charged up the remaining stairs to the opening above, and into it. A figure crouched there. It tried to turn and flee into shadows beyond, but Kardios clutched at a shaggy neck. Powerfully he slammed the captive against the rocky wall and set his sword point at the fellow's throat.

"Were you supposed to kill me?" he inquired softly. "Make ready to depart into whatever reward waits for tricksters."

"No, don't!" cried the other. It was the survivor of the quartet that had challenged Kardios on his way up. "Have mercy—you must be someone great and powerful, and I'm just a minor servitor of Trombroll."

"True on all counts," said Kardios. "You've picked the most unlucky day of your life to ignore Trombroll's orders." And he made his sword point dance against the jugular.

"Wh-what orders?"

"Now you confess to negligence and defective hearing. I'm entrusted with the most vitally important information from out-side, I'm directed to bring it to Trombroll. He left those lower levels before I could reach him, but he must have said I was coming."

"Maybe he told the under-officer." A submissive cringing in Kardios's grasp. "You killed him on the stairs. I'm only a common warder, I thought you were invading. I turned the Flying Fear loose upon you, then tried to crush you with a stone from up here." The voice shook miserably. "It's plain from how you handle your sword that you're important. I ask mercy."

Kardios let him go. "Very well, if you prove trustworthy. Begin by conducting me to Trombroll."

"To Trombroll?" a helpless wave of the hands. "Yes, but I won't go in where he is, I'd never dare call myself to his attention."

"Then take me to his door," commanded Kardios. "If you do that promptly and courteously, perhaps I'll say a good word for you when we examine your blundering treatment of me."

. The man led him along a corridor lighted with small crumbs of radiance in its vaulted roof. Other passages showed to either side, but Kardios's guide led him straight ahead, up a ramp, and to where a door stood at the end of the corridor. It was a dark door, of a material hard to identify, without latch or knob in sight.

"Here is where Trombroll makes his quarters," said the guardsman. "How is it you do not know?"

"I knew all the time, I wondered if you did," Kardios replied readily. "Now go back to your post. If you're lonely without your three companions, perhaps you'll have time to think things over."

Gladly the man trotted away. Kardios studied the door, wondering how to enter.

It might swing open outward or inward, but he saw no indication of where hinges might be. He gave his attention to its snug-fitting edge, all the way around. At the bottom appeared a slight gap. Stooping, Kardios investigated the space with his fingers, then got those fingers under the door and dragged upward.

The door rose like a curtain, barely whispering in its grooves. He looked into a soft dimness. Then he walked in and drew the door down again behind him.

For an instant he thought he had stepped into some sort of grove or thicket. Then he saw that the throng of trees had trunks of enamelled bronze, with golden leaves set closely with emeralds. Underfoot, a gravelly mass of rubies crunched beneath his sandals. Walking with the utmost care to keep his feet silent, he moved among those jewelled trees toward light beyond. At the edge of them, with convenient artificial foliage to mask him, he looked into a spacious compartment, lighted by brilliant lamps.

It was a hall ornamented so richly as to bring into question the owner's taste. What the walls were made of Kardios could not see, for they were draped and swaddled in showily embroidered hangings. The ceiling beams were each of a different sort of rare wood, carved in intricate designs and polished to metallic brightness. The floor was a glowing white stone, pretentiously studded with stars, whorls and rings of coins of all sizes and devices. At the very center stood a table, apparently fashioned from a single green gem—if it were an emerald, then that had been the biggest emerald in all the world. Upon it were golden and silver dishes of appetizing foods, flagons for wine and goblets in which to pour it. On two elaborate gold-mounted benches sat Trombroll and the Princess Yann.

Naturally, Kardios first looked at Yann. At that close, clear view, she was even more splendidly beautiful than she had been in the guard chamber. She held her red gown close to her delectable bosom with a white hand sparkling with rings. The rays of the lamps struck blue lights from her heavy hair. Her eyes gleamed the brighter for disdain of Trombroll.

As for Trombroll, he had doffed his unbecoming spiny armor and gloves, and sat in an over-decorated tunic and tights. His legs looked amusingly bandy. One hand held the brownly roasted drumstick of a fowl. He eyed Yann fixedly.

"You won't flourish without eating well, and this dinner is excellent," he droned out as he chewed.

"I urge you to better manners and better sense," smirked Trombroll unpleasantly. "That fool Geothro knows he must lead his army away, to save your life. If your life is saved, you must decide what to do with it."

"You're fantastic," Yann told him.

"True," and Trombroll bowed, "for a wizard deals in fantastics. I'm a distinguished figure in my profession, respected by many and feared wherever I'm known. My fortress is stocked with wealth and power enough to persuade your father, Zapaun of Varlo, that I'd be a proper son-in-law. I'm personally attracted to you. We'd do well together."

She turned her lovely face away.

"Consider me without prejudice," Trombroll urged, biting into the drumstick. "I was considered handsome in my younger days. Many now think me impressive."

"You look like an anteater," pronounced Yann accurately.

"I put off my armor to please you—"

"You put it off because you don't fear that any of your men will venture here and assassinate you." As Yann spoke, her magnificent eyes fixed themselves on Kardios where he lurked. "If one came here, you'd scream with fright."

"I put off my armor," said Trombroll again, "so that I could embrace you without hurting your tender skin. Why don't you look at me?"

Yann's eyes were fixed upon Kardios. She winked one of them, in a fashion dazzlingly conspiratorial.

"Enter the assassin, Trombroll," she said brightly.

Kardios stepped into the open, sword drawn. Trombroll sprang up and whirled around. His eyes popped wide and his nose twitched.

"I've been watching as he stole upon you, Trombroll," said Yann's triumphant voice. "Now I'll watch as he kills you."

Trombroll's face twisted. "I suppose this means another of those conspiracies," he growled. "But I can count on a faithful servant. If I but make the proper sound—"

"You have no servants at hand," said Kardios. "There would have been one at the door to this place. Even if there were any, you wouldn't live to see him answer your call. The business here can best be settled among us three."

"I don't recognize you, you must be one of the least important of my garrison, and one of the most ignorant," said Trombroll. "I keep my men at a distance. The servant on whose faithfulness I count isn't of your sort."

He snapped his fingers. From under the emerald table, a shaggy mass humped itself into view.

Kardios's first impression was of something that might have developed into a wolf, a tiger, or a big ape, and had stopped developing before it had chosen which. It rose on ungainly hind legs, with its forelimbs slightly lifted and handlike paws hooked, talon fashion. Its muscular body was tufted over with dark, coarse hair. It showed unpleasantly dingy fangs, and its gray features writhed and furrowed repulsively. It shuffled toward Kardios, as tall as he and more powerfully built.

"I can trust him," declared Trombroll.

"Can he trust you?" asked Kardios.

He advanced his right foot and lifted his sword. The motion made the strings of his harp whisper at his shoulder. The bizarre creature stopped its advance, staring with eyes like cold pink fire.

"If you're a music lover, I truly hate to do this," said Kardios.

He did it, a swift lunge with the point that gashed the hairy shoulder. The creature retreated with a grating cry of pain.

Trombroll, watching, snapped his fingers twice. His grotesque servitor charged at a crouch, strangely swift.

Kardios sidestepped and slashed. His edge drove into the shallow skull, and the beast went into an uncouth, flopping fall. It writhed its forelimbs, clenched its paws, and lay motionless. Kardios faced toward Trombroll and Yann at the table.

Yann sat at ease. She smiled, as though in applause of sprightly music. Trombroll lounged erect. "I'm amazed that he didn't stand against your blade," he said.

"He was wide open to a drawing cut," said Kardios.

"Something failed of my charm that should have shielded him from you," said Trombroll, drawing his own long sword. "I'll be more careful in shielding myself." He lifted hilt to jaw in salute. "Shall we make sport for the lady?"

"Since she seems to enjoy it," said Kardios, crossing his weapon upon Trombroll's.

Then there was fierce, swift fencing. Kardios wondered if he should not have kept the mail shirt. His own sword seemed to glance away from a cut at Trombroll, who made no effort to parry. It was slice, counter, jab, dodge.

"Ha!" cried Trombroll, lunging. Kardios struck the point out of line and extended his own blade in a swift return. That thrust, too, glided off. Trombroll gave him a lopsided smile.

"A very minor charm, my poor foolish adversary," he mocked. "It keeps metal from approaching me."

Yann watched raptly. If she worried about Kardios, it was not evident in her expression.

"If you're so protected, why fear your own followers?" asked Kardios, dancing clear.

"They know the charm; they might try something other than sword or axe." Trombroll grinned more broadly. He licked his thin lips with a thinner tongue. Suddenly he flung out his arms, sword well out of line.

"Strike at me," he invited. "At the throat, if you like."

Kardios darted his point. It slid harmlessly to the side, as though from an invisible solidity, and he whipped it back only just in time to parry Trombroll's slicing edge.

"You're indeed under magical protection," said Kardios. "Congratulations."

He dropped his own sword. It rang on the floor, close to the silent form of the dead guardian-monster.

"Congratulations accepted," jeered Trombroll, "but not capitulation. I think," and he glanced sidelong at Yann, "that her gracious highness wants to see more bloodshed. I'll shed it, naturally."

"Hardly naturally," amended Kardios, sliding leftward. Trombroll also shifted position. The hairy body lay between them.

"Now," he said, and slid his right foot forward as he extended his arm.

Kardios beat the blade aside with a slap of his left hand. As Trombroll followed the lunge, his foot found a pool of blood. He shambled forward. Kardios spun in close. Down came his spread right hand, its tensed edge striking like a hatchet. It drove against Trombroll's exposed nape, with a sound like that of a shattering stick. Yann cried out in amazement or applause. Trombroll smashed down on his face and lay as motionless as his slain servitor.

Kardios wrung the hand with which he had struck, then stooped and recovered his sword. He wiped it with an embroidered napkin from the table.

"That was a gamble," he said quietly. "Maybe with the odds in my favor, but a gamble anyway. His magic guarded him only from metal. My hand is of flesh and blood and bone."

Yann rose to her feet, her eyes bewitchingly wide. "You killed him," she whispered.

"I always kill when I strike them like that," said Kardios. "It breaks the neck every time."

"You were magnificent," she was saying. "You—but I don't even know your name."

"It's Kardios," he said. "We can go now. But let's take a souvenir to Prince Feothro."

Straddling the body of Trombroll, he smote with the edge of Trombroll's sword. Trombroll's head rolled away from the severed neck.

"Ah," said Kardios. "His magic died with him."

He stooped to lift the head, but Yann was before him. "Let me," she said, and picked it up by the gray locks. "It's a comfort to look at, without hearing his disgusting addresses. But how shall we get out?"

"It can't be far to the door. We won't have to go to those cellars again."

He took her arm, which trembled at his touch. They went out at an inner door. Halfway down a stairway an armored guardsman came hurrying up to them. Kardios set his hand to hilt, but the fellow only goggled at Trombroll's head in Yann's grasp.

"Then it's true," he cried. "He's dead—Trombroll who made us fear him, serve him, steal and kill for him!"

"He's dead enough, yes," Kardios assured him. "If it brings you happiness, that's good."

The guardsman went running back downstairs. "Did you hear, comrades?" he whooped. "Trombroll's dead, we're free! He can't order us any more, and all that treasure we gathered for him is ours now!"

A many-voiced howl of joy rose from below. The guardsman turned and gestured at Kardios.

"We owe you everything," he said happily. "Come on, take your pick of anything in all those treasure rooms."

"No, thank you," said Kardios. "I promised to bring this lady out to where her friends are waiting for her."

They paced along a great hall at the bottom of the stairs. Doors stood open to both sides. In the chambers within these, Kardios saw happy members of the garrison, off duty at last and snatching at things of considerable value.

"Surely you're one of the world's highest heroes," Yann said. "Heedless of peril, heedless of wealth. Kardios is there nothing of reward you want, nothing I can grant you?"

She bestowed upon him her most winning smile. It was very winning indeed.

"Princess, when I left Feothro outside, he was of half a mind to lead his men away," said Kardios. "If we don't hurry, we may find that he hasn't waited for us."

"Feothro?" repeated Yann, as though the name were strange to her.

"Up ahead yonder is what looks like the gate."

They went there together. It was closed with a mighty bar of wrought metal, which Kardios lifted from its brackets. With a push of his foot, he drove one wing of the gate wide open and led Yann out into the last of the afternoon light.

As they emerged side by side, Kardios felt a myriad eyes fixed upon him. Feothro's hosts waited on the plain at the foot of the slope, phalanxes of spearmen, squadrons of cavalry, trains of siege equipment. All those thousands stared upward as sunset dimmed into twilight.

Then a wild chorus of cheers shook the earth and sky. Weapons and banners waved. Kardios escorted Yann down from the doorway.

Resplendent officers surrounded them. Eagerly these questioned, and Kardios told, in as few words as he could manage, of his entry into the fortress and his destruction of Trombroll.

"His men are left leaderless, disorganized," he finished. "They can't plan or act without him. You can round them up before they go away with all the plunder."

"Your Highness," a young officer addressed Yann, "our gracious Prince Feothro will be overjoyed to see you safe."

"I'll take the Princess to him," said Kardios, and led her in the direction the officer pointed.

Feothro came at an undignified run, several commanders following at his heels. He flung wide his arms. "Yann, my beloved," he quavered.

Yann threw Trombroll's head at Feothro's feet. It rolled there like a pumpkin fallen from a shelf. "Kardios, do you know Feothro?" she asked.

"Never mind Kardios, my dearest one," said Feothro. "You and I are together again—"

"Kardios," said Yann again, turning to look for him.

Kardios was gone.

"I want Kardios," said Yann, as one who was used to having whatever she wanted.

Feothro grimaced, for those commanders were listening intently. "Why do you want Kardios, my beloved?" he asked.

"He saved me," she replied. "Single-handed, he saved me, single-handed against all the fortress yonder. He killed Trombroll and I don't know how many others. Find him, I want him."

Feothro tried to take her hand. "But this Kardios is only a vagabond adventurer," he argued. "He doesn't even have a country, his kingdom of Atlantis was swallowed by the sea."

"He shall have a new kingdom," announced Yann authoritatively. "My father, Zapaun of Varlo, will welcome him as a son-in-law. He'll be the handsomest man at our court. All other women will envy me." She turned from Feothro. "Where did he go? Bring him back."

Feothro scowled among those artless listeners.

"Yes, bring Kardios back," he shrilled suddenly. "I'll have a

few words with him, a very few words, and then the executioner."
His voice rose like a scream. "Send my bodyguard to fetch
him!"

Men scurried obediently in the twilight. Shouts answered shouts.
There were orders and inquiries, to little purpose.

Kardios had strode swiftly away through more distant ranks,
and headed around the slope of the crater. He was thankful for
the coming of darkness. The voices of the searchers bellowed
behind him. Usually he enjoyed the admiration of women. But
just now, what with the way Feothro was acting, the situation
might turn out to be awkward; even for Kardios.

Far away to the east, the moon's rim peeped above the
horizon. Kardios pointed his feet in that direction, for he had no
other guide away from where both Yann and Feothro wanted
him, for widely different reasons.

THE WALL AROUND THE WORLD

by
Theodore Cogswell

*A professor of English at Keystone Junior College in
Pennsylvania since 1965, Ted Cogswell has produced a
brace of outstanding short stories in the sf magazines
since the 1950s. These can be found in two collections—
THE WALL AROUND THE WORLD (1962) and THE
THIRD EYE (1968)—and combine creative ideas with
frequent good humor. Unfortunately, his stories do not
appear often enough, and his many admirers wish that
he would give us more. Professor Cogswell has been an
active member of the Science Fiction Writers of America from its founding, serving as editor of its FORUM
and as secretary of the organization.*

*A story about an attempt to discover the nature of
one's own world, "The Wall Around the World" also
illustrates the concept of the self-fulfilling prophecy.*

The wall that went all the way around the World had always
been there, so nobody paid much attention to it—except Porgie.
Porgie was going to find out what was on the other side of

it—assuming there was another side—or break his neck trying. He was going on fourteen, an age that tends to view the word *impossible* as a meaningless term invented by adults for their own peculiar purposes. But he recognized that there were certain practical difficulties involved in scaling a glassy-smooth surface that rose over a thousand feet straight up. That's why he spent a lot of time watching the eagles.

This morning, as usual, he was late for school. He lost time finding a spot for his broomstick in the crowded rack in the school yard, and it was exactly six minutes after the hour as he slipped guiltily into the classroom.

For a moment, he thought he was safe. Old Mr. Wickens had his back to him and was chalking a pentagram on the blackboard.

But just as Porgie started to slide into his seat, the schoolmaster turned and drawled, "I see Mr. Mills has finally decided to join us."

The class laughed, and Porgie flushed.

"What's your excuse this time, Mr. Mills?"

"I was watching an eagle," said Porgie lamely.

"How nice for the eagle. And what was he doing that was of such great interest?"

"He was riding up on the wind. His wings weren't flapping or anything. He was over the box canyon that runs into the East wall, where the wind hits the Wall and goes up. The eagle just floated in circles, going higher all the time. You know, Mr. Wickens, I'll bet if you caught a whole bunch of eagles and tied ropes to them, they could lift you right up to the top of the wall!"

"That," said Mr. Wickens, "is possible—if you could catch the eagles. Now, if you'll excuse me, I'll continue with the lecture. When invoking Elementals of the Fifth Order, care must be taken to . . ."

Porgie glazed his eyes and began to think up ways and means to catch some eagles.

The next period, Mr. Wickens gave them a problem in Practical Astrology. Porgie chewed his pencil and tried to work on it, but couldn't concentrate. Nothing came out right—and when he found he had accidentally transposed a couple of signs of the zodiac at the very beginning, he gave up and began to draw plans for eagle traps. He tried one, decided it wouldn't work, started another—

"Porgie!"

He jumped. Mr. Wickens, instead of being in front of the

class, was standing right beside him. The schoolmaster reached down, picked up the paper Porgie had been drawing on, and looked at it. Then he grabbed Porgie by the arm and jerked him from his seat.

"Go to my study!"

As Porgie went out the door, he heard Mr. Wickens say, "The class is dismissed until I return!"

There was a sudden rush of large, medium, and small-sized boys out of the classroom. Down the corridor to the front door they pelted, and out into the bright sunshine. As they ran past Porgie, his cousin Homer skidded to a stop and accidentally on purpose jabbed an elbow into his ribs. Homer, usually called "Bull Pup" by the kids because of his squat build and pugnacious face, was a year older than Porgie and took his seniority seriously.

"Wait'll I tell Dad about this. You'll catch it tonight!" He gave Porgie another jab and then ran out into the schoolyard to take command of a game of Warlock.

Mr. Wickens unlocked the door to his study and motioned Porgie inside. Then he shut and locked it carefully behind him. He sat down in the high-backed chair behind his desk and folded his hands.

Porgie stood silently, hanging his head, filled with that helpless guilty anger that comes from conflict with superior authority.

"What were you doing instead of your lesson?" Mr. Wickens demanded.

Porgie didn't answer.

Mr. Wickens narrowed his eyes. The large hazel switch that rested on top of the bookcase beside the stuffed owl lifted lightly into the air, drifted across the room, and dropped into his hand.

"Well?" he said, tapping the switch on the desk.

"Eagle traps," admitted Porgie. "I was drawing eagle traps. I couldn't help it. The Wall made me do it."

"Proceed."

Porgie hesitated for a moment. The switch tapped. Porgie burst out, "I want to see what's on the other side! There's no magic that will get me over, so I've got to find something else!"

Tap, went the switch. "Something else?"

"If a magic way was in the old books, somebody would have found it already!"

Mr. Wickens rose to his feet and stabbed one bony finger accusingly at Porgie. "Doubt is the mother of damnation!"

Porgie dropped his eyes to the floor and wished he was someplace else.

"I see doubt in you. Doubt is evil, Porgie, *evil!* There are ways permitted to men and ways forbidden. You stand on the brink of the fatal choice. Beware that the Black Man does not come for you as he did for your father before you. Now, bend over!"

Porgie bent. He wished he'd worn a heavier pair of pants.

"Are you ready?"

"Yes, sir," said Porgie sadly.

Mr. Wickens raised the switch over his head. Porgie waited. The switch slammed—but on the desk.

"Straighten up," Mr. Wickens said wearily. He sat down again. "I've tried pounding things into your head, and I've tried pounding things on your bottom, and one end is as insensitive as the other. Porgie, can't you understand that you aren't supposed to try and find out new things? The Books contain everything there is to know. Year by year, what is written in them becomes clearer to us."

He pointed out the window at the distant towering face of the Wall that went around the World. "Don't worry about what is on the other side of that! It may be a place of angels or a place of demons—the Books do not tell us. But no man will know until he is ready for that knowledge. Our broomsticks won't climb that high, our charms aren't strong enough. We need more skill at magic, more understanding of the strange unseen forces that surround us. In my grandfather's time, the best of the broomsticks wouldn't climb over a hundred feet in the air. But Adepts in the Great Tower worked and worked until now, when the clouds are low, we can ride right up among them. Someday we will be able to soar all the way to the top of the Wall—"

"Why not now?" Porgie asked stubbornly. "With eagles."

"Because we're not *ready*," Mr. Wickens snapped. "Look at mind-talk. It was only thirty years ago that the proper incantations were worked out, and even now there are only a few who have the skill to talk across the miles by just thinking out their words. Time, Porgie—it's going to take time. We were placed here to learn the Way, and everything that might divert us from the search is evil. Man can't walk two roads at once. If he tries, he'll split himself in half."

"Maybe so," said Porgie. "But birds get over the Wall, and they don't know any spells. Look, Mr. Wickens, if everything is magic, how come magic won't work on everything? Like this, for instance—''

He took a shiny quartz pebble out of his pocket and laid it on the desk.

Nudging it with his finger, he said:

> *"Stone fly,*
> *Rise on high,*
> *Over cloud*
> *And into sky."*

The stone didn't move.

"You see, sir? If words work on broomsticks, they should work on stones, too."

Mr. Wickens stared at the stone. Suddenly it quivered and jumped into the air.

"That's different," said Porgie. "You took hold of it with your mind. Anybody can do that with little things. What I want to know is why the words won't work by themselves."

"We just don't know enough yet," said Mr. Wickens impatiently. He released the stone and it clicked on the desktop. "Every year we learn a little more. Maybe by your children's time we'll find the incantation that will make everything lift." He sniffed. "What do you want to make stones fly for, anyhow? You get into enough trouble just throwing them."

Porgie's brow furrowed. "There's a difference between *making* a thing do something, like when I lift it with my hand or mind, and putting a spell on it so it does the work by itself, like a broomstick."

There was a long silence in the study as each thought his own thoughts.

Finally Mr. Wickens said, "I don't want to bring up the unpleasant past, Porgie, but it would be well to remember what happened to your father. His doubts came later than yours—for a while he was my most promising student—but they were just as strong."

He opened a dark drawer, fumbled in it for a moment, and brought out a sheaf of papers yellow with age. "This is the paper that damned him—*An Enquiry into Non-Magical Methods of Levitation*. He wrote it to qualify for his Junior Adeptship." He threw the paper down in front of Porgie as if the touch of it defiled his fingers.

Porgie started to pick it up.

Mr. Wickens roared, "Don't touch it! It contains blasphemy!"

Porgie snatched back his hand. He looked at the top paper and saw a neat sketch of something that looked like a bird—except that it had two sets of wings, one in front and one in back.

Mr. Wickens put the papers back in the desk drawer. His disapproving eyes caught and held Porgie's as he said, "If you want to go the way of your father, none of *us* can stop you." His voice rose sternly, "But there is one who can . . . Remember the Black Man, Porgie, for his walk is terrible! There are fires in his eyes and no spell may defend you against him. When he came for your father, there was darkness at noon and a high screaming. When the sunlight came back, they were gone—and it is not good to think where."

Mr. Wickens shook his head as if overcome at the memory and pointed toward the door. "Think before you act, Porgie. Think well!"

Porgie was thinking as he left, but more about the sketch in his father's paper than about the Black Man.

The orange crate with the two boards across it for wings had looked something like his father's drawing, but appearances had been deceiving. Porgie sat on the back steps of his house feeling sorry for himself and alternately rubbing two tender spots on his anatomy. Though they were at opposite ends, and had different immediate causes, they both grew out of the same thing. His bottom was sore as a result of a liberal application of his uncle's hand. His swollen nose came from an aerial crack-up.

He'd hoisted his laboriously contrived machine to the top of the woodshed and taken a flying leap in it. The expected soaring glide hadn't materialized. Instead, there had been a sickening fall, a splintering crash, a momentary whirling of stars as his nose banged into something hard.

He wished now he hadn't invited Bull Pup to witness his triumph, because the story'd gotten right back to his uncle—with the usual results.

Just to be sure the lesson was pounded home, his uncle had taken away his broomstick for a week—and just so Porgie wouldn't sneak out, he'd put a spell on it before locking it away in the closet.

"Didn't feel like flying, anyway," Porgie said sulkily to himself, but the pretense wasn't strong enough to cover up the loss. The gang was going over to Red Rocks to chase bats as soon as the sun went down, and he wanted to go along.

He shaded his eyes and looked toward the western Wall as he heard a distant halloo of laughing voices. They were coming in high and fast on their broomsticks. He went back to the woodshed so they wouldn't see him. He was glad he had when they swung low and began to circle the house yelling for him and Bull Pup. They kept hooting and shouting until Homer flew out of his bedroom window to join them.

"Porgie can't come," he yelled. "He got licked and Dad took his broom away from him. Come on, gang!"

With a quick looping climb, he took the lead and they went hedge-hopping off toward Red Rocks. Bull Pup had been top dog ever since he got his big stick. He'd zoom up to five hundred feet, hang from his broom by his knees and then let go. Down he'd plummet, his arms spread and body arched as if he were making a swan dive—and then, when the ground wasn't more than a hundred feet away, he'd call and his broomstick would arrow down after him and slide between his legs, lifting him up in a great sweeping arc that barely cleared the treetops.

"Showoff!" muttered Porgie and shut the woodshed door on the vanishing stick-riders.

Over on the work bench sat the little model of paper and sticks that had got him into trouble in the first place. He picked it up and gave it a quick shove into the air with his hands. It dove toward the floor and then, as it picked up speed, tilted its nose toward the ceiling and made a graceful loop in the air. Leveling off, it made a sudden veer to the left and crashed against the woodshed wall. A wing splintered.

Porgie went to pick it up. "Maybe what works for little things doesn't work for big ones," he thought sourly. The orange crate and the crossed boards had been as close an approximation of the model as he had been able to make. Listlessly, he put the broken glider back on his work bench and went outside. Maybe Mr. Wickens and his uncle and all the rest were right. Maybe there was only one road to follow.

He did a little thinking about it and came to a conclusion that brought forth a secret grin. He'd do it their way—but there wasn't any reason why he couldn't hurry things up a bit. Waiting for his grandchildren to work things out wasn't getting *him* over the wall.

Tomorrow, after school, he'd start working on his new idea, and this time maybe he'd find the way.

In the kitchen, his uncle and aunt were arguing about him. Porgie paused in the hall that led to the front room and listened.

"Do you think I like to lick the kid? I'm not some kind of an ogre. It hurt me more than it hurt him."

"I notice you were able to sit down afterward," said Aunt Olga dryly.

"Well, what else could I do? Mr. Wickens didn't come right out and say so, but he hinted that if Porgie didn't stop mooning around, he might be dropped from school altogether. He's having an unsettling effect on the other kids. Damn it, Olga, I've done everything for that boy I've done for my own son. What do you want me to do, stand back and let him end up like your brother?"

"You leave my brother out of this! No matter what Porgie does, you don't have to beat him. He's still only a little boy."

There was a loud snort. "In case you've forgotten, dear, he had his thirteenth birthday last March. He'll be a man pretty soon."

"Then why don't you have a man-to-man talk with him?"

"Haven't I tried? You know what happens everytime. He gets off with these crazy questions and ideas of his and I lose my temper and pretty soon we're back where we started." He threw up his hands. "I don't know what to do with him. Maybe that fall he had this afternoon will do some good. I think he had a scare thrown into him that he won't forget for a long time. Where's Bull Pup?"

"Can't you call him Homer? It's bad enough having his friends call him by that horrible name. He went out to Red Rocks with the other kids. They're having a bat hunt or something."

Porgie's uncle grunted and got up. "I don't see why that kid can't stay at home at night for a change. I'm going in the front room and read the paper."

Porgie was already there, flipping the pages of his schoolbooks and looking studious. His uncle settled down in his easy chair, opened his paper, and lit his pipe. He reached out to put the charred match in the ashtray, and as usual the ashtray wasn't there.

"Damn that woman," he muttered to himself and raised his voice: "Porgie."

"Yes, Uncle Veryl?"

"Bring me an ashtray from the kitchen, will you please? Your aunt has them all out there again."

"Sure thing," said Porgie and shut his eyes. He thought of the kitchen until a picture of it was crystal-clear in his mind. The

beaten copper ashtray was sitting beside the sink where his aunt
had left it after she had washed it out. He squinted the little eye
inside his head, stared hard at the copper bowl, and whispered:

> "Ashtray fly,
> Follow eye."

Simultaneously he lifted with his mind. The ashtray quivered
and rose slowly into the air.

Keeping it firmly suspended, Porgie quickly visualized the
kitchen door and the hallway and drifted it through.

"Porgie!" came his uncle's angry voice.

Porgie jumped, and there was a crash in the hallway outside as
the bowl was suddenly released and crashed to the floor.

"How many times have I told you not to levitate around the
house? If it's too much work to go out to the kitchen, tell me and
I'll do it myself."

"I was just practicing," mumbled Porgie defensively.

"Well, practice outside. You've got the walls all scratched up
from banging things against them. You know you shouldn't fool
around with telekinesis outside sight range until you've mastered
full visualization. Now go and get me that ashtray."

Crestfallen, Porgie went out the door into the hall. When he
saw where the ashtray had fallen, he gave a silent whistle.
Instead of coming down the center of the hall, it had been three
feet off course and heading directly for the hall table when he let
it fall. In another second, it would have smashed into his aunt's
precious black alabaster vase.

"Here it is, Uncle," he said, taking it into the front room.
"I'm sorry."

His uncle looked at his unhappy face, sighed and reached out
and tousled his head affectionately.

"Buck up, Porgie. I'm sorry I had to paddle you this afternoon.
It was for your own good. Your aunt and I don't want you to get
into any serious trouble. You know what folks think about
machines." He screwed up his face as if he'd said a dirty word.
"Now, back to your books—we'll forget all about what happened today. Just remember this, Porgie: If there's anything you
want to know, don't go fooling around on your own. Come and
ask me, and we'll have a man-to-man talk."

Porgie brightened. "There's something I have been wondering
about."

"Yes?" said his uncle encouragingly.

"How many eagles would it take to lift a fellow high enough to see what was on the other side of the Wall?"

Uncle Veryl counted to ten—very slowly.

The next day Porgie went to work on his new project. As soon as school was out, he went over to the Public Library and climbed upstairs to the main circulation room.

"Little boys are not allowed in this section," the librarian said. "The children's division is downstairs."

"But I need a book," protested Porgie. "A book on how to fly."

"This section is only for adults."

Porgie did some fast thinking. "My uncle can take books from here, can't he?"

"I suppose so."

"And he could send me over to get something for him, couldn't he?"

The librarian nodded reluctantly.

Porgie prided himself on never lying. If the librarian chose to misconstrue his questions, it was her fault, not his.

"Well, then," he said, "do you have any books on how to make things fly in the air?"

"What kind of things?"

"Things like birds."

"Birds don't have to be made to fly. They're born that way."

"I don't mean real birds," said Porgie. "I mean birds you make."

"Oh, Animation. Just a second, let me visualize." She shut her eyes and a card catalogue across the room opened and shut one drawer after another. "Ah, that might be what he's looking for," she murmured after a moment, and concentrated again. A large brass-bound book came flying out of the stacks and came to rest on the desk in front of her. She pulled the index card out of the pocket in the back and shoved it toward Porgie. "Sign your uncle's name here."

He did and then, hugging the book to his chest, got out of the library as quickly as he could.

By the time Porgie had worked three-quarters of the way through the book, he was about ready to give up in despair. It was all grown-up magic. Each set of instructions he ran into either used words he didn't understand or called for unobtainable ingredients like powdered unicorn horns and the blood of red-headed female virgins.

He didn't know what a virgin was—all his uncle's encyclopedia had to say on the subject was that they were the only ones who could ride unicorns—but there was a red-head by the name of Dorothy Boggs who lived down the road a piece. He had a feeling, however, that neither she nor her family would take kindly to a request for two quarts of blood, so he kept on searching through the book. Almost at the very end he found a set of instructions he thought he could follow.

It took him two days to get the ingredients together. The only thing that gave him trouble was finding a toad—the rest of the stuff, though mostly nasty and odoriferous, was obtained with little difficulty. The date and exact time of the experiment was important and he surprised Mr. Wickens by taking a sudden interest in his Practical Astrology course.

At last, after laborious computations, he decided everything was ready.

Late that night, he slipped out of bed, opened his bedroom door a crack, and listened. Except for the usual night noises and resonant snores from Uncle Veryl's room, the house was silent. He shut the door carefully and got his broomstick from the closet—Uncle Veryl had relented about that week's punishment.

Silently he drifted out through his open window and across the yard to the woodshed.

Once inside, he checked carefully to see that all the windows were covered. Then he lit a candle. He pulled a loose floorboard up and removed the book and his assembled ingredients. Quickly, he made the initial preparations.

First there was the matter of molding the clay he had taken from the graveyard into a rough semblance of a bird. Then, after sticking several white feathers obtained from last Sunday's chicken into each side of the figure to make wings, he anointed it with a noxious mixture he had prepared in advance.

The moon was just setting behind the Wall when he began the incantation. Candlelight flickered on the pages of the old book as he slowly and carefully pronounced the difficult words.

When it came time for the business with the toad, he almost didn't have the heart to go through with it; but he steeled himself and did what was necessary. Then, wincing, he jabbed his forefinger with a pin and slowly dropped the requisite three drops of blood down on the crude clay figure. He whispered:

> *"Clay of graveyard,*
> *White cock's feather,*
> *Eye of toad,*
> *Rise together!"*

Breathlessly he waited. He seemed to be in the middle of a circle of silence. The wind in the trees outside had stopped and there was only the sound of his own quick breathing. As the candlelight rippled, the clay figure seemed to quiver slightly as if it were hunching for flight.

Porgie bent closer, tense with anticipation. In his mind's eye, he saw himself building a giant bird with wings powerful enough to lift him over the Wall around the World. Swooping low over the schoolhouse during recess, he would wave his hands in a condescending gesture of farewell, and then as the kids hopped on their sticks and tried to follow him, he would rise higher and higher until he had passed the ceiling of their brooms and left them circling impotently below him. At last he would sweep over the Wall with hundreds of feet to spare, over it and then down—down into the great unknown.

The candle flame stopped flickering and stood steady and clear. Beside it, the clay bird squatted, lifeless and motionless.

Minutes ticked by and Porgie gradually saw it for what it was—a smelly clod of dirt with a few feathers tucked in it. There were tears in his eyes as he picked up the body of the dead toad and said softly, "I'm sorry."

When he came in from burying it, he grasped the image of the clay bird tightly in his mind and sent it swinging angrily around the shed. Feathers fluttered behind it as it flew faster and faster until in disgust he released it and let it smash into the rough boards of the wall. It crumbled into a pile of foul-smelling trash and fell to the floor. He stirred it with his toe, hurt, angry, confused.

His broken glider still stood where he had left it on the far end of his work bench. He went over and picked it up.

"At least you flew by yourself," he said, "and I didn't have to kill any poor little toads to make you."

Then he juggled it in his hand, feeling its weight, and began to wonder. It had occurred to him that maybe the wooden wings on his big orange-box glider had been too heavy.

"Maybe if I could get some long, thin poles," he thought, "and some cloth to put across the wings . . ."

* * *

During the next three months, there was room in Porgie's mind for only one thing—the machine he was building in the roomy old cave at the top of the long hill on the other side of Arnett's grove. As a result, he kept slipping further and further behind at school.

Things at home weren't too pleasant, either—Bull Pup felt it was his duty to keep his parents fully informed of Porgie's short-comings. Porgie didn't care, though. He was too busy. Every minute he could steal was spent in either collecting materials or putting them together.

The afternoon the machine was finally finished, he could hardly tear himself away from it long enough to go home for dinner. He was barely able to choke down his food, and didn't even wait for dessert.

He sat on the grass in front of the cave, waiting for darkness. Below, little twinkling lights marked the villages that stretched across the plain for a full forty miles. Enclosing them like encircling arms stretched the dark and forbidding mass of the Wall. No matter where he looked, it stood high against the night. He followed its curve with his eyes until he had turned completely around, and then he shook his fist at it.

Patting the ungainly mass of the machine that rested on the grass beside him, he whispered fiercely, "I'll get over you yet. Old *Eagle* here will take me!"

Old *Eagle* was an awkward, boxkite-like affair; but to Porgie she was a thing of beauty. She had an uncovered fuselage composed of four long poles braced together to make a rectangular frame, at each end of which was fastened a large wing.

When it was dark enough, he climbed into the open frame and reached down and grabbed hold of the two lower members. Grunting, he lifted until the two upper ones rested under his armpits. There was padding there to support his weight comfortably once he was airborne. The bottom of the machine was level with his waist and the rest of him hung free. According to his thinking, he should be able to control his flight by swinging his legs. If he swung forward, the shifting weight should tilt the nose down; if he swung back, it should go up.

There was only one way to find out if his ifs were right. The *Eagle* was a heavy contraption. He walked awkwardly to the top of the hill, the cords standing out on his neck. He was scared as he looked down the long steep slope that stretched out before him—so scared that he was having trouble breathing. He swallowed twice in a vain attempt to moisten his dry throat, and then lunged forward, fighting desperately to keep his balance as his wobbling steps gradually picked up speed.

Faster he went, and faster, his steps turning into leaps as the wing surfaces gradually took hold. His toes scraped through the long grass and then they were dangling in free air.

He was aloft.

Not daring to even move his head, he slanted his eyes down and to the left. The earth was slipping rapidly by a dozen feet below him. Slowly and cautiously, he swung his feet back. As the weight shifted, the nose of the glider rose. Up, up he went, until he felt a sudden slowing down and a clumsiness of motion. Almost instinctively, he leaned forward again, pointing the nose down in a swift dip to regain flying speed.

By the time he reached the bottom of the hill, he was a hundred and fifty feet up. Experimentally, he swung his feet a little to the left. The glider dipped slightly and turned. Soaring over a clump of trees, he felt a sudden lifting as an updraft caught him.

Up he went—ten, twenty, thirty feet—and then slowly began to settle again.

The landing wasn't easy. More by luck than by skill, he came down in the long grass of the meadow with no more damage than a few bruises. He sat for a moment and rested, his head spinning with excitement. He had flown like a bird, without his stick, without uttering a word. There *were* other ways than magic!

His elation suddenly faded with the realization that, while gliding down was fun, the way over the Wall was *up*. Also, and of more immediate importance, he was half a mile from the cave with a contraption so heavy and unwieldy that he could never hope to haul it all the way back up the hill by himself. If he didn't get it out of sight by morning, there was going to be trouble, serious trouble. People took an unpleasant view of machines and those who built them.

Broomsticks, he decided, had certain advantages, after all. They might not fly very high, but at least you didn't have to walk home from a ride.

"If I just had a great big broomstick," he thought, "I could lift the *Eagle* up with it and fly her home."

He jumped to his feet. It might work!

He ran back up the hill as fast as he could and finally, very much out of breath, reached the entrance of the cave. Without waiting to get back his wind, he jumped on his stick and flew down to the stranded glider.

Five minutes later, he stepped back and said:

> *"Broomstick fly,*
> *Rise on high,*
> *Over cloud*
> *And into sky."*

It didn't fly. It couldn't. Porgie had lashed it to the framework of the *Eagle*. When he grabbed hold of the machine and lifted, nine-tenths of its weight was gone, canceled out by the broomstick's lifting power.

He towed it back up the hill and shoved it into the cave. Then he looked uneasily at the sky. It was later than he had thought. He should be home and in bed—but when he thought of the feeling of power he had had in his flight, he couldn't resist hauling the *Eagle* back out again.

After checking the broomstick to be sure it was still fastened tightly to the frame, he went swooping down the hill again. This time when he hit the thermal over the clump of trees, he was pushed up a hundred feet before he lost it. He curved through the darkness until he found it again and then circled tightly within it.

Higher he went and higher, higher than any broomstick had ever gone!

When he started to head back, though, he didn't have such an easy time of it. Twice he was caught in downdrafts that almost grounded him before he was able to break loose from the tugging winds. Only the lifting power of his broomstick enabled him to stay aloft. With it bearing most of the load, the *Eagle* was so light that it took just a flutter of air to sweep her up again.

He landed the glider a stone's throw from the mouth of his cave.

"Tomorrow night!" he thought exultantly as he unleashed his broomstick. "Tomorrow night!"

There was a tomorrow night, and many nights after that. The *Eagle* was sensitive to every updraft, and with care he found he could remain aloft for hours, riding from thermal to thermal. It was hard to keep his secret, hard to keep from shouting the news, but he had to. He slipped out at night to practice, slipping back in again before sunrise to get what sleep he could.

He circled the day of his fourteenth birthday in red and waited. He had a reason for waiting.

In the World within the Wall, fourteenth birthdays marked the boundary between the little and the big, between being a big child and a small man. Most important, they marked the time when one was taken to the Great Tower where the Adepts lived and given a full-sized broomstick powered by the most potent of spells, sticks that would climb to a full six hundred feet, twice the height that could be reached by the smaller ones the youngsters rode.

Porgie needed a man-sized stick, needed that extra power, for he had found that only the strongest of updrafts would lift him past the three-hundred-foot ceiling where the lifting power of his little broomstick gave out. He had to get up almost as high as the Wall before he could make it across the wide expanse of flat plain that separated him from the box canyon where the great wind waited.

So he counted the slowly passing days and practiced flying during the rapidly passing nights.

The afternoon of his fourteenth birthday found Porgie sitting on the front steps expectantly, dressed in his best and waiting for his uncle to come out of the house. Bull Pup came out and sat down beside him.

"The gang's having a coven up on top of old Baldy tonight," he said. "Too bad you can't come."

"I can go if I want to," said Porgie.

"How?" said Bull Pup and snickered. "You going to grow wings and fly? Old Baldy's five hundred feet up and your kid stick won't lift you that high."

"Today's my birthday."

"You think you're going to get a new stick?"

Porgie nodded.

"Well, you ain't. I heard Mom and Dad talking. Dad's mad because you flunked Alchemy. He said you had to be taught a lesson."

Porgie felt sick inside, but he wouldn't let Bull Pup have the satisfaction of knowing it.

"I don't care," he said. "I'll go to the coven if I want to. You just wait and see."

Bull Pup was laughing when he hopped on his stick and took off down the street. Porgie waited an hour, but his uncle didn't come out.

He went into the house. Nobody said anything about his new broomstick until after supper. Then his uncle called him into the living room and told him he wasn't getting it.

"But, Uncle Veryl, you promised!"

"It was a conditional promise, Porgie. There was a big *if* attached to it. Do you remember what it was?"

Porgie looked down at the floor and scuffed one toe on the worn carpet. "I tried."

"Did you really, son?" His uncle's eyes were stern but compassionate. "Were you trying when you fell asleep in school today? I've tried talking with you and I've tried whipping you and neither seems to work. Maybe this will. Now you run upstairs and get started on your studies. When you can show me that your marks are improving, we'll talk about getting you a new broomstick. Until then, the old one will have to do."

Porgie knew that he was too big to cry, but when he got to his room, he couldn't help it. He was stretched out on his bed with his face buried in the pillows when he heard a hiss from the window. He looked up to see Bull Pup sitting on his stick, grinning malevolently at him.

"What do you want?" sniffed Porgie.

"Only little kids cry," said Bull Pup.

"I wasn't crying. I got a cold."

"I just saw Mr. Wickens. He was coming out of that old cave back of Arnett's grove. He's going to get the Black Man, I'll bet."

"I don't know anything about that old cave," said Porgie, sitting bolt upright on his bed.

"Oh, yes, you do. I followed you up there one day. You got a machine in there. I told Mr. Wickens and he gave me a quarter. He was real interested."

Porgie jumped from his bed and ran toward the window, his face red and his fists doubled. "I'll fix you!"

Bull Pup backed his broomstick just out of Porgie's reach, and then stuck his thumbs in his ears and waggled his fingers. When Porgie started to throw things, he gave a final taunt and swooped away toward old Baldy and the coven.

Porgie's uncle was just about to go out in the kitchen and fix himself a sandwich when the doorbell rang. Grumbling, he went out into the front hall. Mr. Wickens was at the door. He came into the house and stood blinking in the light. He seemed uncertain as to just how to begin.

"I've got bad news for you," he said finally. "It's about Porgie. Is your wife still up?"

Porgie's uncle nodded anxiously.

"She'd better hear this, too."

Aunt Olga put down her knitting when they came into the living room.

"You're out late, Mr. Wickens."

"It's not of my own choosing."

"Porgie's done something again," said his uncle.

Aunt Olga sighed. "What is it this time?"

Mr. Wickens hesitated, cleared his throat, and finally spoke in a low, hushed voice: "Porgie's built a machine. The Black Man told me. He's coming after the boy tonight."

Uncle Veryl dashed up the stairs to find Porgie. He wasn't in his room.

Aunt Olga just sat in her chair and cried shrilly.

The moon stood high and silver-lit the whole countryside. Porgie could make out the world far below him almost as if it were day. Miles to his left, he saw the little flickering fires on top of old Baldy where the kids were holding their coven. He fought an impulse and then succumbed to it. He circled the *Eagle* over a clump of trees until the strong rising currents lifted him almost to the height of the Wall. Then he twisted his body and banked over toward the distant red glowing fires.

Minutes later, he went silently over them at eight hundred feet, feeling out the air currents around the rocks. There was a sharp downdraft on the far side of Baldy that dropped him suddenly when he glided into it, but he made a quick turn and found untroubled air before he fell too far. On the other side, toward the box canyon, he found what he wanted, a strong, rising current that seemed to have no upward limits.

He fixed its location carefully in his mind and then began to circle down toward the coven. Soon he was close enough to make out individual forms sitting silently around their little fires.

"Hey, Bull Pup," he yelled at the top of his lungs.

A stocky figure jumped to its feet and looked wildly around for the source of the ghostly voice.

"Up here!"

Porgie reached in his pocket, pulled out a small pebble and chucked it down. It cracked against a shelf of rock four feet from Bull Pup. Porgie's cousin let out a howl of fear. The rest of the kids jumped up and reared back their heads at the night sky, their eyes blinded by firelight.

"I told you I could come to the coven if I wanted to," yelled Porgie, "but now I don't. I don't have any time for kid stuff; I'm going over the Wall!"

During his last pass over the plateau he wasn't more than thirty feet up. As he leaned over, his face was clearly visible in the firelight.

Placing one thumb to his nose, he waggled his fingers and chanted, "nyah, nyah, nyah, you can't catch me!"

His feet were almost scraping the ground as he glided over the drop-off. There was an anxious second of waiting and then he felt the sure, steady thrust of the up-current against his wings.

He looked back. The gang was milling around, trying to figure out what had happened. There was an angry shout of command from Bull Pup, and after a moment of confused hesitation they all made for their brooms and swooped up into the air.

Porgie mentally gauged his altitude and then relaxed. He was almost at their ceiling and would be above it before they reached him.

He flattened out his glide and yelled, "Come on up! Only little kids play that low!"

Bull Pup's stick wouldn't rise any higher. He circled impotently, shaking his fist at the machine that rode serenely above him.

"You just wait," he yelled. "You can't stay up there all night. You got to come down some time, and when you do, we'll be waiting for you."

"Nyah, nyah, nyah," chanted Porgie and mounted higher into the moonlit night.

When the updraft gave out, he wasn't as high as he wanted to be, but there wasn't anything he could do about it. He turned and started a flat glide across the level plain toward the box canyon. He wished now that he had left Bull Pup and the other kids alone. They were following along below him. If he dropped down to their level before the canyon winds caught him, he was in trouble.

He tried to flatten his glide still more, but instead of saving altitude, he went into a stall that dropped him a hundred feet before he was able to regain control. He saw now that he could never make it without dropping to Bull Pup's level.

Bull Pup saw it, too, and let out an exultant yell: "Just you wait! You're going to get it good!"

Porgie peered over the side into the darkness where his cousin rode, his pug face gleaming palely in the moonlight.

"Leave him alone, gang," Bull Pup shouted. "He's mine!"

The rest pulled back and circled slowly as the *Eagle* glided quietly down among them. Bull Pup darted in and rode right alongside Porgie.

He pointed savagely toward the ground: "Go down or I'll knock you down!"

Porgie kicked at him, almost upsetting his machine. He wasn't fast enough. Bull Pup dodged easily. He made a wide circle and came back, reaching out and grabbing the far end of the *Eagle's* front wing. Slowly and maliciously, he began to jerk it up and down, twisting violently as he did so.

"Get down," he yelled, "or I'll break it off!"

Porgie almost lost his head as the wrenching threatened to throw him out of control.

"Let go!" he screamed, his voice cracking.

Bull Pup's face had a strange excited look on it as he gave the wing another jerk. The rest of the boys were becoming frightened as they saw what was happening.

"Quit it, Bull Pup!" somebody called. "Do you want to kill him?"

"Shut up or you'll get a dose of the same!"

Porgie fought to clear his head. His broomstick was tied to the frame of the *Eagle* so securely that he would never be able to free it in time to save himself. He stared into the darkness until he caught the picture of Bull Pup's broomstick sharply in his mind. He'd never tried to handle anything that big before, but it was that or nothing.

Tensing suddenly, he clamped his mind down on the picture and held it hard. He knew that words didn't help, but he uttered them anyway:

> *"Broomstick stop,*
> *Flip and Flop!"*

There was a sharp tearing pain in his head. He gritted his teeth and held on, fighting desperately against the red haze that threatened to swallow him. Suddenly there was a half-startled, half-frightened squawk from his left wingtip, and Bull Pup's stick jerked to an abrupt halt, gyrating so madly that its rider could hardly hang on.

"All right, the rest of you," screamed Porgie. "Get going or I'll do the same thing to you!"

They got, arcing away in terrified disorder. Porgie watched as they formed a frightened semicircle around the blubbering Bull Pup. With a sigh of relief, he let go with his mind.

As he left them behind in the night, he turned his head back and yelled weakly, "Nyah, nyah, nyah, you can't catch me!"

He was only fifty feet off the ground when he glided into the far end of the box canyon and was suddenly caught by the strong updraft. As he soared in a tight spiral, he slumped down against the arm-rests, his whole body shaking in delayed reaction.

The lashings that held the front wing to the frame were dangerously loose from the manhandling they had received. One more tug and the whole wing might have twisted back, dumping him down on the sharp rocks below. Shudders ran through the *Eagle* as the supports shook in their loose bonds. He clamped both hands around the place where the rear wing spar crossed the frame and tried to steady it.

He felt his stick's lifting power give out at three hundred feet. The *Eagle* felt clumsy and heavy, but the current was still enough to carry him slowly upward. Foot by foot he rose toward the top of the Wall, losing a precious hundred feet once when he spiraled out of the updraft and had to circle to find it. A wisp of cloud curled down from the top of the Wall and he felt a moment of panic as he climbed into it.

Momentarily, there was no left or right or up or down. Only damp whiteness. He had the feeling the *Eagle* was falling out of control; but he kept steady, relying on the feel for the air he had gotten during his many practice flights.

The lashings had loosened more. The full strength of his hands wasn't enough to keep the wing from shuddering and trembling. He struggled resolutely to maintain control of ship and self against the strong temptation to lean forward and throw the *Eagle* into a shallow dive that would take him back to normalcy and safety.

He was almost at the end of his resolution when with dramatic suddenness he glided out of the cloud into the clear moon-touched night. The up-current under him seemed to have lessened. He banked in a gentle arc, trying to find the center of it again.

As he turned, he became aware of something strange, something different, something almost frightening. For the first time in his life, there was no Wall to block his vision, no vast black line stretching through the night.

He was above it!

There was no time for looking. With a loud *ping*, one of the lashings parted and the leading edge of the front wing flapped violently. The glider began to pitch and yaw, threatening to nose over into a plummeting dive. He fought for mastery, swinging his legs like desperate pendulums as he tried to correct the erratic side swings that threatened to throw him out of control. As he fought, he headed for the Wall.

If he were to fall, it would be on the other side. At least he would cheat old Mr. Wickens and the Black Man.

Now he was directly over the Wall. It stretched like a wide road underneath him, its smooth top black and shining in the moonlight. Acting on quick impulse, he threw his body savagely forward and to the right. The ungainly machine dipped abruptly and dove toward the black surface beneath it.

Eighty feet, seventy, sixty, fifty—he had no room to maneuver, there would be no second chance—thirty, twenty—

He threw his weight back, jerking the nose of the *Eagle* suddenly up. For a precious second the wings held, there was a sharp breaking of his fall; then, with a loud, cracking noise, the front wing buckled back in his face. There was a moment of blind whirling fall and a splintering crash that threw him into darkness.

Slowly, groggily, Porgie pulled himself up out of the broken wreckage. The *Eagle* had made her last flight. She perched precariously, so near the outside edge of the wall that part of her rear wing stretched out over nothingness.

Porgie crawled cautiously across the slippery wet surface of the top of the Wall until he reached the center. There he crouched down to wait for morning. He was exhausted, his body so drained of energy that in spite of himself he kept slipping into an uneasy sleep.

Each time he did, he'd struggle back to consciousness trying to escape the nightmare figures that scampered through his brain. He was falling, pursued by wheeling, batlike figures with pug faces. He was in a tiny room and the walls were inching in toward him and he could hear the voice of Bull Pup in the distance chanting, "You're going to get it." And then the room turned into a long, dark corridor and he was running. Mr. Wickens was close behind him, and he had long, sharp teeth and he kept yelling, "Porgie! Porgie!"

He shuddered back to wakefulness, crawled to the far edge of the Wall and, hanging his head over, tried to look down at the Outside World. The clouds had boiled up and there was nothing underneath him but gray blankness hiding the sheer thousand foot drop. He crawled back to his old spot and looked toward the east, praying for the first sign of dawn. There was only blackness there.

He started to doze off again and once more he heard the voice: "Porgie! Porgie!"

He opened his eyes and sat up. The voice was still calling, even though he was awake. It seemed to be coming from high up and far away.

It came closer, closer, and suddenly he saw it in the darkness—a black figure wheeling above the Wall like a giant crow. Down it came, nearer and nearer, a man in black with arms outstretched and long fingers hooked like talons!

Porgie scrambled to his feet and ran, his feet skidding on the slippery surface. He looked back over his shoulder. The black figure was almost on top of him. Porgie dodged desperately and slipped.

He felt himself shoot across the slippery surface toward the edge of the Wall. He clawed, scrabbling for purchase. He couldn't stop. One moment he felt wet coldness slipping away under him; the next, nothingness as he shot out into the dark and empty air.

He spun slowly as he fell. First the clouds were under him and they tipped and the star-flecked sky took their places. He felt cradled, suspended in time. There was no terror. There was nothing.

Nothing—until suddenly the sky above him was blotted out by a plummeting black figure that swooped down on him, hawk-like and horrible.

Porgie kicked wildly. One foot slammed into something solid and for an instant he was free. Then strong arms circled him from behind and he was jerked out of the nothingness into a world of falling and fear.

There was a sudden strain on his chest and then he felt himself being lifted. He was set down gently on the top of the Wall.

He stood defiant, head erect, and faced the black figure.

"I won't go back. You can't make me go back."

"You don't have to go back, Porgie."

He couldn't see the hooded face, but the voice sounded strangely familiar.

"You've earned your right to see what's on the other side," it said. Then the figure laughed and threw back the hood that partially covered his face.

In the bright moonlight, Porgie saw Mr. Wickens!

The schoolmaster nodded cheerfully. "Yes, Porgie, I'm the Black Man. Bit of a shock, isn't it?"

Porgie sat down suddenly.

"I'm from the Outside," said Mr. Wickens, seating himself

carefully on the slick black surface. "I guess you could call me a sort of observer."

Porgie's spinning mind couldn't catch up with the new ideas that were being thrown at him. "Observer?" he said uncomprehendingly. "Outside?"

"Outside. That's where you'll be spending your next few years. I don't think you'll find life better there, and I don't think you'll find it worse. It'll be different, though, I can guarantee that." He chuckled. "Do you remember what I said to you in my office that day—that Man can't follow two paths at once, that Mind and Nature are bound to conflict? That's true, but it's also false. You can have both, but it takes two worlds to do it.

"Outside, where you're going, is the world of the machines. It's a good world, too. But the men who live there saw a long time ago that they were paying a price for it; that control over Nature meant that the forces of the Mind were neglected, for the machine is a thing of logic and reason, but miracles aren't. Not yet. So they built the Wall and they placed people within it and gave them such books and such laws as would insure development of the powers of the Mind. At least they hoped it would work that way—and it did."

"But—but why the Wall?" asked Porgie.

"Because their guess was right. There is magic." He pulled a bunch of keys from his pocket. "Lift it, Porgie."

Porgie stared at it until he had the picture in his mind and then let his mind take hold, pulling with invisible hands until the keys hung high in the air. Then he dropped them back into Mr. Wickens' hand.

"What was that for?"

"Outsiders can't do that," said the schoolmaster. "And they can't do conscious telepathy—what you call mind-talk—either. They can't because they really don't believe such things can be done. The people inside the Wall do, for they live in an atmosphere of magic. But once these things are worked out, and become simply a matter of training and method, then the ritual, the mumbo-jumbo, the deeply ingrained belief in the existence of supernatural forces will be no longer necessary.

"These phenomena will be only tools that anybody can be trained to use, and the crutches can be thrown away. Then the Wall will come tumbling down. But until then—" he stopped and frowned in mock severity—"there will always be a Black

Man around to see that the people inside don't split themselves up the middle trying to walk down two roads at once.''

There was a lingering doubt in Porgie's eyes. "But you flew without a machine.''

The Black Man opened his cloak and displayed a small, gleaming disk that was strapped to his chest. He tapped it. "A machine, Porgie. A machine, just like your glider, only of a different sort and much better. It's almost as good as levitation. Mind and Nature . . . magic and science . . . they'll get together eventually.''

He wrapped his cloak about him again. "It's cold up here. Shall we go? Tomorrow is time enough to find out what is Outside the Wall that goes around the World.''

"Can't we wait until the clouds lift?'' asked Porgie wistfully. "I'd sort of like to see it for the first time from up here.''

"We could,'' said Mr. Wickens, "but there is somebody you haven't seen for a long time waiting for you down there. If we stay up here, he'll be worried.''

Porgie looked up blankly. "I don't know anybody Outside. I—'' He stopped suddenly. He felt as if he were about to explode. "Not my father!''

"Who else? He came out the easy way. Come, now, let's go and show him what kind of man his son has grown up to be. Are you ready?''

"I'm ready,'' said Porgie.

"Then help me drag your contraption over to the other side of the Wall so we can drop it inside. When the folk find the wreckage in the morning, they'll know what the Black Man does to those who build machines instead of tending to their proper business. It should have a salutary effect on Bull Pup and the others.''

He walked over to the wreckage of the *Eagle* and began to tug at it.

"Wait,'' said Porgie. "Let me.'' He stared at the broken glider until his eyes began to burn. Then he gripped and pulled.

Slowly, with an increasing consciousness of mastery, he lifted until the glider floated free and was rocking gently in the slight breeze that rippled across the top of the great Wall. Then, with a sudden shove, he swung it far out over the abyss and released it.

The two stood silently, side by side, watching the *Eagle* pitch downward on broken wings. When it was lost in the darkness below, Mr. Wickens took Porgie in his strong arms and stepped confidently to the edge of the Wall.

"Wait a second," said Porgie, remembering a day in the schoolmaster's study and a switch that had come floating obediently down through the air. "If you're from Outside, how come you can do lifting?"

Mr. Wickens grinned. "Oh, I was born Inside. I went over the Wall for the first time when I was just a little older than you are now."

"In a glider?" asked Porgie.

"No," said the Black Man, his face perfectly sober. "I went out and caught myself a half-dozen eagles."

THE PEOPLE OF THE BLACK CIRCLE

by
Robert E. Howard

The story of Robert E. Howard is truly stranger than fiction. A physically robust young man, he could not cope with the death of his mother in 1936 and killed himself. He was thirty years old. Before his tragic death he had produced a considerable body of fiction which has been undergoing an enormous revival in recent years. Howard wrote many different kinds of fiction and poetry, but his fame rests largely on his creation of Conan the Barbarian, a muscular axe-man who has become one of the most popular characters in the fantasy field, single-handedly creating the sub-genre of "heroic fantasy." The Conan character has been continued by such authors as Lin Carter and L. Sprague de Camp, and he was the subject of a major motion picture in 1982.

One of the longest and most memorable of the Conan stories, "The People of the Black Circle" deals with a royal family's attempts to revenge themselves against an attack by wizardry.

1. Death Strikes a King

The king of Vendhya was dying. Through the hot, stifling night the temple gongs boomed and the conchs roared. Their clamor was a faint echo in the gold-domed chamber where Bhunda Chand struggled on the velvet-cushioned dais. Beads of sweat glistened on his dark skin; his fingers twisted the gold-worked fabric beneath him. He was young; no spear had touched him, no poison lurked in his wine. But his veins stood out like blue cords on his temples, and his eyes dilated with the nearness of death. Trembling slave-girls knelt at the foot of the dais, and leaning down on him, watching him with passionate intensity, was his sister, the Devi Yasmina. With her was the *wazam*, a noble grown old in the royal court.

She threw up her head in a gusty gesture of wrath and despair as the thunder of the distant drums reached her ears.

"The priests and their clamor!" she exclaimed. "They are no wiser than the leeches, who are helpless! Nay, he dies and none can say why. He is dying now—and I stand here helpless, who would burn the whole city and spill the blood of thousands to save him."

"Not a man of Ayodhya but would die in his place, if it might be, Devi," answered the *wazam*. "This poison——"

"I tell you it is not poison!" she cried. "Since his birth he has been guarded so closely that the cleverest poisoners of the East could not reach him. Five skulls bleaching on the Tower of the Kites can testify to attempts which were made—and which failed. As you well know, there are ten men and ten women whose sole duty is to taste his food and wine, and fifty armed warriors guard his chambers as they guard it now. No, it is not poison; it is sorcery—black, ghastly magic——"

She ceased as the king spoke; his livid lips did not move, and there was no recognition in his glassy eyes. But his voice rose in an eery call, indistinct and far away, as if he called to her from beyond vast, wind-blown gulfs.

"Yasmina! Yasmina! My sister, where are you? I can not find you. All is darkness, and the roaring of great winds!"

"Brother!" cried Yasmina, catching his limp hand in a convulsive grasp. "I am here! Do you not know me——"

Her voice died at the utter vacancy of his face. A low, confused moaning waned from his mouth. The slave-girls at the foot of the dais whimpered with fear, and Yasmina beat her breast in her anguish.

*   *   *

In another part of the city, a man stood in a latticed balcony overlooking a long street in which torches tossed luridly, smokily revealing upturned dark faces and the whites of gleaming eyes. A long-drawn wailing rose from the multitude.

The man shrugged his broad shoulders and turned back into the arabesqued chamber. He was a tall man, compactly built and richly clad.

"The king is not yet dead, but the dirge is sounded," he said to another man who sat cross-legged on a mat in a corner. This man was clad in a brown camel-hair robe and sandals, and a green turban was on his head. His expression was tranquil, his gaze impersonal.

"The people know he will never see another dawn," this man answered.

The first speaker favored him with a long, searching stare.

"What I can not understand," he said, "is why I have had to wait so long for your masters to strike. If they have slain the king now, why could they not have slain him months ago?"

"Even the arts you call sorcery are governed by cosmic laws," answered the man in the green turban. "The stars direct these actions, as in other affairs. Not even my masters can alter the stars. Not until the heavens were in the proper order could they perform this necromancy." With a long, stained fingernail he mapped the constellations on the marble-tiled floor. "The slant of the moon presaged evil for the king of Vendhya; the stars are in turmoil, the Serpent in the House of the Elephant. During such juxtaposition, the invisible guardians are removed from the spirit of Bhunda Chand. A path is opened in the unseen realms, and once a point of contact was established, mighty powers were put in play along that path."

"Point of contact?" inquired the other. "Do you mean that lock of Bhunda Chand's hair?"

"Yes. All discarded portions of the human body still remain part of it, attached to it by intangible connections. The priests of Asura have a dim inkling of this truth, and so all nail-trimmings, hair, and other waste products of the persons of the royal family are carefully reduced to ashes and the ashes hidden. But at the urgent entreaty of the princess of Kosala, who loved Bhunda Chand vainly, he gave her a lock of his long black hair as a token of remembrance. When my masters decided upon his doom, the lock, in its golden, jewel-crusted case, was stolen from under her pillow while she slept, and another substituted, so like the first that she never knew the difference. Then the genuine lock traveled by camel-caravan up the long, long road to Peshkhauri, thence up the Zhaibar Pass, until it reached the hands of those for whom it was intended."

"Only a lock of hair," murmured the nobleman.

"By which a soul is drawn from its body and across gulfs of echoing space," returned the man on the mat.

The nobleman studied him curiously.

"I do not know if you are a man or a demon, Khemsa," he said at last. "Few of us are what we seem. I, whom the Kshatriyas know as Kerim Shah, a prince from Iranistan, am no greater a masquerader than most men. They are all traitors in the one way or another, and half of them know not whom they serve. There at least I have no doubts; for I serve King Yezdigerd of Turan."

"And I the Black Seers of Yimsha," said Khemsa; "and my masters are greater than yours, for they have accomplished by their arts what Yezdigerd could not with a hundred thousand swords."

Outside, the moan of the tortured thousands shuddered up to the stars which crusted the sweating Vendhyan night, and the conchs bellowed like oxen in pain.

In the gardens of the palace the torches glinted on polished helmets and curved swords and gold-chased corselets. All the noble-born fighting-men of Ayodhya were gathered in the great palace or about it, and at each broad-arched gate and door fifty archers stood on guard, with bows in their hands. But Death stalked through the royal palace and none could stay his ghostly tread.

On the dais under the golden dome the king cried out again, racked by awful paroxysms. Again his voice came faintly and far away, and again the Devi bent to him, trembling with a fear that was darker than the terror of death.

"Yasmina!" Again that far, weirdly dreeing cry, from realms immeasurable. "Aid me! I am far from my mortal house! Wizards have drawn my soul through the wind-blown darkness. They seek to snap the silver cord that binds me to my dying body. They cluster around me; their hands are taloned, their eyes are red like flame burning in darkness. *Aie*, save me, my sister! Their fingers sear me like fire! They would slay my body and damn my soul! What is this they bring before me?—*Aie!*"

At the terror in his hopeless cry Yasmina screamed uncontrollably and threw herself bodily upon him in the abandon of her anguish. He was torn by a terrible convulsion; foam flew from his contorted lips and his writhing fingers left their marks on the girl's shoulders. But the glassy blankness passed from his eyes like smoke blown from a fire, and he looked up at his sister with recognition.

"Brother!" she sobbed. "Brother——"

"Swift!" he gasped, and his weakening voice was rational. "I know now what brings me to the pyre. I have been on a far journey and I understand. I have been ensorceled by the wizards of the Himelians. They drew my soul out of my body and far away, into a stone room. There they strove to break the silver cord of life, and thrust my soul into the body of a foul night-weird their sorcery summoned up from Hell. Ah! I feel their pull upon me now! Your cry and the grip of your fingers brought me back, but I am going fast. My soul clings to my body, but its hold weakens. Quick—kill me, before they can trap my soul for ever!"

"I can not!" she wailed, smiting her naked breasts.

"Swiftly, I command you!" There was the old imperious note in his flailing whisper. "You have never disobeyed me—obey my last command! Send my soul clean to Asura! Haste, lest you damn me to spend eternity as a filthy gaunt of darkness. Strike, I command you! *Strike!*"

Sobbing wildly, Yasmina plucked a jeweled dagger from her girdle and plunged it to the hilt in his breast. He stiffened and then went limp, a grim smile curving his dead lips. Yasmina hurled herself face-down on the rush-covered floor, beating the reeds with her clenched hands. Outside, the gongs and conchs brayed and thundered and the priests gashed themselves with copper knives.

2. A Barbarian from the Hills

Chunder Shan, governor of Peshkhauri, laid down his golden pen and carefully scanned that which he had written on parchment that bore his official seal. He had ruled Peshkhauri so long only because he weighed his every word, spoken or written. Danger breeds caution, and only a wary man lives long in that wild country where the hot Vendhyan plains meet the crags of the Himelians. An hour's ride westward or northward and one crossed the border and was among the Hills where men lived by the law of the knife.

The governor was alone in his chamber, seated at his ornately-carven table of inlaid ebony. Through the wide window, open for the coolness, he could see a square of the blue Himelian night, dotted with great white stars. An adjacent parapet was a shadowy line, and further crenelles and embrasures were barely hinted at in the dim starlight. The governor's fortress was strong, and situated outside the walls of the city it guarded. The breeze that stirred the tapestries on the wall brought faint noises from the streets of Peshkhauri—occasional snatches of wailing song, or the thrum of a cithern.

The governor read what he had written, slowly, with his open hand shading his eyes from the bronze butter-lamp, his lips moving. Absently, as he read, he heard the drum of horses' hoofs outside the barbican, the sharp staccato of the guards' challenge. He did not heed, intent upon his letter. It was addressed to the *wazam* of Vendhya, at the royal court of Ayodhya, and it stated, after the customary salutations:

> Let it be known to your Excellency that I have faith-fully carried out your Excellency's instructions. The seven tribesmen are well guarded in their prison, and I have repeatedly sent word into the hills that their chief come in person to bargain for their release. But he has made no move, except to send word that unless they are freed he will burn Peshkhauri and cover his saddle with my hide, begging your Excellency's indulgence. This he is quite capable of attempting, and I have tripled the numbers of the lance guards. The man is not a native of Ghulistan. I can not with certainty predict his next move. But since it is the wish of the Devi——

He was out of his ivory chair and on his feet facing the arched door, all in one instant. He snatched at the curved sword lying in its ornate scabbard on the table, and then checked the movement.

It was a woman who had entered unannounced, a woman whose gossamer robes did not conceal the rich garments beneath any more than they concealed the suppleness and beauty of her tall, slender figure. A filmy veil fell below her breasts, supported by a flowing headdress bound about with a triple gold braid and adorned with a golden crescent. Her dark eyes regarded the astonished governor over the veil, and then with an imperious gesture of her white hand, she uncovered her face.

"Devi!" The governor dropped to his knee before her, his

surprise and confusion somewhat spoiling the stateliness of his obeisance. With a gesture she motioned him to rise, and he hastened to lead her to the ivory chair, all the while bowing level with his girdle. But his first words were of reproof.

"Your Majesty! This was most unwise! The border is unsettled. Raids from the hills are incessant. You came with a large attendance?"

"An ample retinue followed me to Peshkhauri," she answered. "I lodged my people there and came on to the fort with my maid, Gitara."

Chunder Shan groaned in horror.

"Devi! You do not understand the peril. An hour's ride from this spot, the hills swarm with barbarians who make a profession of murder and rapine. Women have been stolen and men stabbed between the fort and the city. Peshkhauri is not like your southern provinces——"

"But I am here, and unharmed," she interrupted with a trace of impatience. "I showed my signet ring to the guard at the gate, and to the one outside your door, and they admitted me unannounced, not knowing me, but supposing me to be a secret courier from Ayodhya. Let us not now waste time. You have received no word from the chief of the barbarians?"

"None save threats and curses, Devi. He is wary and suspicious. He deems it a trap, and perhaps he is not to be blamed. The Kshatriyas have not always kept their promises to the hill people."

"He must be brought to terms!" broke in Yasmina, the knuckles of her clenched hands showing white.

"I do not understand." The governor shook his head. "When I chanced to capture these seven hillmen, I reported their capture to the *wazam,* as the custom, and then, before I could hang them, there came an order to hold them and communicate with their chief. This I did, but the man holds aloof, as I have said. These men are of the tribe of Afghulis, but he is a foreigner from the West, and he is called Conan. I have threatened to hang them tomorrow at dawn, if he does not come."

"Good!" exclaimed the Devi. "You have done well. And I will tell you why I have given these orders. My brother——" she faltered, choking, and the governor bowed his head, with the customary gesture of respect for a departed sovereign.

"The king of Vendhya was destroyed by magic," she said at last. "I have devoted my life to the destruction of his murderers. As he died he gave me a clue, and I have followed it. I have read the Book of Skelos, and talked with nameless hermits in the

:aves below Jhelai. I learned how, and by whom, he was destroyed. His enemies were the Black Seers of Mount Yimsha.''

"Asura!" whispered Chunder Shan, paling.

Her eyes knifed him through. "Do you fear them?"

"Who does not, your Majesty?" he replied. "They are black devils, haunting the uninhabited hills beyond the Zhaibar. But he sages say that they seldom interfere in the lives of mortal nen.''

"Why they slew my brother I do not know," she answered. 'But I have sworn on the altar of Asura to destroy them! And I need the aid of a man beyond the border. A Kshatriya army, inaided, would never reach Yimsha.''

"Aye," muttered Chunder Shan. "You speak the truth there. It would be a fight every step of the way, with hairy hillmen iurling down boulders from every height, and rushing us with heir long knives in every valley. The Turanians fought their way hrough the Himelians once, but how many returned to Khurusun? Few of those who escaped the swords of the Kshatriyas, after the king, your brother, defeated their host on the Jhumda River, ever saw Secunderam again.''

"And so I must control men across the border," she said, "men who know the way to Mount Yimsha——''

"But the tribes fear the Black Seers and shun the unholy mountain," broke in the governor.

"Does the chief, Conan, fear them?" she asked.

"Well, as to that," muttered the governor, "I doubt if there is anything that devil fears.''

"So I have been told. Therefore he is the man I must deal with. He wishes the release of his seven men. Very well; their ransom shall be the heads of the Black Seers!" Her voice thrummed with hate as she uttered the last words, and her hands clenched at her sides. She looked an image of incarnate passion as she stood there with her head thrown high and her bosom heaving.

Again the governor knelt, for part of his wisdom was the knowledge that a woman in such an emotional tempest is as perilous as a blind cobra to any about her.

"It shall be as you wish, your Majesty." Then as she presented a calmer aspect, he rose and ventured to drop a word of warning. "I can not predict what the chief Conan's action will be. The tribesmen are always turbulent, and I have reason to believe that emissaries from the Turanians are stirring them up to raid our borders. As your majesty knows, the Turanians have

established themselves in Secunderam and other northern cities,
though the hill tribes remain unconquered. King Yezdigerd ha,
long looked southward with greedy lust and perhaps is seeking to
gain by treachery what he could not win by force of arms. I have
thought that Conan might well be one of his spies."

"We shall see," she answered. "If he loves his followers, he
will be at the gates at dawn, to parley. I shall spend the night in
the fortress. I came in disguise to Peshkhauri, and lodged my
retinue at an inn instead of the palace. Besides my people, only
yourself knows of my presence here."

"I shall escort you to your quarters, your Majesty," said the
governor, and as they emerged from the doorway, he beckoned
the warrior on guard there, and the man fell in behind them,
spear held at a salute.

The maid waited, veiled like her mistress, outside the door,
and the group traversed a wide, winding corridor, lighted by
smoky torches, and reached the quarters reserved for visiting
notables—generals and viceroys, mostly; none of the royal family had ever honored the fortress before. Chunder Shan had a
perturbed feeling that the suite was not suitable to such an
exalted personage as the Devi, and though she sought to make
him feel at ease in her presence, he was glad when she dismissed
him and he bowed himself out. All the menials of the fort had
been summoned to serve his royal guest—though he did not
divulge her identity—and he stationed a squad of spearmen
before her doors, among them the warrior who had guarded his
own chamber. In his preoccupation he forgot to replace the man.

The governor had not been gone long from her when Yasmina
suddenly remembered something else which she had wished to
discuss with him, but had forgotten until that moment. It concerned the past actions of one Kerim Shah, a nobleman from
Iranistan, who had dwelt for a while in Peshkhauri before coming on to the court at Ayodhya. A vague suspicion concerning
the man had been stirred by a glimpse of him in Peshkhauri that
night. She wondered if he had followed her from Ayodhya.
Being a truly remarkable Devi, she did not summon the governor
to her again, but hurried out into the corridor, and hastened
toward his chamber.

Chunder Shan, entering his chamber, closed the door and went
to his table. There he took the letter he had been writing and tore
it to bits. Scarcely had he finished when he heard something
drop softly onto the parapet adjacent to the window. He looked

p to see a figure loom briefly against the stars, and then a man
ropped lightly into the room. The light glinted on a long sheen
f steel in his hand.

"Shhhh!" he warned. "Don't make a noise, or I'll send the
Devil a henchman!"

The governor checked his motion toward the sword on the
able. He was within reach of the yard-long Zhaibar knife that
littered in the intruder's fist, and he knew the desperate quick-
ess of a hillman.

The invader was a tall man, at once strong and supple. He was
ressed like a hillman, but his dark features and blazing blue
yes did not match his garb. Chunder Shan had never seen a man
ike him; he was not an Easterner, but some barbarian from the
Vest. But his aspect was as untamed and formidable as any of
ne hairy tribesmen who haunt the hills of Ghulistan.

"You come like a thief in the night," commented the governor,
ecovering some of his composure, although he remembered that
here was no guard within call. Still, the hillman could not know
hat.

"I climbed a bastion," snarled the intruder. "A guard thrust
is head over the battlement in time for me to rap it with my
knife-hilt."

"You are Conan?"

"Who else? You sent word into the hills that you wished for
ne to come and parley with you. Well, by Crom, I've come!
Keep away from that table or I'll gut you."

"I merely wish to seat myself," answered the governor,
arefully sinking into the ivory chair, which he wheeled away
rom the table. Conan moved restlessly before him, glancing
uspiciously at the door, thumbing the razor edge of his three-
oot knife. He did not walk like an Afghuli, and was bluntly
lirect where the East is subtle.

"You have seven of my men," he said abruptly. "You re-
used the ransom I offered. What the devil do you want?"

"Let us discuss terms," answered Chunder Shan cautiously.

"Terms?" There was a timbre of dangerous anger in his
voice. "What do you mean? Haven't I offered you gold?"

Chunder Shan laughed.

"Gold? There is more gold in Peshkhauri than you ever saw."

"You're a liar," retorted Conan. "I've seen the *suk* of the
goldsmiths in Khurusun."

"Well, more than any Afghuli ever saw," amended Chunder
Shan. "And it is but a drop of all the treasure of Vendhya. Why

should we desire gold? It would be more to our advantage t
hang these seven thieves.''

Conan ripped out a sulfurous oath and the long blade quivere
in his grip as the muscles rose in ridges on his brown arm.

"I'll split your head like a ripe melon!''

A wild blue flame flickered in the hillman's eyes, but Chunde
Shan shrugged his shoulders, though keeping an eye on the kee
steel.

"You can kill me easily, and probably escape over the wa
afterward. But that would not save the seven tribesmen. My me
would surely hang them. And these men are headmen among th
Afghulis.''

"I know it,'' snarled Conan. "The tribe is baying like wolve
at my heels because I have not procured their release. Tell me i
plain words what you want, because, by Crom! if there's n
other way, I'll raise a horde and lead it to the very gates o
Peshkhauri!''

Looking at the man as he stood squarely, knife in fist and eyes
glaring, Chunder Shan did not doubt that he was capable of it
The governor did not believe any hill-horde could take Peshkhauri
but he did not wish a devastated countryside.

"There is a mission you must perform,'' he said, choosing his
words with as much care as if they had been razors. "There——''

Conan had sprung back, wheeling to face the door at the same
instant, lips asnarl. His barbarian ears had caught the quick tread
of soft slippers outside the door. The next instant the door was
thrown open and a slim, silk-robed form entered hastily, pulling
the door shut—then stopping short at sight of the hillman.

Chunder Shan sprang up, his heart jumping into his mouth.

"Devi!'' he cried involuntarily, losing his head momentarily
in his fright.

"Devi!'' It was like an explosive echo from the hillman's
lips. Chander Shan saw recognition and intent flame up in the
fierce blue eyes.

The governor shouted desperately and caught at his sword, but
the hillman moved with the devastating speed of a hurricane. He
sprang, knocked the governor sprawling with a savage blow of
his knife-hilt, swept up the astounded Devi in one brawny arm
and leaped for the window. Chunder Shan, struggling frantically
to his feet, saw the man poise an instant on the sill in a flutter of
silken skirts and white limbs that was his royal captive, and
heard his fierce, exultant snarl: *"Now* dare to hang my men!''

nd then Conan leaped to the parapet and was gone. A wild
cream floated back to the governor's ears.

"Guard! *Guard!*" screamed the governor, struggling up and
unning drunkenly to the door. He tore it open and reeled into
he hall. His shouts re-echoed along the corridors, and warriors
ame running, gaping to see the governor holding his broken
ead, from which the blood streamed.

"Turn out the lancers!" he roared. "There has been an
bduction!" Even in his frenzy he had enough sense left to
vithhold the full truth. He stopped short as he heard a sudden
rum of hoofs outside, a frantic scream and a wild yell of
arbaric exultation.

Followed by the bewildered guardsmen, the governor raced
or the stair. In the courtyard of the fort a force of lancers always
cood by saddled steeds, ready to ride at an instant's notice.
Chunder Shan led his squadron flying after the fugitive, though
is head swam so he had to hold with both hands to the saddle.
Ie did not divulge the identity of the victim, but said merely that
he noblewoman who had borne the royal signet ring had been
arried away by the chief of the Afghulis. The abductor was out
f sight and hearing, but they knew the path he would strike—
he road that runs straight to the mouth of the Zhaibar. There was
o moon; peasant huts rose dimly in the starlight. Behind them
ell away the grim bastion of the fort, and the towers of Peshkhauri.
head of them loomed the black walls of the Himelians.

3. Khemsa Uses Magic

In the confusion that reigned in the fortress while the guard
vas being turned out, no one noticed that the girl who had
ccompanied the Devi slipped out the great arched gate and
anished in the darkness. She ran straight for the city, her
arments tucked high. She did not follow the open road, but cut
traight through fields and over slopes, avoiding fences and
eaping irrigation ditches as surely as if it were broad daylight, and
s easily as if she were a trained masculine runner. The hoof-drum
f the guardsmen had faded away up the hill road before she
eached the city wall. She did not go to the great gate, beneath
vhose arch men leaned on spears and craned their necks into the
larkness, discussing the unwonted activity about the fortress.
She skirted the wall until she reached a certain point where the
pire of a tower was visible above the battlements. Then she

placed her hands to her mouth and voiced a low, weird call th
carried strangely.

Almost instantly a head appeared at an embrasure and a rop
came wriggling down the wall. She seized it, placed a foot in th
loop at the end, and waved her arm. Then quickly and smoothl
she was drawn up the sheer stone curtain. An instant later sh
scrambled over the merlons and stood up on a flat roof whic
covered a house that was built against the wall. There was a
open trap there, and a man in a camel-hair robe who silentl
coiled the rope, not showing in any way the strain of hauling
full-grown woman up a forty-foot wall.

"Where is Kerim Shah?" she gasped, panting after a lon
run.

"Asleep in the house below. You have news?"

"Conan has stolen the Devi out of the fortress and carried he
away into the hills!" She blurted out her news in a rush, th
words stumbling over one another.

Khemsa showed no emotion, but merely nodded his turbane
head. "Kerim Shah will be glad to hear that," he said.

"Wait!" The girl threw her supple arms about his neck. Sh
was panting hard, but not only from exertion. Her eyes blaze
like black jewels in the starlight. Her upturned face was close t
Khemsa's, but though he submitted to her embrace, he did no
return it.

"Do not tell the Hyrkanian!" she panted. "Let us use thi
knowledge ourselves! The governor has gone into the hills wit
his riders, but he might as well chase a ghost. He has not tol
anyone that it was the Devi who was kidnapped. None i
Peshkhauri or the fort knows it except us."

"But what good does it do us?" the man expostulated. "M
masters sent me with Kerim Shah to aid him in every way——"

"Aid yourself!" she cried fiercely. "Shake off your yoke!"

"You mean—disobey my masters?" he gasped, and she fel
his whole body turn cold under her arms.

"Aye!" she shook him in the fury of her emotion. "You too
are a magician! Why will you be a slave, using your powers onl
to elevate others? Use your arts for yourself!"

"That is forbidden!" He was shaking as if with an ague. "I
am not one of the Black Circle. Only by the command of the
masters do I dare to use the knowledge they have taught me."

"But you *can* use it!" she argued passionately. "Do as I beg
you! Of course Conan has taken the Devi to hold as hostage
against the seven tribesmen in the governor's prison. Destroy

hem, so Chunder Shan can not use them to buy back the Devi.
Then let us go into the mountains and take her from the Afghulis.
They can not stand against your sorcery with their knives. The
treasure of the Vendhyan kings will be ours as ransom—and then
when we have it in our hands, we can trick them, and sell her to
the king of Turan. We shall have wealth beyond our maddest
dreams. With it we can buy warriors. We will take Khorbhul,
oust the Turanians from the hills, and send our hosts southward;
become king and queen of an empire!''

Khemsa too was panting, shaking like a leaf in her grasp; his
face showed gray in the starlight, beaded with great drops of
perspiration.

''I love you!'' she cried fiercely, writhing her body against
his, almost strangling him in her wild embrace, shaking him in
her abandon. ''I will make a king of you! For love of you I
betrayed my mistress; for love of me betray your masters! Why
fear the Black Seers? By your love for me you have broken one
of their laws already! Break the rest! You are as strong as they!''

A man of ice could not have withstood the searing heat of her
passion and fury. With an inarticulate cry he crushed her to him,
bending her backward and showering gasping kisses on her eyes,
face, and lips.

''I'll do it!'' His voice was thick with laboring emotions. He
staggered like a drunken man. ''The arts they have taught me
shall work for me, not for my masters. We shall be rulers of the
world—of the world——''

''Come then!'' Twisting lithely out of his embrace, she seized
his hand and led him toward the trap-door. ''First we must make
sure that the governor does not exchange those seven Afghulis
for the Devi.''

He moved like a man in a daze, until they had descended a
ladder and she paused in the chamber below. Kerim Shah lay on
a couch motionless, an arm across his face as though to shield
his sleeping eyes from the soft light of a brass lamp. She plucked
Khemsa's arm and made a quick gesture across her own throat.
Khemsa lifted his hand; then his expression changed and he drew
away.

''I have eaten his salt,'' he muttered. ''Besides, he can not
interfere with us.''

He led the girl through a door that opened on a winding stair.
After their soft tread had faded into silence, the man on the
couch sat up. Kerim Shah wiped the sweat from his face. A

knife-thrust he did not dread, but he feared Khemsa as a ma
fears a poisonous reptile.

"People who plot on roofs should remember to lower the
voices," he muttered. "But as Khemsa has turned against h
masters, and as he was my only contact with them, I can cou
on their aid no longer. From now on I play the game in my ow
way."

Rising to his feet he went quickly to a table, drew pen an
parchment from his girdle, and scribbled a few succinct lines:

> To Khosru Khan, governor of Secunderam: the
> Cimmerian Conan has carried the Devi Yasmina to
> the villages of the Afghulis. It is an opportunity to
> get the Devi into our hands, as the king has so long
> desired. Send three thousand horsemen at once. I
> will meet them in the Valley of Gurashah with native
> guides.

And he signed it with a name that was not in the least lik
Kerim Shah.

Then from a golden cage he drew forth a carrier pigeon, t
whose leg he made fast the parchment, rolled into a tiny cylinde
and secured with gold wire. Then he went quickly to a casemen
and tossed the bird into the night. It wavered on fluttering wings
balanced, and was gone like a flitting shadow. Catching u
helmet, sword, and cloak, Kerim Shah hurried out of the cham
ber and down the winding stair.

The prison quarters of Peshkhauri were separated from the res
of the city by a massive wall, in which was set a single iron-
bound door under an arch. Over the arch burned a lurid re
cresset, and beside the door squatted a warrior with spear an
shield.

This warrior, leaning on his spear, and yawning from time t
time, started suddenly to his feet. He had not thought he hac
dozed, but a man was standing before him, a man he had no
heard approach. The man wore a camel-hair robe and a green
turban. In the flickering light of the cresset his features were
shadowy, but a pair of lambent eyes shone surprisingly in the
lurid glow.

"Who comes?" demanded the warrior, presenting his spear.
"Who are you?"

The stranger did not seem perturbed, though the spear-point

touched his bosom. His eyes held the warrior's with strange intensity.

"What are you obliged to do?" he asked, strangely.

"To guard the gate!" The warrior spoke thickly and mechanically; he stood rigid as a statue, his eyes slowly glazing.

"You lie! You are obliged to obey me! You have looked into my eyes, and your soul is no longer your own. Open that door!"

Stiffly, with the wooden features of an image, the guard wheeled about, drew a great key from his girdle, turned it in the massive lock, and swung open the door. Then he stood at attention, his unseeing stare straight ahead of him.

A woman glided from the shadows and laid an eager hand on the mesmerist's arm.

"Bid him fetch us horses, Khemsa," she whispered.

"No need of that," answered the Rakhsha. Lifting his voice slightly he spoke to the guardsman. "I have no more use for you. Kill yourself!"

Like a man in a trance, the warrior thrust the butt of his spear against the base of the wall and placed the keen head against his body, just below the ribs. Then slowly, stolidly, he leaned against it with all his weight, so that it transfixed his body and came out between his shoulders. Sliding down the shaft he lay still, the spear jutting above him its full length, like a horrible stalk growing out of his back.

The girl stared down at him in morbid fascination, until Khemsa took her arm and led her through the gate. Torches lighted a narrow space between the outer wall and a lower inner one, in which were arched doors at regular intervals. A warrior paced this enclosure, and when the gate opened he came sauntering up, so secure in his knowledge of the prison's strength that he was not suspicious until Khemsa and the girl emerged from the archway. Then it was too late. The Rahksha did not waste time in hypnotism, though his action savored of magic to the girl. The guard lowered his spear threateningly, opening his mouth to shout an alarm that would bring spearmen swarming out of the guardrooms at either end of the alleyway. Khemsa flicked the spear aside with his left hand, as a man might flick a straw, and his right flashed out and back, seeming gently to caress the warrior's neck in passing. And the guard pitched on his face without a sound, his head lolling on a broken neck.

Khemsa did not glance at him, but went straight to one of the arched doors and placed his open hand against the heavy bronze lock. With a rending shudder the portal buckled inward. As the girl followed him through, she saw that the thick teakwood hung in splinters, the bronze bolts were bent and twisted from their sockets, and the great hinges broken and disjointed. A thousand-pound battering-ram with forty men to swing it could have shattered the barrier no more completely. Khemsa was drunk with freedom and the exercise of his power, glorying in his might and flinging his strength about as a young giant exercises his thews with unnecessary vigor in the exultant pride of his prowess.

The broken door let them into a small courtyard, lit by a cresset. Opposite the door was a wide grille of iron bars. A hairy hand was visible, gripping one of these bars, and in the darkness behind them glimmered the whites of eyes.

Khemsa stood silent for a space, gazing into the shadows from which those glimmering eyes gave back his stare with burning intensity. Then his hand went into his robe and came out again, and from his opening fingers a shimmering feather of sparkling dust shifted to the flags. Instantly a flare of green fire lighted the enclosure. In the brief glare the forms of seven men, standing motionless behind the bars, were limned in vivid detail; tall, hairy men in ragged hillmen's garments. They did not speak, but in their eyes blazed the fear of death, and their hairy fingers gripped the bars.

The fire died out but the glow remained, a quivering ball of lambent green that pulsed and shimmered on the flags before Khemsa's feet. The wide gaze of the tribesmen was fixed upon it. It wavered, elongated; it turned into a luminous green smoke spiraling upward. It twisted and writhed like a great shadowy serpent, then broadened and billowed out in shining folds and whirls. It grew to a cloud moving silently over the flags—straight toward the grille. The men watching its coming with dilated eyes; the bars quivered with the grip of their desperate fingers. Bearded lips parted but no sound came forth. The green cloud rolled on the bars and blotted them from sight. Like a fog it oozed through the grille and hid the men within. From the enveloping folds came a strangled gasp, as of a man plunged suddenly under the surface of water. That was all.

Khemsa touched the girl's arm, as she stood with parted lips and dilated eyes. Mechanically she turned away with him, looking back over her shoulder. Already the mist was thinning; close to the bars she saw a pair of sandaled feet, the toes turned upward—she glimpsed the indistinct outlines of seven still, prostrate shapes.

"And now for a steed swifter than the fastest horse ever bred in a mortal stable," Khemsa was saying. "We will be in Afghulistan before dawn."

4. An Encounter in the Pass

Yasmina Devi could never clearly remember the details of her abduction. The unexpectedness and violence stunned her; she had only a confused impression of a whirl of happenings—the terrifying grip of a mighty arm, the blazing eyes of her abductor, and his hot breath burning on her flesh. The leap through the window to the parapet, the mad race across battlements and roofs when the fear of falling froze her, the reckless descent of a rope bound to a merlon—he went down almost at a run, his captive folded limply over his brawny shoulder—all this was a befuddled tangle in the Devi's mind. She retained a more vivid memory of him running fleetly into the shadows of the trees, carrying her like a child, and vaulting into the saddle of a fierce Bhalkhana stallion which reared and snorted. Then there was a sensation of flying, and the racing hoofs were striking sparks of fire from the flinty road as the stallion swept up the slopes.

As the girl's mind cleared, her first sensations were furious rage and shame. She was appalled. The rulers of the golden kingdoms south of the Himelians were considered little short of divine; and she was the Devi of Vendyha! Fright was submerged in regal wrath. She cried out furiously and began struggling. She, Yasmina, to be carried on the saddle-bow of a hill chief, like a common wench of the market place! He merely hardened his massive thews slightly against her writhings, and for the first time in her life she experienced the coercion of superior physical strength. His arms felt like iron about her slender limbs. He glanced down at her and grinned hugely. His teeth glimmered whitely in the starlight. The reins lay loose on the stallion's flowing mane, and every thew and fiber of the great beast strained as he hurtled along the boulder-strew trail. But Conan sat easily, almost carelessly, in the saddle, riding like a centaur.

"You hill-bred dog!" she panted, quivering with the impact of shame, anger, and the realization of helplessness. "You dare—you *dare!* Your life shall pay for this! Where are you taking me?"

"To the villages of Afghulistan," he answered, casting a glance over his shoulder.

Behind them, beyond the slopes they had traversed, torches

were tossing on the walls of the fortress, and he glimpsed a flare of light that meant the great gate had been opened. And he laughed a deep-throated boom gusty as the hill wind.

"The Governor has sent his riders after us," he laughed. "By Crom, we will lead him a merry chase! What do you think, Devi—will they pay seven lives for a Kshatriya princess?"

"They will send an army to hang you and your spawn of devils," she promised him with conviction.

He laughed gustily and shifted her to a more comfortable position in his arms. But she took this as a fresh outrage, and renewed her vain struggles, until she saw that her efforts were only amusing him. Besides, her light silken garments, floating on the wind, were being outrageously disarranged by her struggles. She concluded that a scornful submission was the better part of dignity, and lapsed into a smoldering quiescence.

She felt even her anger being submerged by awe as they entered the mouth of the Pass, lowering like a black well mouth in the blacker walls that rose like colossal ramparts to bar their way. It was as if a gigantic knife had cut the Zhaibar out of walls of solid rock. On either hand sheer slopes pitched up for thousands of feet, and the mouth of the Pass was dark as hate. Even Conan could not see with any accuracy, but he knew the road, even by night. And knowing that armed men were racing through the starlight after him, he did not check the stallion's speed. The great brute was not yet showing fatigue. He thundered along the road that followed the valley bed, labored up a slope, swept along a low ridge where treacherous shale on either hand lurked for the unwary, and came upon a trail that followed the lap of the left-hand wall.

Not even Conan could spy, in that darkness, an ambush set by Zhaibar tribesmen. As they swept past the black mouth of a gorge that opened into the Pass, a javelin swished through the air and thudded home behind the stallion's straining shoulder. The great beast let out his life in a shuddering sob and stumbled, going headlong in mid-stride. But Conan had recognized the flight and stroke of the javelin, and he acted with spring-steel quickness.

As the horse fell he leaped clear, holding the girl aloft to guard her from striking boulders. He lit on his feet like a cat, thrust her into a cleft of rock, and wheeled toward the outer darkness, drawing his knife.

Yasmina, confused by the rapidity of events, not quite sure just what had happened, saw a vague shape rush out of the arkness, bare feet slapping softly on the rock, ragged garments whipping on the wind of his haste. She glimpsed the flicker of steel, heard the lightning crack of stroke, parry, and counter-stroke, and the crunch of bone as Conan's long knife split the other's skull.

Conan sprang back, crouching in the shelter of the rocks. Out in the night men were moving and a stentorian voice roared: "What, you dogs! Do you flinch? In, curse you, and take them!"

Conan started, peered into the darkness and lifted his voice.

"Yar Afzal! Is it you?"

There sounded a startled imprecation, and the voice called warily.

"Conan? Is that you, Conan?"

"Aye!" The Cimmerian laughed. "Come forth, you old war-dog. I've slain one of your men."

There was movement among the rocks, a light flared dimly, and then a flame appeared and came bobbing toward him, and as it approached, a fierce bearded countenance grew out of the darkness. The man who carried it held it high, thrust forward, and craned his neck to peer among the boulders it lighted; the other hand gripped a great curved tulwar. Conan stepped forward, sheathing his knife, and the other roared a greeting.

"Aye, it is Conan! Come out of your rocks, dogs! It is Conan!"

Others pressed into the wavering circle of light—wild, ragged, bearded men, with eyes like wolves, and long blades in their fists. They did not see Yasmina, for she was hidden by Conan's massive body. But peeping from her covert, she knew icy fear for the first time that night. These men were more like wolves than human beings.

"What are you hunting in the Zhaibar by night, Yar Afzal?" Conan demanded of the burly chief, who grinned like a bearded ghoul.

"Who knows what might come up the Pass after dark? We Wazulis are nighthawks. But what of you, Conan?"

"I have a prisoner," answered the Cimmerian. And moving aside he disclosed the cowering girl. Reaching a long arm into the crevice he drew her trembling forth.

Her imperious bearing was gone. She stared timidly at the ring of bearded faces that hemmed her in, and was grateful for the strong arm that clasped her possessively. The torch was thrust

close to her, and there was a sucking intake of breath about th
ring.

"She is my captive," Conan warned, glancing pointedly
the feet of the man he had slain, just visible within the ring
light. "I was taking her to Afghulistan, but now you have slai
my horse, and the Kshatriyas are close behind me."

"Come with us to my village," suggested Yar Afzal. "W
have horses hidden in the gorge. They can never follow us in th
darkness. They are close behind you, you say?"

"So close that I hear now the clink of their hoofs on th
flint," answered Conan grimly.

Instantly there was movement; the torch was dashed out an
the ragged shapes melted like phantoms into the darkness. Cona
swept up the Devi in his arms, and she did not resist. Th
rocky ground hurt her slim feet in their soft slippers and she fe
very small and helpless in that brutish, primordial blacknes
among those colossal, nighted crags.

Feeling her shiver in the wind that moaned down the defiles
Conan jerked a ragged cloak from its owner's shoulders an
wrapped it about her. He also hissed a warning in her ear
ordering her to make no sound. She did not hear the distant clin
of shod hoofs on rock that warned the keen-eared hillmen; bu
she was far too frightened to disobey, in any event.

She could see nothing but a few faint stars far above, but sh
knew by the deepening darkness when they entered the gorg
mouth. There was a stir about them, the uneasy movement o
horses. A few muttered words, and Conan mounted the horse o
the man he had killed, lifting the girl up in front of him. Lik
phantoms except for the click of their hoofs, the band swep
away up the shadowy gorge. Behind them on the trail they lef
the dead horse and the dead man, which were found less than
half an hour later by the riders from the fortress, who recognize
the man as a Wazuli and drew their own conclusions accordingly

Yasmina, snuggled warmly in her captor's arms, grew drowsy
in spite of herself. The motion of the horse, though it wa
uneven, uphill and down, yet possessed a certain rhythm which
combined with weariness and emotional exhaustion to forc
sleep on her. She had lost all sense of time or direction. They
moved in soft thick darkness, in which she sometimes glimpse
vaguely gigantic walls sweeping up like black ramparts, or grea
crags shouldering the stars; at times she sensed echoing depths
beneath them, or felt the wind of dizzy heights blowing col
about her. Gradually these things faded into a dreamy unwake-

fulness in which the clink of hoofs and the creak of saddles were like the irrelevant sounds in a dream.

She was vaguely aware when the motion ceased and she was lifted down and carried a few steps. There she was laid down on something soft and rustling, and something—a folded coat, perhaps—was thrust under her head, and the cloak in which she was wrapped was carefully tucked about her. She heard Yar Afzal laugh.

"A rare prize, Conan; fit mate for a chief of the Afghulis."

"Not for me," came Conan's answering rumble. "This wench will buy the lives of my seven headmen, blast their souls."

That was the last she heard as she sank into dreamless slumber.

She slept while armed men rode through the dark hills; and the fate of kingdoms hung in the balance. Through the shadowy gorges and defiles that night there rang the hoofs of galloping horses, and the starlight glimmered on helmets and curved blades, until the ghoulish shapes that haunt the crags stared into the darkness from ravine and boulder and wondered what things were afoot.

A band of these sat gaunt horses in the black pit-mouth of a gorge as the hurrying hoofs swept past. Their leader, a well-built man in a helmet and gilt-braided cloak, held up his hand warningly, until the riders had sped on. Then he laughed softly.

"They must have lost the trail! Or else they have found that Conan has already reached the Afghuli villages. It will take many riders to smoke out that hive. There will be squadrons riding up the Zhaibar by dawn."

"If there is fighting in the hills there will be looting," muttered a voice behind him, in the dialect of the Irakzai.

"There will be looting," answered the man with the helmet. "But first it is our business to reach the valley of Gurashah and await the riders that will be galloping southward from Secunderam before daylight."

He lifted his reins and rode out of the defile, his men falling in behind him—thirty ragged phantoms in the starlight.

5. The Black Stallion

The sun was well up when Yasmina awoke. She did not start and stare blankly, wondering where she was. She awoke with full knowledge of all that had occurred. Her supple limbs were stiff from her long ride, and her firm flesh still seemed to feel the contact of the muscular arm that had borne her so far.

She was lying on a sheepskin covering a pallet of leaves on hard-beaten dirt floor. A folded sheepskin coat was under her head, and she was wrapped in a ragged cloak. She was in a large room, the walls of which were crudely but strongly built of uncut rocks, plastered with sun-baked mud. Heavy beams supported a roof of the same kind, in which showed a trap-door up to which led a ladder. There were no windows in the thick walls, only loopholes. There was one door, a sturdy bronze affair that must have been looted from some Vendhyan border tower. Opposite it was a wide opening in the wall, with no door, but several strong wooden bars in place. Beyond them Yasmina saw a magnificent black stallion munching a pile of dried grass. The building was fort, dwelling place, and stable in one.

At the other end of the room a girl in the vest and baggy trousers of a hillwoman squatted beside a small fire, cooking strips of meat on an iron grid laid over blocks of stone. There was a sooty cleft in the wall a few feet from the floor, and some of the smoke found its way out there. The rest floated in blue wisps about the room.

The hill girl glanced at Yasmina over her shoulder, displaying a bold, handsome face, and then continued her cooking. Voices boomed outside; then the door was kicked open, and Conan strode in. He looked more enormous than ever with the morning sunlight behind him, and Yasmina noted some details that had escaped her the night before. His garments were clean and not ragged. The broad Bakhariot girdle that supported his knife in its ornamented scabbard would have matched the robes of a prince, and there was a glint of fine Turanian mail under his shirt.

"Your captive is awake, Conan," said the Wazuli girl, and he grunted, strode up to the fire, and swept the strips of mutton off into a stone dish.

The squatting girl laughed up at him, with some spicy jest, and he grinned wolfishly, and hooking a toe under her haunches, tumbled her sprawling onto the floor. She seemed to derive considerable amusement from this bit of rough horseplay, but Conan paid no more heed to her. Producing a great hunk of bread from somewhere, with a copper jug of wine, he carried the lot to Yasmina, who had risen from her pallet and was regarding him doubtfully.

"Rough fare for a Devi, girl, but our best," he grunted. "It will fill your belly, at least."

He set the platter on the floor, and she was suddenly aware of a ravenous hunger. Making no comment, she seated herself cross-legged on the floor, and taking the dish in her lap, she began to eat, using her fingers, which were all she had in the way of table utensils. After all, adaptability is one of the tests of true aristocracy. Conan stood looking down at her, his thumbs hooked in his girdle. He never sat cross-legged, after the Eastern fashion.

"Where am I?" she asked abruptly.

"In the hut of Yar Afzal, the chief of the Khurum Wazulis," he answered. "Afghulistan lies a good many miles farther on to the west. We'll hide here awhile. The Kshatriyas are beating up the hills for you—several of their squads have been cut up by the tribes already."

"What are you going to do?" she asked.

"Keep you until Chundar Shan is willing to trade back my seven cow-thieves," he grunted. "Women of the Wazulis are crushing ink out of *shoki* leaves, and after a while you can write a letter to the governor."

A touch of her old imperious wrath shook her, as she thought how maddeningly her plans had gone awry, leaving her captive of the very man she had plotted to get into her power. She flung down the dish, with the remnants of her meal, and sprang to her feet, tense with anger.

"I will not write a letter! If you do not take me back, they will hang your seven men, and a thousand more besides!"

The Wazuli girl laughed mockingly, Conan scowled, and then the door opened and Yar Afzal came swaggering in. The Wazuli chief was as tall as Conan, and of greater girth, but he looked fat and slow beside his hard compactness of the Cimmerian. He plucked his red-stained beard and stared meaningly at the Wazuli girl, and that wench rose and scurried out without delay. Then Yar Afzal turned to his guest.

"The damnable people murmur, Conan," quoth he. "They wish me to murder you and take the girl to hold for ransom. They say that anyone can tell by her garments that she is a noble lady. They say why should the Afghuli dogs profit by her, when it is the people who take the risk of guarding her?"

"Lend me your horse," said Conan. "I'll take her and go."

"Pish!" boomed Yar Afzal. "Do you think I can't handle my own people? I'll have them dancing in their shirts if they cross me! They don't love you—or any other outlander—but you saved my life once, and I will not forget. Come out, though, Conan; a scout has returned."

Conan hitched at his girdle and followed the chief outside.

They closed the door after them, and Yasmina peeped through a loop-hole. She looked out on a level space before the hut. At the farther end of that space there was a cluster of mud and stone huts, and she saw naked children playing among the boulders, and the slim erect women of the hills going about their tasks.

Directly before the chief's hut a circle of hairy, ragged men squatted, facing the door. Conan and Yar Afzal stood a few paces before the door, and between them and the ring of warriors another man sat cross-legged. This one was addressing his chief in the harsh accents of the Wazuli which Yasmina could scarcely understand, though as part of her royal education she had been taught the languages of Iranistan and the kindred tongues of Ghulistan.

"I talked with a Dagozai who saw the riders last night," said the scout. "He was lurking near when they came to the spot where we ambushed the lord Conan. He overheard their speech. Chunder Shan was with them. They found the dead horse, and one of the men recognized it as Conan's. Then they found the man Conan slew, and knew him for a Wazuli. It seemed to them that Conan had been slain and the girl taken by the Wazuli; so they turned aside from their purpose of following to Afghulistan. But they did not know from which village the dead man was come, and we had left no trail a Kshatriya could follow.

"So they rode to the nearest Wazuli village, which was the village of Jugra, and burnt it and slew many of the people. But the men of Khojur came upon them in darkness and slew some of them, and wounded the governor. So the survivors retired down the Zhaibar in the darkness before dawn, but they returned with reinforcements before sunrise, and there has been skirmishing and fighting in the hills all morning. It is said that a great army is being raised to sweep the hills about the Zhaibar. The tribes are whetting their knives and laying ambushes in every pass from here to Gurashah valley. Moreover, Kerim Shah has returned to the hills."

A grunt went around the circle, and Yasmina leaned closer to the loop-hole at the name she had begun to mistrust.

"Where went he?" demanded Yar Afzal.

"The Dagozai did not know; with him were thirty Irakzai of the lower villages. They rode into the hills and disappeared."

"These Irakzai are jackals that follow a lion for crumbs," growled Yar Afzal. "They have been lapping up the coins Kerim Shah scatters among the border tribes to buy men like horses. I like him not, for all he is our kinsman from Iranistan."

"He's not even that," said Conan. "I know him of old. He's an Hyrkanian, a spy of Yezdigerd's. If I catch him I'll hang his hide to a tamarisk."

"But the Kshatriyas!" clamored the men in the semi-circle. "Are we to squat on our haunches until they smoke us out? They will learn at last in which Wazuli village the wench is held. We are not loved by the Zhaibari; they will help the Kshatriyas hunt us out."

"Let them come," grunted Yar Afzal. "We can hold the defiles against a host."

One of the men leaped up and shook his fist at Conan.

"Are we to take all the risks while he reaps the rewards?" he howled. "Are we to fight his battles for him?"

With a stride Conan reached him and bent slightly to stare full into his hairy face. The Cimmerian had not drawn his long knife, but his left hand grasped the scabbard, jutting the hilt suggestively forward.

"I ask no man to fight my battles," he said softly. "Draw your blade if you dare, you yapping dog!"

The Wazuli started back, snarling like a cat.

"Dare to touch me and here are fifty men to rend you apart!" he screeched.

"What!" roared Yar Afzal, his face purpling with wrath. His whiskers bristled, his belly swelled with his rage. "Are you chief of Khurum? Do the Wazulis take orders from Yar Afzal, or from a low-bred cur?"

The man cringed before his invincible chief, and Yar Afzal, striding up to him, seized him by the throat and choked him until his face was turning black. Then he hurled the man savagely against the ground and stood over him with his tulwar in his hand.

"Is there any who questions my authority?" he roared, and his warriors looked down sullenly as his bellicose glare swept their semicircle. Yar Afzal grunted scornfully and sheathed his weapon with a gesture that was the apex of insult. Then he kicked the fallen agitator with a concentrated vindictiveness that brought howls from his victim.

"Get down the valley to the watchers on the heights and bring word if they have seen anything," commanded Yar Afzal, and the man went, shaking with fear and grinding his teeth with fury.

Yar Afzal then seated himself ponderously on a stone, growling in his beard. Conan stood near him, legs braced apart, thumbs hooked in his girdle, narrowly watching the assembled warriors. They stared at him sullenly, not daring to brave Yar Afzal's fury, but hating the foreigner as only a hillman can hate.

"Now listen to me, you sons of nameless dogs, while I tell you what the lord Conan and I have planned to fool the Kshatriyas" —the boom of Yar Afzal's bull-like voice followed the discomfited warrior as he slunk away from the assembly.

The man passed by the cluster of huts, where women who had seen his defeat laughed at him and called stinging comments, and hastened on along the trail that wound among spurs and rocks toward the valley head.

Just as he rounded the first turn that took him out of sight of the village, he stopped short, gaping stupidly. He had not believed it possible for a stranger to enter the valley of Khurum without being detected by the hawk-eyed watchers along the heights; yet a man sat cross-legged on a low ledge beside the path—a man in a camel-hair robe and a green turban.

The Wazuli's mouth gaped for a yell, and his hand leaped to his knife-hilt. But at that instant his eyes met those of the stranger and the cry died in his throat, his fingers went limp. He stood like a statue, his own eyes glazed and vacant.

For minutes the scene held motionless; then the man on the ledge drew a cryptic symbol in the dust on the rock with his forefinger. The Wazuli did not see him place anything within the compass of that emblem, but presently something gleamed there—a round, shiny black ball that looked like polished jet. The man in the green turban took this up and tossed it the Wazuli, who mechanically caught it.

"Carry this to Yar Afzal," he said, and the Wazuli turned like an automaton and went back along the path, holding the black jet ball in his outstretched hand. He did not even turn his head to the renewed jeers of the women as he passed the huts. He did not seem to hear.

The man on the ledge gazed after him with a cryptic smile. A girl's head rose above the rim of the ledge and she looked at him with admiration and a touch of fear that had not been present the night before.

"Why did you do that?" she asked.

He ran his fingers through her dark locks caressingly.

"Are you still dizzy from your flight on the horse-of-air, that you doubt my wisdom?" he laughed. "As long as Yar Afzal lives, Conan will bide safe among the Wazuli fighting-men. Their knives are sharp, and there are many of them. What I plot will be safer, even for me, than to seek to slay him and take her from among them. It takes no wizard to predict what the Wazulis will do, and what Conan will do, when my victim hands the globe of Yezud to the chief of Khurum.''

Back before the hut, Yar Afzal halted in the midst of some tirade, surprised and displeased to see the man he had sent up the valley, pushing his way through the throng.

''I bade you go to the watchers!'' the chief bellowed. ''You have not had time to come from them.''

The other did not reply; he stood woodenly, staring vacantly into the chief's face, his palm outstretched holding the jet ball. Conan, looking over Yar Afzal's shoulder, murmured something and reached to touch the chief's arm, but as he did so, Yar Afzal, in a paroxysm of anger, struck the man with his clenched fist and felled him like an ox. As he fell, the jet sphere rolled to Yar Afzal's foot, and the chief, seeming to see it for the first time, bent and picked it up. The men, staring perplexedly at their senseless comrade, saw their chief bend, but they did not see what he picked up from the ground.

Yar Afzal straightened, glanced at the jet, and made a motion to thrust it into his girdle.

''Carry that fool to his hut,'' he growled. ''He has the look of a lotus-eater. He returned me a blank stare. I—*aie!''*

In his right hand, moving toward his girdle, he had suddenly felt movement where movement should not be. His voice died away as he stood and glared at nothing; and inside his clenched right hand he felt the quivering of *change,* of *motion,* of *life.* He no longer held a smooth shining sphere in his fingers. And he dared not look; his tongue clove to the roof of his mouth, and he could not open his hand. His astonished warriors saw Yar Afzal's eyes distend, the color ebb from his face. Then suddenly a bellow of agony burst from his bearded lips; he swayed and fell as if struck by lightning, his right arm tossed out in front of him. Face down, he lay, and from between his opening fingers crawled a spider—a hideous, black, hairy-legged monster whose body shone like black jet. The men yelled and gave back suddenly, and the creature scuttled into a crevice of the rocks and disappeared.

The warriors started up, glaring wildly, and a voice rose above their clamor, a far-carrying voice of command which came from none knew where. Afterward each man there—who still lived— denied that he had shouted, but all there heard it.

''Yar Afzal is dead! Kill the outlander!''

That shout focused their whirling minds as one. Doubt, bewilderment and fear vanished in the uproaring surge of the blood-lust. A furious yell rent the skies as the tribesmen responded instantly to the suggestion. They came headlong across the open space, cloaks flapping, eyes blazing, knives lifted.

Conan's action was as quick as theirs. As the voice shouted he sprang for the hut door. But they were closer to him than he was to the door, and with one foot on the sill he had to wheel and parry the swipe of a yard-long blade. He split the man's skull—ducked another swinging knife and gutted the wielder—felled a man with his left fist and stabbed another in the belly—and heaved back mightily against the closed door with his shoulders. Hacking blades were nicking chips out of the jambs about his ears, but the door flew open under the impact of his shoulders, and he went stumbling backward into the room. A bearded tribesman, thrusting with all his fury as Conan sprang back, over-reached and pitched headfirst through the doorway. Conan stooped, grasped the slack of his garments and hauled him clear, and slammed the door in the faces of the men who came surging into it. Bones snapped under the impact, and the next instant Conan slammed the bolts into place and whirled with desperate haste to meet the man, who sprang from the floor and tore into action like a madman.

Yasmina cowered in a corner, staring in horror as the two men fought back and forth across the room, almost trampling her at times; the flash and clangor of their blades filled the room, and outside the mob clamored like a wolf-pack, hacking deafeningly at the bronze door with their long knives, and dashing huge rocks against it. Somebody fetched a tree trunk, and the door began to stagger under the thunderous assault. Yasmina clasped her ears, staring wildly. Violence and fury within, cataclysmic madness without. The stallion in his stall neighed and reared, thundering with his heels against the walls. He wheeled and launched his hoofs through the bars just as the tribesman, backing away from Conan's murderous swipes, stumbled against them. His spine cracked in three places like a rotten branch and he was hurled headlong against the Cimmerian, bearing him backward so that they both crashed to the beaten floor.

Yasmina cried out and ran forward; to her dazed sight it seemed that both were slain. She reached them just as Conan threw aside the corpse and rose. She caught his arm, trembling from head to foot.

"Oh, you live! I thought—I thought you were dead!"

He glanced down at her quickly, into the pale, upturned face and the wide staring dark eyes.

"Why are you trembling?" he demanded. "Why should you care if I live or die?"

A vestige of her poise returned to her, and she drew away, making a rather pitiful attempt at playing the Devi.

"You are preferable to those wolves howling without," she answered, gesturing toward the door, the stone sill of which was beginning to splinter away.

"That won't hold long," he muttered, then turned and went swiftly to the stall of the stallion.

Yasmina clenched her hands and caught her breath as she saw him tear aside the splintered bars and go into the stall with the maddened beast. The stallion reared above him, neighing terribly, hoofs lifted, eyes and teeth flashing and ears laid back, but Conan leaped and caught his mane with a display of sheer strength that seemed impossible, and dragged the beast down on his forelegs. The steed snorted and quivered, but stood still while the man bridled him and clapped on the gold-worked saddle, with the wide silver stirrups.

Wheeling the beast around in the stall, Conan called quickly to Yasmina, and the girl came, sidling nervously past the stallion's heels. Conan was working at the stone wall, talking swiftly as he worked.

"A secret door in the wall here; that not even the Wazuli know about. Yar Afzal showed it to me once when he was drunk. It opens out into the mouth of the ravine behind the hut. Ha!"

As he tugged at a projection that seemed casual, a whole section of the wall slid back on oiled iron runners. Looking through, the girl saw a narrow defile opening in a sheer stone cliff within a few feet of the hut's back wall. Then Conan sprang into the saddle and hauled her up before him. Behind them the great door groaned like a living thing and crashed in, and a yell rang to the roof as the entrance was instantly flooded with hairy faces and knives in hairy fists. And then the great stallion went through the wall like a javelin from a catapult, and thundered into the defile, running low, foam flying from the bit-rings.

That move came as an absolute surprise to the Wazulis. It was a surprise, too, to those stealing down the ravine. It happened so quickly—the hurricane-like charge of the great horse—that a man in a green turban was unable to get out of the way. He went down under the frantic hoofs, and a girl screamed. Conan got one glimpse of her as they thundered by—a slim, dark girl in silk trousers and a jeweled breast-band, flattening herself against the ravine wall. Then the black horse and his riders were gone up the gorge like the spume blown before a storm, and the men who came tumbling through the wall into the defile after them met that which changed their yells of bloodlust to shrill screams of fear and death.

6. The Mountain of the Black Seers

"Where now?" Yasmina was trying to sit erect on the rocking saddlebow, clutching her captor. She was conscious of a recognition of shame that she should not find unpleasant the feel of his muscular flesh under her fingers.

"To Afghulistan," he answered. "It's a perilous road, but the stallion will carry us easily, unless we fall in with some of your friends, or my tribal enemies. Now that Yar Afzal is dead, those damned Wazulis will be on our heels. I'm surprised we haven't sighted them behind us already."

"Who was that man you rode down?" she asked.

"I don't know. I never saw him before. He's no Ghuli, that's certain. What the devil he was doing there is more than I can say. There was a girl with him, too."

"Yes." Her gaze was shadowed. "I can not understand that. That girl was my maid, Gitara. Do you suppose she was coming to aid me? That the man was a friend? If so, the Wazulis have captured them both."

"Well," he answered, "there's nothing we can do. If we go back, they'll skin us both. I can't understand how a girl like that could get this far into the mountains with only one man—and he a robed scholar, for that's what he looked like. There's something infernally queer in all this. That fellow Yar Afzal beat and sent away—he moved like a man walking in his sleep. I've seen the priests of Zamora perform their abominable rituals in their forbidden temples, and their victims had a stare like that man. The priests looked into their eyes and muttered incantations, and then the people became like walking dead men, with glassy eyes, doing as they ordered.

"And then I saw what the fellow had in his hand, which Yar Afzal picked up. It was like a big black jet bead, such as the temple girls of Yezud wear when they dance before the black stone spider which is their god. Yar Afzal held it in his hand, and he didn't pick up anything else. Yet when he fell dead, a spider, like the god at Yezud, only smaller, ran out of his fingers. And then, when the Wazulis stood uncertain there, a voice cried out for them to kill me, and I know that voice didn't come from any of the warriors, nor from the women who watched by the huts. It seemed to come from *above*.''

Yasmina did not reply. She glanced at the stark outlines of the mountains all about them and shuddered. Her soul shrank from their gaunt brutality. This was a grim, naked land where anything might happen. Age-old traditions invested it with shuddery horror for anyone born in the hot, luxuriant southern plains.

The sun was high, beating down with fierce heat, yet the wind that blew in fitful gusts seemed to sweep off slopes of ice. Once she heard a strange rushing above them that was not the sweep of the wind, and from the way Conan looked up, she knew it was not a common sound to him, either. She thought that a strip of the cold blue sky was momentarily blurred, as if some all but invisible object had swept between it and herself, but she could not be sure. Neither made any comment, but Conan loosened his knife in his scabbard.

They were following a faintly marked path dipping down into ravines so deep the sun never struck bottom, laboring up steep slopes where loose shale threatened to slide from beneath their feet, and following knife-edge ridges with blue-hazed echoing depths on either hand.

The sun had passed its zenith when they crossed a narrow trail winding among the crags. Conan reined the horse aside and followed it southward, going almost at right angles to their former course.

"A Galzai village is at one end of the trail," he explained. "Their women follow it to a well, for water. You need new garments."

Glancing down at her filmy attire, Yasmina agreed with him. Her cloth-of-gold slippers were in tatters, her robes and silken under-garments torn to shreds that scarcely held together decently. Garments meant for the streets of Peshkhauri were scarcely appropriate for the crags of the Himelians.

Coming to a crook in the trail, Conan dismounted, helped Yasmina down and waited. Presently he nodded, though she heard nothing.

"A woman coming along the trail," he remarked. In sudden panic she clutched his arm.

"You will not—not kill her?"

"I don't kill women ordinarily," he grunted; "though some of these hillwomen are she-wolves. No,'' he grinned as at a huge jest. ''By Crom, I'll *pay* for her clothes! How is that?'' He displayed a handful of gold coins, and replaced all but the largest. She nodded, much relieved. It was perhaps natural for men to slay and die; her flesh crawled at the thought of watching the butchery of a woman

Presently, a woman appeared around the crook of the trail—a tall, slim Galzai girl, straight as a young sapling, bearing a great empty gourd. She stopped short and the gourd fell from her hands when she saw them; she wavered as though to run, then realized that Conan was too close to her to allow her to escape, and so stood still, staring at them with a mixed expression of fear and curiosity.

Conan displayed the gold coin.

''If you will give this woman your garments,'' he said, ''I will give you this money.''

The response was instant. The girl smiled broadly with surprise and delight, and, with the disdain of a hillwoman for prudish conventions, promptly yanked off her sleeveless embroidered vest, slipped down her wide trousers and stepped out of them, twitched off her wide-sleeved shirt, and kicked off her sandals. Bundling them all in a bunch, she proffered them to Conan, who handed them to the astonished Devi.

''Get behind that rock and put these on,'' he directed, further proving himself no native hillman. ''Fold your robes up into a bundle and bring them to me when you come out.''

''The money!'' clamored the hill girl, stretching out her hands eagerly. ''The gold you promised me!''

Conan flipped the coin to her, she caught it, bit, then thrust it into her hair, bent and caught up the gourd and went on down the path, as devoid of self-consciousness as of garments. Conan waited with some impatience while the Devi, for the first time in her pampered life, dressed herself. When she stepped from behind the rock he swore in surprise, and she felt a curious rush of emotions at the unrestrained admiration burning in his fierce blue eyes. She felt shame, embarrassment, yet a stimulation of vanity she had never before experienced, and a tingling when meeting the impact of his eyes. He laid a heavy hand on her shoulder and turned her about, staring avidly at her from all angles.

''By Crom!'' said he. ''In those smoky, mystic robes you were aloof and cold and far off as a star! Now you are a woman of warm flesh and blood! You went behind that rock as the Devi of Vendhya; you come out as a hill girl—though a thousand times more beautiful than any wench of the Zhaibar! You were a goddess—now you are real!''

He spanked her resoundingly, and she, recognizing this as merely another expression of admiration, did not feel outraged. It was indeed as if the changing of her garments had wrought a change in her personality. The feelings and sensations she had suppressed rose to domination in her now, as if the queenly robes she had cast off had been material shackles and inhibitions.

But Conan, in his renewed admiration, did not forget that peril lurked all about them. The farther they drew away from the region of the Zhaibar, the less likely he was to encounter any Kshatriya troops. On the other hand, he had been listening all throughout their flight for sounds that would tell him the vengeful Wazulis of Khurum were on their heels.

Swinging the Devi up, he followed her into the saddle and again reined the stallion westward. The bundle of garments she had given him, he hurled over a cliff, to fall into the depths of a thousand-foot gorge.

''Why did you do that?'' she asked. ''Why did you not give them to the girl?''

''The riders from Peshkhauri are combing these hills,'' he said. ''They'll be ambushed and harried at every turn, and by way of reprisal they'll destroy every village they can take. They may turn westward any time. If they found a girl wearing your garments, they'd torture her into talking, and she might put them on my trail.''

''What will she do?'' asked Yasmina.

''Go back to her village and tell her people that a stranger attacked her,'' he answered. ''She'll have them on our track, all right. But she had to go on and get the water first; if she dared go back without it, they'd whip the skin off her. That gives us a long start. They'll never catch us. By nightfall we'll cross the Afghuli border.''

''There are no paths or signs of human habitation in these parts,'' she commented. ''Even for the Himelians this region seems singularly deserted. We have not seen a trail since we left the one where we met the Galzai woman.''

For answer he pointed to the northwest, where she glimpsed a peak in a notch of the crags.

''Yimsha,'' grunted Conan. ''The tribes build their villages as far from that mountain as they can.''

She was instantly rigid with attention.

"Yimsha!" she whispered. "The mountain of the Black Seers!"

"So they say," he answered. "This is as near as I ever approached it. I have swung north to avoid any Kshatriya troops that might be prowling through the hills. The regular trail from Khurum to Afghulistan lies farther south. This is an ancient one, and seldom used."

She was staring intently at the distant peak. Her nails bit into her pink palms.

"How long would it take to reach Yimsha from this point?"

"All the rest of the day, and all night," he answered, and grinned. "Do you want to go there? By Crom, it's no place for an ordinary human, from what the hill people say."

"Why do they not gather and destroy the devils that inhabit it?" she demanded.

"Wipe out wizards with swords? Anyway, they never interfere with people, unless the people interfere with them. I never saw one of them, though I've talked with men who swore they had. They say they've glimpsed people from the tower among the crags at sunset or sunrise—tall, silent men in black robes."

"Would you be afraid to attack them?"

"I?" The idea seemed a new one to him. "Why, if they imposed upon me, it would be my life or theirs. But I have nothing to do with them. I came to these mountains to raise a following of human beings, not to war with wizards."

Yasmina did not at once reply. She stared at the peak as at a human enemy, feeling all her anger and hatred stir in her bosom anew. And another feeling began to take dim shape. She had plotted to hurl against the masters of Yimsha the man in whose arms she was now carried. Perhaps there was another way, besides the method she had planned, to accomplish her purpose. She could not mistake the look that was beginning to dawn in this wild man's eyes as they rested on her. Kingdoms have fallen when a woman's slim white hands pulled the strings of destiny. Suddenly she stiffened, pointing.

"Look!"

Just visible on the distant peak there hung a cloud of peculiar aspect. It was a frosty crimson in color, veined with sparkling gold. This cloud was in motion; it rotated, and as it whirled it contracted. It dwindled to a spinning taper that flashed in the sun. And suddenly it detached itself from the snow-tipped peak, floated out over the void like a gay-hued feather, and became invisible against the cerulean sky.

"What could that have been?" asked the girl uneasily, as a shoulder of rock shut the distant mountain from view; the phenomenon had been disturbing, even its beauty.

"The hillmen call it Yimsha's Carpet, whatever that means," answered Conan. "I've seen five hundred of them running as if the devil were at their heels, to hide themselves in caves and crags, because they saw that crimson cloud float up from the peak. What in——"

They had advanced through a narrow, knife-cut gash between turreted walls and emerged upon a broad ledge, flanked by a series of rugged slopes on one hand, and a gigantic precipice on the other. The dim trail followed this ledge, bent around a shoulder and reappeared at intervals far below, working a tedious way downward. And emerging from the gut that opened upon the ledge, the black stallion halted short, snorting. Conan urged him on impatiently, and the horse snorted and threw his head up and down, quivering and straining as if against an invisible barrier.

Conan swore and swung off, lifting Yasmina down with him. He went forward, with a hand thrown out before him as if expecting to encounter unseen resistance, but there was nothing to hinder him, though when he tried to lead the horse, it neighed shrilly and jerked back. Then Yasmina cried out, and Conan wheeled, hand starting to knife-hilt.

Neither of them had seen him come, but he stood there, with his arms folded, a man in a camel-hair robe and a green turban. Conan grunted with surprise to recognize the man the stallion had spurned in the ravine outside the Wazuli village.

"Who the devil are you?" he demanded.

The man did not answer. Conan noticed that his eyes were wide, fixed, and of a peculiar luminous quality. And those eyes held his like a magnet.

Khemsa's sorcery was based on hypnotism, as is the case with most Eastern magic. The way has been prepared for the hypnotist for untold centuries of generations who have lived and died in the firm conviction of the reality and power of hypnotism, building up, by mass thought and practice, a colossal though intangible atmosphere against which the individual, steeped in the traditions of the land, finds himself helpless.

But Conan was not a son of the East. Its traditions were meaningless to him; he was the product of an utterly alien atmosphere. Hypnotism was not even a myth in Cimmeria. The heritage that prepared a native of the East for submission to the mesmerist was not his.

He was aware of what Khemsa was trying to do to him; but he felt the impact of the man's uncanny power only as a vague impulsion, a tugging and pulling that he could shake off as a man shakes spider webs from his garments.

Aware of hostility and black magic, he ripped out his long knife and lunged, as quick on his feet as a mountain lion.

But hypnotism was not all of Khemsa's magic. Yasmina, watching, did not see by what roguery of movement or illusion the man in the green turban avoided the terrible disemboweling thrust. But the keen blade whickered between side and lifted arm, and to Yasmina it seemed that Khemsa merely brushed his open palm lightly against Conan's bullneck. But the Cimmerian went down like a slain ox.

Yet Conan was not dead; breaking his fall with his left hand, he slashed at Khemsa's legs even as he went down, and the Rakhsha avoided the scythe-like swipe only by a most unwizardly bound backward. Then Yasmina cried out sharply as she saw a woman she recognized as Gitara glide out from among the rocks and come up to the man. The greeting died in the Devi's throat as she saw the malevolence in the girl's beautiful face.

Conan was rising slowly, shaken and dazed by the cruel craft of that blow which, delivered with an art forgotten of men before Atlantis sank, would have broken like a rotten twig the neck of a lesser man. Khemsa gazed at him cautiously and a trifle uncertainly. The Rakhsha had learned the full flood of his own power when he faced at bay the knives of the maddened Wazulis in the ravine behind Khurum village; but the Cimmerian's resistance had perhaps shaken his newfound confidence a trifle. Sorcery thrives on success, not on failure.

He stepped forward, lifting his hand—then halted as if frozen, head tilted back, eyes wide open, hand raised. In spite of himself Conan followed his gaze, and so did the women—the girl cowering by the trembling stallion, and the girl beside Khemsa.

Down the mountain slopes, like a whirl of shining dust blown before the wind, a crimson, conoid cloud came dancing. Khemsa's dark face turned ashen; his hand began to tremble, then sank to his side. The girl beside him, sensing the change in him, stared at him inquiringly.

The crimson shape left the mountain slope and came down in a long arching swoop. It struck the ledge between Conan and Khemsa, and the Rakhsha gave back with a stifled cry. He backed away, pushing the girl Gitara back with groping, fending hands.

The crimson cloud balanced like a spinning top for an instant, whirling in a dazzling sheen on its point. Then without warning it was gone, vanished as a bubble vanishes when burst. There on the ledge stood four men. It was miraculous, incredible, impossible, yet it was true. They were not ghosts or phantoms. They were four tall men, with shaven, vulture-like heads, and black robes that hid their feet. Their hands were concealed by their wide sleeves. They stood in silence, their naked heads nodding slightly in unison. They were facing Khemsa, but behind them Conan felt his own blood turning to ice in his veins. Rising, he backed stealthily away, until he felt the stallion's shoulder trembling against his back, and the Devi crept into the shelter of his arm. There was no word spoken. Silence hung like a stifling pall.

All four of the men in black robes stared at Khemsa. Their vulture-like faces were immobile, their eyes introspective and contemplative. But Khemsa shook like a man in an ague. His feet were braced on the rock, his calves straining as if in physical combat. Sweat ran in streams down his dark face. His right hand locked on something under his brown robe so desperately that the blood ebbed from that hand and left it white. His left hand fell on the shoulder of Gitara and clutched in agony like the grasp of a drowning man. She did not flinch or whimper, though his fingers dug like talons into her firm flesh.

Conan had witnessed hundreds of battles in his wild life, but never one like this, wherein four diabolical wills sought to beat down one lesser but equally devilish will that opposed them. But he only faintly sensed the monstrous quality of that hideous struggle. With his back to the wall, driven to bay by his former masters, Khemsa was fighting for his life with all the dark power, all the frightful knowledge they had taught him through long, grim years of neophytism and vassalage.

He was stronger than even he had guessed, and the free exercise of his powers in his own behalf had tapped unsuspected reservoirs of forces. And he was nerved to super-energy by frantic fear and desperation. He reeled before the merciless impact of those hypnotic eyes, but he held his ground. His features were distorted into a bestial grin of agony, and his limbs were twisted as in a rack. It was a war of souls, of frightful brains steeped in lore forbidden to men for a million years, of mentalities which had plumbed the abysses and explored the dark stars where spawn the shadows.

Yasmina understood this better than did Conan. And she dimly understood why Khemsa could withstand the concentrated impact of those four hellish wills which might have blasted into atoms the very rock on which he stood. The reason was the girl that he clutched with the strength of his despair. She was like an anchor to his staggering soul, battered by the waves of those psychic emanations. His weakness was now his strength. His love for the girl, violent and evil though it might be, was yet a tie that bound him to the rest of humanity, providing an earthly leverage for his will, a chain that his inhuman enemies could not break; at least not break through Khemsa.

They realized that before he did. And one of them turned his gaze from the Rakhsha full upon Gitara. There was no battle there. The girl shrank and wilted like a leaf in the drought. Irresistibly impelled, she tore herself from her lover's arms before he realized what was happening. Then a hideous thing came to pass. She began to back toward the precipice, facing her tormentors, her eyes wide and blank as dark gleaming glass from behind which a lamp has been blown out. Khemsa groaned and staggered toward her, falling into the trap set for him. A divided mind could not maintain the unequal battle. He was beaten, a straw in their hands. The girl went backward, walking like an automaton, and Khemsa reeled drunkenly after her, hands vainly outstretched, groaning, slobbering in his pain, his feet moving heavily like dead things.

On the very brink she paused, standing stiffly, her heels on the edge, and he fell on his knees and crawled whimpering toward her, groping for her, to drag her back from destruction. And just before his clumsy fingers touched her, one of the wizards laughed, like the sudden, bronze note of a bell in Hell. The girl reeled suddenly and, consummate climax of exquisite cruelty, reason and understanding flooded back into her eyes, which flared with awful fear. She screamed, clutched wildly at her lover's straining hands, and then, unable to save herself, fell headlong with a moaning cry.

Khemsa hauled himself to the edge and stared over, haggardly, his lips working as he mumbled to himself. Then he turned and stared for a long minute at his torturers, with wide eyes that held no human light. And then with a cry that almost burst the rocks, he reeled up and came rushing toward them, a knife lifted in his hand.

One of the Rakhshas stepped forward and stamped his foot, and as he stamped, there came a rumbling that grew swiftly to a grinding roar. Where his foot struck, a crevice opened in the solid rock that widened instantly. Then, with a deafening crash, a whole section of the ledge gave way. There was a last glimpse of Khemsa, with arms wildly upflung, and then he vanished amidst the roar of the avalanche that thundered down into the abyss.

The four looked contemplatively at the ragged edge of the rock that formed the new rim of the precipice, and then turned suddenly. Conan, thrown off his feet by the shudder of the mountain, was rising, lifting Yasmina. He seemed to move as slowly as his brain was working. He was befogged and stupid. He realized that there was desperate need for him to lift the Devi on the black stallion, and ride like the wind, but an unaccountable sluggishness weighed his every thought and action.

And now the wizards had turned toward him; they raised their arms, and to his horrified sight, he saw their outlines fading, dimming, becoming hazy and nebulous, as a crimson smoke billowed around their feet and rose about them. They were blotted out by a sudden whirling cloud—and then he realized that he too was enveloped in a blinding crimson mist—he heard Yasmina scream, and the stallion cried out like a woman in pain. The Devi was torn from his arm, and as he lashed out with his knife blindly, a terrific blow like a gust of storm wind knocked him sprawling against a rock. Dazedly he saw a crimson conoid cloud spinning up and over the mountain slopes. Yasmina was gone, and so were the four men in black. Only the terrified stallion shared the ledge with him.

7. On to Yimsha

As mists vanish before a strong wind, the cobwebs vanished from Conan's brain. With a searing curse he leaped into the saddle and the stallion reared neighing beneath him. He glared up the slopes, hesitated, and then turned down the trail in the direction he had been going when halted by Khemsa's trickery. But now he did not ride at a measured gait. He shook loose the reins and the stallion went like a thunderbolt, as if frantic to lose hysteria in violent physical exertion. Across the ledge and around the crag and down the narrow trail threading the great steep they plunged at breakneck speed. The path followed a fold of rock, winding interminably down from tier to tier of striated escarpment, and once, far below, Conan got a glimpse of the ruin that had fallen—a mighty pile of broken stone and boulders at the foot of a gigantic cliff.

The valley floor was still far below him when he reached a

long and lofty ridge that led out from the slope like a natural causeway. Out upon this he rode, with an almost sheer drop on either hand. He could trace ahead of him the trail he had to follow; far ahead it dropped down from the ridge and made a great horseshoe back into the river bed at his left hand. He cursed the necessity of traversing those miles, but it was the only way. To try to descend to the lower lap of the trail here would be to attempt the impossible. Only a bird could get to the river-bed with a whole neck.

So he urged on the wearying stallion, until a clink of hoofs reached his ears, welling up from below. Pulling up short and reining to the lip of the cliff, he stared down into the dry river-bed that wound along the foot of the ridge. Along that gorge rode a motley throng—bearded men on half-wild horses, five hundred strong, bristling with weapons. And Conan shouted suddenly, leaning over the edge of the cliff, three hundred feet above them.

At his shout they reined back, and five hundred bearded faces were tilted up toward him; a deep, clamorous roar filled the canyon. Conan did not waste words.

"I was riding for Ghor!" he roared. "I had not hoped to meet you dogs on the trail. Follow me as fast as your nags can push! I'm going to Yimsha, and——"

"Traitor!" The howl was like a dash of ice-water in his face.

"What?" He glared down at them, jolted speechless. He saw wild eyes blazing up at him, faces contorted with fury, fists brandishing blades.

"Traitor!" they roared back, wholeheartedly. "Where are the seven chiefs held captive in Peshkhauri?"

"Why, in the governor's prison, I suppose," he answered.

A bloodthirsty yell from a hundred throats answered him with such a waving of weapons and a clamor that he could not understand what they were saying. He beat down the din with a bull-like roar, and bellowed: "What devil's play is this? Let one of you speak, so I can understand what you mean!"

A gaunt old chief elected himself to this position, shook his tulwar at Conan as a preamble, and shouted accusingly: "You would not let us go raiding Peshkhauri to rescue our brothers!"

"No, you fools!" roared the exasperated Cimmerian. "Even if you'd breached the wall, which is unlikely, they'd have hanged the prisoners before you could reach them."

"And you went alone to traffic with the governor!" yelled the Afghuli, working himself into a frothing frenzy.

"Well?"

"Where are the seven chiefs?" howled the old chief, making his tulwar into a glimmering wheel of steel about his head. "Where are they? Dead!"

"What!" Conan nearly fell off his horse in his surprise.

"Aye, dead!" five hundred bloodthirsty voices assured him.

The old chief brandished his arms and got the floor again. "They were not hanged!" he screeched. "A Wazuli in another cell saw them die! The governor sent a wizard to slay them by craft!"

"That must be a lie," said Conan. "The governor would not dare. Last night I talked with him——"

The admission was unfortunate. A yell of hate and accusation split the skies.

"Aye! You went to him alone! To betray us! It is no lie. The Wazuli escaped through the doors the wizard burst in his entry, and told the tale to our scouts whom he met in the Zhaibar. They had been sent forth to search for you, when you did not return. When they heard the Wazuli's tale, they returned with all haste to Ghor, and we saddled our steeds and girt our swords!"

"And what do you fools mean to do?" demanded the Cimmerian.

"To avenge our brothers!" they howled. "Death to the Kshatriyas! Slay him, brothers, he is a traitor!"

Arrows began to rattle around him. Conan rose in his stirrups, striving to make himself heard above the tumult, and then, with a roar of mingled rage, defiance, and disgust, he wheeled and galloped back up the trail. Behind him and below him the Afghulis came pelting, mouthing their rage, too furious even to remember that the only way they could reach the height whereon he rode was to traverse the river-bed in the other direction, make the broad bend, and follow the twisting trail up over the ridge. When they did remember this, and turned back, their repudiated chief had almost reached the point where the ridge joined the escarpment.

At the cliff he did not take the trail by which he had descended, but turned off on another, a mere trace along a rock-fault, where the stallion scrambled for footing. He had not ridden far when the stallion snorted and shied back from something lying in the trail. Conan stared down on the travesty of a man, a broken, shredded, bloody heap that gibbered and gnashed splintered teeth.

Only the dark gods that rule over the grim destinies of wizards know how Khemsa dragged his shattered body from beneath that awful cairn of fallen rocks and up the steep slope to the trail.

Impelled by some obscure reason, Conan dismounted and stood looking down at the ghastly shape, knowing that he was witness of a thing miraculous and opposed to nature. The Rakhsha lifted his gory head, and his strange eyes, glazed with agony and approaching death, rested on Conan with recognition.

"Where are they?" It was a racking croak not even remotely resembling a human voice.

"Gone back to their damnable castle on Yimsha," grunted Conan. "They took the Devi with them."

"I will go!" muttered the man. "I will follow them! They killed Gitara; I will kill them—the acolytes, the Four of the Black Circle, the Master himself! Kill—kill them all!" He strove to drag his mutilated frame along the rock, but not even his indomitable will could animate that gory mass longer, where the splintered bones hung together only by torn tissue and ruptured fiber.

"Follow them!" raved Khemsa, drooling a bloody slaver. "Follow!"

"I'm going to," growled Conan. "I went to fetch my Afghulis, but they've turned on me. I'm going on to Yimsha alone. I'll have the Devi back if I have to tear down that damned mountain with my bare hands. I didn't think the governor would dare kill my headmen, when I had the Devi, but it seems he did. I'll have his head for that. She's no use to me now as a hostage, but——"

"The curse of Yizil on them!" gasped Khemsa. "Go! I—Khemsa—am dying. Wait—take my girdle."

He tried to fumble with a mangled hand at his tatters, and Conan, understanding what he sought to convey, bent and drew from about his gory waist a girdle of curious aspect.

"Follow the golden vein through the abyss," muttered Khemsa. "Wear the girdle. I had it from a Stygian priest. It will aid you, though it failed me at last. Break the crystal globe with the four golden pomegranates. Beware of the Master's transmutations—I am going to Gitara—she is waiting for me in Hell—*aie, ya Skelos yar!*" And so he died.

Conan stared down at the girdle. The hair of which it was woven was not horsehair. He was convinced that it was woven of the thick black tresses of a woman. Set in the thick mesh were tiny jewels such as he had never seen before. The buckle was strangely made, in the form of a golden serpent head, flat, wedge-shaped, and scaled with curious art. A strong shudder shook Conan as he handled it, and he turned as though to cast it over the precipice; then he hesitated, and finally buckled it about his waist, under the Bakhariot girdle. Then he mounted and pushed on.

The sun had sunk behind the crags. He climbed the trail in the vast shadow of the cliffs that was thrown out like a dark blue mantle over valleys and ridges far below. He was not far from the crest when, edging around the shoulder of a jutting crag, he heard the clink of shod hoofs ahead of him. He did not turn back. Indeed, so narrow was the path that the stallion could not have wheeled his great body upon it. He rounded the jut of the rock and came upon a portion of the path that broadened somewhat. A chorus of threatening yells broke on his ear, but his stallion pinned a terrified horse hard against the rock, and Conan caught the arm of the rider in an iron grip, checking the lifted sword in midair.

"Kerim Shah!" muttered Conan, red glints smoldering luridly in his eyes. The Turanian did not struggle; they sat their horses almost breast to breast, Conan's fingers locking the other's sword arm. Behind Kerim Shah filed a group of lean Irakzai on gaunt horses. They glared like wolves, fingering bows and knives, but rendered uncertain because of the narrowness of the path and the perilous proximity of the abyss that yawned beneath them.

"Where is the Devi?" demanded Kerim Shah.

"What's it to you, you Hyrkanian spy?" snarled Conan.

"I know you have her," answered Kerim Shah. "I was on my way northward with some tribesmen when we were ambushed by enemies in Shalizah Pass. Many of my men were slain, and the rest of us harried through the hills like jackals. When we had beaten off our pursuers, we turned westward, toward Amir Jehun Pass, and this morning we came upon a Wazuli wandering through the hills. He was quite mad, but I learned much from his incoherent gibberings before he died. I learned that he was the sole survivor of a band which followed a chief of the Afghulis and a captive Kshatriya woman into a gorge behind Khurum village. He babbled much of a man in a green turban whom the Afghuli rode down, but who, when attacked by the Wazulis who pursued, smote them with a nameless doom that wiped them out as a gust of wind-driven fire wipes out a cluster of locusts.

"How that one man escaped, I do not know, nor did he; but I knew from his maunderings that Conan of Ghor had been in

Khurum with his royal captive. And as we made our way through the hills, we overtook a naked Galzai girl bearing a gourd of water, who told us a tale of having been stripped and ravished by a giant foreigner in the garb of an Afghuli chief, who, she said, gave her garments to a Vendhyan woman who accompanied him. She said you rode westward.''

Kerim Shah did not consider it necessary to explain that he had been on his way to keep his rendezvous with the expected troops from Secunderam when he found his way barred by hostile tribesmen. The road to Gurashah valley through Shalizah Pass was longer than the road that wound through Amir Jehun Pass, but the latter traversed part of the Afghuli country, which Kerim Shah had been anxious to avoid until he came with an army. Barred from the Shalizah road, however, he had turned to the forbidden route, until news that Conan had not yet reached Afghulistan with his captive had caused him to turn southward and push on recklessly in the hope of overtaking the Cimmerian in the hills.

"So you had better tell me where the Devi is," suggested Kerim Shah. "We outnumber you—"

"Let one of your dogs nock a shaft and I'll throw you over the cliff," Conan promised. "It wouldn't do you any good to kill me, anyhow. Five hundred Afghulis are on my trail, and if they find you've cheated them, they'll flay you alive. Anyway, I haven't got the Devi. She's in the hands of the Black Seers of Yimsha."

"*Tarim!*" swore Kerim Shah softly, shaken out of his poise for the first time. "Khemsa—"

"Khemsa's dead," grunted Conan. "His masters sent him to Hell on a landslide. And now get out of my way. I'd be glad to kill you if I had the time, but I'm on my way to Yimsha."

"I'll go with you," said the Turanian abruptly.

Conan laughed at him. "Do you think I'd trust you, you Hyrkanian dog?"

"I don't ask you to," returned Kerim Shah. "We both want the Devi. You know my reason; King Yezdigerd desires to add her kingdom to his empire, and herself in his seraglio. And I knew you, in the days when you were a hetman of the *kozak* steppes; so I know your ambition is wholesale plunder. You want to loot Vendhya, and to twist out a huge ransom for Yasmina. Well, let us for the time being, without any illusion about each other, unite our forces, and try to rescue the Devi from the Seers. If we succeed, and live, we can fight it out to see who keeps her."

Conan narrowly scrutinized the other for a moment, and then nodded, releasing the Turanian's arm. "Agreed; what about your men?"

Kerim Shah turned to the silent Irakzai and spoke briefly: "This chief and I are going to Yimsha to fight the wizards. Will you go with us, or stay here to be flayed by the Afghulis who are following this man?"

They looked at him with eyes grimly fatalistic. They were doomed and they knew it—had known it ever since the singing arrows of the ambushed Dagozai had driven them back from the pass of Shalizah. The men of the lower Zhaibar had too many reeking blood-feuds among the crag-dwellers. They were too small a band to fight their way back through the hills to the villages of the border, without the guidance of the crafty Turanian. They counted themselves as dead already, so they made the reply that only dead men would make: "We will go with thee and die on Yimsha."

"Then in Crom's name let us be gone," grunted Conan, fidgeting with impatience as he stared into the blue gulfs of the deepening twilight. "My wolves were hours behind me, but we've lost a devilish lot of time."

Kerim Shah backed his steed from between the black stallion and the cliff, sheathed his sword and cautiously turned the horse. Presently the band was filing up the path as swiftly as they dared. They came out upon the crest nearly a mile east of the spot where Khemsa had halted the Cimmerian and the Devi. The path they had traversed was a perilous one, even for hillmen, and for that reason Conan had avoided it that day when carrying Yasmina, though Kerim Shah, following him, had taken it supposing the Cimmerian had done likewise. Even Conan sighed with relief when the horses scrambled up over the last rim. They moved like phantom riders through an enchanted realm of shadows. The soft creak of leather, the clink of steel marked their passing, then again the dark mountain slopes lay naked and silent in the starlight.

8. *Yasmina Knows Stark Terror*

Yasmina had time but for one scream when she felt herself enveloped in that crimson whirl and torn from her protector with appalling force. She screamed once, and then she had no breath to scream. She was blinded, deafened, rendered mute and eventually senseless by the terrific rushing of the air about her. There was a dazed consciousness of dizzy height and numbing speed, a confused impression of natural sensations gone mad, and then vertigo and oblivion.

A vestige of these sensations clung to her as she recovered consciousness; so she cried out and clutched wildly as though to stay a headlong and involuntary flight. Her fingers closed on soft fabric, and a relieving sense of stability pervaded her. She took cognizance of her surroundings.

She was lying on a dais covered with black velvet. This dais stood in a great, dim room whose walls were hung with dusky tapestries across which crawled dragons reproduced with repellent realism. Floating shadows merely hinted at the lofty ceiling, and gloom that lent itself to illusion lurked in the corners. There seemed to be neither windows nor doors in the walls, or else they were concealed by the nighted tapestries. Where the dim light came from, Yasmina could not determine. The great room was a realm of mysteries, of shadows, and shadowy shapes in which she could not have sworn to observe movement, yet which invaded her mind with a dim and formless terror.

But her gaze fixed itself on a tangible object. On another, smaller dais of jet, a few feet away, a man sat cross-legged, gazing contemplatively at her. His long black velvet robe, embroidered with gold thread, fell loosely about him, masking his figure. His hands were folded in his sleeves. There was a velvet cap upon his head. His face was calm, placid, not unhandsome, his eyes lambent and slightly oblique. He did not move a muscle as he sat regarding her, nor did his expression alter when he saw she was conscious.

Yasmina felt fear crawl like a trickle of ice-water down her supple spine. She lifted herself on her elbows and stared apprehensively at the stranger.

"Who are you?" she demanded. Her voice sounded brittle and inadequate.

"I am Master of Yimsha." The tone was rich and resonant, like the mellow notes of a temple bell.

"Why did you bring me here?" she demanded.

"Were you not seeking me?"

"If you are one of the Black Seers—yes!" she answered recklessly, believing that he could read her thoughts anyway.

He laughed softly, and chills crawled up and down her spine again.

"You would turn the wild children of the hills against the Seers of Yimsha!" he smiled. "I have read it in your mind, princess. Your weak, human mind, filled with petty dreams of hate and revenge."

"You slew my brother!" A rising tide of anger was vying with her fear; her hands were clenched, her lithe body rigid. "Why did you persecute him? He never harmed you. The priests say the Seers are above meddling in human affairs. Why did you destroy the king of Vendhya?"

"How can an ordinary human understand the motives of a Seer?" returned the Master calmly. "My acolytes in the temples of Turan, who are the priests behind the priests of Tarim, urged me to bestir myself in behalf of Yezdigerd. For reasons of my own, I complied. How can I explain my mystic reasons to your puny intellect? You could not understand."

"I understand this: my brother died!" Tears of grief and rage shook in her voice. She rose upon her knees and stared at him with wide blazing eyes, as supple and dangerous in that moment as a she-panther.

"As Yezdigerd desired," agreed the Master calmly. "For a while it was my whim to further his ambitions."

"Is Yezdigerd your vassal?" Yasmina tried to keep the timbre of her voice unaltered. She had felt her knee pressing something hard and symmetrical under a fold of velvet. Subtly she shifted her position, moving her hand under the fold.

"Is the dog that licks up the offal in the temple yard the vassal of the god?" returned the Master.

He did not seem to notice the actions she sought to dissemble. Concealed by the velvet, her fingers closed on what she knew was the golden hilt of a dagger. She bent her head to hide the light of triumph in her eyes.

"I am weary of Yezdigerd," said the Master. "I have turned to other amusements—ha!"

With a fierce cry Yasmina sprang like a jungle cat, stabbing murderously. Then she stumbled and slid to the floor, where she cowered, staring up at the man on the dais. He had not moved; his cryptic smile was unchanged. Tremblingly she lifted her hand and stared at it with dilated eyes. There was no dagger in her fingers; they grasped a stalk of golden lotus, the crushed blossoms drooping on the bruised stem.

She dropped it as if it had been a viper, and scrambled away from the proximity of her tormenter. She returned to her own dais, because that was at least more dignified for a queen than groveling on the floor at the feet of a sorcerer, and eyed him apprehensively, expecting reprisals.

But the Master made no move.

"All substance is one to him who holds the key of the cosmos," he said cryptically. "To an adept nothing is immutable. At will, steel blossoms bloom in unnamed gardens, or flower-swords flash in the moonlight."

"You are a devil," she sobbed.

"Not I!" he laughed. "I was born on this planet, long ago. Once I was a common man, nor have I lost all human attributes in the numberless eons of my adeptship. A human steeped in the dark arts is greater than a devil. I am of human origin, but I rule demons. You have seen the Lords of the Black Circle—it would blast your soul to hear from what far realm I summoned them and from what doom I guard them with ensorceled crystal and golden serpents.

"But only I can rule them. My foolish Khemsa thought to make himself great—poor fool, bursting material doors and hur-tling himself and his mistress through the air from hill to hill! Yet if he had not been destroyed, his power might have grown to rival mine."

He laughed again. "And you, poor, silly thing! Plotting to send a hairy hill chief to storm Yimsha! It was such a jest that I myself could have designed, had it occurred to me, that you should fall into his hands. And I read in your childish mind an intention to seduce by your feminine wiles to attempt your purpose, anyway.

"But for all your stupidity, you are a woman fair to look upon. It is my whim to keep you for my slave."

The daughter of a thousand proud emperors gasped with shame and fury at the word.

"You dare not!"

His mocking laughter cut her like a whip across her naked shoulders.

"The king dares not trample a worm in the road? Little fool, do you not realize that your royal pride is no more to me than a straw blown on the wind? I, who have known the kisses of the queens of Hell! You have seen how I deal with a rebel!"

Cowed and awed, the girl crouched on the velvet-covered dais. The light grew dimmer and more phantom-like. The fea-tures of the Master became shadowy. His voice took on a newer tone of command.

"I will never yield to you!" Her voice trembled with fear but it carried a ring of resolution.

"You will yield," he answered with horrible conviction. "Fear

and pain shall teach you. I will lash you with horror and agony
to the last quivering ounce of your endurance, until you become
as melted wax to be bent and molded in my hands as I desire.
You shall know such discipline as no mortal woman ever knew,
until my slightest command is to you as the unalterable will of
the gods. And first, to humble your pride, you shall travel back
through the lost ages, and view all the shapes that have been
you. *Aie, yil la khosa!''*

At these words the shadowy room swam before Yasmina's
affrighted gaze. The roots of her hair prickled her scalp, and her
tongue clove to her palate. Somewhere a gong sounded a deep,
ominous note. The dragons on the tapestries glowed like blue
fire, and then faded out. The Master on his dais was but a
shapeless shadow. The dim light gave way to soft, thick darkness,
almost tangible, that pulsed with strange radiations. She could no
longer see the Master. She could see nothing. She had a strange
sensation that the walls and ceiling had withdrawn immensely
from her.

Then somewhere in the darkness a glow began, like a firefly
that rhythmically dimmed and quickened. It grew to a golden
ball, and as it expanded its light grew more intense, flaming
whitely. It burst suddenly, showering the darkness with white
sparks that did not illumine the shadows. But like an impression
left in the gloom, a faint luminance remained, and revealed a
slender dusky shaft shooting up from the shadowy floor. Under
the girl's dilated gaze it spread, took shape; stems and broad
leaves appeared, and great black poisonous blossoms that towered above her as she cringed against the velvet. A subtle
perfume pervaded the atmosphere. It was the dread figure of the
black lotus that had grown up as she watched, as it grows in the
haunted, forbidden jungles of Khitai.

The broad leaves were murmurous with evil life. The blossoms bent toward her like sentient things, nodding serpent-like
on pliant stems. Etched against soft, impenetrable darkness, it
loomed over her, gigantic, blackly visible in some mad way. Her
brain reeled with the drugging scent and she sought to crawl
from the dais. Then she clung to it as it seemed to be pitching at
an impossible slant. She cried out with terror and clung to the
velvet, but she felt her fingers ruthlessly torn away. There was a
sensation as of all sanity and stability crumbling and vanishing.
She was a quivering atom of sentiency driven through a black,
roaring, icy void by a thundering wind that threatened to extin-

guish her feeble flicker of animate life like a candle blown out in a storm.

Then there came a period of blind impulse and movement, when the atom that was she mingled and merged with myraid other atoms of spawning life in the yeasty morass of existence, molded by formative forces until she emerged again a conscious individual, whirling down an endless spiral of lives.

In a mist of terror she relived all her former existences, recognized and *was* again all the bodies that had carried her ego throughout the changing ages. She bruised her feet again over the long, weary road of life that stretched out behind her into the immemorial Past. Back beyond the dimmest dawns of Time she crouched shuddering in primordial jungles, hunted by slavering beasts of prey. Skin-clad, she waded thigh-deep in rice-swamps, battling with squawking waterfowl for the precious grains. She labored with the oxen to drag the pointed stick through the stubborn soil, and she crouched endlessly over looms in peasant huts.

She saw walled cities burst into flame, and fled screaming before the slayers. She reeled naked and bleeding over burning sands, dragged at the slaver's stirrup, and she knew the grip of hot, fierce hands on her writhing flesh, the shame and agony of brutal lust. She screamed under the bite of the lash, and moaned on the rack; mad with terror she fought against the hands that forced her head inexorably down on the bloody block.

She knew the agonies of childbirth, and the bitterness of love betrayed. She suffered all the woes and wrongs and brutalities that man has inflicted on woman throughout the eons; and she endured all the spite and malice of woman for woman. And like the flick of a fiery whip throughout was the consciousness she retained of her Devi-ship. She was all the women she had ever been, yet in her knowing she was Yasmina. This consciousness was not lost in the throes of reincarnation. At one and the same time she was a naked slave-wench groveling under the whip, and the proud Devi of Vendhya. And she suffered not only as the slave-girl suffered, but as Yasmina, to whose pride the whip was like a white-hot brand.

Life merged into life in flying chaos, each with its burden of woe and shame and agony, until she dimly heard her own voice screaming unbearably, like one long-drawn cry of suffering echoing down the ages.

Then she awakened on the velvet-covered dais in the mystic room.

In a ghostly gray light she saw again the dais and the cryptic robed figure seated upon it. The hooded head was bent, the high shoulders faintly etched against the uncertain dimness. She could make out no details clearly, but the hood, where the velvet cap had been, stirred a formless uneasiness in her. As she stared, there stole over her a nameless fear that froze her tongue to her palate—a feeling that it was not the Master who sat so silently on that black dais.

Then the figure moved and rose upright, towering above her. It stooped over her and the long arms in their wide black sleeves bent about her. She fought against them in speechless fright, surprised by their lean hardness. The hooded head bent down toward her averted face. And she screamed, and screamed again in poignant fear and loathing. Bony arms gripped her lithe body, and from that hood looked forth a countenance of death and decay—features like rotting parchment on a moldering skull.

She screamed again, and then, as those champing, grinning jaws bent toward her lips, she lost consciousness. . . .

9. *The Castle of the Wizards*

The sun had risen over the white Himelian peaks. At the foot of a long slope, a group of horsemen halted and stared upward. High above them a stone tower poised on the pitch of the mountainside. Beyond and above that gleamed the walls of a greater keep, near the line where the snow began that capped Yimsha's pinnacle. There was a touch of unreality about the whole—purple slopes pitching up to that fantastic castle, toy-like with distance, and above it the white glistening peak shouldering the cold blue.

"We'll leave the horses here," grunted Conan. "That treacherous slope is safer for a man on foot. Besides, they're done."

He swung down from the black stallion which stood with wide-braced legs and drooping head. They had pushed hard throughout the night, gnawing at scraps from saddle-bags, and pausing only to give the horses the rests they had to have.

"That first tower is held by the acolytes of the Black Seers," said Conan. "Or so men say; watch-dogs for their masters—lesser sorcerers. They won't sit sucking their thumbs as we climb this slope."

Kerim Shah glanced up the mountain, then back the way they had come; they were already far up on Yimsha's side, and a vast expanse of lesser peaks and crags spread out beneath them.

Among those labyrinths the Turanian sought in vain for a move ment of color that would betray men. Evidently the pursuin Afghulis had lost their chief's trail in the night.

"Let us go, then."

They tied the weary horses in a clump of tamarisk and witho further comment turned up the slope. There was no cover. It wa a naked incline, strewn with boulders not big enough to conce a man. But they did conceal something else.

The party had not gone fifty steps when a snarling shape bur from behind a rock. It was one of the gaunt savage dogs th infested the hill villages, and its eyes glared redly, its jaw dripped foam. Conan was leading, but it did not attack him. dashed past him and leaped at Kerim Shah. The Turanian leape aside, and the great dog flung itself upon the Irakzai behind him The man yelled and threw up his arm, which was torn by th brute's fangs as it bore him backward, and the next instant half dozen tulwars were hacking at the beast. Yet not until it wa literally dismembered did the hideous creature cease its efforts seize and rend its attackers.

Kerim Shah bound up the wounded warrior's gashed arm looked at him narrowly, and then turned away without a word He rejoined Conan, and they renewed the climb in silence.

Presently Kerim Shah said: "Strange to find a village dog i this place."

"There's no offal here," grunted Conan.

Both turned their heads to glance back at the wounded warrio toiling after them among his companions. Sweat glistened on hi dark face and his lips were drawn back from his teeth in grimace of pain. Then both looked again at the stone towe squatting above them.

A slumberous quiet lay over the uplands. The tower showe no sign of life, nor did the strange pyramidal structure beyond it But the men who toiled upward went with the tenseness of me walking on the edge of a crater. Kerim Shah had unslung th powerful Turanian bow that killed at five hundred paces, and th Irakzai looked to their own lighter and less lethal bows.

But they were not within bow-shot of the tower when some thing shot down out of the sky without warning. It passed s close to Conan that he felt the wind of the rushing wings, but i was an Irakzai who staggered and fell, blood jetting from a severed jugular. A hawk with wings like burnished steel shot up again, blood dripping from the scimitar-beak, to reel against the sky as Kerim Shah's bowstring twanged. It dropped like a plummet, but no man saw where it struck the earth.

Conan bent over the victim of the attack, but the man was already dead. No one spoke; useless to comment on the fact that never before had a hawk been known to swoop on a man. Red rage began to vie with fatalistic lethargy in the wild souls of the Irakzai. Hairy fingers nocked arrows and men glared vengefully at the tower whose very silence mocked them.

But the next attack came swiftly. They all saw it—a white puffball of smoke that tumbled over the tower-rim and came drifting and rolling down the slope toward them. Others followed it. They seemed harmless, mere woolly globes of cloudy foam, but Conan stepped aside to avoid contact with the first. Behind him one of the Irakzai reached out and thrust his sword into the unstable mass. Instantly a sharp report shook the mountainside. There was a burst of blinding flame, and then the puffball had vanished, and of the too-curious warrior remained only a heap of charred and blackened bones. The crisped hand still gripped the ivory sword-hilt, but the blade was gone—melted and destroyed by that awful heat. Yet men standing almost within reach of the victim had not suffered except to be dazzled and half blinded by the sudden flare.

"Steel touches it off," grunted Conan. "Look out—here they come!"

The slope above them was almost covered by the billowing spheres. Kerim Shah bent his bow and sent a shaft into the mass, and those touched by the arrow burst like bubbles in spurting flame. His men followed his example and for the next few minutes it was as if a thunderstorm raged on the mountain slope, with bolts of lightning striking and bursting in showers of flame. When the barrage ceased, only a few arrows were left in the quivers of the archers.

They pushed on grimly, over soil charred and blackened, where the naked rock had in places been turned to lava by the explosion of those diabolical bombs.

Now they were almost within arrowflight of the silent tower, and they spread their line, nerves taut, ready for any horror that might descend upon them.

On the tower appeared a single figure, lifting a ten-foot bronze horn. Its strident bellow roared out across the echoing slopes, like the blare of trumpets on Judgment Day. And it began to be fearfully answered. The ground trembled under the feet of

the invaders, and the rumblings and grindings welled up from th
subterranean depths.

The Irakzai screamed, reeling like drunken men on the shud
dering slope, and Conan, eyes glaring, charged recklessly up th
incline, knife in hand, straight at the door that showed in th
tower-wall. Above him the great horn roared and bellowed i
brutish mockery. And then Kerim Shah drew a shaft to his ea
and loosed.

Only a Turanian could have made that shot. The bellowing o
the horn ceased suddenly, and a high, thin scream shrilled in it
place. The green-robed figure on the tower staggered, clutchin;
at the long shaft which quivered in its bosom, and then pitche
across the parapet. The great horn tumbled upon the battlemen
and hung precariously, and another robed figure rushed to seiz
it, shrieking in horror. Again the Turanian bow twanged, an
again it was answered by a death-howl. The second acolyte, i
falling, struck the horn with his elbow and knocked it clatterin;
over the parapet to shatter on the rocks far below.

At such headlong speed had Conan covered the ground tha
before the clattering echoes of that fall had died away, he wa
hacking at the door. Warned by his savage instinct, he gave bacl
suddenly as a tide of molten lead splashed down from above. Bu
the next instant he was back again, attacking the panels with
redoubled fury. He was galvanized by the fact that his enemies
had resorted to earthly weapons. The sorcery of the acolytes wa:
limited. Their necromantic resources might well be exhausted.

Kerim Shah was hurrying up the slope, his hillmen behind him
in a straggling crescent. They loosed as they ran, their arrows
splintering against the walls or arching over the parapet.

The heavy teak portal gave way beneath the Cimmerian's
assault, and he peered inside warily, expecting anything. He was
looking into a circular chamber from which a stair wound upward.
On the opposite side of the chamber a door gaped open, revealing the outer slope—and the backs of half a dozen green-robed
figures in full retreat.

Conan yelled, took a step into the tower, and then native
caution jerked him back, just as a great block of stone fell
crashing to the floor where his foot had been an instant before.
Shouting to his followers, he raced around the tower.

The acolytes had evacuated their first line of defense. As
Conan rounded the tower he saw their green robes twinkling up
the mountain ahead of him. He gave chase, panting with earnest
blood-lust, and behind him Kerim Shah and the Irakzai came

pelting, the latter yelling like wolves at the flight of their enemies, their fatalism momentarily submerged by temporary triumph.

The tower stood on the lower edge of a narrow plateau whose upward slant was barely perceptible. A few hundred yards away, this plateau ended abruptly in a chasm, which had been invisible farther down the mountain. Into this chasm the acolytes apparently leaped without checking their speed. Their pursuers saw the green robes flutter and disappear over the edge.

A few moments later they themselves were standing on the brink of the mighty moat that cut them off from the castle of the Black Seers. It was a sheer-walled ravine that extended in either direction as far as they could see, apparently girdling the mountain, some four hundred yards in width and five hundred feet deep. And in it, from rim to rim, a strange, translucent mist sparkled and shimmered.

Looking down, Conan grunted. Far below him, moving across the glimmering floor, which shone like burnished silver, he saw the forms of the green-robed acolytes. Their outline was wavering and indistinct, like figures seen under deep water. They walked in single file, moving toward the opposite wall.

Kerim Shah nocked an arrow and sent it singing downward. But when it struck the mist that filled the chasm it seemed to lose momentum and direction, wandering widely from its course.

"If they went down, so can we!" grunted Conan, while Kerim Shah stared after his shaft in amazement. "I saw them last at this spot——"

Squinting down he saw something shining like a golden thread across the canyon floor far below. The acolytes seemed to be following this thread, and there suddenly came to him Khemsa's cryptic words—"Follow the golden vein!" On the brink, under his very hand as he crouched, he found it, a thin vein of sparkling gold running from an outcropping of ore to the edge and down across the silvery floor. And he found something else, which had before been invisible to him because of the peculiar refraction of the light. The gold vein followed a narrow ramp, which slanted down into the ravine, fitted with niches for hand and foot hold.

"Here's where they went down," he grunted to Kerim Shah. "They're no adepts, to waft themselves through the air! We'll follow them——"

It was at that instant that the man who had been bitten by the mad dog cried out horribly and leaped at Kerim Shah, foaming and gnashing his teeth. The Turanian, quick as a cat on his feet,

sprang aside and the madman pitched head-first over the brink.
The others rushed to the edge and glared after him in amazement.
The maniac did not fall plummetlike. He floated slowly down
through the rosy haze like a man sinking in deep water. His
limbs moved like a man trying to swim, and his features were
purple and convulsed beyond the contortions of his madness. Far
down at last on the shining floor his body settled and lay still.

"There's death in that chasm," muttered Kerim Shah, drawing back from the rosy mist that shimmered almost at his feet.
"What now, Conan?"

"On!" answered the Cimmerian grimly. "Those acolytes are
human; if the mist doesn't kill them, it won't kill me."

He hitched his belt, and his hands touched the girdle Khemsa
had given him; he scowled, then smiled bleakly. He had forgotten that girdle; yet thrice had death passed him by to strike
another victim.

The acolytes had reached the farther wall and were moving up
it like great green flies. Letting himself upon the ramp, he
descended warily. The rosy cloud lapped about his ankles, as-
cending as he lowered himself. It reached his knees, his thighs,
his waist, his armpits. He felt it as one feels a thick heavy fog on
a damp night. With it lapping about his chin he hesitated, and
then ducked under. Instantly his breath ceased; all air was shut
off from him and he felt his ribs caving in on his vitals. With a
frantic effort he heaved himself up, fighting for life. His head
rose above the surface and he drank air in great gulps.

Kerim Shah leaned down toward him, spoke to him, but
Conan neither heard nor heeded. Stubbornly, his mind fixed on
what the dying Khemsa had told him, the Cimmerian groped for
the gold vein, and found that he had moved off it in his descent.
Several series of hand-holds were niched in the ramp. Placing
himself directly over the thread, he began climbing down once
more. The rosy mist rose about him, engulfed him. Now his head
was under, but he was still drinking pure air. Above him he saw
his companions staring down at him, their features blurred by the
haze that shimmered over his head. He gestured for them to
follow and went down swiftly, without waiting to see whether
they complied or not.

Kerim Shah sheathed his sword without comment and followed,
and the Irakzai, more fearful of being left alone than of the
terrors that might lurk below, scrambled after him. Each man
clung to the golden thread as they saw the Cimmerian do.

Down the slanting ramp they went to the ravine floor and

moved out across the shining level, treading the gold vein like rope-walkers. It was as if they walked along an invisible tunnel through which air circulated freely. They felt death pressing in on them above and on either hand, but it did not touch them.

The vein crawled up a similar ramp on the other wall up which the acolytes had disappeared, and up it they went with taut nerves, not knowing what might be waiting for them among the jutting spurs of rock that fanged the lip of the precipice.

It was the green-robed acolytes who awaited them, with knives in their hands. Perhaps they had reached the limits to which they could retreat. Perhaps the Stygian girdle about Conan's waist could have told why their necromantic spells had proven so weak and so quickly exhausted. Perhaps it was a knowledge of death decreed for failure that sent them leaping from among the rocks, eyes glaring and knives glittering, resorting in their desperation to material weapons.

There among the rocky fangs on the precipice lip was no war of wizard craft. It was a whirl of blades, where real steel bit and real blood spurted, where sinewy arms dealt forthright blows that severed quivering flesh, and men went down to be trodden under foot as the fight raged over them.

One of the Irakzai bled to death among the rocks, but the acolytes were down—slashed and hacked asunder or hurled over the edge to float sluggishly down to the silver floor that shone so far below.

Then the conquerors shook blood and sweat from their eyes, and looked at one another. Conan and Kerim Shah still stood upright and four of the Irakzai.

They stood among the rocky teeth that serrated the precipice brink, and from that spot a path wound up a gentle slope to a broad stair, consisting of half a dozen steps, a hundred feet across, cut out of a green jade-like substance. They led up to a broad stage or roofless gallery of the same polished stone, and above it rose, tier upon tier, the castle of the Black Seers. It seemed to have been carved out of the sheer stone of the mountain. The architecture was faultless, but unadorned. The many casements were barred and masked with curtains within. There was no sign of life, friendly or hostile.

They went up the path in silence, and warily as men treading the lair of a serpent. The Irakzai were dumb, like men marching to a certain doom. Even Kerim Shah was silent. Only Conan seemed unaware what a monstrous dislocating and uprooting of accepted thought and action their invasion constituted, what an unprecedented violation of tradition. He was not of the East; and he came of a breed who fought devils and wizards as promptly and matter-of-factly as they battled human foes.

He strode up the shining stairs and across the wide green gallery straight toward the great golden-bound teak door that opened upon it. He cast but a single glance upward at the higher tiers of the great pyramidal structure towering above him. He reached a hand for the bronze prong that jutted like a handle from the door—then checked himself, grinning hardly. The handle was made in the shape of a serpent, head lifted on arched neck; and Conan had a suspicion that that metal head would come to grisly life under his hand.

He struck it from the door with one blow, and its bronze clink on the glassy floor did not lessen his caution. He flipped it aside with his knife-point, and again turned to the door. Utter silence reigned over the towers. Far below them the mountain slopes fell away into a purple haze of distance. The sun glittered on snow-clad peaks on either hand. High above, a vulture hung like a black dot in the cold blue of the sky. But for it, the men before thg gold-bound door were the only evidence of life, tiny figures on a green jade gallery poised on the dizzy height, with that fantastic pile of stone towering above them.

A sharp wind off the snow slashed them, whipping their tatters about. Conan's long knife splintering through the teak panels roused the startled echoes. Again and again he struck, hewing through polished wood and metal bands alike. Through the sundered ruins he glared into the interior, alert and suspicious as a wolf. He saw a broad chamber, the polished stone walls untapestried, the mosaic floor uncarpeted. Square, polished ebon stools and a stone dais formed the only furnishings. The room was empty of human life. Another door showed in the opposite wall.

"Leave a man on guard outside," grunted Conan. "I'm going in."

Kerim Shah designated a warrior for that duty, and the man fell back toward the middle of the gallery, bow in hand. Conan strode into the castle, followed by the Turanian and the three remaining Irakzai. The one outside spat, grumbled in his beard, and started suddenly as a low mocking laugh reached his ears.

He lifted his head and saw, on the tier above him, a tall, black-robed figure, naked head nodding slightly as he stared down. His whole attitude suggested mockery and malignity.

Quick as a flash the Irakzai bent his bow and loosed, and the arrow streaked upward to strike full in the black-robed breast. The mocking smile did not alter. The Seer plucked out the missile and threw it back at the bowman, not as a weapon is hurled, but with a contemptuous gesture. The Irakzai dodged, instinctively throwing up his arm. His fingers closed on the revolving shaft.

Then he shrieked. In his hand the wooden shaft suddenly *writhed*. Its rigid outline became pliant, melting in his grasp. He tried to throw it from him, but it was too late. He held a living serpent in his naked hand, and already it had coiled about his wrist and its wicked wedge-shaped head darted at his muscular arm. He screamed again and his eyes became distended, his features purple. He went to his knees shaken by an awful convulsion, and then lay still.

The men inside had wheeled at his first cry. Conan took a swift stride toward the open doorway, and then halted short, baffled. To the men behind him it seemed that he strained against empty air. But though he could see nothing, there was a slick, smooth, hard surface under his hands, and he knew that a sheet of crystal had been let down in the doorway. Through it he saw the Irakzai lying motionless on the glassy gallery, an ordinary arrow sticking in his arm.

Conan lifted his knife and smote, and the watchers were dumbfounded to see his blow checked apparently in midair, with the loud clang of steel that meets an unyielding substance. He wasted no more effort. He knew that not even the legendary tulwar of Amir Khurum could shatter that invisible curtain.

In a few words he explained the matter to Kerim Shah, and the Turanian shrugged his shoulders. "Well, if our exit is barred, we must find another. In the meanwhile our way lies forward, does it not?"

With a grunt the Cimmerian turned and strode across the chamber to the opposite door, with a feeling of treading on the threshold of doom. As he lifted his knife to shatter the door, it swung silently open as if of its own accord. He strode into a great hall, flanked with tall glassy columns. A hundred feet from the door began the broad jade-green steps of a stair that tapered toward the top like the side of a pyramid. What lay beyond that stair he could not tell. But between him and its shimmering foot stood a curious altar of gleaming black jet. Four great golden serpents twined their tails about this altar and reared their wedge-shaped heads in the air, facing the four quarters of the compass like the enchanted guardians of a fabled treasure. But on the altar, between the arching necks, stood only a crystal globe filled with a cloudy smoke-like substance, in which floated four golden pomegranates.

The sight stirred some dim recollection in his mind; then Conan heeded the altar no longer, for on the lower steps of the stair stood four black-robed figures. He had not seen them come. They were simply there, tall, gaunt, their vulture-heads nodding in unison, their feet and hands hidden by their flowing garments.

One lifted his arm and the sleeve fell away revealing his hand—and it was not a hand at all. Conan halted in midstride, compelled against his will. He had encountered a force differing subtly from Khemsa's mesmerism, and he could not advance, though he felt it in his power to retreat if he wished. His companions had likewise halted, and they seemed even more helpless than he, unable to move in either direction.

The Seer whose arm was lifted beckoned to one of the Irakzai, and the man moved toward him like one in a trance, eyes staring and fixed, blade hanging in limp fingers. As he pushed past Conan, the Cimmerian threw an arm across his breast to arrest him. Conan was so much stronger than the Irakzai that in ordinary circumstances he could have broken his spine between his hands. But now the muscular arm was brushed aside like a straw and the Irakzai, moved toward the stair, treading jerkily and mechanically. He reached the steps and knelt stiffly, proffering his blade and bending his head. The Seer took the sword. It flashed as he swung it up and down. The Irakzai's head tumbled from his shoulders and thudded heavily on the black marble floor. An arch of blood jetted from the severed arteries and the body slumped over and lay with arms spread wide.

Again a malformed hand lifted and beckoned, and another Irakzai stumbled stiffly to his doom. The ghastly drama was re-enacted and another headless form lay beside the first.

As the third tribesman clumped his way past Conan to his death, the Cimmerian, his veins bulging in his temples with his efforts to break past the unseen barrier that held him, was suddenly aware of allied forces, unseen, but waking into life about him. This realization came without warning, but so powerfully that he could not doubt his instinct. His left hand slid involuntarily under his Bakhariot belt and closed on the Stygian girdle. And as he gripped it he felt new strength flood his numbed limbs; the will to live was a pulsing white-hot fire, matched by the intensity of his burning rage.

The third Irakzai was a decapitated corpse, and the hideous finger was lifting again when Conan felt the bursting of the invisible barrier. A fierce, involuntary cry burst from his lips as he leaped with the explosive suddenness of pent-up ferocity. His left hand gripped the sorcerer's girdle as a drowning man grips a floating log, and the long knife was a sheen of light in his right. The men on the steps did not move. They watched calmly, cynically; if they felt surprise they did not show it. Conan did not allow himself to think what might chance when he came within knife-reach of them. His blood was pounding in his temples, a mist of crimson swam before his sight. He was afire with the urge to kill—to drive his knife deep into flesh and bone, and twist the blade in blood and entrails.

Another dozen strides would carry him to the steps where the sneering demons stood. He drew his breath deep, his fury rising redly as his charge gathered momentum. He was hurtling past the altar with its golden serpents when like a levin-flash there shot across his mind again as vividly as if spoken in his external ear, the cryptic words of Khemsa: *"Break the crystal ball!"*

His reaction was almost without his own volition. Execution followed impulse so spontaneously that the greatest sorcerer of the age would not have had time to read his mind and prevent his action. Wheeling like a cat from his headlong charge, he brought his knife crashing down upon the crystal. Instantly the air vibrated with a peal of terror, whether from the stairs, the altar, or the crystal itself he could not tell. Hisses filled his ears as the golden serpents, suddenly vibrant with hideous life, writhed and smote at him. But he was fired to the speed of a maddened tiger. A whirl of steel sheared through the hideous trunks that waved toward him, and he smote the crystal sphere again and yet again. And the globe burst with a noise like a thunder-clap, raining fiery shards on the black marble, and the gold pomegranates, as if released from captivity, shot upward toward the lofty roof and were gone.

A mad screaming, bestial and ghastly, was echoing through the great hall. On the steps wirthed four black-robed figures, twisting in convulsions, froth dripping from their livid mouths. Then with one frenzied crescendo of inhuman ululation they stiffened and lay still, and Conan knew that they were dead. He stared down at the altar and the crystal shards. Four headless golden serpents still coiled about the altar, but no alien life now animated the dully gleaming metal.

Kerim Shah was rising slowly from his knees, whither he had

been dashed by some unseen force. He shook his head to clear the ringing from his ears.

"Did you hear that crash when you struck? It was as if a thousand crystal panels shattered all over the castle as that globe burst. Were the souls of the wizards imprisoned in those golden balls?—Ha!"

Conan wheeled as Kerim Shah drew his sword and pointed.

Another figure stood at the head of the stair. His robe, too, was black, but of richly embroidered velvet, and there was a velvet cap on his head. His face was calm, and not unhandsome.

"Who the devil are you?" demanded Conan, staring up at him, knife in hand.

"I am the Master of Yimsha!" His voice was like the chime of a temple bell, but a note of cruel mirth ran through it.

"Where is Yasmina?" demanded Kerim Shah.

The Master laughed down at him.

"What is that to you, dead man? Have you so quickly forgotten my strength, once lent to you, that you come armed against me, you poor fool? I think I will take your heart, Kerim Shah!"

He held out his hand as if to receive something, and the Turanian cried out sharply like a man in mortal agony. He reeled drunkenly, and then, with a splintering of bones, a rending of flesh and muscle, and a snapping of mail-links, his breast burst outward with a shower of blood, and through the ghastly aperture something red and dripping shot through the air into the Master's outstretched hand, as a bit of steel leaps to the magnet. The Turanian slumped to the floor and lay motionless, and the Master laughed and hurled the object to fall before Conan's feet—a still-quivering human heart.

With a roar and a curse Conan charged the stair. From Khemsa's girdle he felt strength and deathless hate flow into him to combat the terrible emanation of power that met him on the steps. The air filled with a shimmering steely haze through which he plunged like a swimmer, head lowered, left arm bent about his face, knife gripped low in his right hand. His half-blinded eyes, glaring over the crook of his elbow, made out the hated shape of the Seer before and above him, the outline wavering as a reflection wavers in disturbed water.

He was racked and torn by forces beyond his comprehension, but he felt a driving power outside and beyond his own lifting him inexorably upward and onward, despite the wizard's strength and his own agony.

Now he had reached the head of the stairs, and the Master's

face floated in the steely haze before him, and a strange fear shadowed the inscrutable eyes. Conan waded through the mist as through a surf, and his knife lunged upward like a live thing. The keen point ripped the Master's robe as he sprang back with a low cry. Then before Conan's gaze, the wizard vanished—simply disappeared like a burst bubble, and something long and undulating darted up one of the smaller stairs that led up to the left and right from the landing.

Conan charged after it, up the left-hand stair, uncertain as to just what he had seen whip up those steps, but in a berserk mood that drowned the nausea and horror whispering at the back of his consciousness.

He plunged out into a broad corridor whose uncarpeted floor and untapestried walls were of polished jade, and something long and swift whisked down the corridor ahead of him, and into a curtained door. From within the chamber rose a scream of urgent terror. The sound lent wings to Conan's flying feet, and he hurtled through the curtains and headlong into the chamber within.

A frightful scene met his glare. Yasmina cowered on the farther edge of a velvet-covered dais, screaming her loathing and horror, an arm lifted as if to ward off attack, while before her swayed the hideous head of a giant serpent, shining neck arching up from dark-gleaming coils. With a choked cry Conan threw his knife.

Instantly the monster whirled and was upon him like the rush of wind through tall grass. The long knife quivered in its neck, point and a foot of blade showing on one side, and the hilt and a hand's-breadth of steel on the other, but it only seemed to madden the giant reptile. The great head towered above the man who faced it, and then darted down, the venom-dripping jaws gaping wide. But Conan had plucked a dagger from his girdle and he stabbed upward as the head dipped down. The point tore through the lower jaw and transfixed the upper, pinning them together. The next instant, the great trunk had looped itself about the Cimmerian as the snake, unable to use its fangs, employed its remaining form of attack.

Conan's left arm was pinioned among the bone-crushing folds, but his right was free. Bracing his feet to keep upright, he stretched forth his hand, gripped the hilt of the long knife jutting from the serpent's neck, and tore it free in a shower of blood. As if divining his purpose with more than bestial intelligence, the snake writhed and knotted, seeking to cast its loops about his right arm. But with the speed of light the long knife rose and fell, shearing half-way through the reptile's giant trunk.

Before he could strike again, the great, pliant loops fell from him and the monster dragged itself across the floor, gushing blood from its ghastly wounds. Conan sprang after it, knife lifted, but his vicious swipe cut empty air as the serpent writhed away from him and struck its blunt nose against a paneled screen of sandalwood. One of the panels gave inward and the long, bleeding barrel whipped through it and was gone.

Conan instantly attacked the screen. A few blows rent it apart and he glared into the dim alcove beyond. No horrific shape coiled there; there was blood on the marble floor, and bloody tracks led to a cryptic arched door. Those tracks were of a man's bare feet. . . .

"Conan!" He wheeled back into the chamber just in time to catch the Devi of Vendhya in his arms as she rushed across the room and threw herself upon him, catching him about the neck with a frantic clasp, half hysterical with terror and gratitude and relief.

His wild blood had been stirred to its uttermost by all that had passed. He caught her to him in a grasp that would have made her wince at another time, and crushed her lips with his. She made no resistance; the Devi was drowned in the elemental woman. She closed her eyes and drank in his fierce, hot, lawless kisses with all the abandon of passionate thirst. She was panting with his violence when he ceased for breath, and glared down at her lying limp in his mighty arms.

"I knew you'd come for me," she murmured. "You would not leave me in this den of devils."

At her words, recollection of their environment came to him suddenly. He lifted his head and listened intently. Silence reigned over the castle of Yimsha, but it was a silence impregnated with menace. Peril crouched in every corner, leered invisibly from every hanging.

"We'd better go while we can," he muttered. "Those cuts were enough to kill any common beast—or *man*—but a wizard has a dozen lives. Wound one, and he writhes away like a crippled snake to soak up fresh venom from some source of sorcery."

He picked up the girl and, carrying her in his arms like a child, he strode out into the gleaming jade corridor and down the stairs, nerves tautly alert for any sign or sound.

"I met the Master," she whispered, clinging to him and shuddering. "He worked his spells on me to break my will. The most awful was a moldering corpse which seized me in its arms—I fainted then and lay as one dead, I do not know how long. Shortly after I regained consciousness I heard sounds of strife below, and cries, and then that snake came slithering through the curtains—ah!" She shook at the memory of that horror. "I knew somehow that it was not an illusion, but a real serpent that sought my life."

"It was not a shadow, at least," answered Conan cryptically. "He knew he was beaten, and chose to slay you rather than let you be rescued."

"What do you mean, *he?*" she asked uneasily, and then shrank against him, crying out, and forgetting her question. She had seen the corpses at the foot of the stairs. Those of the Seers were not good to look at; as they lay twisted and contorted, their hands and feet exposed to view, and at the sight Yasmina went livid and hid her face against Conan's powerful shoulder.

10. Yasmina and Conan

Conan passed through the hall quickly enough, traversed the outer chamber, and approached the door that led upon the gallery. Then he saw the floor sprinkled with tiny, glittering shards. The crystal sheet that had covered the doorway had been shivered to bits, and he remembered the crash that had accompanied the shattering of the crystal globe. He believed that every piece of crystal in the castle had broken at that instant, and some dim instinct or memory of esoteric lore vaguely suggested the truth of the monstrous connection between the Lords of the Black Circle and the golden pomegranates. He felt the short hair bristle chilly at the back of his neck and put the matter hastily out of his mind.

He breathed a deep sigh of relief as he stepped out upon the green jade gallery. There was still the gorge to cross, but at least he could see the white peaks glistening in the sun, and the long slopes falling away into the distant blue hazes.

The Irakzai lay where he had fallen, an ugly blotch on the glassy smoothness. As Conan strode down the winding path, he was surprised to note the position of the sun. It had not yet passed its zenith; and yet it seemed to him that hours had passed since he plunged into the castle of the Black Seers.

He felt an urge to hasten, not a mere blind panic, but an instinct of peril growing behind his back. He said nothing to

Yasmina, and she seemed content to nestle her dark head against his arching breast and find security in the clasp of his iron arms. He paused an instant on the brink of the chasm, frowning down. The haze which danced in the gorge was no longer rose-hued and sparkling. It was smoky, dim, ghostly, like the life-tide that flickered thinly in a wounded man. The thought came vaguely to Conan that the spells of magicians were more closely bound to their personal beings than were the actions of common men to the actors.

But far below, the floor shone like tarnished silver, and the gold thread sparkled undimmed. Conan shifted Yasmina across his shoulder, where she lay docilely, and began the descent. Hurriedly he descended the ramp, and hurriedly he fled across the echoing floor. He had a conviction that they were racing with time, that their chances of survival depended upon crossing that gorge of horrors before the wounded Master of the castle should regain enough power to loose some other doom upon them.

When he toiled up the farther ramp and came out upon the crest, he breathed a gusty sigh of relief and stood Yasmina upon her feet.

"You walk from here," he told her; "it's downhill all the way."

She stole a glance at the gleaming pyramid across the chasm; it reared up against the snowy slope like the citadel of silence and immemorial evil.

"Are you a magician, that you have conquered the Black Seers of Yimsha, Conan of Ghor?" she asked, as they went down the path, with his heavy arm about her supple waist.

"It was a girdle Khemsa gave me before he died," Conan answered. "Yes, I found him on the trail. It is a curious one, which I'll show you when I have time. Against some spells it was weak, but against others it was strong, and a good knife is always a hearty incantation."

"But if the girdle aided you in conquering the Master," she argued, "why did it not aid Khemsa?"

He shook his head. "Who knows? But Khemsa had been the Master's slave; perhaps that weakened its magic. He had no hold on me as he had on Khemsa. Yet I can't say that I conquered him. He retreated, but I have a feeling that we haven't seen the last of him. I want to put as many miles between us and his lair as we can."

He was further relieved to find horses tethered among the

tamarisks as he had left them. He loosed them swiftly and mounted the black stallion, swinging the girl up before him. The others followed, freshened by their rest.

"And what now?" she asked. "To Afghulistan?"

"Not just now!" He grinned hardly. "Somebody—maybe the governor—killed my seven headmen. My idiotic followers think I had something to do with it, and unless I am able to convince them otherwise, they'll hunt me like a wounded jackal."

"Then what of me? If the headmen are dead, I am useless to you as a hostage. Will you slay me to avenge them?"

He looked down at her, with eyes fiercely aglow, and laughed at the suggestion.

"Then let us ride to the border," she said. "You'll be safe from the Afghulis there——"

"Yes, on a Vendhyan gibbet."

"I am queen of Vendhya," she reminded him with a touch of her old imperiousness. "You have saved my life. You shall be rewarded."

She did not intend it as it sounded, but he growled in his throat, ill pleased.

"Keep your bounty for your city-bred dogs, princess! If you're a queen of the plains, I'm chief of the hills, and not one foot toward the border will I take you!"

"But you would be safe——" she began bewilderedly.

"And you'd be the Devi again," he broke in. "No, girl; I prefer you as you are now—a woman of flesh and blood, riding on my saddle bow."

"But you can't *keep* me!" she cried. "You can't——"

"Watch and see!" he advised grimly.

"But I will pay you a vast ransom——"

"Devil take your ransom!" he answered roughly, his arms hardening around her supple figure. "The kingdom of Vendhya could give me nothing I desire half so much as I desire you. I took you at the risk of my neck; if your courtiers want you back, let them come up the Zhaibar and fight for you."

"But you have no followers now!" she protested. "You are hunted! How can you preserve your own life, much less mine?"

"I still have friends in the hills," he answered. "There is a chief of the Khurakzai who will keep you safely while I bicker with the Afghulis. If they will have none of me, by Crom! I will ride northward with you to the steppes of the *kozaki*. I was a hetman among the Free Companions before I rode southward. I'll make you a queen on the Zaporoska River!''

''But I can not!'' she objected. ''You must not hold me——''

''If the idea's so repulsive,'' he demanded, ''why did you yield your lips to me so willingly?''

''Even a queen is human,'' she answered, coloring. ''But because I am a queen, I must consider my kingdom. Do not carry me away into some foreign country. Come back to Vendhya with me!''

''Would you make me your king?'' he asked sardonically.

''Well, there are customs——'' she stammered, and he interrupted her with a hard laugh.

''Yes, civilized customs that won't let you do as you wish. You'll marry some withered old king of the plains, and I can go my way with only the memory of a few kisses snatched from your lips. Ha!''

''But I must return to my kingdom!'' she repeated helplessly.

''Why?'' he demanded angrily. ''To chafe your rump on gold thrones, and listen to the plaudits of smirking, velvet-skirted fools? Where is the gain? Listen: I was born in the Cimmerian hills where the people are all barbarians. I have been a mercenary soldier, a corsair, a *kozak*, and a hundred other things. What king has roamed the countries, fought the battles, loved the women, and won the plunder that I have?

''I came into Ghulistan to raise a horde and plunder the kingdoms to the south—your own among them. Being chief of the Afghulis was only a start. If I can conciliate them, I'll have a dozen tribes following me within a year. But if I can't, I'll ride back to the steppes and loot the Turanian borders with the *kozaki*. And you'll go with me. To the devil with your kingdom; they fended for themselves before you were born.''

She lay in his arms looking up at him, and she felt a tug at her spirit, a lawless, reckless urge that matched his own and was by it called into being. But a thousand generations of sovereignship rode heavy upon her.

''I can't! I can't!'' she repeated helplessly.

''You haven't any choice,'' he assured her. ''You—what the devil!''

They had left Yimsha some miles behind them, and were riding along a high ridge that separated two deep valleys. They had just topped a steep crest where they could gaze down into the valley on their right hand. And there a running fight was in progress. A strong wind was blowing away from them, carrying the sound from their ears, but even so the clashing of steel and thunder of hoofs welled up from far below.

They saw the glint of the sun on lancetip and spired helmet. Three thousand mailed horsemen were driving before them a ragged band of turbaned riders, who fled snarling and striking like fleeing wolves.

"Turanians!" muttered Conan. "Squadrons from Secunderam. What the devil are they doing here?"

"Who are the men they pursue?" asked Yasmina. "And why do they fall back so stubbornly? They can not stand against such odds."

"Five hundred of my mad Afghulis," he growled, scowling down into the vale. "They're in a trap, and they know it."

The valley was indeed a cul-de-sac at the end. It narrowed to a high-walled gorge, opening out further into a round bowl, completely rimmed with lofty, unscalable walls.

The turbaned riders were being forced into this gorge, because there was nowhere else for them to go, and they went reluctantly, in a shower of arrows and a whirl of swords. The helmeted riders harried them, but did not press in too rashly. They knew the desperate fury of the hill tribes, and they knew too that they had their prey in a trap from which there was no escape. They had recognized the hillmen as Afghulis, and they wished to hem them in and force a surrender. They needed hostages for the purpose they had in mind.

Their emir was a man of decision and initiative. When he reached Gurashah valley, and found neither guides nor emissary waiting for him, he pushed on, trusting to his own knowledge of the country. All the way from Secunderam there had been fighting, and tribesmen were licking their wounds in many a crag-perched village. He knew there was a good chance that neither he nor any of his helmeted spearmen would ever ride through the gates of Secunderam again, for the tribes would all be up behind him now, but he was determined to carry out his orders—which were to take Yasmina Devi from the Afghulis at all costs, and to bring her captive to Secunderam or, if confronted by impossibility, to strike off her head before he himself died.

Of all this, of course, the watchers on the ridge were not aware. But Conan fidgeted with nervousness.

"Why the devil did they get themselves trapped?" he demanded of the universe at large. "I know what they're doing in these parts—they were hunting me, the dogs! Poking into every valley—and found themselves penned in before they knew it.

The poor fools! They're making a stand in the gorge, but they can't hold out for long. When the Turanians have pushed them back into the bowl, they'll slaughter them at their leisure."

The din welling up from below increased in volume and intensity. In the strait of the narrow gut, the Afghulis, fighting desperately, were for the time holding their own against the mailed riders, who could not throw their whole weight against them.

Conan scowled darkly, moved restlessly, fingering his hilt, and finally spoke bluntly: "Devi, I must go down to them. I'll find a place for you to hide until I come back to you. You spoke of your kingdom—well, I don't pretend to look on those hairy devils as my children, but after all, such as they are, they're my henchmen. A chief should never desert his followers, even if they desert him first. They think they were right in kicking me out—Hell, I won't be cast off! I'm still chief of the Afghulis, and I'll prove it! I can climb down on foot into the gorge."

"But what of me?" she queried. "You carried me away forcibly from *my* people; now will you leave me to die in the hills alone while you go down and sacrifice yourself uselessly?"

His veins swelled with the conflict of his emotions.

"That's right," he muttered helplessly. "Crom knows what I *can* do."

She turned her head slightly, a curious expression dawning on her beautiful face. Then:

"Listen!" she cried. "Listen!"

A distant fanfare of trumpets was borne faintly to their ears. They stared into the deep valley on the left and caught a glint of steel on the farther side. A long line of lances and polished helmets moved along the vale, gleaming in the sunlight.

"The riders of Vendhya!" she cried exultingly.

"There are thousands of them!" muttered Conan. "It has been long since a Kshatriya host has ridden this far into the hills."

"They are searching for me!" she exclaimed. "Give me your horse! I will ride to my warriors! The ridge is not so precipitous on the left, and I can reach the valley floor. Go to your men and make them hold out a little longer. I will lead my horsemen into the valley at the upper end and fall upon the Turanians! We will crush them in the vise! Quick, Conan! Will you sacrifice your men to your own desire?"

The burning hunger of the steppes and the wintry forests glared out of his eyes, but he shook his head and swung off the stallion, placing the reins in her hands.

"You win!" he grunted. "Ride like the devil!"

She wheeled away down the left-hand slope, and he ran swiftly along the ridge until he reached the long ragged cleft that was the defile in which the fight raged. Down the rugged wall he scrambled like an ape, clinging to projections and crevices, to fall at last, feet first, into the mêlée that raged in the mouth of the gorge. Blades were whickering and clanging about him, horses rearing and stamping, helmet plumes nodding among turbans that were stained crimson.

As he hit, he yelled like a wolf, caught a gold-worked rein, and dodging the sweep of a scimitar, drove his long knife upward through the rider's vitals. In another instant he was in the saddle, yelling ferocious orders to the Afghulis. They stared at him stupidly for an instant; then as they saw the havoc his steel was wreaking among their enemies, they fell to their work again, accepting him without comment. In that inferno of licking blades and spurting blood there was no time to ask or answer questions.

The riders in their spired helmets and gold-worked hauberks swarmed about the gorge mouth, thrusting and slashing, and the narrow defile was packed and jammed with horses and men, the warriors crushed breast to breast, stabbing with shortened blades, slashing murderously when there was an instant's room to swing a sword. When a man went down he did not get up from beneath the stamping, swirling hoofs. Weight and sheer strength counted heavily there, and the chief of the Afghulis did the work of ten. At such times accustomed habits sway men strongly, and the warriors, who were used to seeing Conan in their vanguard, were heartened mightily, despite their distrust of him.

But superior numbers counted too. The pressure of the men behind forced the horsemen of Turan deeper and deeper into the gorge, in the teeth of the flickering tulwars. Foot by foot the Afgulis were shoved back, leaving the defile-floor carpeted with dead, on which the riders trampled. As he hacked and smote like a man possessed, Conan had time for some chilling doubts—would Yasmina keep her word? She had but to join her warriors, turn southward, and leave him and his band to perish.

But at last, what seemed centuries of desperate battling, in the valley outside there rose another sound above the clash of steel and yells of slaughter. And then with a burst of trumpets that shook the walls, and rushing thunder of hoofs, five thousand riders of Vendhya smote the hosts of Secunderam.

That stroke split the Turanian squadrons asunder, shattered, tore, and rent them and scattered their fragments all over the valley. In an instant the surge had ebbed back out of the gorge; there was a chaotic, confused swirl of fighting, horsemen wheeling and smiting singly and in clusters, and then the emir went down with a Kshatirya lance through his breast, and the riders in their spired helmets turned their horses down the valley, spurring like mad and seeking to slash a way through the swarms which had come upon them from the rear. As they scattered in flight, the conquerors scattered in pursuit, and all across the valley floor, and up on the slopes near the mouth and over the crests streamed the fugitives and the pursuers. The Afghulis, those left to ride, rushed out of the gorge and joined in the harrying of their foes, accepting the unexpected alliance as unquestionably as they had accepted the return of their repudiated chief.

The sun was sinking toward the distant crags when Conan, his garments hacked to tatters and the mail under them reeking and clotted with blood, his knife dripping and crusted to the hilt, strode over the corpses to where Yasmina Devi sat her horse among her nobles on the crest of the ridge, near a lofty precipice.

"You kept your word, Devi!" he roared. "By Crom, though, I had some bad seconds down in that gorge—*look out!*"

Down from the sky swooped a vulture of tremendous size with a thunder of wings that knocked men sprawling from their horses.

The scimitar-like beak was slashing for the Devi's soft neck, but Conan was quicker—a short run, a tigerish leap, the savage thrust of a dripping knife, and the vulture voiced a horribly human cry, pitched sideways and went tumbling down the cliffs to the rocks and river a thousand feet below. As it dropped, its black wings thrashing the air, it took on the semblance, not of a bird, but of a black-robed human body that fell, arms in wide black sleeves thrown abroad.

Conan turned to Yasmina, his red knife still in his hand, his blue eyes smoldering, blood oozing from wounds on his thickly-muscled arms and thighs.

"You are the Devi again," he said, grinning fiercely at the gold-clasped gossamer robe she had donned over her hill-girl attire, and awed not at all by the imposing array of chivalry about him. "I have you to thank for the lives of some three hundred and fifty of my rogues, who are at least convinced that I didn't betray them. You have put my hands on the reins of conquest again."

"I still owe you a ransom," she said, her dark eyes glowing as they swept over him. "Ten thousand pieces of gold I pay you——"

He made a savage, impatient gesture, shook the blood from his knife and thrust it back in its scabbard, wiping his hand on his mail.

"I will collect your ransom in my own way, at my own time," he said. "I will collect it in your palace at Ayodhya, and I will come with fifty thousand men to see that the scales are fair."

She laughed, gathering her reins into her hands. "And I will meet you on the shores of the Jhumda with a hundred thousand!"

His eyes shone with fierce appreciation and admiration as, stepping back, he lifted his hand with a gesture that was like the assumption of kingship, indicating that her road was clear before her.

ABOUT THE EDITORS

Isaac Asimov has been called "one of America's treasures." Born in the Soviet Union, he was brought to the United States at the age of three (along with his family) by agents of the American government in a successful attempt to prevent him from working for the wrong side. He quickly established himself as one of this country's foremost science fiction writers and writer about everything, and although now approaching middle age, he is going stronger than ever. He long ago passed his age and weight in books, and with some 270 to his credit threatens to close in on his I.Q. His sequel to THE FOUNDATION TRILOGY— FOUNDATION'S EDGE—was one of the best-selling books of 1982 and 1983.

Martin H. Greenberg has been called (in THE SCIENCE FICTION AND FANTASY BOOK REVIEW) "The King of the Anthologists"; to which he replied—"It's good to be the King!" He has produced more than seventy of them, usually in collaboration with a multitude of co-conspirators, most frequently the two who have given you WIZARDS. A Professor of Regional Analysis and Political Science at the University of Wisconsin–Green Bay, he is still trying to publish his weight.

Charles G. Waugh is a king-sized (6'4") Professor of Psychology and Communications at the University of Maine at Augusta who would be happy if he could keep his weight below Asimov's I.Q. Basically a very friendly fellow, he has done some fifty anthologies and single-author collections and especially enjoys locating overlooked stories. Perhaps his most unique characteristic is that he met his wife via computer, a machine his wife claims must have been an IB(E)M.